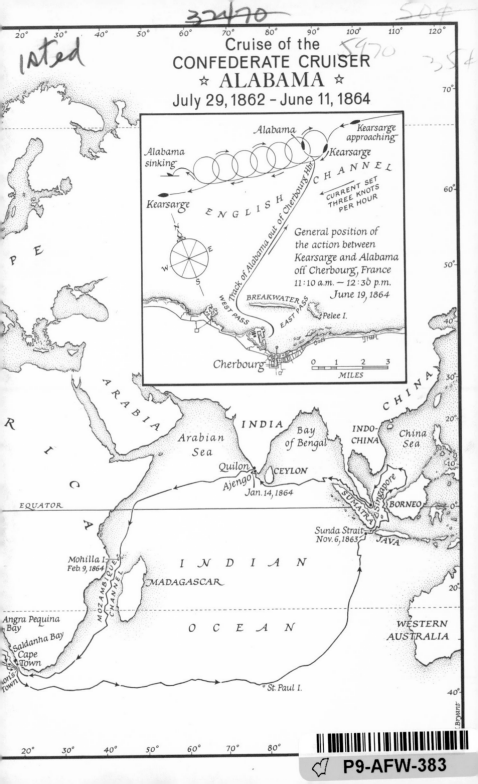

Cruise of the CONFEDERATE CRUISER ☆ ALABAMA ☆
July 29, 1862 – June 11, 1864

Alabama

Kearsarge approaching

Alabama sinking

Kearsarge

Kearsarge

ENGLISH CHANNEL

CURRENT SET THREE KNOTS PER HOUR

Track of Alabama out of Cherbourg Hbr.

General position of the action between Kearsarge and Alabama off Cherbourg, France
11:10 a.m. – 12:30 p.m.
June 19, 1864

N E W S

WEST PASS

BREAKWATER

EAST PASS

Pelee I.

Cherbourg

0 1 2 3
MILES

PE

ARABIA

INDIA

Arabian Sea

Bay of Bengal

INDO-CHINA

CHINA

China Sea

R

RICA

A

Quilon

Ajengo

CEYLON

Jan. 14, 1864

SUMATRA

Singapore

BORNEO

EQUATOR

Sunda Strait
Nov. 6, 1863

JAVA

Mohilla I.
Feb 9, 1864

INDIAN

MADAGASCAR

MOZAMBIQUE CHANNEL

Angra Pequina Bay

OCEAN

WESTERN AUSTRALIA

Saldanha Bay

Cape Town

ton's Town

St. Paul I.

Bryant

The Raiders

BOOKS BY WILLARD M. WALLACE

Nonfiction

APPEAL TO ARMS
A Military History of the American Revolution

TRAITOROUS HERO
The Life and Fortunes of Benedict Arnold

SIR WALTER RALEIGH

SOUL OF THE LION
A Biography of General Joshua L. Chamberlain

INTERVIEW IN WEEHAWKEN
The Burr-Hamilton Duel as told in the Original Documents
(Edited by Harold C. Syrett and Jean G. Cook
With an Introduction and Conclusion by Willard M. Wallace)

Fiction

EAST TO BAGADUCE
JONATHAN DEARBORN
THE RAIDERS

Juvenile

FRIEND WILLIAM

The Raiders

A Novel of the Civil War at Sea

by WILLARD M. WALLACE

Little, Brown and Company · Boston · Toronto

Published simultaneously in Canada
by Little, Brown & Company (Canada) Limited

PRINTED IN THE UNITED STATES OF AMERICA

To
Elizabeth M. Wallace
and
Gorham Munson

Contents

[vii]

Contents

[vii]

ONE

Attaché in England

I

JUST after one o'clock on the morning of March 5, 1862, I awoke to an unaccustomed silence. The monotonous churning of the paddle wheels had stilled, although the British and North American steamer *Arcadia*, Boston to Liverpool, was not yet halfway across the Atlantic. Quickly I dressed and shrugged into my overcoat. Then, pulling the flaps of my cap down over my ears, I hurried up the nearest gangway to the main deck.

Outside, the snow, driven on a quartering wind, stung my cheeks. The sea was running steeply. Off to starboard shone the lights of a steamer. By the *Arcadia's* starboard rail, aft of the paddle box, lanterns blossomed, and seamen stood by the bulwarks with lines dangling down the iron side. Finding an opening among the crush of curious passengers, I slid through to the rail and peered over.

Alongside the *Arcadia* tossed a small boat with six or eight people. There was a good deal of shouting between the boat and the steamer; then four seamen hauled hard and drew a person up the steamer's side.

"Easy — it's a woman!" someone shouted from below.

"Easy does it!" an officer said harshly, and the detail smoothed out its pulling.

As she came over the side and two seamen lifted her gently to the deck, releasing the line about her, her hair came loose and spilled over her face and shoulders. She flung it back, thick and blonde in the lantern light.

"Are you all right, madam?" the officer asked.

"Yes, I'm quite all right, thank you. Now, do please get my companion aboard."

The ship's officer bowed in quick acknowledgment of what was both plea and order, and a tall man was soon drawn over the side. The boat crew then cast off from the *Arcadia*, and rowed back to the other ship. Presently the *Arcadia*'s great paddle wheels began again to churn. We quickly resumed our course and speed.

Though the couple from the boat were soon escorted below, speculation rose among those passengers who dared keep the deck in the face of the nasty weather. Where had the man and the woman come from? Who were they?

I, too, was mystified, but my eyes and ears had registered certain facts. One was that each had brought aboard several pieces of luggage. A second was that both had accents that ever so faintly reflected an origin south of the Mason-Dixon line. A third was that the man had attempted to take the girl in his arms when he landed on the deck, and that she had slipped to one side so naturally and unhurriedly that probably few noticed her evasion.

Returning to my stateroom, I found that I was both amused and pleased that the woman had acted as she did. I also began to wonder on what blockade runner and from what Southern port they had sailed and what their purpose was in Europe. But such speculation hardly prevented me from falling asleep again. I did not reawake until a heavy sea rolled me against the bedrail and started my wound aching. By now it was seven A.M.

I eased myself out of bed, cursing the Rebel gunner at Fort Pulaski who was responsible. I had pushed my little blockader, really only a fast, large tugboat with its deck reinforced to support one twenty-four-pounder and one twelve-pounder, close to shore in pursuit of a steamer running for the Savannah River.

One of Pulaski's gunners, dead-eyeing on our gun-flashes, took the roof off the pilothouse with a thirty-two-pound solid shot that killed the pilot and wounded two crewmen. It also slammed me around so that three of my ribs buckled and a flying splinter sliced the skin above them for eight inches as neatly as a surgeon's knife. The wound was now practically healed, but the ribs still gave me trouble when I took a deep breath or, as now, when my body's weight pressed upon them. One thing I dreaded was to trim my whiskers because of the painful stretching of the arm, but I hated a scraggly beard. After dressing, I went on to the dining saloon.

There were perhaps a half-dozen passengers present out of one hundred aboard whose stomachs were hardy enough to endure breakfast. My own rarely troubled me except for the first twenty-four hours or so after departure, and then I was usually miserable. It was now thoroughly adjusted, or so I thought, but the redolence of fried fish, of which the English were so fond for breakfast, made me hasten through the bacon and eggs I had ordered and seek the deck.

Outside, the sea was still running high, but the sky had cleared somewhat. I walked the deck, setting not too brisk a pace in order to avoid breathing deeply. As I walked, I watched now the passengers who began to appear and now the sea, and marveled that I should be heading away from the war I had deliberately chosen to enter.

After my graduation from Bowdoin College, when I was still uncertain how I wished to spend my life, I had gone to sea for two years with Captain Nathan Cummings of Cape Elizabeth, Maine. By the time he brought his barkentine, the *Grace Stone*, back to Portland from Canton, I was third mate. But I had had enough of the boredom of the sea, and in my off-watch hours read enough law to please my grandfather, Bradford Pettigrew, Chief Justice of the Maine Supreme Court, who had brought me up. When I told him that now I wanted to go to Harvard for further study, he was delighted. And when, after a year of intensive study and a summer of reading with him, I passed the bar examination and was accepted as a practicing attorney of the State of Maine, his cup was full to overflowing. He and my grandmother, who had been Eliza Dearborn before her marriage, gave a dinner for me to which the family and friends were invited.

Among those present were my great-uncle Jonathan Dearborn, the famous newspaper editor, and a younger friend of his, the editor of the *Hartford Times* and a power in the new Republican party, one Gideon Welles.

I was just recalling my impression of Welles when the *Arcadia* struck an especially heavy sea. As the deck mounted under me, I caught a glimpse of passengers trying to keep their balance. Then a body fell against me, and I quickly braced myself against a stanchion to support our weight. As I did so, my ribs seemed again to cave in. For a moment, the pain was like hot fire against my flesh. I grew dizzy and burst into a sudden sweat on a very cold day.

"Have I hurt you?" a voice asked.

I could not reply.

"Tell me, sir, are you all right?"

"Thank you, ma'am," I said, and turned to face her. I now saw that she was a rather small person, slim, with blonde hair and large blue eyes that appeared solicitous. I should have preferred to have done something for which they were admiring.

"Weren't you brought aboard from the boat last night?" I asked.

"Yes, I was, Mr. —"

"I beg your pardon," I said. "I'm Scott Pettigrew."

"And I am Tamara Ravenel."

I bowed. I looked carefully at her as she stood with one gloved hand holding to the rail and the other to her perky bonnet, which, despite its ribbon tied under her chin, threatened to blow off. With wisps of blonde hair defying the bonnet and the wind blowing her black coat and gray traveling

[6]

dress against her, with her cheeks turning pink in the air and her eyes brightly animated, I thought she would have been an appealing subject for a portrait artist.

"I hope I didn't hurt you, Mr. Pettigrew," she said; and I caught again, as I had during the night, the tone of vigor, "but I am afraid I did. Have you been ill?"

I shook my head. "No, no, I'm quite all right, thank you. It was simply the surprise of meeting you this way! I wasn't prepared."

"I don't think you were," she said. "I hope you're not angry at the wave!"

"I'm grateful to the wave, Miss Ravenel," I said.

"But what were you looking at, Mr. Pettigrew? No, don't answer . . . I'm being too curious."

"Nothing, really."

"Then you must have had serious thoughts. If you could have seen how forbidding you looked! I thought I was brave even to approach you." She was just short of being what my Grandmother Pettigrew would call "forward."

"Perhaps my thoughts were serious," I said.

She shrugged. "Well, it is no business of mine."

"No, it is no business of yours," I said.

"Mr. Pettigrew, you are rude!" she exclaimed. "Good day."

She walked away, her head held high. Several of the passengers looked at her and then at me. I stared them coldly and briefly down, and turned back to my view of the ocean.

Miss Ravenel was clearly a person to reckon with. Though her manner was so friendly I could not take real offense, I was annoyed by her persistence. But I was cautious about pursuing the opening made possible by the manner of our meeting. Though I had no means of telling, apart from her accent, I felt sure she was Southern. Because of the islands of Northern sympathizers scattered through the South, particularly in Tennessee and North Carolina, I couldn't be certain she was a Confederate simply because she had a Southern accent. Until I

[7]

learned for sure, however, I would consider her one, as well as the man with whom she came aboard the *Arcadia*. What my attitude should be toward a female Confederate I couldn't be sure. But I had been fighting Confederate males, if only from the deck of a ship, for months, and, for the present, I had no desire to make their closer acquaintance.

I presume my being bound for Europe had its origin in my meeting Gideon Welles at the dinner my Grandfather Pettigrew gave for me. The conversation had turned political before the evening was over. Unlike my Uncle Jonathan, Welles had swung over from the Democratic to the Republican party. When he asked me what my views were on states' rights and slavery, I replied that I was opposed to both the hotheaded states' rightists of the South, largely Democratic, and the more rabid abolitionists of the North, largely Republican, since each group seemed determined in its own way to wreck the Union. I was strongly opposed to slavery, too, but I thought that, before the issue became hopelessly divisive and a major cause for civil strife, the federal government should liberate the slaves by purchasing their freedom, provide for their acceptance into the economy as free laborers, and educate them in the rights and responsibilities of voting citizens.

"Admirable," said Welles with a smile, "in fact, highly commendable. But also naive and unrealistic if you believe either that the Buchanan Administration would promote such a program or that the South would ever listen to such a proposal. Slavery is still big business, with the investment capitalized at about two billion dollars."

"Paying out that amount would still be preferable to a war, sir."

"Of course. But I'm afraid we are likely to come to a war instead. Now, what about your party affiliation, Mr. Pettigrew?"

"I presume you would be happy, sir, if I said I am a Republi-

[8]

can." I didn't mean to offend him, but Mr. Welles's abrupt manner nettled me.

"Yes, I certainly would. Democrats with their states'-rights obsession will be the death of this country yet. I know — I was one myself."

"And you were fired from the *Hartford Times*, Gideon, for becoming a Republican," Uncle Jonathan said. But his smile took the edge off his remark.

"It may have amounted to that, Jonathan," Welles said, "but the time comes when a man has to declare himself. You are standing four-square on the principles of the Democratic party, or almost so. I think you are wrong. Judge Pettigrew over here has become a leader in the Republican party. I think he is right. Now where do you stand, young man?"

I glanced at my grandfather, so spare and elegant, and at my big and fleshy great-uncle. Both were looking at me.

"Before I went to sea, I was a Democrat," I said to Mr. Welles. "Aboard ship, I recognized the need of authority. I don't mean to compare our country with a ship — aboard ship there must be at all times absolute control by the captain, else the ship and all aboard may be lost. Our country is a democracy, not a ship at sea, but there are times when a strong central authority is needed to preserve the Union. Some people may not think a union of states worth preserving; I happen to believe it is. I therefore registered as a Republican, sir."

"Good for you, young man!"

"But let me be quite candid, sir," I said. "When this crisis is over, if the Republican party becomes what I consider excessively authoritarian, I may well return to the Democratic party."

"That is fair enough, Scott," my grandfather said, coming forward and taking me by the arm. "Now let us go back to the ladies."

I didn't know what Mr. Welles thought, but he must have remembered me. At any rate, when war broke out, I received a

[9]

navy commission as an acting volunteer master. After taking a seamanship examination and a brief course at Newport, where the Annapolis Naval Academy had been moved, I was given a small gunboat of shallow draft and sent down to assist the tiny squadron off Fort Pulaski. I had been instrumental in helping chase one blockade runner ashore, and scored a lucky hit on another that blew her boiler. She was loaded with arms and was otherwise so valuable, too, that, while recovering from my wound, which I received soon afterward, I was given the thanks of Congress, which made my promotion to acting volunteer lieutenant almost automatic. Later, such a feat as mine would have passed practically unnoticed.

While recuperating in Washington, I was summoned by Welles to his office. He was making a splendid Secretary of the Navy, in my opinion, though I was aware there were those who differed. Certainly he and the genial Assistant Secretary, Gustavus Vasa Fox, were creating a formidable navy; Welles was lucky to have the large, heavily bearded and enormously competent Fox with him. Welles now told me that he wanted me to go to London to serve on the staff of our Minister to England, Charles Francis Adams. The appointment, Mr. Welles assured me, had been approved by Secretary of State Seward. He instructed me to keep an eye, while abroad, on the activities of Captain James Bulloch, who was arranging to have the British build ships for the Confederacy. Bulloch, who had once served in the United States Navy, was believed to have left England for the Confederacy but was expected to return. I had an idea of the importance attached to my assignment when I found myself aboard the *Arcadia*, out of Boston, bound for Liverpool, only four days later.

Now, three days after the *Arcadia*'s departure, though I was heading away from the war, the war had come to me. Or so I was persuaded. I did not for a moment believe that there was any connection between my being on board the *Arcadia* and our picking up passengers at sea. But neither did I believe that

Tamara Ravenel's falling against me was entirely the fault of a great wave. Yet, if neither of these, what did she want? And why should she have sought out me from among all the male passengers aboard? Surely neither my name nor my appearance was that distinguished. It must, then, be my mission, about which I had naturally said nothing.

Suddenly weary of this speculation, I turned away and sought the smoking room for a cigar and coffee. As I entered the crowded room where none but men were permitted, I noticed Miss Ravenel's companion of the night before. He was talking with the *Arcadia*'s second officer, Guy Allen. While I waited for the steward to bring my coffee, I felt the new passenger giving me a look at once cool and studied. My own eyes, I was sure, must have reflected my annoyance, but his had appraised me without apparent emotion. When he had seen as much as he wanted to see, he looked away. I leisurely finished my cigar and coffee. Without having any gift of clairvoyance, however, I had a disquieting sense of something happening which involved me. I do not like mysteries.

II

As the *Arcadia*, moving swiftly the next few days after the storm, approached Europe, I became increasingly curious about Tamara Ravenel and her companion. Occasionally I encountered them on deck or in the dining saloon. The first time I saw them together, Tamara introduced him to me as her cousin Roger Clavering. A distant cousin, no doubt; his behavior when he had boarded the *Arcadia* had been anything but cousinly.

Still, the introduction to Clavering, though brief, was long enough for me to see that this was a formidable man. It wasn't only that he was tall and lean and walked with a kind of catlike grace. Nor was it the long, aristocratic face and nose. I suppose it was more the way his eyes, cold and gray and seemingly

[11]

unblinking, bored through me. He knew who I was before Tamara introduced us; Guy Allen had told him, I was sure. And though he bowed and smiled, his eyes flickered over me, and, possibly disdaining what he saw, he took her arm and moved away.

What piqued me was not so much his brush-off as the flash of amusement on Tamara's face. Was I being made fun of? I have yet to see the man who accepts ridicule without becoming angry. I hugged to myself the satisfaction that my face revealed little of how I really felt. Moreover, I had a faint hope that I might not be the one that amused her — that it might, indeed, be the situation or possibly Clavering himself.

It was at one of those interminable British teas in the dark-paneled main saloon of the *Arcadia* that I talked with Clavering for the first time. People were standing or sitting in small groups, and as I strolled through the crowd, Tamara Ravenel called and asked if I would like to join them. They were not alone. Guy Allen was there, too, a tall, gay-mannered man with intensely blue eyes. He introduced himself at once and acknowledged that naturally he knew me from the passenger list.

" 'Naturally,' Mr. Allen?" I asked, accepting tea from one of the stewards and declining a cupcake with a watery, thin white frosting.

"The passenger list is small, Mr. Pettigrew," he smiled, "and you walk like a man who knows a deck."

"But why are you so sure that Mr. Pettigrew has been to sea before, Mr. Allen?" Tamara asked.

"He didn't say that, my dear," Clavering cut in. "Mr. Allen said that Mr. Pettigrew walks like a man who knows a deck, which isn't precisely the same thing."

"Oh, bother such hairsplitting! You have been to sea before, haven't you, Mr. Pettigrew?"

"Yes," I said, "I've been to sea before. I spent two years, mostly in Indian and Chinese waters."

"Indeed." Clavering's voice was rich and deep.

[12]

"Did you have any trouble out there?" Allen asked.

"I got to China sometime after you Britishers and the French whipped China in 1856," I said. "But I saw the Emperor's summer palace your troops burned outside Peking, and the ship I was on lay in Bombay for a while during your Indian Mutiny."

"What I meant was whether you had been in any action yourself," Allen said.

"Why should I have been? Our country was at peace. Yes, we tangled with pirates off the Malayan coast, but that was all."

"Did you win, Mr. Pettigrew?" Tamara asked.

I looked at her, then at Clavering, who said, "I daresay Mr. Pettigrew wouldn't be here now if the Malays had taken his ship. Is that not right, Pettigrew?"

"Quite right," I said. "As it was, we escaped only because a breeze came up."

"I always considered those Eastern peoples poor fighters until the Mutiny," Allen said. "I still think they are, for the most part."

I shrugged. The subject was distasteful to me, and I had no desire to pursue it.

"Aren't we lucky to be safe aboard the *Arcadia*, away from any raiders!" Tamara said.

"All we have to fear is some Yankee cruiser stopping us," Allen said.

But Clavering shook his head. "Not much fear of that, Allen, since your government objected to Captain Wilkes's taking the Confederate emissaries, Mr. Mason and Mr. Slidell, off the British mail steamer *Trent*. If the Lincoln Administration had not apologized and agreed to return the men, there would have been war. No captain in the United States Navy will make the same mistake again. Don't you agree, Mr. Pettigrew?"

I could not make the man out. He didn't say "our emissaries" or "the Yankee government." He spoke almost like a neutral; in fact, it had been Allen, an Englishman, who had used the term "Yankee." But quickly I told him I agreed with him. And I did.

[13]

Charles Wilkes, for all the hero's welcome he received in the North, including an expression of appreciation by Congress and elaborate banquets in his honor, had made a great mistake when his *San Jacinto* halted the *Trent*. Had he taken the ship into port, that would have been bad enough, but the issue could have been adjudicated. But to halt the *Trent* on the high seas, take the Confederate commissioners off her, and permit her to continue was a humiliating affront to the British. As President Lincoln admitted, it was what we accused the British of doing to our ships and citizens before the War of 1812.

"I tell you, if Her Majesty's government had sent the fleet over, it would have been the end of the United States," Allen said warmly. "As it was, we've sent troops."

"Indeed, yes," Clavering agreed, although his tone was very dry. "But you may remember there was so much ice in the St. Lawrence that Secretary Seward actually offered to provide facilities for moving both the troops and their baggage from Portland to Montreal. I don't think the offer was accepted, but the situation must have been a little embarrassing for the British."

"What a lovely irony!" Tamara exclaimed.

If Allen was discomfited by all this, I was puzzled. I couldn't figure out just where these people stood in relation to the war, though I sensed they were Southerners without doubt. Nor did the girl help clarify the situation when she said, "You would think the British government would have had enough pride and resolution to send the fleet, wouldn't you? Besides, British mills need Southern cotton, and if they don't get it, thousands of their workers will go hungry."

"I daresay," Clavering said, "but governments have often ignored the fate of little people."

"Quite so!" Allen cut in. "Mind you, I don't go along with giving authority to the little people, Mr. Clavering, but I have no respect for the present ministry. As long as Lord Palmerston is the Prime Minister and Lord Russell is at the Foreign Office,

[14]

there'll be no recognition of the South. They're quick to wave the flag in China or Europe, but they seem shy about offending the Yankees."

"What do you have against Americans, Mr. Allen?" I asked.

"I think you Yanks are hypocrites!" he blazed back at me. "You're beginning to talk a lot now about freeing the slaves, but what you really mean is that you'll deny the South the right to set up a sovereign nation. Your people were rebels in your Revolution and now you are refusing the South a right to the same role. Liberty!"

"There does seem something in what you say, Mr. Allen," Tamara said. Then she turned to me. "Don't you agree, Mr. Pettigrew?"

I had no intention of agreeing or disagreeing; I had heard enough of arguments about the war. But I was saved, or so I thought for a moment, from what might have become an uncomfortable situation, by Clavering himself.

"I doubt that there is any need to excite yourself, Mr. Allen," he said. "After all, Mr. Pettigrew is just another passenger bound for Europe. Isn't that so, Mr. Pettigrew?"

I nodded. "And I believe the same is true of you and Miss Ravenel."

"We were on our way to Europe when our steamer developed engine trouble and had to turn back to Bermuda. Luckily, we were near the *Arcadia* and our captain was good enough to put us aboard."

I could only wonder at the emergency that had prompted them to chance the rough water between their steamer and the *Arcadia*. Was their purpose in going to Europe to sell cotton stocks? To buy a blockade runner? To lecture to English audiences on the virtues of the Confederacy and the evils of the North? I almost felt sorry for them because I was certain the South would eventually lose the war. Still, there was a quality of assurance not unmixed with danger about Roger Clavering that stopped pity in mid-stride. He spoke with surprising objectivity

[15]

about the South, and without rancor of the North. Yet of his commitment I had no doubt.

"Pettigrew," he went on, "I presume you're for the North."

"Yes, I'm for the North," I acknowledged.

"Yet from your speech I would say you must have lived for some time in the South."

"I spent my childhood until I was ten years old in Charleston. Then my parents took me with them to Havana, where my father had business. While there, they came down with yellow fever and died. I stayed with the American consul until my grandfather brought me to Portland, Maine, to live with him."

"Then you must have relatives in South Carolina," Tamara said.

"Yes, my mother's people."

"What was their name, may I ask?"

"Middleton — oh, not *the* Middletons," I added hastily as her eyes widened, "in fact, no relation at all to them, but I can understand your surprise. Middleton is a name that has magic in South Carolina."

"Indeed, yes," Clavering said. "Signers of the Declaration of Independence and the Constitution, and now loyal Confederates. Well, well, so you are of both Northern and Southern ancestry and Northern in your sympathies."

"My loyalties are with the Union," I said.

"Yet you take no part in the war," Allen said.

I stared at him, simply stared at him. He had the grace to grow brick-red, then recollected that he had duties to attend to and excused himself. Still, though Allen annoyed me with his breeziness and insolence, Clavering, for all his suave manners and judicious air, seemed more formidable. His eyes remained cold and constantly appraising.

"I'm afraid Allen was rude," Clavering said.

"Of course he was," Tamara said, "but you are an enemy of the South, Mr. Pettigrew, so I can't feel sorry for you at all."

[16]

"Even an enemy who doesn't fight the South?" Clavering asked.

"Especially such an enemy!" she said.

Clavering's question had been an insult. It was deliberate — of this I was sure. But I declined to respond to it. "Then if you feel as you do, Miss Ravenel," I said, "you'd be well advised not to talk any longer with this particular Yankee. It would be unpatriotic."

At this, Clavering chuckled deep in his throat and said, "Mr. Pettigrew may be right, Tamara. Perhaps you'd better leave us."

"I'll leave when I want to leave, thank you, Roger!"

"Just as you wish," he said, "but as for me, I am retreating. Anyone who calls my cousin unpatriotic had best look for a bombproof, Pettigrew." Smiling, he tipped his hat and left.

Tamara gave an impatient twitch to her shoulders. "Tell me, Mr. Pettigrew, are you going to be in London?"

"Yes, I expect I shall. Will you?"

"Who knows? And surely it can't interest a Yankee where I am."

"Well, perhaps you're right," I said. "Perhaps it wouldn't do for us to meet in London, now that we're at war."

She looked at me for a long moment, then she smiled. "How right you are, Mr. Pettigrew. Now do be careful of the North's reputation and, of course, your own! Good-bye, Mr. Pettigrew."

I bowed, and as I watched the straight, trim back disappearing, I regretted having said anything to shut off our acquaintance. The truth was I had never seen such a mercurial person. Probably it was my good fortune that the *Arcadia* was due to arrive on the morrow, before I fell even more deeply under the spell of that pair of blue eyes. As I left for my stateroom to put on clean linen for dinner, I thought of the incongruity of such a shipboard acquaintanceship and my service to come with Charles Francis Adams, our Minister to England.

III

WE landed at Liverpool on a gray, rainy morning, and as soon as I cleared the customs, I boarded a train for London. I saw little of Liverpool but was impressed by the swarm of ships there and the bustle of activity at the docks and in the streets. The smell of coal smoke, which hung low over the city, was so rank that I started to cough.

Nowhere did I see Tamara Ravenel and Clavering. I decided they must have slept late and left the *Arcadia* after I did, for I was one of the first passengers ashore.

I noticed a short, stocky man among the visitors on the wharf waiting for the passengers to come ashore, and I saw him again in the railway station as many of the passengers boarded the train for London. He stood with his hands in his coat pockets, hat pulled down nearly over his eyes. He so resembled Captain Cummings of the *Grace Stone* that I stared at him as I passed. However, he seemed not to notice.

Wherever Clavering and Miss Ravenel had gone, they certainly weren't on the train, for I walked from one end to the other without seeing them. At once disappointed and relieved, I enjoyed the ride to the world's largest city. It seemed a pity, however, to observe the black hand of industrialization clutching at the green countryside of the older England — blackened brick factories and mills with tall chimneys belching smoke, long rows of sooty houses built just alike, rivers covered with black and greenish-yellow scum. Much the same thing was happening in our own New England, but the scale of this was so vast and one is so accustomed to think of England either as London or as country that the effect was depressing. Though my grandfather would have said this was progress, his eyes would have twinkled while he spoke.

The train arrived in London late in the evening, because of a hot box. So I put up for the night at a hotel near the railroad station. This was a mistake; off and on during the night I heard the rumble of trains, the clanging of bells, and the high shriek of the English locomotive whistles. Several times I got up from bed to stand at the grimy window and watch in the white gaslight of the streets below the unceasing flow of wagons and drays. I had never seen London before. The great city fascinated me.

At nine o'clock the next morning, after being lucky enough to secure a hansom cab, I presented myself with my luggage at the legation office at 5 Mansfield Street in Portland Place. I was ushered in at once by the official assistant secretary of the legation, Benjamin Moran. He was a slender man with a high forehead and muttonchop whiskers, grooves between his eyes, and a cleft chin. He was gracious but direct, obviously very busy and anxious for me to state my business and be gone. When I told him that I had been temporarily assigned to Mr. Adams's staff as a naval attaché, he blinked.

"I never heard of you, sir," he said, and his tone was curt. "We have had no notice of your coming. May I see your credentials?"

I carried two passports, one in my name as a lawyer for the benefit of the English customs officers, the other with my rank in the navy. I now produced the latter passport, but after glancing at it and returning it, Moran said, "I refer to your orders, Lieutenant Pettigrew, assigning you to the staff of this legation."

"My orders from Secretary Welles are to present my credentials personally to Mr. Adams."

"It is the Secretary of State, Mr. Seward, who assigns the personnel to this legation, not the Secretary of the Navy. Now may I see your orders?"

"You may not."

I believe I spoke firmly rather than harshly, for I had no doubt that Moran was an efficient, hardworking civil servant,

[19]

anxious to spare Mr. Adams from intruders. But if he had his instructions, I had mine. I was determined to obey them.

"Is something wrong?"

Both of us turned to the young man who entered the room, a notebook in his hand.

"Nothing at all," Moran said, though his irritation was plain. "Lieutenant Pettigrew says that he has been assigned to us, but he refuses to let me see his orders. Lieutenant, this is Mr. Henry Adams, the Minister's son and private secretary."

We shook hands while I looked with interest at this younger Adams, who was only two or three years my junior. A trim, slender man, about middle height, he had the high, broad brow of the Adamses and the glacial blue eyes. He was dressed in the conventional gray pants and black frock coat, his shoes shone with blacking, and he wore a pearl-headed pin in his cravat. Did he fancy fine apparel or was this merely an Adams's respect for convention?

"My father delegates many duties to Mr. Moran," he said, "but if Mr. Welles ordered you to report personally to him, I will find out if this is a convenient time for him to see you."

"The Minister explained that he would be busy with his correspondence this morning, Mr. Adams," Moran said.

"I know — I have some of his dictation with me," Adams replied, tapping the notebook. "Let me ask my father." He left, and I heard him going up the stairs.

"You may as well sit down, lieutenant," Moran said. "You will probably have quite a wait."

But I didn't. Henry Adams was back even before I could settle myself in one of the half-dozen straight-backed chairs in the office.

"If you will follow me, Lieutenant Pettigrew, I will take you to the Minister."

He spoke with a slight but unmistakable note of triumph. I wondered what relations were like between the Minister's private secretary and the official assistant secretary of the legation.

"Thank you," I said. I also thanked Moran.

I found Mr. Adams somewhat shorter but broader than his son, with a wider and sterner face, and a distant but not unpleasant manner. He rose from his desk, where he had been writing, and shook my hand. It wasn't much of a handclasp, but at least he hadn't given me a "fish," as we say in Maine. Mr. Adams asked me to take a chair opposite his in front of a coal-burning brazier. Then, reading the contents of the sealed envelope I passed to him, he leaned back, crossed his legs, and looked at the smoking coals for a long moment.

"Are you familiar with these instructions, lieutenant?" he asked.

"Yes, sir, in general, though not in detail. I know that Mr. Welles requested me to keep an eye on Captain James Bulloch and to make myself available to you."

"Mr. Moran is right, lieutenant. It is unusual that your assignment should not have been cleared through the State Department."

I said nothing. I knew that Welles and Seward had their differences in the cabinet, but the error of clearance was surely oversight rather than an act of deliberation. Or was it?

"It is clear that Mr. Welles did not intend that you should be an intelligence agent," Adams said, looking at the paper again.

"That is my understanding, sir."

"You have had no training in the techniques of espionage?"

"No, sir."

"So your mission is to be generally available to me, as you say, and to keep an eye on Captain Bulloch. Yet it happens that Captain Bulloch has just returned from the South, and we have our own agents keeping him and his colleagues under surveillance. As for your usefulness to me, perhaps Mr. Welles will communicate to me what precisely he has in mind."

[21]

His curt reduction of my role nettled me; I wondered what Welles could have had in mind sending me off so secretly and quickly. "I'm afraid I am as mystified as you are, sir."

"I think you are indeed mystified," Mr. Adams smiled briefly. "I have but been testing you, Lieutenant Pettigrew."

He went over to his escritoire, picked up a letter, and came back and sat down. "Mr. Welles's letter arrived in this morning's mail. It evidently came on the *Arcadia* with you by diplomatic pouch."

Adams had had his little jest at my expense.

"Lieutenant, have you heard of the *Number 290*?"

"Yes, sir. The newspapers at home have mentioned that she may be a raider the Laird Yard is building for the Rebels at Liverpool."

"I'm convinced that is a possibility, and our consul there, Thomas H. Dudley, is convinced it is a fact. Now, lieutenant, you are to find out everything you can about the 290 and send your reports often and directly to Secretary Welles. You may use the regular mails or the diplomatic pouch if you wish. The navy wants to act as quickly as possible to intercept her if she turns out to be a raider."

"But isn't it against British law for her to be armed and equipped in Britain for a belligerent power, sir?"

The Minister nodded. "It is, indeed. And that is what makes it imperative to keep constantly in touch with what is happening in Liverpool. The *Oreto*, another raider the British have prepared, is ready to leave at any time, and our efforts to hold her have failed so far. We're determined to work harder to forestall the 290. Now be sure to send a copy of your reports to me for forwarding to Mr. Welles through the State Department. In that way, if your originals to him go astray, he will receive my copies."

"Does this mean I should remain in Liverpool?"

Again the stern lines of his face relaxed. "By no means. Mr. Dudley is a good man and he has the 290 under constant watch.

You will need to work closely with him, but you will have other duties here in London."

"I'm afraid I don't follow you, sir."

"Lieutenant, again let us be clear on this: you are not an intelligence agent, you have had no experience in such work. You will be in England only until the 290 mystery is cleared up. Then you will return to Washington. If I were to make you a member of my staff, the Confederates here in London would expect you to watch the *Number 290*. You will be here as a lawyer friend of the family's, particularly of my son Henry's. I doubt that even this will deceive them, but no matter. You should see the sights of London, you should attend whatever festivities Henry goes to — as his guest, of course — and, whatever you do and wherever you go, keep your eyes and ears open. I shall want a report of anything favorable in any way to the Confederacy. But you are not to appear to be more than mildly curious, even in Liverpool. Have you divulged to anyone your status as an officer in our navy?"

It was a long speech for Mr. Adams, but my reply was short. Whatever I had said to Clavering and Tamara on the *Arcadia*, I had not uttered a syllable about my connection with the navy.

"Then I think you should continue discreet. You are traveling, and as a lawyer interested in legal matters pertaining to the sea, you will naturally wish to talk with people in great ports like London and Liverpool. I shall see that you have letters of introduction to a number of barristers. In the meantime, Henry can show you something of London in the evenings when you are in town. I often take a long walk in the evenings myself, and I shall be glad to have your company."

I thanked him, but he brushed off my thanks with a wave of his hand and rang a tiny bell — almost like a Christmas toy. Instantly Henry appeared. As his father explained the arrangements, he nodded. "I'll do what I can, sir, of course. But will you explain the situation to Mr. Moran?"

"I will take care of Moran," Mr. Adams said shortly. "Now

take Lieutenant Pettigrew in tow and do please introduce him to your mother and Mary and Brooks."

"By the bye, lieutenant," he said to me. "I think we'd better stop calling you by that title. From now on, you shall be Mister Pettigrew."

And it was as Mr. Pettigrew that I came to be known in the Adams household.

The members of that household had at least one feature in common: they were all different. Mrs. Adams, a rather ample woman, I found to be unfailingly kind but prone to moods, especially despair, and very nervous about manners and protocol. Her daughter Mary seemed shy and retiring, though there were times when the girl forced herself to appear as poised as if entertaining others were something she excelled in, which it was not. She was given to silences. So, too, was Brooks. Named after his rich mother's family whose fortune had kept the Charles Adamses afloat for years, he was bitingly sarcastic, utterly charming, and silent by turns. Few women could have flashed from mood to mood more quickly than he — and his brilliance and perception shone through even the darkest nimbus of temperament.

I never met Charles, the sturdy, outgoing, astute cavalry officer in the Army of the Potomac, but of those I knew, I liked Henry best. Though he had the same scintillation and acerbic view of his family, he lacked the crustiness of his father and the gloom of his mother and Brooks. A worker like his father, he possessed a certain lightness of mood, even a gaiety, that made him a delightful companion. And if frequently critical of our mistakes and foibles as a nation, he could be a passionate nationalist.

"These British are so confident of themselves and so contemptuous of others," he said one day. We were having tea in a hotel after he called for me at Allen and Doddridge, specialists in admiralty law, with whom I had discussed a range of topics from common cargo insurance to barratry and piracy. "They pride themselves on knowing more about the sea than any other people."

"That's probably the truth," I said.

"Surely they're not more knowledgeable than we are!"

"Henry, you know very well they have the greatest navy and the largest merchant marine in the world. They have a massive experience to draw from, and they are far ahead of us in the construction of iron steamships."

"We must be ahead of them in something!" He looked around the high-ceilinged room with its tables of fashionably dressed English people, and his voice sank to a fierce whisper. "Sometimes I think this Palmerston government will go too far and this damned old country will wake up one morning and find itself at war with us. Then what a squealing there will be! By the Lord, I would almost be willing to submit to our sufferings, just to have the pleasure of seeing our privateers make ducks and drakes of their commerce. You should have been here at the time of the *Trent* crisis. It looked like war for sure then, and I never admired my father more for his coolness."

"It would be hard for me to imagine your father as anything but cool," I said.

Henry's eyebrows rose languidly. "My father has his emotions, do believe me, but he takes them out in work. Luckily he gets on with Lord Russell."

"Not with Palmerston?"

"Oh, they're on acceptable terms, but there is little cordiality in the relationship. Palmerston is definitely a pro-Southern aristocrat who would like nothing better than to humiliate the United States. Yet, to give the devil his due, when many people and some of the newspapers were calling for violent measures to uphold British honor in the *Trent* affair, he merely readied the fleet and ordered a few thousand troops to Canada, as you know. He is a shrewd politician who knows the mass of Englishmen would be opposed to a war with the United States in

[25]

support of a slaveholding cause like the Confederacy. Remember — England freed her slaves in 1833, and despite the war talk by the upper classes, she still has a tradition of being no friend to tyranny."

"But also of being no friend to the United States," I said.

"Have we given them much cause to be friends to us?" he asked. "Have you forgotten 'Fifty-four forty or fight'? And don't tell me you don't remember as a boy the Aroostook War, when your own Maine lumbermen and militia were mustered against New Brunswick. And in the *Trent* affair, Captain Wilkes was treated at home as a hero instead of as an incredible blunderer."

"I know, I know."

Henry was disturbed, and though I meant my voice to be soothing, his eyes grew hard. "I'm boring you," he said. His father could not have sounded more formal.

"On the contrary, you interest me and puzzle me at the same time," I said. "You criticize the British in one breath and defend them in another. Why?"

"I'll tell you. This government I neither like nor trust, and there is a John Bull-ish air of moral and every other kind of superiority toward us that drives me mad. If war comes, I might brave seasickness again and go into the navy just to have a go at them in their own home waters."

"But don't you have many English friends?" I asked.

"Of course I do. Oh, I don't dislike the English as individuals. They are honest and forthright and likable — and very critical of themselves. We can learn a lot from them, believe me. It's this attitude of theirs and the sympathy so many of the upper classes have for the South that I find hard to live with."

"We've been complaining of that superior attitude since before the Revolution."

"Our resentment may spring in part from envy," he said, with a shrug. "After all, they are an ancient and knowledgeable people, and greatly accomplished, compared with ourselves.

Granted that we are raw and aggressive, but they rub our noses in our crudeness."

"We'll learn," I said. "I've an idea that the British are like other nations in that they respect power."

"And morality," Henry added quickly. "Not raw power by itself."

"I'll concede that — at least I will now. But in their own policies they justify themselves by moral reasons so flagrantly that they often seem hypocritical, and I'm not sure they aren't."

"Well, we're not lily-white in that respect. Now look here, I didn't call for you just to argue with you about the British. I've managed to get an invitation for you to accompany me to a reception at Lord Palmerston's tomorrow night. You will meet some interesting gentlemen and a number of beautiful ladies. Besides, staying for the reception will give you a day to recover before you leave for Liverpool. Mr. Dudley has been informed about you and wants to talk with you. Will you come with me to the Palmerstons'?"

"I'll be happy to," I said. Yet I should have preferred to go at once to Liverpool. I had no doubt that I should make the acquaintance of interesting gentlemen. The vaunted beauty of the English ladies I might meet, however, had no such appeal for me as observing that lady of the sea being groomed by the Lairds in Liverpool — the mysterious *Number 290.*

IV

THE Palmerston reception found me having to hire dress clothing from tailors in Savile Row: black broadcloth lined with silk, stiff white shirt, white cravat with pearl pin, cape and top hat, and, of course, white gloves. Henry was dressed in similar attire, though with the greater elegance of black silk lapels. He said that had this been a court affair, he would have worn the court dress resumed during his father's ministry and would have looked like a gay buck straight out of the Regency period. Giving me a critical appraisal before we left, he said that I looked correct but a trifle sinister.

Also going to the reception were Benjamin Moran and the secretary of the legation, Charles Lush Wilson. Moran and I had worked out a reasonably civil relationship, though neither of us liked the other. At the same time, I respected Moran for the hardworking, conscientious man that he was, and felt that he could be trusted. Wilson I was less sure of. Though a native of Connecticut, he had lived in Chicago for years, and owned the *Chicago Daily Journal*. His was strictly a political appointment, owing to his having supported Mr. Lincoln in the campaign of 1860, and he took his paper work so lightly and was so slovenly at it that he kept Moran in a state of almost perpetual exasperation. It was no secret that even Mr. Adams was occasionally annoyed with him. Still, amenities were generally preserved in the legation, while, outside it, none would have guessed that we were not all the best of comrades.

Furthermore, this night was indeed a happy one for all of us. Word had arrived in the forenoon of the great fight in Hampton Roads between the Confederate ram *Virginia*, formerly the U.S.S. *Merrimac*, and John Ericsson's cheesebox-on-a-raft, the *Monitor*. The *Virginia* had destroyed the sloop-of-war *Cumberland* and the frigate *Congress* — both wooden sailing ships — on March 8, and their shot had bounced off the iron monster's sides like India rubber. Only the arrival of the *Monitor* that night kept the *Virginia* from finishing off the federal squadron the next day. The battle between the two ironclads was pretty much of a draw, though the *Virginia* finally withdrew to Norfolk and spared the fleet.

All of us were greatly excited at the news.

"Now we can hold our heads up!" Henry exclaimed and ran with the news to his father.

At my raised eyebrows, Moran said, "You've no idea how galling it has been to listen to these Englishmen brag about what their navy would do to us if trouble broke out between our two countries. Now they just wouldn't dare stand up against us. Why, we'd build a whole fleet of *Monitors*."

"I think we're likely to do that in any event," I said, "but they have ironclads, too — the *Warrior*, for instance, and the French have *La Gloire*."

"But these Europeans have only a few, and we can build *Monitors* in three months — at least that's all the time Ericsson needed. They can't match us. I tell you all this makes me proud."

The carriage deposited Henry and me at Cambridge House at eleven o'clock. The guests were already numerous and stood two abreast on the staircase leading to the drawing rooms. Dukes and duchesses were mixed helter-skelter with the middle class, and people talked without any introduction, though generally with members of their own set. Several steps above us I could see Moran and Wilson. Moran's face was a study in controlled exasperation, obviously at Wilson, whose loud voice carried clearly above the polite murmurs about him. Wilson, however, was so obviously enjoying himself that he ignored both Moran's disapproval and the amused looks of the other guests.

How long we stood on the steps, inching our way upward, I don't know, but it must have been an hour, and it seemed much longer, judging by how cramped my feet felt in a new pair of dress shoes. In the end, we reached the top and gazed out at a sea of crinolines and vivid scarlet and blue uniforms and black frock coats and white cravats. The principal drawing room of Cambridge House faced Piccadilly, and another, a long room, merged with it from the east. Both were brilliantly lighted with ceiling candelabra and wall sconces. We had previously deposited our hats and cloaks in the cloakroom, so we entered the drawing room looking as distinguished as we ever would. After an interminable period, we finally approached

[29]

Lord and Lady Palmerston, the former, at least, no friend to the North.

When Henry introduced me to him as a lawyer friend, Palmerston nodded, uttered a gracious welcome, and then said, with a twinkle in his blue eyes, "Mr. Adams, I would still bet on our *Warrior* over your *Monitor*."

"Then, sir, if you will forgive me, you'd lose."

Henry looked up at the tall old man, a battle light gleaming in his eyes.

"I'll forgive you, young man," Palmerston growled amiably, "for I'd win. Our shells could have penetrated the *Virginia's* armor. The *Monitor's* shot only made dents. We could put the *Monitor* out of action quite as handily as the *Virginia*."

"Perhaps, sir," I said gently, "both ships were not using heavy powder charges."

For an instant he stared at me, then he nodded. "I thought you were a lawyer, Mr. Pettigrew."

"I am, sir, but artillery is a hobbyhorse with me."

"I daresay, I daresay."

Then he introduced us to Lady Palmerston, a woman of aristocratic bearing but kindly manner. She recognized Henry at once, and welcomed both of us. After that we were on our own.

"How did you know about those powder charges?" Henry asked.

"I didn't, but I've seen enough of those Dahlgren cannon to feel certain their construction is stronger than most people think it is. If the powder charge were increased by half or even doubled, it would take more than the four inches of railroad iron the *Merrimac* had to hold out the shot."

"Wouldn't you know Palmerston would call her the *Virginia*?"

I shrugged. "Well, I suppose that's correct, but I think, for most of us, she'll go down in history as the *Merrimac*, and I only wish she had been properly destroyed when the Norfolk Navy Yard was burned."

"A bad job of burning, I'd say."

With that, we passed among the crowd, which grew constantly. When we had entered, there were still a number of gentlemen sitting and conversing with the ladies, but before long only the ladies were seated, and eventually many ladies as well as all the gentlemen were standing. No one seemed to pay much attention to anyone outside of his own little clique, but Henry bravely made the rounds, introducing me. I met the long-faced Earl of Shaftesbury, who had been so active in pressing for reform acts in the factories and mines and for freeing the slaves in the Empire back in 1833. He wondered when Mr. Lincoln would get around to emancipating our slaves. Fortunately his seemed only a rhetorical remark with no answer expected. I also met, more fleetingly, little Lord John Russell, the Foreign Secretary, with his intellectual face and a manner which, however suave, seemed sincere. Henry had mentioned that his father got along much more easily with Russell than Palmerston, but personally I preferred the more direct, forthright manner of the Prime Minister.

One person who caught my eye was Lady Diane de Vere Beauclerk, a descendant of Nell Gwyn's. Tall and slender, she had bright blue eyes, a small nose, and chestnut-brown hair which she wore back from her temples in thick masses. She was surrounded by admirers, among whom I saw Moran and Wilson on the fringes.

Henry and I were about to move over to her group when I heard a voice say, "The South, sir, will lead General McClellan into a trap on the road to Richmond."

Up to this point I had heard nothing but banalities. The men had spoken in the dawdling, languid tone of their class, which made me think they needed a cathartic. Though the women were more animated and cheerful, their voices almost musical and more articulate, they talked of nothing, either. I felt Henry Adams was scarcely exaggerating when he said that these receptions canonized mediocrity. But now someone had expressed an opinion clearly and decisively, and it was not about the weather or some other silly reception he had attended. As a matter of fact, the voice didn't even sound English, and it wasn't unfamiliar. I turned with Henry.

Not ten feet away, though with several couples in between, stood Roger Clavering and, with him, Tamara Ravenel and a tall, deeply tanned man, fair hair flecked with gray, who looked military but without the woodenness of a number of Guards officers present. I had earlier mentioned to Henry having met Clavering and Tamara aboard the *Arcadia*, though I had gone into few details of our conversation. I now quietly identified them for him and asked who their companion was.

"That is Alexander Rushton, Lord Cromyn, a captain in the Royal Navy, and, by all the reports we have heard, a restless, ambitious man."

"I suppose his being with them means that he is sympathetic to the Rebels."

"I shouldn't wonder, although she is lovely enough to attract attention regardless."

"Would you like to meet her? Or wouldn't it be the better part of diplomacy?"

"Of course I'd like to meet her."

"Then come with me."

We moved toward her, Henry nodding to acquaintances. Clavering faced our way even before we reached him, and, to be perfectly honest, I didn't think he knew we were approaching. At once I introduced Henry to them and they, Lord Cromyn to us.

Henry Adams might deplore the lack of depth to the conversation at gatherings like this, but he was adept himself at keeping it from becoming weighty. Tamara Ravenel's eyes sparkled as he drolly compared this reception with one he had attended in Washington in the early winter of 1861, when gentlemen were requested to leave their derringers and loaded canes with the cloakroom attendants.

"Do you mean there might have been a battle right there in the drawing room?" Cromyn asked.

"Oh, I've no doubt of it," Henry said, and his elbow brushed my ribs.

"Oh, come now, surely you Americans aren't that ill-mannered!"

"Perhaps not all of us," Clavering said. "But a man's honor is a sacred thing. Take his weapons away and you leave him only his fists."

"No gentleman uses his fists against another gentleman, Mr. Clavering."

"Then what is left for him to do? Spit tobacco juice over his opponent's shoes?"

"A filthy habit, you Americans with your tobacco-chewing!"

"Lord Cromyn, I couldn't agree more," Tamara said. "Even carpets aren't immune when Americans chew."

"Maybe you Southerners ought to lose this war for having made tobacco-chewing popular. Don't you think so, Mr. Pettigrew?"

I had the impression that Cromyn had merely been leading us along as the sober Englishman, that he hadn't been one whit taken in, and the half-challenging, taunting tone with which he put that simple question convinced me. "Oh, I think the South ought to lose the war," I replied, "but not for raising tobacco for whatever use."

"Mr. Pettigrew has no liking for Southerners, Lord Cromyn," Tamara said.

Clavering nodded. "Yes, there is little doubt that Mr. Pettigrew would like to see all Southerners hanged, drawn and quartered — your lovely old English penalty for treason, Lord Cromyn."

His lordship grunted.

It was Henry who broke the awkward silence when he laughed lightly and said, "All of us should be thankful we live in such civilized times as these."

"Yes, traitors are merely hanged now," Clavering said.

"I doubt there'll be much hanging," Cromyn growled, "if no one can win a clear-cut victory. It's like your two ironclads: a standoff. Sorry I missed seeing that fight."

"It will change the navies of the world," Henry said.

"It will — though, as you know, we and the French are already producing ironclads ourselves. Actually that battle merely confirms what we already knew before, and it introduces no new principle."

"Not even the *Monitor*'s turret?"

"No, Mr. Adams, our Captain Coles already had designed a turret, and a better one than Ericsson put on the *Monitor*."

Tamara Ravenel gave an unmistakable sniff. "You British are always a little smarter than the rest of the world, aren't you?"

His lordship actually smiled. "We'd like to think so, Miss Ravenel, but the truth is we just started earlier and have got more engineering knowledge."

"Enough to build ships fast enough to run the blockade of the Southern ports?" I asked.

Cromyn smiled a thin, rather hard smile. "Yes, Mr. Pettigrew, I'm sure we could build ships fast enough to elude any of your new blockading cruisers."

He didn't have to add, "We're doing that already" — everyone knew it.

"Do you think the blockade ineffective, Lord Cromyn?" Henry asked.

"You're in a better position to know than I am, Mr. Adams," Cromyn countered. "But from over here it seems that a resolute captain in a reasonably swift ship doesn't have much difficulty slipping into at least a half-dozen Southern ports and out again."

"The blockade will tighten as more ships are brought into service," I said.

"Undoubtedly," said Cromyn. "But as your navy gets tougher, runners will become swifter and their masters more skillful."

It struck me now that Clavering and Miss Ravenel had been silent during this exchange. Was it something to do with the blockade that had sent them to England? Were they agents over here to arrange for the construction and fitting out of blockade runners? Was their mission apart from that of Captain Bulloch?

Henry now took my arm. "I think we must pay our respects to a few more people before we leave."

We bowed and bade good night to the others, and began again the endless social rounds.

When we left at two o'clock, the street was lined with coaches, their drivers chatting in groups or dozing over their reins. We caught a cab for the legation, and the heads of both animals and drivers came up with a jerk as we clip-clopped past the carriages down the street. I was puzzled and tired, so held my tongue while Henry went on about what a bore these receptions were, how meaningless was all this rush and fuss of society. No one so much as attempted to have a good time, Henry added, for if he did, he would be thought vulgar. "I tell you, I see nothing to admire in the whole system. It's a nuisance. In fact, it's worse — it's evil."

"I think you need a good sleep, Henry," I said.

He looked at me as if to protest, then subsided, only to rouse himself a moment later and say, "By God, that Miss Ravenel is a pretty woman. But if you ask me, she and Clavering are up to no good."

"And Lord Cromyn?"

"I don't know the connection. While you're off to Liverpool, I'll find out what I can. But Clavering — he's a man to watch out for, if you ask me."

[35]

V

I arrived in Liverpool late the next afternoon. It was as gray a day as when I had first set foot here from the *Arcadia*, and the smoke was as heavy and oppressive. I wondered if the sun ever shone on Liverpool.

Our consul, Thomas H. Dudley, a lawyer and former treasurer of Camden, New Jersey, was a welcome surprise. Though Moran had originally liked Dudley very much and still respected him far more than most consuls who visited the legation office, Dudley's energy, his frequent reports of Confederate activity in the great port city, and his constant suspicions and suggestions annoyed the assistant secretary. I was therefore prepared to meet a real busybody, patriot though he might be.

But the man with the heavy mustache and beard who rose from his desk in an office made cheery by a coal fire and a fine enlarged photograph of President Lincoln on the plain buff wall was hardly what I had expected. He was tall and thin, somewhere in his early forties, with a high, broad forehead barely concealed by a shock of brown, wavy hair. There was an intellectual quality about his face, a refinement in his dress, and an air of energy and force about him which expressed itself at once in the alacrity with which he greeted me and in the vigor and pace of his speech.

"Mr. Pettigrew, I am glad to meet you, sir."

He shook my hand and motioned me to a chair beside his desk.

"Now, then," he said, "Mr. Adams has written about you. My own agents are active, and I shall be glad to keep you posted for your reports to Secretary Welles."

I could scarcely get out a word of thanks before he rushed on.

"You could stay with my family and me, but we are watched by Captain Bulloch's people, so I think that for you to preserve your role as a student of maritime law, you'd best take lodgings elsewhere. I can recommend a modest, respectable place, and you already have letters of introduction from Mr. Adams to a number of the great admiralty law people in this city. Now do you have anything in mind for tomorrow?"

"No, sir," I said.

"Then I shall have one of my assistants show you about Liverpool and take you by one of the ferries up the river past the Laird Yard. In fact, he will conduct you to one of the lodging houses now and will call for you at ten o'clock tomorrow morning. Is this agreeable to you?"

"Very agreeable," I said.

"Good." He rose, opened a door and called, "Bruce!"

A lanky young man appeared, neatly attired but badly needing some of his black hair shorn. His nose was large, and his eyes, almost as dark as his hair, looked friendly but gigantic behind his spectacles. When Dudley introduced him as Bruce Thornton from Bangor, Maine, I felt as if I were meeting a neighbor, but a friendly neighbor. Being from Maine, he didn't break out into an effusion of greetings, but he shook my hand as if he meant it. When Dudley told him where to take me, Thornton got his hat and coat and walked me to my rooming house.

"When were you last in Maine?" I asked on the way.

"Three years ago."

"Then you weren't here when Nathaniel Hawthorne was consul?"

"No, he had left for Italy in 1857. He was here for four years, you know, and is still something of a legend. It isn't every consular post that can lay claim to a first-rate literary man, though I can't say I've as yet read anything he wrote except his reports."

I hadn't, either, though I knew a good deal about his work through my Grandmother Pettigrew, who had read everything he had written and had strong feelings about it, most of them favorable. She objected, however, to *The House of Seven Gables*, in which she thought the wicked escaped unpunished, and she disliked his biography of his friend President Pierce, mainly, I think, because she thought Pierce soft on slavery, and therefore could not abide him.

My lodgings — a large room on the second floor of a three-story brick house — were nothing to celebrate. Luckily the mattress wasn't too lumpy; the linen, the worn carpet, and the furniture were clean, and I could see the river through the small forest of factory chimneys. The landlady, a Mrs. Washburn, assured me that she served a good table. She couldn't remember any objections from Englishmen; she didn't expect any from Americans. And, to give the lady her due, she was a good cook, though the helpings seemed designed to keep her boarders lean.

The next morning, I walked through the neighborhood. It was partly commercial and partly residential, the streets were cobbled, and the great brewery wagons that rumbled through them refused to give way for the lighter vehicles, despite the angry shouts of drivers. The air fairly reeked of fresh manure, and foot travelers like myself had to watch where we stepped.

Promptly at ten o'clock, Thornton appeared. "There are ferries up and down and across this river," he said. "If you're ready, we'll give the Liverpool waterfront a good looking-over."

And that we did. Liverpool, as the chief entrepôt for the cotton that went to the Lancashire mills, as the transatlantic shipping point for passengers, and as a great shipbuilding area, is one of the busiest ports in the world. I marveled at the skillful way in which the ferries we rode dodged the shipping — great passenger steamers and freighters; heavily sparred ships, their canvas drooping, drawn by tugs with high funnels; long lines of barges also under tow, and a multitude of little steam launches plowing furiously through the water filthy with coal dust, oil, garbage and sewage. Finally we took a ferry heading upriver toward Tranmere and Eastham. This took us directly past the Birkenhead Ironworks, which was the Laird Yard, where the 290 was under construction. People crossing the river to the lower landings or even those taking the Woodside Ferry across would not have noticed the 290 because the ironworks lay above and opposite the main commercial establishments of the port. People on this ferry, however, could not help but notice her because along at the south end of the Laird Yard she looked so different from the iron ships being built.

"There she is, and if you ask me, I'd say she's going to be a beauty," Thornton said.

I studied the hull resting on the ways. Though dwarfed by the other large craft in the yard, she so far excelled them in beauty of design, there was no comparison. Depending, too, on how powerful her engines were, she would probably be able to outsail most ships now in the Mersey. Workmen were swarming over her, but she was still weeks, perhaps months, from being finished.

"Do we absolutely know she is being built for the South?" I asked. I had to raise my voice to be heard above the staccato pounding of hammers in the yard, which sounded for all the world like musketry.

He nodded, but frowned me into silence as other passengers moved over to the rail to look at the yard.

I glanced at them. I recognized no one but listened to exclamations of pleasure that puzzled me. No one seemed to know for a certainty that the 290 was destined for the South. While I heard the view expressed that she was probably to be a blockade runner, not all agreed. Some thought she was being built for a mercantile house in a European country — Spain was most often mentioned. One man said that he had heard she was being constructed as a combination carrier and yacht for an industrialist in Hamburg.

"Nay, she's too big for a yacht," a thick voice answered.

Then we swept by the Laird Yard, and people wandered away.

At the landing stage above the ironworks we went ashore and entered a public house.

"It would have been all right to return on the same ferry," Thornton said, "but there's no sense in letting anyone aboard notice that we're curious about what's going on at the yard."

"But don't Bulloch and his crowd know you people are keeping the 290 under surveillance?"

"Oh, of course," he acknowledged. "They're watching us, and we're watching them. As a matter of fact, we know who some of them are, and they know us. I've been in this pub at least twice before, and on the first occasion I sat just behind Bulloch. He's a very decent person — he'll even bid you good day, which is more than most Confederate emissaries to this country will do."

Silently we watched men come and go in this shabby little hole-in-the-wall. Then I came back to my original question and repeated it.

"We're certain, though we don't actually know that Bulloch commissioned the *Number 290*. So we ask workmen in the yard and keep our ears open for anything let slip along the waterfront, particularly by ship chandlers, builders, and lawyers. Mr. Dudley has made up his mind that the 290 won't escape the way the *Oreto* did."

Presently Thornton looked at his watch and asked if there was anything else I wanted to see.

"Is it possible to get closer to the 290?" I asked.

"Only if you get into the yard, and they will let no one in without a pass."

"Is it difficult to get a pass?"

He shrugged. "It's not easy unless you have something to do with one of the ships being constructed there. Even then, they are particular and want identification. You see, these shipyards are in fierce competition with one another and want to guard their secrets. Well, shall we go?"

We were just about to rise when Thornton settled back into

his chair again. I thought he exchanged some sort of eye signal with someone behind me, but for the moment he said nothing. Then he slowly stood up, and we made our way out of the pub. As we did so, I noticed a short, stocky man, hat pushed back from his brow, just addressing himself to his beer and kidney pie. His little eyes looked steadily at us, then he dug deeply into his pie, and we left. I wouldn't have given him a second thought if I hadn't detected Thornton's eye signal, and suddenly I remembered the broad little man who had been at the wharf when the *Arcadia* docked and at the depot when the passengers boarded the train for London. He and this man were one and the same.

"Is he a friend?" I asked Thornton.

"Of a kind."

"Surely you weren't trying to hide the look you gave him!"

"No, not really. The man's named Maguire. He follows Captain Bulloch everywhere — those are Mr. Dudley's orders."

"Everywhere?"

"Well, when Bulloch is in Liverpool. If Maguire is here now, that must mean that Bulloch is up from London to look at the 290."

"Is Bulloch the only man he follows?"

Thornton shook his head. "He keeps an eye on several people for Mr. Dudley, and, of course, he works for others. He has several operatives in his own employ."

"Well, I'd like to meet him," I said. I then told Thornton about my seeing Maguire before and how he had resembled a sea captain I had sailed with. By this time, we had boarded the downriver ferry and found ourselves seats so that we could look at the 290 again.

For the next three days, I saw no one from the consulate. I busied myself calling on legal offices. Discreet inquiries about the 290 got nowhere. Not that there was a conspiracy of silence about that ship; I believe most Englishmen I talked with had

[41]

even less of an idea of her destination than we did — and I reluctantly concluded that ours was barely more than a firmly held suspicion, for all the activity of Mr. Dudley's office. In fact, I began to think that Moran had a point when he said that Dudley saw a Rebel under every bed.

My discussions with English lawyers, however, were very fruitful in further opening up the field of maritime law. I started giving serious thought to its possibilities after the war. It was still too early to gauge in what condition American commerce would find itself when the war was over. If raiders such as the newly escaped *Oreto* and the 290 really got loose on the high seas, they might not only destroy many ships but, far more serious, would also frighten our shipowners into placing their vessels under foreign registry, from which the owners would probably hesitate long before returning them to United States registry. This would cut into the business of maritime law unless a firm could also represent British owners in the United States. However I looked at the present and the future, it all added up to the necessity of preventing the South from sending out commerce raiders. The *Number 290*, if a raider, must never be permitted to leave port if the efforts of Consul Dudley and Mr. Adams could hold her.

At noon on the fourth day, I took my lunch at a restaurant near the Free Public Library. I had no more than given my order when Maguire stood before me.

"Mr. Pettigrew, my name is Maguire. May I join you?"

I rose, and invited him to be my guest. Maguire accepted without demur, and after a suitable taste of ale, was ready to talk.

"Mr. Pettigrew," he said, "I understand you are interested in the *Number 290.*"

When I said that I was, he laughed hugely. "If I had a pound for everyone interested in finding out about the 290, I'd be hiring other people to do the work I do."

"Mr. Dudley has told you who I am?"

[42]

"Young Thornton did, at Mr. Dudley's direction."

"Then can you tell me anything more certain than rumor about the 290?"

"Mr. Pettigrew, what I learn about that ship I report to Mr. Dudley — and only Mr. Dudley. He's my employer. He knows what I know."

The man was blunt. I nodded. "Fair enough. Now can you tell me something that has nothing to do with the 290 or Mr. Dudley, so far as I know?"

"I don't know what you're driving at, Mr. Pettigrew, but I don't work for philanthropy." His jaw crunched on a piece of beef gristle, and with a grunt of distaste he spat it upon his plate.

"That's fair enough, too," I said. "I wouldn't expect you to work for nothing. I'm not even sure there will be any work at all. I wouldn't have mentioned you to Bruce Thornton if I hadn't seen you before in connection with two acquaintances of mine."

He picked up his glass of ale and looked at me steadily after he drank. "Thornton told me about them."

"Did he mention their names?"

Maguire nodded. "He did."

"Do you know them?"

"What's it worth to you, Mr. Pettigrew? How much?"

"It may be worth nothing at all, Mr. Maguire. But if you have some worthwhile information for me, I think we can agree on a price."

"And if I don't have information?"

"Then I may ask if you will obtain some. Pray stop playing with me, Maguire."

Maguire nodded, took the cigar I offered him, and after smelling its length, lighted it with a sigh of appreciation at its aroma. "Mr. Pettigrew, have you ever heard of Colbert and Snow Limited?"

I shook my head.

[43]

"They are a London firm in the import-export trade, specializing in cotton and tobacco from America and spices from the East. Actually they operate much like brokers and have among their clients a number of the textile mills up here. Now with the blockade of the Southern coast, cotton is going to become scarce once the manufacturers over here exhaust their stockpiles. So is Virginia tobacco, for that matter. The longfibered cotton from Egypt and India may take up the slack eventually, but there'll always be a demand here for Southern cotton and tobacco and a demand in the South for munitions, clothing, shoes, medicines — you name them, for whatever the items, the South will need them and will want what it doesn't actually need. Colbert and Snow are therefore considering the ordering of several blockade runners."

"But what is the connection between all this and Miss Ravenel and Roger Clavering?"

"It's possible that they're over here to negotiate with Colbert and Snow on this very point."

"But you do not know for sure?"

"That is right."

"Do you know if they are operating in behalf of the Confederate government?"

"No, I don't know that, either. They may be doing so, or they may be engaged in their own behalf, or maybe for both themselves and their government."

"Do you mind telling me if it was because of them you were watching the passengers when the *Arcadia* docked?"

"That's right, though I didn't know they would be the ones I'd be looking for."

"I don't understand."

He knocked off a long ash from his cigar. "It's like this, Mr. Pettigrew. The consulate learned on the day that Captain Bulloch returned that we could expect more Southern agents. We didn't know how or when they were coming, but every

[44]

English ship arriving here from America has been watched by our own agents. We learned about Ravenel and Clavering within minutes of the *Arcadia's* docking."

"But Thornton told me he had never heard of them."

Maguire shrugged. "That's quite possible, since Mr. Dudley keeps much to himself. Or Mr. Thornton may not have wanted to let you know that he knew of them until he had cleared it with Mr. Dudley. Your consul here keeps his office under very tight control, Mr. Pettigrew."

"But you seem to have no hesitation in speaking to me about Miss Ravenel and Mr. Clavering."

"Mr. Pettigrew, I work for the consulate, but I work independently, too. The only condition Mr. Dudley placed on such an arrangement is that I do nothing to hurt the consulate. He trusts me, and I keep faith with him. Ravenel and Clavering are no friends to your government, so I have no reluctance in helping you. And, of course, anything I discover for you will help the consulate, too."

I liked Maguire up to a point. I had the feeling that I could trust him. I therefore engaged him to learn everything he could about Tamara Ravenel and Roger Clavering. All that had passed between us on the *Arcadia* I revealed to him, including the association of Guy Allen, the *Arcadia's* second officer, with Miss Ravenel and Clavering. Naturally, I also described Henry's and my encounter with them and Lord Cromyn at Palmerston's reception. Maguire made no notes of anything I said. He merely leaned forward with his elbows on the table and listened to me with half-shut eyes. His cigar was now only a stump, but he thrust a toothpick into it and smoked it down to thumbnail length. When I had finished, he grunted and mashed the cigar out.

"Mr. Pettigrew," he now said, "I'll do what I can for you, and I'll let you know when I have anything to report."

For the first time since arriving in England, I felt easy.

[45]

Maguire's unmistakable air of competence was very reassuring. Not only did I feel that whatever was to be learned about the 290 would be learned, but also I was certain that the Ravenel-Clavering mystery was on its way to being unraveled.

VI

THAT evening at dinner the conversation in the rooming house turned to the battle between the *Monitor* and the *Merrimac*. The report of that contest was stale news — in fact, no longer news — by this time, but it was still capable of stirring up a conversation. A stout Liverpool stockbroker named Jenkins gloomed that Britannia no longer ruled the waves. At this, Angus MacNaughton, an engineer at the Laird Yard, shook his shaggy head.

"Tush, tush!" he growled. "Those American ships cannot cross the ocean. Isn't that right, Mr. Pettigrew?"

"They were designed for tasks in American coastal waters," I said, which, I realized, wasn't answering his question directly.

"There, what did I tell you?" MacNaughton gloated.

"But now we must rebuild our entire fleet in iron," Jenkins said. "Think of the expense!"

"But, Mr. Jenkins, think of all the jobs it'll make for people right here in the yards at Liverpool!" Mrs. Washburn, who had stopped at the entrance to the kitchen, cut in.

"Aye, Mrs. Washburn," Angus MacNaughton laughed, "and your little hotel here won't lack for tenants, will it?"

"It never has, Mr. MacNaughton. Oh, I'm all for an iron navy, and a big one, too. And I'd have nothing to do with that little wooden ship of yours that people make so much fuss about, Mr. MacNaughton."

"It isn't my ship, madam," he protested.

"But it is a warship, isn't it?" Jenkins asked.

"Who knows?" And MacNaughton cocked an eye toward me. "But if it should be a Southern cruiser, Mr. Pettigrew, it will do your merchant ships no good."

"I'm sorry to say that's true," I said.

"Aye, that war of yours is a bad thing, Mr. Pettigrew. 'Tis a pity you can't free your slaves without all that bloodletting. A cruel thing, slavery."

"We were wiser to set our slaves free almost thirty years ago," Jenkins said.

I let the conversation run along whatever course it wished, and agreed when I could or disagreed moderately when it was necessary. The longer we talked, however, the clearer became MacNaughton's hatred of slavery as both unchristian and derogatory to the dignity of man.

After dinner, MacNaughton detained me in the small living room where we had our coffee, and asked if I were meeting enough men skilled in maritime law.

"Yes, I think so. I have had a number of useful conversations. But I am also interested in studying types of shipping, particularly the new iron ships — their construction, their weaknesses, their cost of operation, and the like. I believe that a maritime lawyer should be thoroughly familiar with such matters. All I know is wooden ships."

"You've been to sea yourself?"

I told him briefly about my experience under Captain Nathan Cummings.

"Ah, you have a good start on your career, Mr. Pettigrew. Now, how would you like to look at some iron ships being built? I speak of the vessels at Laird's. . . . I shall have to clear you, of course, but I will let you know tomorrow of the exact time."

"You are very kind, Mr. MacNaughton."

"Tush, tush. But just you wait until you see some of our beauties."

That night I had a little difficulty falling asleep. It appeared

[47]

as if I might at last get a close look at the 290. Nor did I feel too wrenched in my conscience at deceiving Angus Mac-Naughton, for I was exceedingly interested in iron ships and their future, and the possible role they might have in my own future as well.

"You'll observe, Mr. Pettigrew, that the old Mersey is busy this time of day."

Angus MacNaughton spoke sober truth. The river in the murky light of early morning was alive with craft large and small, of every description, but notably with steam ferries and launches crowded with workers. We were on a ferry headed upriver, and, time and again, I thought that we might be run down by one of the cross-river ferries. Visibility was poor, between the coal smoke and mist, but the pilots of these river craft were as skillful as they were daring.

"Oh, there's an occasional accident," MacNaughton said when I expressed admiration of the pilots, "but those men know their river and their own ships very well. But your New York waters must be as crowded as the Mersey."

I explained that the waters around New York, busy as they were, were more spacious than the Mersey, hence less hazardous.

As we approached the Birkenhead Ironworks, MacNaughton said, "I can be with you this morning, Mr. Pettigrew, but come noon, you will have to find your own way back home. The Lairds are not philanthropists."

"They must be an interesting family."

"Aye, they're that." He squinted at the yard with its numerous ships under construction, its colonnaded office buildings, and at least four chimneys towering above the foundries.

"The old man of the family is John Laird of Birkenhead," MacNaughton said. "He is as fit and trim now as when he founded the yard. He's actually been building iron ships since 1829. He was one of the first to have faith in iron."

"Does he still supervise the yard?" I asked, my attention

drawn to a great twisting roll of smoke pouring from one of the chimneys where firemen had evidently just spread on coal.

"Oh, he still keeps an eye on the operations, but at a distance. It's John, Jr., and William who actually manage the yard. I would not like to be one of their competitors. They drive a rough bargain, but they press so hard for quality that they never lack for contracts."

"The Laird work is well known and respected in America," I said.

"I've no doubt. We make ships for companies all over the world."

"Mr. MacNaughton, didn't the Lairds build the Confederate raider *Oreto?*"

"That was the Miller Yard — W. C. Miller and Sons, on the Liverpool side of the river. A good firm. Now, then, Mr. Pettigrew, let's go ashore."

We surged forward with the crowd as the steamer docked. From the Birkenhead side, as well as off the ferries from Liverpool, hundreds of workmen, most of them wearing caps and all carrying dinner pails, converged on the gates. A number of them, seeing us, tugged at their caps and bade Mr. MacNaughton good morning. He never failed to respond and seemed to know a surprising number by name. Then, as a whistle blew, the gates opened and the watchmen checked us through. MacNaughton had evidently spoken to them on the previous day, for after entering my name on a list, they let us in without question.

"Now, then, let us go meet John, Jr., first of all," MacNaughton said.

We entered a large building and went up to a long office cluttered with desks and tables, where clerks in dark frock coats were already at work. They barely glanced up as we entered and walked down the side of the room to the door to Mr. Laird's office. At his cheery "Come in," we entered a room, walnut-paneled, with a long table and several desks, books and ledgers rising high along one wall, ship models in glass cases along another wall, and windows overlooking the yard and the river.

John, Jr., came forward to meet us, a slim, vital man with a long face and whiskers on his cheeks but his chin clean-shaven. He welcomed me cordially but briskly; this would not be a long interview. "Mr. MacNaughton tells me that you are a lawyer and interested in ships. Iron ships."

"Yes, sir," I said, "and Mr. MacNaughton has assured me there are none better built than at Laird's."

"Angus has been with us for many years, Mr. Pettigrew."

"Nearly forty years," MacNaughton said.

"And a grand designer and engineer he is, Mr. Pettigrew. You couldn't have a better guide around the yard. You're coming to the meeting at noon, Angus?"

"Aye, I'll be there," MacNaughton said.

A few more pleasantries, and we left.

He conducted me through drafting rooms, a small laboratory, a foundry, and along the stocks where the great iron ships were cradled. I saw eight ships on the ways in the yard, five of them iron; of the five, three were steamers. We went aboard one of the last, and I learned more about the seaworthiness of an iron hull than I ever knew before. The hammering and riveting and pounding on the echoing iron hull prevented me from hearing everything MacNaughton was saying, but there was no doubt of his fascination with what came of the famous recipe of iron ore, coke, limestone, and air.

"People said it was contrary to nature for iron ships to float," MacNaughton shouted. "They said iron ships would sink like stones." He roared with laughter. "I tell you, with good seamen they're indestructible."

He was, of course, exaggerating; iron ships have their own problems. But looking over the Birkenhead Ironworks, I had no doubt that the future lay with ships of metal. Moreover, unlike wooden ships, there seemed no limit to the size and power of

[50]

iron ships, provided their engines were strong enough to drive them and the docks were large enough to accommodate them.

Most of the morning we climbed up, inside, and through the ships in the Laird Yard. It was nearly noon before we got to where the *Number 290* lay.

"Now here is a beauty," I said, "even if she isn't iron."

"You like her, do you?" he asked, looking at me. "Well, she'll be a dandy sailer."

"Yes, I like her, though she's small. But isn't she being fitted for steam as well as sail?"

"Aye, she is."

He made no move to offer to take me aboard her — or indeed to discuss her further. And there was no doubt we'd certainly have been in the way because of the activity aboard her. I didn't press MacNaughton. He'd been accommodating enough as it was. But, observing her, I was sure I was looking at a ship of about 230 feet in length with a beam of 30 feet, and perhaps, when afloat, of a displacement of a thousand tons. I knew my estimates were only approximate, but this was near enough for the time being. How powerful her engines would be there was no telling, but she was to be a screw steamer that, given a limited coal bunker capacity, would depend partially on sail. When in pursuit of prey, if she was truly a cruiser, she would rely on her steam.

"Mr. Pettigrew," MacNaughton said, drawing a gold-capped watch from his vest and opening it by pressing the stem, "we have seen the Laird Yard, and now I must get ready for our officers' meeting at noon. Let me show you to the gate."

As we walked the length of the yard to the gate where we had entered, I told him how deeply I appreciated his kindness. Though he "tush-tushed" me, I think he was pleased. He couldn't know — or at least I was fairly sure he couldn't know — how pleased I really was. And this in spite of our not going aboard the 290. I was certain he had had his orders not to take me aboard. Nor had he said a thing about her that would have

[51]

revealed her dimensions or ownership. He may have known, from my interest in ships, that I could estimate pretty accurately how large she was. But as for her ownership and destination, not only had he said nothing, but I began to wonder if he really knew. On the other hand, there was no doubt of his antislavery sentiments. Had his inviting me to the Birkenhead Ironworks more to it than a desire to accommodate me? Had it been a way of giving me a look at the 290 that no one else had thus far obtained, and thus striking a blow that might, in its peculiar way, be against the slaveholding South? But did this mean that he suspected I was something other than I appeared? I had no answer to these questions.

Since I had a few minutes to wait for the downriver ferry, I strolled around the waterfront, smoking a cigar. I was so engrossed in the river activity and so appalled by the row on identical row of operatives' houses that I came near to missing the ferry. Its whistle startled me into a rapid stride; then, flinging my cigar away, into a run. I made it aboard, but it was close.

As we churned out into the stream, passing the 290, I moved toward the rail. Then I froze. Among the group of passengers just a few feet down the rail from me was Roger Clavering, in deep conversation with three other men.

Turning to look at the Liverpool side of the river, I wondered whether that group could have been in the ironworks when Angus MacNaughton had been showing me around. Had he noticed them aboard the 290, and was this the reason he had not wanted me to go aboard? Actually the yard was so large, Clavering and I need never have seen each other unless we had come together on the deck of that ship. More likely, I suspected, all casual visitors were denied access to the *Number 290*. Clavering, on the other hand, might not fit into my category, though what his role could be, puzzled me. If he was simply in England to invest in blockade runners, the 290 could have been of no concern to him; she was obviously no runner.

With a brief snort from the whistle and a furious churning of water, the ferry worried its way into the slip, and I moved forward with part of the crowd to go ashore. Clavering and his companions must have remained aboard for another landing or hung back to the rear of the crowd. At any rate, I didn't see them as, in the van, I stepped ashore and walked rapidly up to the street. A number of cabs lined the curb, but I decided that I would walk to my lodgings, stopping somewhere along the way at a restaurant for a late noon meal.

Then, as I turned onto the street, I heard my name being called — and knew almost without looking that it was Tamara Ravenel. She was waving at me from a cab. She seemed, indeed, to be beckoning me.

"Miss Ravenel," I said, and tipped my hat. "I didn't know you were in Liverpool."

"There was no reason for you to know I was here. What a dreadfully dirty city!"

"Dirty but busy."

"Your friend, young Mr. Adams," she said, with a swift change of subject, "can't be at all like his father."

"Why do you say that?"

"Oh, he is so courteous and understanding, and witty, too."

"Do you mean his father doesn't have those virtues?"

She shrugged. "I don't know, myself, whether he has or not, but people say he is an old grampus."

"I have found him very considerate," I said.

"Have you got to know him that well?" she asked. "Most people never get past that officious creature Moran, or that silly Mr. Wilson. But, of course, you live at the legation, don't you? So, of course, you have more contact with Mr. Adams than most."

"Perhaps," I conceded. "May I direct the driver to take you somewhere?"

"Oh, not at all, thank you. I am waiting for Roger. Ah, here he is, and with Captain Bulloch, too."

[53]

Bulloch! I turned around, as Clavering and his companion came up to the carriage. Clavering and I shook hands perfunctorily; then he introduced me to Bulloch. I expressed my pleasure at meeting the remarkable Confederate agent, a stocky man with shaven chin and muttonchop whiskers.

For all he was a Rebel, James Dunwoody Bulloch was a man of enormous integrity. A shipping expert and former navy officer, Bulloch had commanded a steamer, the *Bienville*, on the New Orleans–New York run when the war broke out. When several New Orleans men expressed a wish to buy the steamer, Bulloch said he had no authority to execute the sale. He insisted on sailing to New York to deliver the ship to its owners. Then Bulloch returned south, and received a commission from the Davis Administration to go to Europe and buy and outfit ships for the Confederacy. He had done so, and, almost at once, ordered the *Oreto* built. Meanwhile, he procured the swift steamer *Fingal* in Scotland and sailed her, loaded with guns and ammunition, uniforms and medicines, to the Southern coast via Bermuda, and ran the blockade into Savannah. I was only too well acquainted with the *Fingal's* exploit, for she slid past my little blockader in a fog one early November night without anyone on board being aware of her until, with daylight, she made her dash up the river. Bulloch had returned to England just before I arrived, and in time to see his *Oreto* put to sea.

"Have you been in England long, Mr. Pettigrew?" he asked.

"We were fellow passengers on the *Arcadia*," Tamara broke in.

"For part of the way," I said.

"Yes," said Clavering, "ever since our boat was picked up by the *Arcadia*."

"I'm not sure Mr. Pettigrew approves of us," Tamara said. "If you scratch him deeply enough, you'll find a real Yankee."

"I'm sorry," Bulloch said. "I don't know what this is all about. . . . But if Mr. Pettigrew prefers the North, that's his privilege, just as it is mine to prefer the South."

"Thank you, sir," I said.

"You may not know it," Tamara said, "but Mr. Pettigrew must have been on the same ferry as you."

"Indeed." And Clavering stared. "Did you see the Laird Yard, Mr. Pettigrew?"

"Who could help seeing it?" I said. "It's a busy, noisy place."

"And the *Number 290*?" Clavering asked.

"Of course. And an interesting ship she is. It's hard to see just what she'll be like, but my guess is that she'll be a beauty."

"Like her, do you?" Bulloch asked.

"What I could see of her," I said. "Whoever gets her will be lucky."

"I couldn't agree more," Clavering said. "Now, captain, if we could be on our way with Tamara."

Bulloch nodded. "Of course, of course. We're late already. Mr. Pettigrew," he bowed lightly. But this time he didn't give me his hand.

As I walked away from the curb and up the street, I was brimming with questions to which I had no conclusive answers. Only slowly did I recollect that, after all, I was not an espionage agent. Mine was the role of a general observer and a liaison officer between the legation, on the one hand, and the Navy Department, on the other. The questions that had occurred to me intrigued me, but they were personally irrelevant.

With this resolution to my perplexity, I realized I was hungry. Even though it was early afternoon by this time, I turned in at a restaurant and ordered roast mutton. It was barely warm, the roast potatoes only half-done, and the quince jelly so weak it failed to cut the strong taste of the mutton. Luckily I was so hungry, the dreadful meal tasted almost savory — at least, until I glanced out the window.

Across the street, standing in the recessed doorway of a tobacconist's shop, was one of the two men who had been with Clavering and Bulloch. My eyesight has always been excellent for distance, and I easily recognized the broad face, hat pulled down over the eyes, and the hulking shoulders that seemed ready to burst through the black overcoat. I looked carefully up and down the street but failed to see his companion.

So I was under surveillance myself now. But for what reason? Was it for the purpose of finding out where I lived, or was it to learn whether I would now go to the consulate to deliver a report on what I had seen this day? If the latter, the man across the street would soon discover that I had no intention of seeing Mr. Dudley, and if this reassured Clavering and Bulloch, it would probably also puzzle them. For that matter, I decided to give my watcher a long afternoon.

After taking my time over my meal, I lighted a cigar, and, ordering a glass of Tokay wine, smoked the cigar down to a rather short butt. Then I paid my bill, and, going outdoors, hailed a cab. I noticed that there was now no one near the tobacconist's window, but I had little doubt that I was still being observed. I directed the cabbie to drive to the office of Mr. F. S. Hull, a celebrated solicitor who, so Bruce Thornton had told me, had also been consulted by Captain Bulloch.

Hull I found to be a gracious but busy man, who talked with me for a half hour after his secretary presented him with my letter of introduction from Mr. Adams. I realized I was in the presence of a very acute legal mind. But if noncommittal on a number of points, he did say he thought Secretary Seward somewhat rash, though infinitely more judicious than Mr. Lincoln. I told him that he was profoundly mistaken in the comparison, though he might have a point as to Mr. Seward's rashness. We parted amicably.

Outside I hailed another cab and had the driver take me home. When we pulled out into the street and had gone a full block, I glanced back. A cab with a pair of dirty grays that I had observed waiting four cabs down from mine was also coming up the street. I then directed my driver to take me two blocks out of my way so that I might look at one of the new hotels springing up. After we had passed the hotel, I leaned deliberately out of the cab to gaze at it, and casually glanced back. The grays were moving along at a leisurely pace behind a private carriage and a heavy dray.

I now bade my driver take me to my lodgings. I had no desire to conceal where I lived; my pursuer may have known the location anyway. What I wanted to make sure of was whether or not I was still being followed. Now that I knew, I didn't feel any more at ease, but I'd be better prepared for whatever might happen.

Later that evening, I unlocked my valise and drew out a little blunt-nosed derringer. For a moment I considered my navy Colt, but that was too bulky. The derringer, though limited in range, would fit comfortably into my overcoat pocket. Henceforth it would be my companion on the streets and along the waterfront of Liverpool.

VII

ON the following day I wrote Secretary Welles a full report of my visit to the Laird Yard, with copies to Mr. Adams and Consul Dudley. I mailed the original, and Mr. Adams's copy, directly to the legation, for transmission through diplomatic pouch to Washington. Mr. Dudley's copy I intended to deliver to Thornton in the evening.

One thing I did not mention in my report, which contained rough sketches of the 290, was my being followed. It seemed both unnecessary and overly dramatic for inclusion in an official report. Nor was I at all certain it had anything to do with my having seen the 290 from close at hand. Clavering and Tamara Ravenel may have had an idea from the time I had first encountered them aboard the *Arcadia* that I was something other than I really was. I speculated often and at length as to what I might appear to them to be, but all I could be reasonably sure of was that they thought I was engaged in some clandestine mission. Whether that mission was official or private in their minds was something of which I was also uncertain. I even wondered if I was for them a case of mistaken identity. Still, I had been deliberately followed, and there was no uncertainty at all about this.

That evening, when I was driven to Bruce Thornton's, I went with the derringer in my pocket. I also took another precaution. When I came to Europe, I brought three weapons with me: the derringer; the Colt, which I left behind now in favor of the smaller, lighter weapon, and a bowie knife. A crewman on the *Grace Stone*, a real trickster with this blade, had taught me how to use it. Only once had I employed it in a fight. Since then, I had had a special belt made and a loop in the sheath through which the belt passed. The knife snugged my left hip. I hoped I should never have to use it again — I hate a blade against a man — but the derringer would take care of only one opponent, while the bowie could give me assurance with a second.

When I reached the Thorntons', Bruce's wife Sally, whom I had met only once before and then briefly, opened the door for me. A slender girl, brown-eyed and brown-haired, she welcomed me warmly, then frowned. "Bruce isn't back yet. He sent a runner about five o'clock saying he would be late. That Consul Dudley is like an overseer on a slave plantation."

"Perhaps I'd better come back later," I said.

"Nonsense, Mr. Pettigrew, please do come in."

The Thorntons occupied half of the second floor of a three-story house on Duke Street. Though most of the furniture was the landlord's and clearly looked like discarded relics of his, Sally Thornton had draped large India-print scarves over several of the larger pieces so that, with a few artfully chosen paintings and statuettes, many books, and coals glowing in the living-room grate, the lodgings looked most attractive.

"What is the news of the 290?" Sally asked.

"Nothing new, really. But when she's launched and the Lairds start installing her engines and equipping her, there will be some excitement at your husband's office and at the legation in London, too."

"I'm certain of that, and the excitement may not end then," she said, sitting down and picking up some knitting. "Have you heard the rumor here in Liverpool that the South may place an order for an ironclad strong enough to break the blockade?"

A seagoing ironclad. Now, that really would be something to contend with. As more vessels were added to the blockade, they would invariably include monitors, but monitors couldn't really keep the sea in heavy weather. This could mean our wooden cruisers would be brushed aside by an ironclad built for oceanic travel. Still, it would take a long time before such a monster became a reality.

"If it's only a rumor, I wouldn't worry," I said, "for if the British do start building such a ship, Mr. Adams may be able to persuade Lord Russell that it would be dangerous to good relations between our two countries to permit the South to have it."

"Not if England recognizes the South," she said.

"You're right, of course," I conceded. "But if McClellan can whip Joe Johnston's army this spring, the problem of recognition is likely to become an academic one — and the ironclad problem, too, for that matter."

"Let's hope so."

She excused herself to attend to something on the stove. Bruce's long delay had obviously upset her dinner plans. When she returned, her face flushed from the heat of the kitchen, she said, "Tell me, Scott, does your grandmother do her own cooking?"

"Most of the time. But why do you ask?"

"I was thinking that since your grandfather is Chief Justice of the State of Maine, he must surely do a lot of entertaining."

"I wouldn't say a great deal. But when they do, my grandmother has someone in to help her, of course. When we're alone, she insists on doing the cooking herself. She's a wizard. Something magical happens when she steps into a kitchen."

Sally Thornton smiled warmly. "You're very fond of your grandparents, aren't you, Scott?"

"I am." And I let it go at that.

"Do you hope to return to Maine after the war?"

"Yes, I hope to, but that depends, of course, on what opportunities are available at that time. I imagine Bruce feels the same, though if he stays in the consular service, he won't see much of Maine."

She shrugged. "He wouldn't be sorry about that. I'm the one who loves Maine. I sometimes wonder whether Bruce would go back there to live if his life depended on it. He likes the cultural advantages that one has in large cities and foreign lands, and he enjoys meeting the people who make the world run, especially those in government. I do, too — up to a point."

> " 'Towered cities please us then
> And the busy hum of men.' "

"Why, Scott, I wouldn't have thought you knew poetry. I didn't think Maine people had any use or liking for poetry."

"Why, my grandfather often cites Shakespeare and Milton in his rulings. Besides, have you forgotten that Longfellow comes from Maine? My uncle Jonathan Dearborn published some of his early poems in the *Eastern Courier*, and I even sat in on a course of lectures by Professor Longfellow at Harvard. It was he who introduced me to the poetry of the Brownings, though I haven't read much of Mrs. Browning's work."

"A pity she died last year," Sally sighed. "I love her 'Napoleon III in Italy.' Perhaps you remember those lines that run:

> Great is he
> Who uses his greatness for all.
> His name shall stand, perpetually,
> As a name to applaud and cherish,

> Not only within the civic wall
> For the loyal, but also without
> For the generous and free."

"Napoleon III may have helped free Italy, but I'm sure it was as much for his own purposes as for the Italians."

"You just don't like him."

"I neither like nor admire him, and if he could, he would recognize the Confederacy — you know that. He just doesn't dare go it alone without England."

"That may be — I won't argue with you. But though Mrs. Browning wrote those lines with Napoleon III in mind, I see them applying to Mr. Lincoln as well. Just think, Scott,

> Great is he
> Who uses his greatness for all. . . .

Isn't Mr. Lincoln trying to do that? If only our own countrymen could see it that way — and the British, too, for that matter."

"My Grandmother Pettigrew would agree with you," I said with a smile. "For her, Lincoln can do no wrong."

"I'd like to meet her," she said.

"Well, who knows? Perhaps you will have the opportunity someday. But my Uncle Jonathan is a little less convinced. He thinks that Lincoln acts more the politician than the statesman."

"I disagree with him," she said. "What does his wife think?"

"Aunt India? She died during the year of the Indian Mutiny. She and Uncle Jonathan were visiting there, and she came down with blackwater fever and died very suddenly. Uncle Jonathan has never really recovered."

"How sad. Did they have any children?"

"Two. Bradford and Alice. Alice died of pneumonia when a year old. Uncle Bradford rents the Dearborn farm on Cape Elizabeth from Grandmother Pettigrew. She and her brother Paul were the only children of my great-grandfather Tom

[61]

Dearborn, who fought in the Revolution. Paul had no children, so my grandparents bought out his share of the farm and let Uncle Bradford work it."

"Does he have any children?"

"Two. He and Aunt Ruth had five, but three died young. My cousin Clara teaches school in Portland and wouldn't leave her students for a husband. And then there's my cousin Jedediah, who's a better farmer than his father but who's itching to join the army, and probably will one of these months. When I want to do some duck-shooting, I go out to the farm and Jed and I take our shotguns and have ourselves a time."

Of a sudden it seemed that I could smell the balsam forest and the salt marsh that still cover much of Cape Elizabeth, could feel first the piercing cold of the early dawn, then the beat of anticipation as a black, irregular line in the sky flew close to the marsh. For a moment, I was homesick. I glanced at Sally Thornton and saw her smile. Then someone shouted for help from down in the street.

"That's Bruce!" Sally cried out.

I went for the door, told Sally to bring the derringer from my coat pocket, and ran down the stairs.

It was dark outside, and the gas lamps were few, but I could see a small knot of struggling men.

"Bruce!" I shouted.

"Be quick!" he said in a strangled voice. "Over — " He stopped as if someone had clamped a hand over his mouth or hit him.

I drew my bowie and plunged toward him, using the butt like a hammer to pound one of the group over the head. Then as two broke off from Bruce and headed for me, I brought the bowie down. As one lunged, his own knife swung upward. The bowie caught in his coatsleeve, which parted, and the point ripped his arm. He screamed and backed away. The second jumped me. I collapsed in a rough-and-tumble trick, and he rolled over me. Then as I turned toward him, a third man

[62]

landed on my back, and I felt my shoulder suddenly burn as his knife point slid along the top of the bone.

Suddenly a clear voice, a woman's, cut through the darkness. "You men, there, put down those knives or I'll fire!"

God bless you, Sally Thornton, I thought. But I prayed she wouldn't have to use the derringer. We were so close that she might hit any one of us. Our assailants were as startled as Bruce and I, and for a moment they stared, without moving, at Sally, the gaslight making the derringer in her hand glitter.

"Can't you hear the lady?" I shouted. "She's a dead shot."

Three knives clattered to the cobblestones. The fourth man had already fled. I backed up and took the derringer from Sally, while she got an arm around Bruce to hold him up.

By this time people were beginning to come out of their houses, and I could hear the jingle of bells on a constabulary wagon.

"Scott," Bruce called out, "let them go, let the bastards go now."

"Are you mad?"

"I say let them go before the constables get here. Sally, you tell him to let them go."

His voice was feeble but frantic. Sally turned to me. "Do as he says, Scott."

"All right, you heard the gentleman," I said. "Now get the hell out of here and take your pig-stickers with you." I kicked their knives toward them and kept them covered as they scrambled for the weapons and then took off up a dark alley.

At that moment, the constabulary wagon clattered into the street, and as people rushed to meet it, Sally and I half ran with Bruce to the Thorntons' and up the stairs to their flat. Together we cleaned Bruce up. So far as I could see, he had some slight facial wounds that had bled freely, a couple of lumps on his head, and a soreness in his body where he had been pummeled when the men had jumped him. I offered to go for a doctor, but he insisted he was all right.

[63]

While a couple of fingers of brandy were reviving him, I stripped off my suit coat, and Sally bandaged the wound in my shoulder, which was more messy than serious. She wanted to mend the coat, but I told her that I would take it to a tailor to have it cleaned and that he would stitch the torn cloth.

Meanwhile, Bruce had recovered sufficiently to explain what had happened. "They jumped me just as I turned into Bridgewater Street. I got away from them and almost reached the house. Then one of them caught up with me and grappled with me until the others arrived."

"But what were they trying to do?" Sally asked. "Were they crimpers?"

The same thought had been on my mind, for Liverpool, like a number of European ports and our own New York, had a reputation for muscling men aboard ships whose crews could not be completed by lawful hire. The hitch here was that the Thorntons didn't live within the proximity of the waterfront where such crimp details usually operated. And I said as much now. Bruce agreed.

"If they had intended killing me," he added, "they could have done so easily. All of them had knives."

"Did they steal your wallet?" I asked.

"Yes, but I had the feeling they were looking for something more than that. See how they ripped up my pockets."

"But, Bruce, why on earth didn't you want those men arrested?" Sally asked, tucking a blanket around him as he lay on the couch.

"You know as well as I do that Dudley doesn't want unfavorable publicity — or any kind of publicity. We simply can't afford it. We're unpopular enough as it is. Besides, I don't think those men really meant any harm to me. It was Scott they were after. I'm sure of it now."

"What do you mean?" I asked.

"I stopped by your place to ask you to come over for a glass of wine but learned that you had already left the house. Your

[64]

landlady didn't know where you were going. But those bastards must have tailed me home from there. You're a little taller than I am, Scott, and perhaps a bit heavier, but in the darkness, isn't it possible people who didn't know us well might confuse us?"

"Is it possible?" I demanded of Sally.

She looked at her husband and then at me, and nodded slowly. "Yes, I suppose it's possible so long as they couldn't see your faces clearly. You don't look alike at all."

Bruce closed his eyes. "This still leaves us the question of motive."

"Perhaps not," I said, and stood up. "You may not know, but I paid a visit to Birkenhead yesterday and made a complete report of it today. One copy I mailed to Mr. Adams. The other I brought along tonight for you to give to Mr. Dudley in the morning. Both the landlady and the maid saw me writing this morning and have keys to my room. Those thugs may have been paid to find out if I had written such a report and to get it from me."

"They really mean business, don't they?" Bruce pursed his lips.

"Their employer certainly does, and it could be either Bulloch or Clavering," I said.

"Or someone else."

"I'd bet on one of those two."

"Scott, do you still have that letter with you?" Sally asked.

"It's right here," I said, patting my inside coat pocket, "and I am taking it to the consulate myself in the morning."

"But you're not going back to your room tonight, Scott," Bruce said.

"Bruce is right," Sally said vehemently. "You must sleep here, Scott. Why, they may be waiting for you outside at this very moment."

I began to think that perhaps the Thorntons were right. So far as his assailants knew, Bruce still had the letter. They might

[65]

attack me as I left, but more likely they would try to get into Bruce's lodgings during the night.

"All right, I'll stay," I said. "I'll be a watchdog for you."

"I hadn't thought of that," Sally said.

"I know you haven't, and let's hope the watchdog and his weapons won't be needed. . . . Well, Sally, you handled the derringer like a veteran and spoke out with a real quarterdeck voice. How long has it been since you fired a pistol?"

To my surprise Bruce began to laugh. "A shotgun, possibly, for hunting. But a derringer? Scott, Sally never handled a pistol in her life."

VIII

THE next morning, my shoulder still smarting, I accompanied the bruised and aching Bruce Thornton to the consulate, where we told Consul Dudley what had happened. Then I handed him the copy of my report.

"They're getting rough," Dudley said. "But I doubt that Bulloch was directly responsible. He'll use every device he can think of to throw our agents off the track, yet so far he hasn't resorted to violence."

"Then Clavering," I said.

"Bruce may have told you we're trying to find out what we can about him. Not much luck, so far . . . Now just let me glance at this report of yours."

He did more than glance at it — he studied it, while I smoked one of his cigars. When he finished, he stared out the window, still holding the report in his hands.

"Mr. Pettigrew," he turned suddenly and came to his feet, "my agents have traveled up and down the river, they have talked with workmen in the Laird Yard, they have shadowed Bulloch all over England. We still don't really know just what the actual ownership, purpose, and destination of the 290 are.

[66]

We can guess, however, and I think pretty accurately. What you have given us here is the best description to date of this ship. Now, with what you have told me of Bulloch and Clavering probably being in the yard, your being followed, and the attack, I'm more certain than ever that ship is to be a Rebel raider. Of course I can't prove it yet. But those people were afraid we'd learn too much from your report."

He paused, again stared out the window, then resumed his pacing. "Mr. Pettigrew, this city is friendly to the South — I suppose it has too many maritime rivalries with our Northern shipping. Now you take Manchester, and you'll find most of the people, at least the working people, friendly to the North. That's because of John Bright and their own feeling about slavery. Have you met Bright?"

"No, sir. I know, of course, that he's a rich man, a Quaker, and a potent member of the Liberal party."

"He's more than that. He *hates* slavery, Mr. Pettigrew, and he commands the loyalties of the textile workers, the very people who are being laid off their jobs because of the cotton shortage. If this rebellion of ours continues much longer, the Lincoln Administration will have to take a stand against slavery. That will give the war a moral issue, which it really has now, though many people here and at home don't realize it, and it will rally more of the English workers and middle class to Bright's side. We'll need that support. Otherwise the upper classes here would have the government recognize the South right now."

He stopped as suddenly as he had begun, bade me be careful, and dismissed me, with the understanding that we would continue to keep in touch with each other.

We did, and I was careful, particularly as I walked along the great docks — those to the north, such as the Prince, the Waterloo, the Victoria, and the Trafalgar; and those to the south, such as George's, the Canning, the Albert, the Queen's, the Coburg, and the Brunswick (which was the largest, devoted to the timber trade and covering more than twelve acres, with two graving docks and a basin linking it with the Mersey). The varieties of ships and cargoes loading and unloading at these and other Liverpool docks fascinated me, especially the Coburg, where the transatlantic steamers docked. But I never forgot that these were areas where some of the roughest, toughest people of the world worked and lived. Nor did I forget Consul Dudley's words that this was a pro-Southern city.

Ample evidence of this sentiment was furnished on Sunday, April 20. The Thorntons and I were out walking that afternoon, as were many citizens of Liverpool after their Sunday dinners, when we heard cheering down along the docks. We had intended to take a ferry ride upriver, but this we postponed and, on impulse, followed the crowd to where a big, full-rigged ship was moored. A cordon of constables held back the onlookers as a handful of men were permitted ashore. Three were obviously Englishmen, and they were talking with two Royal Navy officers and a civilian who, Bruce said, was from the mayor's office. A fourth man was in the uniform of the United States Navy and kept loudly insisting on seeing the United States consul.

"What on earth —?" Sally began, but Bruce cut her off.

"Scott, stay with Sally, please. I'd better look into this!"

We saw him speak to the constable in charge, then to the civilian and the Royal Navy officers, but the din was so terrific, we couldn't hear a word that was said. From the crowd, however, came all manner of jeers at "those bloody Yanks" and "those goddamned Yankees," then a roar of cheering for the three Englishmen who had come ashore from the ship.

Presently Bruce spoke to a constable, who sent one of his men whistling for a cab. When it arrived, Bruce and the American walked over to us, and Bruce introduced him as Acting Master Josiah Stone.

"We're all going to the consulate," Bruce said. "Afterward,

I'll have the cab take you home, Sal. Could you go with her, Scott?"

As we drove away, the crowd hissed and booed us, then broke into cheering again, and the last we heard they were putting their lungs into "Rule, Britannia!"

"I wish you or Mr. Stone would tell us what all this is about," Sally said.

As Bruce glanced at Stone's sober face, the officer said, in a deep and troubled voice, "You might as well tell it, sir."

Bruce then related briefly the extraordinary story of the ship *Emily St. Pierre*. The *Emily* was owned by Fraser, Trenholm and Company, a Liverpool firm with a branch in Charleston, and was bound for Charleston from India with a cargo of gunny cloth. She had been stopped on March 18 off the Carolina coast by a federal cruiser which put a prize crew aboard her under Acting Master Stone and ordered her to Philadelphia. The *Emily*'s captain, William Wilson, and two men were taken along to testify in her defense before the prize court and were given the run of the ship. All went well until off Hatteras, when Stone was surprised by Captain Wilson and, with the help of the captain's steward, put in irons. Assisted by the third Englishman, they then surprised most of the officers and prize crew while asleep, bound them, and persuaded several men who were on deck that Stone wanted them to bring up a coil of heavy rope from a scuttle. When the men disappeared below, Wilson put the hatches on. Three men had thus mastered sixteen. To make the situation even more humiliating, Wilson persuaded several of the Union prize crew to help work the *Emily* across the Atlantic to Liverpool.

Bruce told the story simply, without adornment of any kind; after all, Stone himself was present. I felt sympathetic with the man but found myself admiring Wilson's exploit and amazed at Stone's stupidity in not having confined Wilson and his two crewmen in the first place. I didn't envy him the reprimand he was sure to receive from Admiral Du Pont when he returned.

[69]

"And now what happens?" Sally asked.

"We must try to recover the *Emily* for the United States government, Mrs. Thornton," Stone said.

Her husband nodded. "The first step is to register a protest with the United States consul. Meanwhile, British officials have impounded the *Emily* and will hold her until the government makes a decision one way or another."

"I think international law is reasonably clear on such an issue," I said. "But if the British insist on the right of the owners to the ship, they will have to consult rulings on blockade precedents during their previous wars. This could take some time."

"Knowing the British as little as I do," Sally said, "I'm still certain this will take time."

The settlement of the *Emily*'s case not only took time, it also led to my departure from Liverpool.

The very next morning, a runner arrived from Consul Dudley with a request that I report at once to his office. When I arrived, his secretary led me through a roomful of people waiting to see him. Dudley was busy writing at his desk when I entered. He waved me to a chair and continued a furious scratching. Then he rang a bell for his secretary, and when the busy little frock coat reappeared, Dudley practically flung him the letter he had been writing.

"Two copies, quick now!" he snapped. "Mr. Pettigrew," and he turned to stare at me while his right hand drummed the desk top, "can you leave for London this evening?"

"Yes, sir, of course."

"Good!" Dudley got up and started to pace the floor. "I wired Mr. Adams about the *Emily St. Pierre,* and he should have received the telegram this morning. What I'd like you to do is to take my report and Acting Master Stone's deposition to Mr. Adams. I'm sure he will make strong representations to Lord Russell to release the *Emily* to us. By Heaven, the British had better do something to demonstrate their neutrality. You might also mention to Mr. Adams that in my report I have reminded him of three ships being loaded here to run the blockade."

The wretched train lumbered along all night to arrive in London just when the street traffic was the most dense. I had to walk to the legation.

"Mr. Pettigrew, you've arrived just in time — you can help us move." Moran greeted me as I handed him the packet.

"Move!"

"On Friday. To Five Upper Portland Place. This will be the fifth location since Mr. Adams arrived. I pray it will be the last."

He went off with the packet while I sat down to wait. It was still early and the secretary, Charles Wilson, had not come in yet. His desk, however, with its newspapers and clippings stacked helter-skelter, looked more like an editor's desk than the neat, clean desk of the secretary of a legation, or at least, the kind of desk top I knew Mr. Adams preferred.

Then Moran reappeared and said that Mr. Adams was having breakfast and had asked if I would join him and Henry.

Already by the time I entered the dining room he had glanced over the letters and had passed them to Henry. Both greeted me warmly. Even before I was well into my bacon, they were plying me with questions about the *Number 290*, the *Emily*, and sentiment in Liverpool.

As for the last, I said there was no doubt that Mr. Dudley was convinced most of Liverpool was pro-Southern.

"But what do you think?" Mr. Adams asked sharply.

"I think he is right, sir. At the same time, there are some people who hate slavery so much they favor the North," and I cited MacNaughton.

"That's a negative form of sympathy," Henry said.

[71]

"We can't afford to turn up our noses, boy," his father said. "We'll accept any kind and degree of support and be grateful for it."

With that, he waved us to the office with the request that Henry send in Moran and Wilson to confer with him. Wilson greeted me breezily but refrained from a backslap. Moran, meanwhile, waited for Wilson to lead the way to Mr. Adams. Not only was his mouth turned down at the corners; his foot tapped the floor. Moran despised Wilson, yet observed strictly the latter's right, as secretary of the legation, to precede him.

Later, when they returned from the conference and Wilson buried his head in the morning newspapers, Moran came over to Henry's desk. Standing near my chair beside the end of the desk, he said, "Henry, Mr. Adams would like you and Mr. Pettigrew to go to the British Museum and look up some of the cases like the *Emily*'s that rose during the Napoleonic Wars, when Sir William Scott was on the bench. Mind you, be careful," and he shook his finger at us as we rose. "If you don't find the right cases, I'll have to go over myself and hunt."

"I can't tell you the number of times that man makes me want to throw up," Henry said as we looked around for a cab, then decided to walk.

"But I have the impression he's very efficient," I said.

"Efficient, yes, but officious, my God!"

Henry was edgy. As I listened to him speak of General McClellan's massing of troops before Yorktown on the Peninsula, preparatory to a drive on Richmond, it was easy to detect the longing in his voice; his brother was in service, and he would have preferred to be there also instead of doing the very useful but frustrating work of assisting his father's shorthanded legation. I suppose he knew that even in the army he would meet men as annoying to him as Moran, but Moran, with his love of detail and attention to punctilio, was a reality that he had to live with and was what pious people would call his cross.

At the British Museum, where sooner or later one seems to meet all the educated great and humble of London, we followed Moran's advice and searched very carefully the court decisions on cases resembling the *Emily*'s. I had the feeling that Moran would probably not accept our own findings completely and would do his own research afterwards, but this didn't prevent Henry and me from being extraordinarily careful. At length, I whispered to Henry that the decisions of the great justice Sir William Scott left no doubt that it was the duty of the British government to hand the *Emily* back to the United States.

"They won't do it!" Henry said out loud.

"Hush!"

The low-spoken but stern order of the clerk on duty reminded us that in the library of the Museum silence was to be preserved. And the indignant looks from the pale, scholarly men and women reading or taking notes at the tables were momentarily awesome. I wondered what would happen if I laughed aloud. I suppose it would have been as horrifying as when a little girl I heard of accidentally set off a music box at the funeral of an aunt.

We gathered up the copies we had made of the cases during the Napoleonic Wars, which clearly revealed, as I had whispered, that according to precedent, Captain Wilson's recapture of the *Emily* assured the forfeiture of both ship and cargo to the United States. Then we left the Museum.

"I agree with you," I said, as we walked down Great Russell Street. "I don't think the British will concede to us, but at least this material gives your father judicial support for a protest."

"And Father will make that protest firm and at once. He wants it written by tomorrow and intends to submit it to Lord Russell the next day."

"He and Mr. Dudley make a good team."

"Yes, but Dudley keeps sending him so many reports, Father can hardly keep up with them."

"Did you find out anything more about Tamara Ravenel and Roger Clavering?" And I told him briefly about my encounter with them in Liverpool.

"Considerably," Henry said. "We know they are Confederate agents, that they have spent some time with the Confederate mission in London, and that they manage to get invitations to various important 'at homes' here. They have also been in Liverpool, Bristol, and Southampton."

"All ports," I said.

"Yes, and with good reason. Through Colbert and Snow Limited, they have bought two small steamers, one in Bristol and the other in Southampton, and these will undoubtedly be blockade runners. The Bristol steamer is due to leave sometime this week, probably for Bermuda."

"They certainly haven't been sitting on their hands. I suppose their presence in Liverpool now means more of the same activity there."

"I shouldn't wonder." Then he gave me an odd, appraising look. "I met your Miss Ravenel again while you were away, this time at the Earl of Derby's. She inquired after you."

"Was Clavering with her?"

"You don't suppose one of these London hostesses invites a stray woman, do you? Of course, if the woman is of high station, that might be different. Otherwise, an escort for a woman is imperative."

"Did you talk with Clavering, too?"

He shook his head. "Very little. He was off chatting with Thomas Baring, head of Baring Brothers, the great banking house."

"Probably raising a loan," I said.

"That may well be." Then he waited until several people coming toward us had passed, and said, "Scott, Miss Ravenel spoke at least twice of your South Carolina background. She made a considerable point of it. So I have a mad idea that she may think you're a renegade Southerner helping the North, or a Confederate agent disguised as a Yankee."

"I can't believe it. She's called me a Yankee all along."

He shrugged. "If she *is* finally persuaded you're either of these roles, she'll fear you and hate you. I don't doubt she will hurt you."

"As a fellow Southerner, competing for blockade runners?"

"Absolutely," he said. "The Rebels have many agents here in England, and most of them seem to be working at cross-purposes. There's no coordination of their efforts, and they'll do anything to trip one another up. Believe me, there's precious little evidence of any politeness or goodwill among them. So you will do well to be careful."

Careful! I'd been careful ever since I had taken to carrying the derringer and the bowie in Liverpool. But if what Henry was saying had any basis in fact, I'd have to be more careful still. I had no desire to end a corpse on a dark London street, or floating face down in the Thames or in the Mersey.

IX

THE next day, with part of the legation office a shambles from boxes of papers piled up for the move on Friday, Wilson and Moran worked on the message for Lord Russell, while Henry and I continued to pack more of the official papers and books. Then Mr. Adams himself came in and asked Henry and me to come to his study. This, too, was all torn up, but he had continued at his desk as if all were calm and orderly about him. We drew up chairs.

"Henry," he said, and he riffled the edges of a telegram he held, "do you know the Morley Hotel in Euston Square?"

"Of course, but I have never been in it," Henry replied.

"Well, we in this legation have evidently been asleep. Over the weekend it had a distinguished visitor."

The Minister's voice was dry and hard. We looked intently at him.

"This is a telegram from Mr. Dudley, whose antennae are obviously far more sensitive than ours. Captain Raphael Semmes and one of his officers, Lieutenant John Kell, arrived in London over the weekend and are lodging there."

Semmes, the captain of the Confederate raider *Sumter*, had left a wake of burning ships in his cruise in the Caribbean and across the Atlantic. Incredibly skillful in dodging traps set for him by federal men-of-war, he had been finally hemmed in at Gibraltar. It didn't seem possible that he had slipped through the Union cordon.

"You surely can't mean that the *Sumter* escaped, sir," I said.

Adams shook his head. "He abandoned her and came here by British steamer. Now I'd like both of you to go down to the Morley, see if he is still there, and pick up any information you can about him."

We wasted no time in arriving at the Morley but learned from the clerk that Semmes was receiving no more visitors for the day.

"He's been like a king holding court," the clerk said. "But, of course, he is a very important man, you know."

The condescension in the man's voice was understandable. It wasn't an everyday occurrence to have as a guest at the hotel a man so loudly acclaimed a hero in his homeland and England, or so vehemently denounced as a pirate in the United States. But contrary to the clerk's assumption, we had had no hope of a personal interview with him; Semmes would have indignantly disdained it.

We were about to leave when three men came down the stairs, two of them carrying a valise apiece. One of the two I recognized at once as Captain Bulloch. The other with the valise was a stocky, deeply tanned man slightly above middle height, with high cheekbones, dark pinpoints of eyes above a strong nose, and a dashing mustache with waxed tips somewhat

[76]

in the style of Napoleon III. I had no doubt of it: this was Raphael Semmes. The third man, who was hatless and was obviously coming down to see them off, was tall, with a broad auburn-whiskered face, and blue eyes that missed nothing. This must be Semmes's skillful second-in-command, Lieutenant Kell. The group in the lobby broke into a subdued handclapping as Semmes and Bulloch left, and Semmes tipped his hat to them. Kell spoke to the clerk at the desk, then walked slowly upstairs, while people now dispersed, with Semmes gone.

As for ourselves, I turned to Henry when we reached the street. "Henry, have you ever met Captain Bulloch?"

"No, I've never seen him. Was that Bulloch?"

"It was, and if you were to ask me, I'd say he is taking Semmes home with him."

"Well, isn't it natural that the principal purchasing agent for the Rebel navy should meet with the most successful Rebel raider?"

"It certainly is natural, which is my point precisely."

His face suddenly lighted up, the cold Adams countenance warmed by an idea. "Of course! What could be more natural than to show Semmes the *Number 290*?"

"Now that the *Sumter* is no longer a threat," I said, "Semmes is the obvious choice."

"Unless it's Bulloch himself, with this meeting being a means for Bulloch's getting advice from the principal raider."

"Perhaps," I said. "But whatever all this means, I think we'd best get word of their departure to your father and Consul Dudley."

The upshot was that in addition to a telegram alerting Dudley, I presently found myself, by Mr. Adams's instructions, taking the night train for Liverpool. Whenever the jolting and swaying and numerous stops woke me, I consoled myself for the uncomfortable ride by realizing that I shouldn't have to help the legation move to its new home.

On arriving in Liverpool, I went directly to the consulate. I was hungry and unshaven, but Mr. Adams had impressed upon me the urgency of reporting at once to Mr. Dudley, giving him a letter from Mr. Adams, and telling him what I had observed at the Morley Hotel.

Dudley himself had just entered his office, the first of the consulate staff to arrive. When he saw me, he rose and shook hands vigorously. Then, even as he bade me be seated, he took Mr. Adams's letter and, with a word of apology, opened and read it.

"Well, well, things are starting to move," he said, his fingers drumming the desk. "Now tell me about Semmes and Bulloch."

What I had to say was soon said, and when I finished, he jumped to his feet and started pacing his office.

"Mr. Pettigrew, we lost sight of Bulloch, he left town so suddenly. When your telegram — or, rather, Mr. Adams's — arrived yesterday, I got in touch with Maguire, who made it a point to be at the station when Bulloch's train came in. Bulloch lives with his wife in a cottage in Waterloo just outside of Liverpool — very decorative, with trellised roses — and he took Semmes there at once. Maguire will see that that house is kept under constant surveillance. Incidentally, Maguire will be in town this noon and would like to talk with you. He has an idea you can help him. If it is agreeable to you, he'll meet you at the King's Arms Hotel at one o'clock."

As I entered the lobby of the King's Arms, Maguire greeted me with outstretched hand, and we were escorted through a crowded dining room to a table against the wall. When I mentioned my surprise at meeting again in such a public place, Maguire said that sometimes attempts at secrecy were more revealing to observers than openness. Then, as we sawed away at ancient mutton, he repeated much of what Dudley had told me.

"This I know," I said, and I did not conceal my impatience.

"Good," he said, not at all ruffled. "Now that we know what the situation is, you can be of real help."

"How?"

"By traveling up and down the steamers that pass the Laird Yard. I have operatives doing the same, but you have a decided advantage over all but one or two of them. You have seen Bulloch and Semmes face-to-face — a number of my men have not seen Bulloch, and none has laid eyes on Semmes. If they should be together, there is no problem. The rub would be if they went separately, and this is when you could be useful."

"Bulloch's own men know who I am by now."

"It doesn't matter. The main point is for you to identify Semmes."

Thus it was that I began again to ferry up and down the river, but now not so much to keep an eye on the *Number 290* as to look for an individual. Yet, as often as I made the passage, I never laid eyes on Semmes. In the end, Maguire told me that he had returned to London without having visited the Laird Yard. Maguire doubted that Semmes had even seen the *Number 290*. This last I questioned. As Consul Dudley, Bruce, and I talked over the situation, I said that I thought that Semmes had surely seen the 290 from a distance at least, though it was not necessary for him to have done so, since so experienced a seaman would need only Bulloch's detailed description to visualize her. "I simply think the man would have been overwhelmingly curious to look at his command," I added.

Dudley frowned slightly. "That's assuming the 290 will be a Rebel cruiser and Semmes has the appointment."

"Semmes or Bulloch," I said. "I realize that Bulloch is a capable officer and that he would probably like to take over the 290."

"He might like to, but it could be that their Secretary of the Navy, Mallory, will order him to remain in England. He's much too useful to the Confederacy placing contracts for supplies and ships."

"Such as ironclads?" I asked.

Dudley got up and started to pace back and forth. "I wish I knew for sure, I certainly wish I knew."

"All we have to go on is rumor, Scott," Bruce said.

"Yes, that's all," Dudley said, "but we've learned to appraise our sources of information pretty accurately, and this particular rumor has substance, I'm convinced."

I thought of Henry Adams's remark about Dudley's continually bombarding his father with suspicions. I was inclined to agree, but even Henry had admitted that some of Dudley's suspicions seemed to have a basis in fact. The consul did not now disclose the source of the ironclad rumor, but he was sufficiently disturbed for me to feel again the fears I had previously felt when Sally Thornton had first mentioned the possibility of a Confederate seagoing ironclad. What such a ship would do to our wooden blockaders was a dreadful thing to contemplate.

As if he sensed what I was thinking, Dudley said, "If the *Number 290* turns out to be the raider I believe she is, and if she escapes the way the *Oreto* did, she'll do immense harm to our shipping. But an ironclad or two loose against our blockaders might cost us the war."

"Two ironclads?"

He stared at me. "Did I say two ironclads?"

"You said 'an ironclad or two,' sir," Bruce put in.

Dudley shrugged. "All right, two. Acting in concert, they wouldn't need to fear anything we have, even monitors. Isn't that so, Mr. Pettigrew?"

"Monitors would give them trouble only when close to shore and then only in fair weather."

"Who is going to build these ironclads, sir?" Bruce asked.

"No one knows anything definite yet — not about plans, cost, builders, or anything, I tell you. All that exists is a rumor. Meanwhile, let's keep our eyes on the 290."

[80]

With that he dismissed us.

While Bruce went back to his work, I strolled toward the customs house, one of the better places to catch up on maritime gossip. On the way I heard screams up the street, then shouts of alarm from men behind me. Quickly I swung about.

A hansom cab was swerving from side to side, the horse rearing and out of control of its driver. Bystanders had backed against the walls and into the doorways of buildings as the furious animal, foam like a beard gathering around its mouth, and its eyes rolling, fought its bit. Inside the cab was a man being thrown about. Even as I glanced back, the right wheel of the cab struck a lamppost, and the cab, slewing around, nearly capsized, then straightened, and the horse dashed on again.

What I did was sheer response to impulse. I did not spring into the horse's way — that would have been madness. Rather, I ran into the street on a slant and ahead of the horse, as if racing it. When he was almost abreast of me, I had edged him toward the wall of buildings. Then I reached for the bridle. I didn't dare put much strength on it for fear it would snap, but the horse, running faster than I, began to drag me, and my weight acted as a brake. For a minute or two I fought to keep from being dragged under his hooves. Flecks of foam from his mouth almost blinded me, and his breathing was like that of a locomotive panting. All the while, I kept speaking to him, trying to calm him. Then, when I thought I could hold on no longer, he slackened and halted.

For a long moment, I stood holding onto the bridle, breathing almost as heavily as the horse and trying to ignore the twinges of pain in my ribs.

"I want to thank you, sir. You may have saved my life and the driver's, too."

I turned around, and recognized at once the round-bearded face with the shaven chin. It was Captain Bulloch himself, and for the moment he looked quite as shaken as I felt. As the cabbie took over the bridle, I shook Bulloch's outstretched hand. "There was a moment when I didn't think I could hold onto him," I said.

"Why don't we step into this pub and have a glass of ale?" he asked.

I could have used something stronger than ale at the moment, and said as much.

The light was dim inside and the air heavy with tobacco smoke. We were near the customs house, and judging from the conversation, which was all about the shipping business, the pub had a heavy sprinkling of shipowners, chandlers, and captains for customers. A number recognized Bulloch and spoke to him. I saw two lawyers from a firm I had consulted, and even as they nodded to me, I noticed their looks of surprise when they saw me with Bulloch.

When our drinks were at hand and our cigars were lighted, we found ourselves taking each other's measure. What Bulloch saw I couldn't guess, but, as before on meeting him, I was impressed by an air of competence and integrity about the man. I wished with all my heart he were on our side.

"Miss Ravenel is convinced you are a Northerner," he said pleasantly.

"Is she?" I asked. "I sometimes think she really believes me a Southerner only pretending to be for the Union."

"But you have lived in the South, I understand, Mr. Pettigrew."

"Yes, in Charleston for a few years as a boy, Captain Bulloch."

"It is a lovely town, but I prefer a lively, progressive city like New Orleans."

"Or Liverpool?" I ventured.

"Yes, Liverpool, too. This is a great port, Mr. Pettigrew, and due to become more important. There's a warmth of life and friendliness in this city, not at all like London. Oh, London has its points, to be sure, but I prefer it here."

[82]

"Liverpool is certainly friendly toward the South," I said.

"For which we can all be grateful, can't we, Mr. Pettigrew?"

"All Southerners should be grateful," I said. "And if the *Number 290* gets to sea, captain, the Confederacy will probably have more reason to be grateful to you than to Liverpool."

He laughed and carefully tapped the ash from his cigar. "I wish she were destined for the Confederacy, but I've heard she is being built for the Spanish government, Mr. Pettigrew."

With neither of us getting anywhere, I suddenly said, "Personally I believe the Confederacy would fare better if its ship orders were coordinated under you, sir, or someone with your knowledge and ability, rather than there being a number of agents — Miss Ravenel and Clavering, for example — all competing with one another."

I was taking a chance, but Bulloch's long silence and intent study of my face were rewarding. I thought he was on the point of agreeing when he glanced over my shoulder and the oddest expression flashed across his face. "It's Roger Clavering, Mr. Pettigrew."

We rose as Clavering joined us. I could well imagine he was curious to see the two of us together. Even when Bulloch briefly explained about the runaway horse, Clavering's "How extraordinary!" sounded suspicious and skeptical.

"Extraordinary, perhaps," Bulloch said, "but damned lucky for me. Will you have a glass, Clavering?"

"I'd love to, captain, but there are matters I wish to confer with you about, if I may."

"Don't let me detain you, gentlemen," I said, picking up my hat. "I must run along, myself."

"Mr. Pettigrew, I'm sorry," Bulloch said, rising and shaking my hand. "Perhaps we can have a longer chat another time."

I left with at least one firm impression, namely, that Clavering was definitely another purchasing agent for the Confederacy, and one who seemed to have a certain authority over Bulloch. But whereas Bulloch was an honest man, I was as certain as daylight tomorrow that Clavering would not hesitate to consider his own financial interests in any arrangements for getting ships and cargoes to the Confederacy.

X

I saw little of Bulloch after the incident of the runaway horse, only occasional glimpses in Liverpool, and always from a distance. I saw even less of Clavering; once in the railway station, as I bought a ticket for London, he was leaving a train that had just come in. He nodded, as did I. Of Tamara Ravenel I saw nothing at all.

Gradually I grew restless. Writing frequent and lengthy reports to Secretary of the Navy Welles, talking with ministerial and consular officials, and conferring with English lawyers provided but a small outlet for my energy. I therefore commenced to write a treatise on maritime law which was both historical and current in its emphasis. Initially this was intended purely for my own edification. Then, as I worked in the British Museum and the law libraries, looking for cases during the Napoleonic Wars which would throw light on British activities at sea and might thereby justify and legally extend the actions of our own blockaders, I had the idea that an up-to-date book of precedents and current practice of maritime law in war and peace would be a very helpful adjunct to any law student or law office. Henry Adams evinced what was at first a mild interest; then, his concern for matters historical gradually deepening, he sometimes assisted me. This was not so much by way of research as by questions that went far beyond what I was attempting but which brought me to a greater understanding of the particular problem confronting me.

"Did the judgment in this case represent a victory for the British merchants as well as a justification of British naval action?" he would ask, whereas I had merely been concerned about the law.

Or on another occasion, "Have you ever thought that a study of the laws of a people may be the most illuminating way of studying that people — their ideas of property, of the worth of the individual, of the importance of the group? Law is organic and continuous."

Such questions and comments not only told me much about Henry Adams, they also gave me much to think about that spring as I watched the *Number 290* literally take shape in the Laird Yard.

Then, one evening in mid-May, my fellow boarder, Angus MacNaughton, drew me aside after dinner. "Would you like to see the *Number 290* go down the ways tomorrow?"

Would I! "For the moment I can think of no greater pleasure," I said.

"Well, then, prepare to enjoy yourself, Mr. Pettigrew," and he handed me a ticket that would admit me to the launching.

He interrupted my thanks, in fact rather brusquely. "I do urge you to conduct yourself with care. For there will be two kinds of watchers at the launching."

"Two?"

"Aye. Those watching the *Number 290* and those watching the watchers."

Later that evening, I went over to the Thorntons'. Word of the launching had been news to me, for I had just arrived from London, but I discovered that both Sally and Bruce already knew about it.

"The announcement was made in the newspapers today," Sally said, knitting on an afghan that was now almost the size of a blanket.

"They're not trying to keep it a secret," Bruce said. "A launching is always a gala event, even in a busy yard like the Lairds'. If the Lairds tried to keep it secret, we'd know for sure the ship was destined for the Rebels. As it is, we'll still be in doubt."

"But you are convinced that ship is to be a Rebel raider, aren't you?" Sally asked.

Bruce and I looked at each other and slowly nodded.

"Then what of this speculation in the papers that she is destined for Spain?"

"Whitewash — or ignorance," Bruce said.

"But isn't your opinion and Scott's based on speculation, too?"

"Yes," he admitted, "but there is some basis for it."

"We may know more after the launching," I said. "She's bound to be given a name."

"I wouldn't count heavily on the name they give her," Bruce said. "They renamed the *Oreto* the *Florida* once she was at sea."

"But if your speculation has some basis, what is it?" Sally asked.

"For one thing, reports from Maguire, who has done a fairly thorough job," her husband said. "He's had his own operatives, and they have talked with workmen in the yard, clerks in the office, and suppliers in the city. And, as Scott knows, Bulloch himself, as well as Clavering and Miss Ravenel and all members of the Confederate mission to England, have been kept under surveillance largely by direction of Mr. Adams."

"You see, Sally," I cut in, "our officials need evidence that can stand up legally, and once they have that, Mr. Adams has a real basis of protest to Lord Russell. The British government might then be induced to intervene. It is contrary to law to fit out a ship with her guns and crew here in England to serve against another power. The Foreign Enlistment Act is clear on this."

"So until there is enough evidence, you go on spying, is that it?" Sally asked.

"That's about it," Bruce said.

[86]

I entered the Laird Yard shortly after noon for the launching. Perhaps three hundred people had been invited for the event. Flags, flying from the ship, now drooped, now slatted in the fitful breeze. The *Number 290* looked sleek in her fresh black topsides and red bottom, and her lines gave the impression of speed. At the same time, there appeared to be a certain delicacy about her; if she was to be a man-of-war, hers was obviously not to be a stand-up, knock-down role.

As I pressed toward her bow and the christening platform, I could see Bulloch aboard with a number of men, one of whom I thought I recognized as a Laird. Then Bulloch walked down a gangway to the christening platform and took a position beside a trim, graceful woman, her blonde hair golden in the sun. As she turned to greet Bulloch, I saw that it was Tamara Ravenel. Beside her stood Clavering in somber black. They were soon joined by other dignitaries, and the bowing and handshaking reminded me of a marionette show.

Then a voice, that of the yardmaster, rang out, almost harshly. At once the crowd became quiet. I thought there might have been a speech or two, but instead, workmen took their places at the blocks, ready with great hammers to send the 290 into the Mersey. John Laird, Jr., whom I had met, now handed a bottle of wine dangling from a line to Tamara.

Grasping the bottle, she stepped forward and said in a voice audible to most of us, "I christen you *Enrica!*" She swung the bottle against the bow and stepped back as the bottle splintered.

Instantly the hammers swung, and the ship, almost without a pause, slid down the ways to the accompaniment of cheers from the crowd and the tooting of whistles from two tugs standing by to take her in tow. Her stern sank deep into the water even as friction smoke rose briefly from the ways. Then she came up like a cork and bobbed gently on the river surface.

As we watched, the tugs nudged her to the graving dock, where she was warped in. She had scarcely been secured there before a derrick moved over her and started lowering parts of her heavy machinery aboard. It was as if all this movement were part of the actual launching, and the crowd lingered, watching it with avid interest. It was obvious, too, that the Lairds were wasting no time in getting her ready for sea, though I knew, from the nature of the work now to be done, that weeks would still pass before the *Enrica* steamed out of Liverpool.

But was she destined for the Confederacy or for Spain, as so many around us were speculating? This was a question that the Union had to find the answer for. If meant to fly the Stars and Bars as a raider, she must not be permitted to put to sea. If legal steps were not sufficient to prevent her leaving, she should be stopped and seized by a federal warship as soon as she was beyond British territorial waters. If no man-of-war was available, someone would have to try to sabotage her. Mr. Adams, I felt sure, would have nothing to do with such a measure. Officially Consul Dudley wouldn't, either, but I didn't think him above arranging surreptitiously to have this done; nor could I feel too critical of him if he should.

As I turned to leave with the crowd, most of whom were already streaming out of the yard, someone jostled my arm. Glancing about, I saw Tamara and Clavering, with Bulloch and John Laird, Jr., a few steps behind them, talking earnestly.

"Did you like the launching, Mr. Pettigrew?"

"I did, Miss Ravenel," I said.

"The Spaniards should find the *Enrica* a welcome addition to their merchant marine, eh, Pettigrew?" Clavering said.

"She certainly is a handsome ship. Your builders have done well by you," I said, addressing myself to Laird.

"Thank you." Laird was impatient to move on.

"Miss Ravenel, you must surely feel honored to have christened the *Enrica*."

"Deeply honored, Mr. Pettigrew."

"But, of course," I added, "one must do something deserving to be so honored — or be related to the builder."

Clavering began to laugh an easy, unconstrained laugh.

"Who can tell, Mr. Pettigrew, perhaps Tamara is a bit of both. Look how she swung that bottle. For a moment I thought it was she and not the workmen's releasing the blocks that sent the *Enrica* into the river."

"You were indeed very efficient, Miss Ravenel," I said. "You smashed the bottle, and I could hear every word distinctly."

She thanked me and left, her hand resting on Clavering's arm.

XI

THE two months following the launching of the *Enrica* were an uncomfortable period for the legation personnel in London and Consul Dudley's office in Liverpool. We were worried about the *Enrica*, ironclads, and pro-Southern sentiment in England. In reports of the launching of the *Enrica* to Mr. Adams and Secretary Welles, I recommended that the Navy Department assign a fast man-of-war to a station off Liverpool in the event that representations to the British government failed and the *Enrica* put to sea. As far as ironclads were concerned, I took an anxious interest, but neither Mr. Adams's office nor Consul Dudley's operatives had turned up anything definite as yet. The development of pro-Southern feeling, however, was something that must have concerned every loyal United States citizen in Great Britain. Certainly, by early summer it began to appear that Palmerston's ministry, which was generally cautious on recognition of the Confederacy, might find its hand forced by the Southern sympathizers in and out of Parliament. Liverpool I knew to be a nest of Southern sympathy, but several events occurred that alarmed me about the government and Parliament.

The first concerned the North's seizure of New Orleans. The British were shocked that Admiral David Farragut and his Gulf squadron were able to hammer their way past the defending forts. What really touched off their anger was General Benjamin Butler's order to the ladies of New Orleans that if they continued to insult our troops, he would treat them as women of the streets. Although this meant only that the occupation authorities would apply the same regulations to them as applied to prostitutes, the British assumed the worst and concluded that they would be turned over to the troops as common whores. Staid British newspapers shrieked their indignation, but the situation didn't become serious until Mr. Adams received, on June 12, a private and confidential note from Lord Palmerston expressing disgust and asserting that if the authorities in Washington insisted on having public officials like Butler, they could expect to be held in ill repute by men everywhere.

Never had I seen Mr. Adams so agitated as during the days following. As Henry explained to me, when we were walking after lunch one day following the arrival of the note, "This note of Palmerston's is outrageous. However it was intended, whether as an official or a private communication, it is unacceptable. If official, it is an insult to our country and should in any case have come through Lord Russell. If private, it is an affront to Father personally and makes his relations with Palmerston very difficult from now on."

"It looks to me, Henry, as if the government were getting ready to recognize the South."

But Henry was not convinced. "I realize it looks that way, but the government has stood up under a lot of pressure so far, and despite Palmerston's feelings on the Butler issue, I don't think they're likely to give in just when it appears that the North is winning."

Henry was right, of course. His father whipped off a note requesting an explanation from Palmerston, and a tart correspondence ensued, with the Prime Minister evasive as to whether his own communication had been private or official. Mr. Adams then went to Lord Russell, who appeared surprised that his chief had not communicated through him. Russell thought the note private, and finally Palmerston replied, on June 19, in such a vein that Mr. Adams could construe the note as essentially private and indicating no real change in the policy of the government. Though personal relations between Henry's father and Palmerston were likely to be frigid for a while, the two governments veered away from a break.

This was especially gratifying to those of us at the legation who occasionally confronted members of the Confederate mission. Mr. Mason, the leading delegate, from the little I had observed him, was a boastful man who rarely opened his mouth except to curse or spit tobacco juice — Henry said that London hostesses lived in terror of his visits. His pleasure if Washington and London should break off relations would be extreme and loud.

It was entirely possible, of course, that Mason and other Confederates in England would still have cause to rejoice, for powerful forces were at work in Parliament in favor of the South. One of these was William Lindsay, the greatest ship-owner in England, who seemed to have appointed himself a liaison agent between the Emperor Napoleon III and the Palmerston government. How much influence he wielded was a question we at the legation often considered. He was all set to propose a motion for recognition of the Confederacy in late June, but evidently thought better of it and postponed action until the government would be more receptive. But that he would bring up his motion I was convinced after I saw Clavering let him off from a cab one day to enter the House of Commons.

Occasionally I attended a session of the House, sitting in the visitors' gallery with Henry, and once in a while I stood outside with the crowd of onlookers as the members of Parliament assembled for their sessions, which began in the late afternoon. It was fascinating for a foreigner to observe many of the distinguished men one read about getting out of cabs and fashionable carriages, some acting like the lords of creation with their elegant clothes and lofty manners. Others behaved like the solid Victorian businessmen they were, though even these had a manner of easy assurance. In fact, all of these Englishmen seemed a confident lot, and I found myself often envying their comparatively untroubled minds when I thought of my own divided country. Most of them, moreover, though by no means all, were unmistakably pro-Southern in their sympathies, if few were as vehement or persistent as William Lindsay. And even he was hardly as insulting as the newspapers, which were in full cry for mediation when word arrived, on July 10, that the North had suffered a defeat on James Island near Charleston, South Carolina.

Earlier, Captain Thomas A. M. Craven of the U.S.S. *Tuscarora* had arrived to pay his respects to Mr. Adams and, before he returned to Southampton, invited members of the legation to visit the man-of-war. A number of us went down on Saturday, the 12th, including Wilson, Moran, Henry, and myself, and a friend of Moran's, a minister named Kittridge, whom Craven had asked to speak to his crew on Sunday. Ostensibly, there was nothing official about our visit, but Mr. Adams had instructed me to give Captain Craven all the information available about the *Enrica*.

On the train to Southampton, Wilson did most of the talking, in a voice that carried easily above the rattling of the coach. For a diplomatic official he was so outspoken in his opinions about the English that Moran, who couldn't stand him, shushed him several times, albeit with a pained smile, for Wilson ranked him. Kittridge tried occasionally to change the subject, as did Henry, but Wilson was fuming over the London press, the anti-American statements in Parliament, and the refusal of the government to do anything to prevent the *Enrica* from sailing. I think that to a man we shared his opinions, but he was unforgivably indiscreet. Though we were alone in the compartment, I'm sure that his voice was audible to anyone

[92]

passing in the corridor. I don't know whether he had consumed too much liquor or was too passionate with anger to contain himself. No one, not even Henry, dared tell him to shut his mouth, even politely; after all, he was the secretary of the legation. Nor was it my place to do so.

Then the flying train suddenly lurched, and Wilson stood up to save his valise from falling on the floor. As he did so, he staggered and would have pitched against the outside door of the compartment had I not reached up and steadied him.

For a moment he stared at me, then growled, "This God-damned train's worse than a ship. I think I'm going to be sick."

"I'll walk with you to the washroom," I said.

"I don't need any help. What the hell, do you — "

Another lurch of the coach, and his face grew strained and very white around the mouth. "All right, Pettigrew, if you'll help me, fine."

Down the narrow corridor we went until we found the washroom, fortunately unoccupied, where I left him and waited in the corridor.

Smoke and sparks whipped along the side of the train, blotting out much of the green countryside, while the shrieking of the whistle for crossroads never seemed to stop. I saw black-legged sheep running frantically in the fields, frightened by the rattling, roaring monster.

Then Wilson rejoined me, and we slowly worked our way back. I let him go ahead and was ready to support him in case he needed assistance.

As we passed the compartments, we glanced through the glass partitions with only a casual curiosity. Most of the compartments were filled, some with family groups evidently going on holiday. I noticed one woman trying to get a cinder out of a boy's right eye. Then I saw a gray and white plumed hat next to the mother and had a glimpse of blonde hair and a familiar profile. I dared not pause to make certain, for she was watching the mother. But after I had steered Wilson to his seat, I turned to Henry, as Kittridge and Moran began to talk with Wilson. "We have company aboard." When Henry's eyebrows lifted, I said, "Tamara Ravenel."

For a moment, he looked at me without speaking. "No one else you recognized?"

I shook my head.

"Did she see you?"

"Not on the way back, but I can't vouch for the way down. Afraid I had eyes only for Wilson."

He stared out the window, then shrugged. "Well, I can't see that it makes any difference whether she saw you or not — or, for that matter, that she is on this train. What harm could she do?"

"To us personally? None. But she could be interested in learning just where three of the four principal officers of the United States legation are going this weekend."

"What good would that do her?"

"Clavering and Bulloch would be interested to know we shall be visiting the *Tuscarora*."

"They would be more interested in the *Tuscarora* herself."

"Right, but they wouldn't treat lightly what we have to say to Captain Craven."

Again the shrug, delicate, almost Continental. "But we don't have anything to say to Craven, do we, outside of what you know of the *Enrica?*"

"That's true, Henry, but they don't know that. If I were a Confederate officer here in England, I'd consider the visit we're making to Craven likely to be an important conference."

"Miss Ravenel certainly won't have much to report to the others," he said with a slight smile. "I wish she would question me. I could lead her a merry chase through a maze of pretty fabrications."

"She might find Wilson or Moran more vulnerable."

"Not Moran," he said, glancing at the acidulous assistant secretary. "I think he's immune to anything that's human."

"Wilson?"

"He admires a pretty face and a shapely ankle, and he loves to talk, but I don't think he's easily taken in by blandishments, and she would probably resort to those with someone she doesn't know."

"That leaves Captain Craven and myself."

"I don't know whether she could reach Craven, or, if she did, how he would respond. As for you — "

Henry glanced at the others, who had started arguing as to whether President Lincoln should issue a proclamation freeing the slaves and, if so, when. Wilson and Moran were like cocks in a pit, with Mr. Kittridge trying to keep them from becoming too vehement. Henry raised an eyebrow and gave me a knowing look. I wasn't amused by the abandon with which those two men argued, but I think Henry felt not only amused, but a little superior as well. In fact, for all his own passionate support of the Union cause, Henry could be detached when others were involved and, in his detachment, was something of a snob. I was even experiencing the beginnings of annoyance at his appraisal of me in relation to Tamara Ravenel. At any rate, I didn't respond to the lifted eyebrow.

"What you want me to tell you, Scott, is that you're invulnerable to Miss Ravenel. But if you think you are, you're mistaken. You may not like her, but she intrigues you. You may keep her at a distance — I suspect she may even scare you — but I'd bet you'll see more of her before the *Enrica* issue is disposed of."

We arrived at Southampton in the late afternoon, and the port was aswarm with liners and freighters, some at dock, others at anchor. Tugs puffed busily about, and the harbor seemed filled with sails and smoke.

Then I saw the *Tuscarora* lying some distance out, and a midshipman who met our train escorted us to a steam launch.

The Southampton docks were crowded with ships: deep-sea screw passenger steamers, big coastal freighters — most of them side-wheelers, a few clippers, and numerous small steamers and sail-driven craft. One ship in particular caught my eye, a gray, low-decked side-wheeler with an extravagantly rakish tilt to her funnel and masts that made her look like a racer. I was about to draw Henry's attention to her when our launch loosed a tremendous blast on her whistle for so tiny a craft, and swept out into the harbor. It soon puffed us beyond most of the shipping and alongside the glistening black hull of the trim *Tuscarora*.

Captain Craven met us and introduced us to his officers, one of whom, a Lieutenant Jones, was a Southerner who had remained loyal to the Union. Since we were to be guests overnight, officers had been turned out of their berths for us. Personally I felt like an intruder as well as an imposter; these were men on sea duty, something I had a much higher regard for than my own role here in England. We had tea, were taken through the ship, and, after cleaning up, had dinner and cigars with Craven and his officers.

It was pleasant there in the lamplight of the paneled cabin. Wilson and Moran were on their best behavior; in fact, Wilson could tell a good story when he wanted to, mostly about the politics and politicians of our country, while Moran knew the European political situation and prominent personalities very well, owing to his years of foreign service. Craven, moreover, was a genial and generous host. There was something about his manner, which was almost fussy, and his face — perhaps it was his high forehead — that suggested a scholar to me, a rather pedantic scholar, at that. I could not help comparing him with the impression I had formed of Raphael Semmes, whose *Sumter* had repeatedly eluded traps set for her by Union warships and, until finally cornered at Gibraltar, had seized or burned a score of Northern merchantmen. If the *Enrica* finally got to sea and if Semmes became her commander, could Craven be relied upon to capture or destroy her? Semmes was ruthless, bold, imaginative, and efficient.

Before that weekend, Mr. Adams had notified Craven that I had been instructed to confer with him on the *Tuscarora*, so as our party broke up later in the evening, it came as no surprise that the captain asked me to breakfast privately with him in his cabin.

The next day was bright, and I could hear activity on the deck above as the crew prepared the ship for a church service at which the Reverend Mr. Kittridge was to speak. Through the port I could see rolling green country beyond the smoky town. The entire aspect was so pleasing and peaceful that it seemed incongruous to be informing Craven of the urgent situation developing at Birkenhead and the possibility that the *Enrica* might escape.

"But am I correct in inferring that you don't really know that this ship is for the Rebels, Mr. Pettigrew?"

"That is correct, sir," I said.

Craven pursed his lips like a disapproving schoolmaster. "So far as I can see, all the legation and Consul Dudley have to go on is a hunch."

"It's not quite as insubstantial as that, sir," I said, "but if it should turn out to be right, Mr. Adams would like reassurance from you, sir, that the *Tuscarora* will be able to handle the *Enrica*."

"You say the *Enrica* has no guns yet?"

"That is correct, sir."

"And you don't know her tonnage, though you guess it to be about like this ship?"

"Yes, sir."

"Nor do you know the *Enrica*'s speed?"

"She has fast lines, but, of course, no one will know what she will do until she has her trials."

"I realize that, Mr. Pettigrew," Craven said in a testy voice.

[97]

He then went on to give me some of the *Tuscarora's* vital statistics, many of which I already knew. She was one of the screw steam sloops of war laid down in the summer after the surrender of Fort Sumter. Commissioned in December, 1861, she was completed in January, 1862, and soon sent to the European station. She had an armament consisting of two eleven-inch Dahlgren smoothbores, six thirty-two-pounders, and one thirty-pounder — a Parrot rifle. As for speed, she maintained an average of seven knots, which struck me as a little slow if she ever had to catch the *Enrica*. When I made the mistake of expressing surprise that the *Tuscarora* wasn't faster, Craven flushed.

"I'll have you understand that if she has to, my ship can make eleven knots, possibly twelve. That ought to be fast enough for your *Enrica!*"

"Yes, sir, I'm sure you are right," though I really had no idea whether he was or not.

"I have an experienced crew, too. Don't ever forget that."

"Of course not, sir."

And naturally he had a point. Whatever kind of crew Bulloch might recruit for his ship, they would be green, as a group. The *Tuscarora's* crew, on the other hand, had had months to work together.

Craven's impatience to greet his other guests and finish preparations for the religious service was so patent that I saw no point in prolonging the conversation. We soon broke it off with his assuring Mr. Adams through me that he would hold the *Tuscarora* in readiness and would act as soon as he received a wire from the legation.

Promptly at eleven o'clock the Bethel flag was run up at the peak and our national flag was unfurled. A desk was brought on deck as a pulpit and was draped with a flag. The crew was assembled, neat lines of blue, very respectful in attitude but with a tendency for both the unshaven boys and the bearded tars to glance at the shipping and especially at a handful of racing sloops gathering outside the harbor. The officers, as well as we ourselves, stood by the guns aft.

As Mr. Kittridge spoke, praising the patriotism of the men and officers and the justice of the cause for which they stood ready to fight, I found myself greatly admiring the immaculate condition of the holystoned decks, the shimmer of burnished cannon, and the beauty of a bright sun in one of the bluest skies I had seen since arriving in England. For a few moments, I thought war was not such an ugly thing after all.

After dinner, we went ashore and took the train for London, but not before I saw something that whetted my interest. My eyesight for distance has always been very good, far better than for objects close at hand. As our launch drew near the wharves with their docked ships, I looked again at the rakish steamer I had admired the previous day. Though the Red Duster flew at her stern, I saw no name or port on her, which wasn't too surprising in view of the fact that obviously she had been freshly painted. I nudged Henry.

"Do you see what I see aboard that gray steamer?"

"There's a woman aboard, if that's what you mean. But what is exciting about that?"

I studied the steamer again. "Yes," I said, "there's a woman talking with two men on her afterdeck, and they are giving this launch a pretty careful examination. One of them has field glasses."

"So our fair friend has been keeping a watch on us after all."

"Did you think she wouldn't? But I don't think we were the only reason she came down to Southampton. If ever a ship was built to slip through our blockade of Southern ports, that's one."

"Is Clavering one of those men with her?"

"Yes, the one nearest her without the glasses."

"And the other?"

"I don't know, Henry. It's hard to tell a person who has field

[99]

glasses to his eyes. But there's something familiar about him. I'll place him eventually, though I can't at the moment."

Aboard the train that afternoon we continued to speculate about Tamara Ravenel and Clavering. We were quite certain they were unaware we had spotted them aboard that ship. Not that it could have mattered greatly to them if they knew we had recognized them and had guessed the purpose of that sleek gray craft. After all, that steamer, if truly a blockade runner, would sail under the British ensign to Bermuda or the Bahamas and was completely safe until then from the *Tuscarora* in these waters, or a Union cruiser on the high seas. But it was comforting, all the same, to be one up on the enemy.

When we were close to London, I remembered the third person aboard the gray steamer. It was Alexander Rushton, Lord Cromyn.

XII

"WE'RE not likely to hear many words of friendship for our country tonight, Mr. Pettigrew."

I nodded to Moran as I glanced about the crowded House of Commons from our seats under the Speaker's Gallery. The House was nearly filled, and men were wondering aloud how the government would respond to William Lindsay, who was at last going to move for recognition of the Confederacy.

This speculation had been going on ever since late afternoon. Hearing of the impending Lindsay motion, Mr. Adams had sent Moran and me to the House to observe how men felt and to report on the proceedings. The House usually convened at about five o'clock, but this day it adjourned until six. In the meantime, scores of spectators crowded St. Stephen's porch and almost filled the outside lobby. Everywhere among them was talk of recognition and what it might mean, and from the frequent allusions to cotton manufacturing, it was clear that many of these were businessmen. Most of them seemed to be worried lest the motion succeed and intervention subsequently occur, for they were still trying to get rid of their surplus from the two bumper cotton crops before the war, and any new influx of cotton would force the price down. It was evident that though the unemployed cotton-mill worker and his family might be suffering, the same ill fortune scarcely extended to the millowner.

While I was listening and trying to avoid being trampled, Moran prodded my ribs. As I glanced in the direction he indicated, I saw Mr. Mason, of the Confederate mission, and Roger Clavering standing together. Mason was talking with a tobacco-chewer even more slovenly dressed than himself, whom Moran identified as Colonel James Williams, a Confederate who had served until the war as the United States Minister to Constantinople. Clavering was chatting with a slim, rather elegant young man whose name Moran didn't know but who, he said, was one of Lord Russell's numerous secretaries at the Foreign Office.

"Does this mean that Clavering is privy to all the decisions that Russell makes?" I asked.

"How should I know?" Moran's irritation came through in his voice, but I suspected he was annoyed not so much by my question, which was meant only half seriously, as by his ignorance of the young man's name.

Finally the doorkeepers let us in. A number of Mason's followers went to the Speaker's Gallery, but Mason himself, with Clavering and Williams, took seats under it on the floor. Moran and I could have gone to the Diplomatic Gallery, but being offered seats under the Speaker's Gallery, we, too, went there. In this way we could keep ourselves better informed about the response of the Confederates to what went on, as well as hear more comments as the members of Parliament chatted with one another.

It was just before William Lindsay rose to speak that Moran

[101]

had whispered about the lack of friendly words this evening. He was certainly correct about a number of the speakers, particularly Lindsay. I had rarely heard such a mixture of lies, misinformation, and curious reasoning. Yet his main points were clear. He wanted mediation. The United States had been intolerably severe, even cruel, to the South, particularly with respect to the tariff. Nor was it to England's interest to permit such a great power to develop on the American continent.

He went on for the better part of an hour, while half the House drifted into the lobbies from sheer boredom and Mason chewed away and squirted tobacco juice. Clavering sat almost motionless, but once he turned his head when Mason spat, and the expression of incredulity on his face came and went so quickly, I wasn't certain whether it was directed at Mason or at Lindsay.

After the cheers, mostly from Tories, there was a brief pause, during which a number of Tories went over to speak to Mason. Sight of them and their expressions of hope that Lindsay's motion might succeed, stirred up my Yankee nationalism. Momentarily I wished they would pass the resolution. Recognition of the Confederacy might then mean intervention, and intervention would mean war, and if war should come, the North would rally as never against the South, and I, for one, would like nothing better than to sail a privateer into these waters and declare Britain under a blockade as our Captain Thomas Boyle of Baltimore had done during the War of 1812, aided by Captain Ben Vail of Portland, under whom my Grandfather Pettigrew had sailed on the privateer *Argus*.

"Look at those smug bastards," Moran hissed.

I liked him for the first time.

Then as Moran left to go to the Diplomatic Gallery, a serious, youngish-looking man with a pale, intellectual face stood up to speak. An Englishman next to me identified him as a Mr. Philip Taylor who had been newly elected for Leicester and was a member of the London Emancipation Society. If ever there was a friend of the North, I soon found out it was Taylor, and he stood up manfully against the storm of jeers when he deplored the import of Lindsay's speech and the pro-Southern sentiment in the House. "This war is between freedom and slavery," he said, and the roar of "No!" was like the blast of a cannon. Mediation was an insult and would lead to war, he insisted, and the jeers and catcalls and foot-thumping made me wonder about the celebrated English freedom of speech. But it was when he brought the name of Abraham Lincoln into his reply that the shouts and hooting and shrieks of derisive laughter set me afire. "Clown! Bumpkin!" they shouted. Lord Palmerston removed his hat, wiped his forehead, and stared at Taylor.

That young man, meanwhile, looked disdainfully at his hecklers. Then he said, in a voice that carried without his having to shout, "Yes, I say honest Abraham Lincoln — a name that will be remembered and honored when all the smooth-tongued diplomats and statesmen of the day are forgotten." He went on to point out the incongruity of England's supporting the slaveholding South when the trend of English history in the modern era had been in favor of freedom. Was England to abandon its historic and honorable position?

When he sat down to more cheers than jeers, others rose to challenge his points, but he received strong support from a famous Liberal, William E. Forster, who blasted Lindsay's speech with a carefully framed rebuttal. One particularly telling point of Forster's was that the North had taxed itself as well as the South, and South Carolina had not even mentioned tariffs or taxes in her declaration of independence.

Both Palmerston and beetle-browed William E. Gladstone, the Chancellor of the Exchequer, who was very friendly to the South, were now paying close attention, and well it was, for the time had come for someone in the Liberal government to make known its position on the Lindsay motion.

In the end, Palmerston himself rose to speak. It was already half-past one in the morning, and the old man should have been home in bed. Indeed, he even tottered when he stood up. Yet the Prime Minister, despite his age and evident sleepiness most of the evening, settled everything in a masterly three-minute speech that revealed he had missed nothing significant that had happened all evening. He even quoted previous speakers. He said, in effect, that mediation would mean war and that the government should somehow refrain from going that far in wounding Northern feelings and thus endangering relations between England and the United States. The result of Palmerston's speech was that Lindsay withdrew his motion.

Mason, of course, was terribly cast down and showed it, and not even the Tories who came over to commiserate with him could remove the sullen look from his face.

Clavering looked much more in control of himself, but as he was leaving and saw me, he said, "I wouldn't feel too encouraged if I were you, Pettigrew."

"We'll take every bit of help and like it," I said.

"You'll need every bit you can get, my friend."

Defeat must have been bitter for him, and what he said was only too true when I thought of how poorly McClellan's Peninsula campaign was faring and how rapidly the *Enrica* was being prepared for escape. There had even been reports in the press that McClellan had surrendered, then fled to a gunboat in the James River. This we at the legation knew to be untrue, but his campaign had been a bitter disappointment.

Over the weekend, Consul Dudley wired that he was coming to London for a consultation about the *Enrica,* and on Tuesday he arrived with Bruce.

Before their conference with Mr. Adams that afternoon, Bruce took me aside and said that if the legation could not persuade the government to intervene, the ship would soon make her escape. "She's ready for her trials anytime, as far as Maguire can find out."

"Does Bulloch still pretend she isn't a Rebel cruiser?" I asked.

"Naturally. And, of course, she isn't a cruiser, since she still hasn't guns or crew. She'll probably take both aboard once she's on the high seas."

"But she'll have to have a skeleton crew to get to sea, and a captain, too."

"Bulloch has a real bulldog in command, a man named Matthew Butcher. No one believes he'll be her fighting commander, but he's taken her over for the time being. We've an affidavit from a sailor that Butcher has said the *Enrica* is going to fight for the Rebels."

"The *Tuscarora* is standing by at Southampton," I said.

"Good, I wish to God she were off Liverpool right now. I hope her commander is a man who can act decisively."

I shrugged. I had doubts about Captain Craven, but there was no point in worrying Bruce — he appeared as deeply concerned as Dudley.

That very day, and the next two as well, the legation submitted a batch of depositions to the Foreign Office, supporting the Rebel character of the *Enrica*. Furthermore, at Mr. Adams's request, Consul Dudley and Bruce went to see the Judge Advocate of the Fleet, Robert Powett Collier. They returned, grateful that he had heard them out, but hardly hoping that he would do anything for us.

Then, on the 24th, Collier gave his learned opinion that under British law, particularly the Foreign Enlistment Act, our government in Washington would have serious cause for complaint if the *Enrica* were not prevented from sailing.

Unfortunately, we had had time to do no more than raise a cheer at the legation when a courier arrived from the Foreign Office with a report that the customs officers at Liverpool, after another inspection, saw no reason to prevent the ship from sailing and would not do so.

"It's back to Liverpool for us now," Bruce said when Dudley came out of a conference with Mr. Adams, following this news.

That evening, all of us at the legation assembled the remaining evidence available on the *Enrica*, and Mr. Adams composed the strongest letter yet to Lord Russell, asking for her detention. He requested me, the next morning, to accompany the regular courier and see that, if possible, the missives reached Russell personally, or at least his secretary.

"I do not need to remind you how urgent it is that Lord Russell give this matter his immediate attention," Mr. Adams said. His eyes were faintly bloodshot, and the inverted V-lines from his nose to the corners of his lips were deeply fissured, always a sign of fatigue and worry with him. But there was nothing tired about his voice.

At the Foreign Office I fully expected to be ignored, especially since Mr. Adams's dispatches had apparently been completely ignored. Much to my surprise, however, Russell was very cordial. At least he remembered my name after his secretary introduced me, and asked me to sit down. His office was all high windows — not too clean — faded Turkey carpets, and mahogany furniture polished to a high luster. The Earl had on what looked like a dark velvet smoking jacket, and seemed as relaxed as if this had been his own study in one of his numerous houses. He spoke quietly, stating that he was fully aware of how perturbed Mr. Adams must feel at the possibility that the *Enrica* might prove to be a Confederate cruiser and what havoc she might create among United States merchant vessels.

"If you will pardon me, sir, for interrupting," I said, "we feel we now have enough evidence to convince the government she really is a raider even if, as yet, she has no guns aboard."

"I understand," he said. "On the other hand, you have no positive proof, and, lacking that, Her Majesty's government must naturally proceed with the utmost care and caution."

"Naturally, sir," I said, echoing him. "But Mr. Collier appears to see sufficient basis in Mr. Adams's protests for the government to detain the ship."

"We are inquiring into the matter, Mr. Pettigrew. All the documents submitted have been sent, as these will be, to the senior law officer of the Crown, Sir John Harding. We shall have to await his opinion before taking any action, if indeed any will be necessary."

He looked at me as he spoke, his blue eyes mild and his voice and manner very bland. He sounded a little like a scholar, and I reminded myself the Russells were an intellectual family. At the same time, I wondered whether he realized how serious this matter was. Once the *Enrica* started raiding Northern commerce, there would be, throughout our country, such a clamor for action against the British that another war crisis might easily rise. I did not doubt that if Harding's opinion agreed with Collier's, the government would issue a restraining order. In the meantime, of course, the *Enrica* might put to sea. There being nothing further to say now, however, I rose, thanked Lord Russell for his attention, and left.

As I walked up the street, I suddenly remembered something that had not occurred to me before. The young man who had ushered me into Lord Russell's office had been the very person with whom Clavering had been chatting the night the Commons had debated the Lindsay motion to recognize the South. On impulse I whirled about, half expecting to see Clavering enter the building. Of course, I didn't. If Clavering and Russell's secretary had some sort of pact, the latter would still have to notify Clavering that the United States legation had made a last attempt to persuade the government to halt the *Enrica*. Moreover, Harding would still have to look at the latest batch of depositions, largely the fruit — like the other depositions — of Maguire's work. On the other hand, the secretary might not wait to warn Clavering if, in his opinion, Harding might endorse Collier's judgment. Both the Attorney General and the

Solicitor General, the legation had heard, were impressed with Collier's findings.

When I reported to Mr. Adams about the interview, his grave acknowledgment increased my concern. It was hard to think of a male member of the Adams family as helpless, but that was the impression he gave me. I knew that I was probably mistaken, but I resolved to talk with Henry. Fortunately, I was able to get Henry away from his desk at noontime, and over lunch in a small hotel nearby, I told him of my fears that Bulloch would send the *Enrica* off as soon as he heard from Clavering, and that he was likely to hear at any hour.

"But it isn't possible!" Henry was more vehement than I had seen him for weeks.

"Of course it's possible!" I snapped back. "You don't know Clavering or Bulloch if you think —"

"I don't mean that at all," Henry said hastily. "I mean it's not possible that Russell should decide to wait for Sir John Harding's opinion."

"Why not? It's a dangerous delay for us, but it seems to make sense to them."

"Well, it shouldn't! Either they're trying to evade meeting the issue head on or they're more ignorant than seems possible."

I shook my head in bewilderment. "For God's sake, make sense, Henry! I must be stupid, for I don't follow you at all."

He took a drink of water before replying. There were times when I thought Henry had a sense of theater, and if this was such a time, he was playing to an attentive but increasingly resentful audience. Just when I thought I had reached the limit of my patience, he put down his glass and touched his lips with his napkin.

"Scott," he said, glancing around and speaking so softly I could barely hear him, "Harding is a very sick man. He is in no condition to read and comment on documents. In fact, his illness may be partly in his head."

"Good God," I exclaimed, "do you mean the government may not even be aware of this?"

"I just don't know. But it's almost certain that before Harding can recover enough to express an opinion, the *Enrica* will have flown."

"She's got to be stopped, Henry."

"The *Tuscarora* couldn't be permitted to touch the *Enrica* in Liverpool, and not even outside, if that ship flies the British flag and is under British registry."

"Yes, I realize that," I said. "If only we could get someone aboard her in her engine room. A little sand in her bearings would slow her down enough on her final trials to cause concern, and might delay her departure long enough for the government to act with or without Harding's opinion."

"I hope you're not thinking of anything so rash. That's not what you were sent over here for."

"It was just a thought, though Bulloch and his captain will have too many guards posted against that very kind of thing. But what I'm seriously thinking of is some way to keep track of the *Enrica* if she gets to sea."

"The *Tuscarora* should be able to take care of that."

"Perhaps," I admitted, "but if the *Enrica* should elude her, we'll have a raider against us that must be gunned down as soon as possible. All our men-of-war will have to be alerted to her probable course and destination."

"But how can we know her course and destination unless we have a spy aboard?"

"Exactly," I said. "Maguire or Dudley or someone must try to bribe one of her crew."

"I think this could be arranged." He studied me with those cold, blue Adams eyes; then his mouth twisted upward with a hint of a skeptical smile. "But, of course, Father must first approve, so you will have to explain your plan in detail. Personally I think it's a reasonable solution, though it won't save some of our merchantmen from the *Enrica*, if she escapes from the *Tuscarora*."

Mr. Adams was not so amenable to the idea as his son. He considered that it was neither fitting nor wise to involve the legation, representing the United States at the highest level, in so equivocal a transaction. He thought the honor of our country would be jeopardized, and he was very brusque. At the same time, he did not deny that the situation might well necessitate recourse to every acceptable means at the legation's command.

Henry was not surprised when I told him of my conversation with his father. "He is a man of honor," Henry said, "and he thinks there is not enough of a carry-over of the principles of private morality into public life."

"I don't say he's wrong," I said. "In fact, at his age and with his experience, probably I should think the same. But, right now, there is at least one element of the national enterprise — the maritime element — in grave danger, and if I were a great minister of state like Mr. Adams, I don't think I'd let my private scruples interfere with my sense of duty."

"Perhaps Father has a higher sense of duty than that, Scott. I admit I share your view at the moment, but if nations start playing fast and loose with principles of morality, we might face a future with every man's hand turned against his neighbor's. It could be like Hobbes's description of man's life in a precivilized condition — 'solitary, poor, nasty, brutish, and short.' "

"You may be right," I conceded, impatient at the philosophical turn, "but what I propose is hardly going to upset international morality or the balance of power."

"It's a beginning," he said. "However, to be realistic, you'd better look for help from someone as eager as Father to stop the *Enrica* and not so easily deterred by the morality of a little bribery."

"I think you're alluding to Consul Dudley," I said.

"Oh? Did I mention his name?" Henry's eyebrows rose with his voice.

[110]

"If you did, I didn't hear you."

I could still see the faintly skeptical smile and the amusement in his eyes when I boarded the train that night for Liverpool. Henry Adams I respected almost as much as Charles Francis Adams, and liked a great deal more. I hoped the time would come when I might know Henry well, a time untroubled by matters affecting Clavering, Bulloch, the *Enrica,* or even Consul Dudley of Liverpool.

XIII

As soon as I reached Liverpool in the morning, I went directly to Mrs. Washburn's boardinghouse (where I had regularly paid rent on my room), shaved, washed, changed my linen, and caught a cab for the consulate. When I arrived, I found Consul Dudley, Bruce, and Maguire already in conference. They greeted me enthusiastically until I had to inform them that the government had still taken no action to detain the *Enrica.* I told them about Harding's illness.

"Damn it, man," Dudley fumed, "it's not possible they're doing nothing about her! To let her go is against their own Enlistment Act. They don't need legal advice beyond their own Attorney General to see that."

"Maybe they don't want to see it that quickly," Bruce said. "A carefully considered opinion from counsel, particularly a sick man, will take enough time to allow her to escape."

Dudley paced the room. "Maguire," he barked, "we've looked at so many possible legal angles, I sometimes think I'm back learning mathematics again. Is there any way you can think of that we could stop that ship?"

Maguire hunched his broad shoulders. "Yes, sir, there are ways. If we could get by her guards, we could cripple her machinery, we could set her afire, we could place a charge of powder aboard with a well-laid fuse — there are a number of ways we could prevent her from sailing. But she is so well guarded that her watchmen would have to be doped or bribed or knocked on the head before we could do anything. Still" — and here he shrugged — "there are those who would do a thorough job for you regardless of the risk."

"Would you, Maguire?"

Maguire looked steadily at Consul Dudley. "No, sir." He offered no explanation, and I respected him for it.

"Mr. Maguire," I said, "for the moment let's assume the *Enrica* eludes the *Tuscarora* and reaches the high seas. Our first duty will then be to know where she's going."

"Our first duty will be to destroy her," Dudley growled.

"But first we must know where she is, Mr. Dudley. Then we can order men-of-war into those waters, and we may hope that they will find her and destroy her. Is that not so, sir?"

As he made no reply, but merely inclined his head, I continued. "Wherever she stops, whether to coal or to provision and water, we shall soon know from the United States consul or someone in the native government. But by the time you or Mr. Adams or Secretary Welles finds out her locale, she will have been gone for days or weeks. What our government must learn is what will be her next port of call and the one after that, if possible."

"But our government isn't clairvoyant, Scott," Bruce said. "We're all betting here that Semmes, not Bulloch, will be her eventual commander — you think so yourself — and Semmes is a wily old bird who keeps things to himself."

"True, but even captains talk to their officers, and officers talk among themselves, and a ship is a whispering gallery. Moreover, a raider will go where the pickings are richest — to the regular shipping lanes. If we know she is at Kingston, Jamaica, with only one hundred tons of coal, we can make a calculated guess as to the area of future activity and possible coaling stations."

"What if she loads at sea from some collier meeting her at a prearranged place?" Dudley asked.

"That's more difficult, but it, too, can be anticipated. What gives this raider her strength is the flexibility she has because of steam. But coal is also her weakness — once she runs out of it. Now what I propose is that someone aboard her be found who can be persuaded to pass on to the United States consul at any port of call any rumors of her ensuing destination and the amount of her existing coal supplies."

"A hireling," Dudley said.

I nodded. "An old-fashioned term, sir, but that's the kind of person we'd look for. Nor would it be a case of a Southerner selling out, if rumor is true that the crew, except for the officers, is almost completely non-Southern. Now could such a person be found, Mr. Maguire?"

"Such a person can always be found, Mr. Pettigrew," Maguire said, lighting his short stubby pipe with a match that gave off a rank smell of sulfur.

He was right, of course. Trading in men's honor is as old as warfare or the desire for gain. I turned to Dudley.

"Would you have any objection, Mr. Dudley, to such a recourse on our part?" I told him of my lack of success with Mr. Adams, and the necessity, should the plan be agreeable to him, of making the bribe sufficiently generous.

To my relief Dudley shook his head. "I'd have no objections whatsoever in principle, Pettigrew, and somehow we'd find the money. My doubts are about the practicality of the plan. It's a long, long shot, indeed."

"It certainly is," I said, "but until there are more oceanic cables than there are now and until ships find some means of communicating with one another apart from visual signals, what other procedure would be more practicable? It might not succeed at all. On the other hand, if it did, the destruction of the raider would certainly be worth the small investment."

"Yes, yes, of course." Dudley thought for a moment, then looked at Bruce. "How do you feel about it?"

"I say let's try it if Mr. Maguire can find the man," Bruce said.

"Can you?" Dudley asked Maguire.

The detective removed his pipe and carefully blew a perfect smoke ring. "I think likely, but there's not much time."

"Good man!" Dudley started to pace again. "Let's get to work at once. Meanwhile, we'll make another plea to the customs people here, and I'll send another warning to Mr. Adams that time is growing short. That damned ship is taking on more coal this morning, Pettigrew."

"Did you know that Clavering was on the train that got in from London before yours, Mr. Pettigrew?" Maguire asked.

"I had no idea," I said. "Is there some connection between his arrival and the *Enrica*'s coaling?"

"When he arrived, he went directly to the Laird Yard and handed Bulloch a message. He must have known what it was, for he spoke to Bulloch and Bulloch barely glanced at the paper. Since then, the *Enrica* has started taking aboard coal and stores."

"Scott," said Bruce, "we think someone in the government warned Clavering that Bulloch had better get the *Enrica* to sea as soon as possible."

"I'm not sure that means the government is about to act," I said. "As of yesterday, they were being very deliberate. But it may mean that someone in Russell's office has heard that if Sir John Harding doesn't give an opinion in, say, forty-eight hours more, the Attorney General will present his ruling to Lord Russell." I recalled the pale, intellectual face of the secretary in Russell's office, the very person whom I had once seen talking with Clavering, and felt certain he was the one responsible for the information sent to Bulloch.

"Well, whatever Clavering told Bulloch," Dudley broke in impatiently, "it was bad news for us if it speeds the *Enrica*'s

[114]

departure. Pettigrew, if you will, help Thornton get these last depositions in shape to send to London. I'm off for the Customs Office."

He returned in the afternoon, bitterly critical. "They say there are no guns and no munitions aboard that ship so they can't in all conscience recommend her seizure as a man-of-war. Can't they see by the way she's constructed that she *is* one? Bulloch's hard at work digging up a crew, too. Did you ever hear of a little steamer like her with a hundred men or more for a crew unless she's a man-of-war? Now, where in hell is Maguire?"

But Maguire didn't appear again that day, and when Bruce and I left, late that afternoon, Dudley continued to fume. I promised Bruce to come over to his place later that evening but declined his invitation to dine. I wanted to talk with Angus MacNaughton about the *Enrica*.

Angus invited me up to his room after we had eaten. In fact, to my surprise, he had met me before we went into the dining room and asked me to have a brandy with him after our coffee. "Until, then, no word of the *Enrica*, please," he said.

His room was spartan except for a bookcase containing well-worn sets of Shakespeare, Ossian, Burns, and Scott. By his bedside was a broken-backed Bible.

"Now, then," he said, when he had poured me a glass of brandy from a decanter he kept locked in a walnut cabinet, "I have something for you." He drew an envelope from the inside pocket of his jacket.

Mystified, I took it — a squarish envelope addressed to "Mr. Scott Pettigrew" — thanked him, and started to put it in my own pocket.

"Why don't you open it?" he asked.

Glancing at him, I took the letter opener he passed me, a brass knife with a bust of Burns for a handle, and slit the seal. Pulling out the thick, folded stationery, I read a formal invitation, handwritten, to me to be aboard the *Enrica* for a sailing party on the steamer's second trial run at nine o'clock Tuesday morning, the 29th. It was signed by John Laird.

Carefully tamping down every shred of tobacco into a fierce-looking briar, MacNaughton struck a match on his sole. He had a miniature Vesuvius going before he spoke.

"So you do not understand, eh?" he finally remarked.

"I certainly do not."

"Now, Mr. Pettigrew, it's no secret here in Liverpool that you probably saved Mr. Bulloch from serious harm that day you stopped his horse and carriage. The Lairds and Mr. Bulloch are friends, and it's clear they thought you would enjoy a run aboard the *Enrica*."

"But how did they know I was back in Liverpool?"

"They may not have known, but Mr. Laird knew I had brought you to the yard that day, weeks ago, and when he asked if I could see that this invitation reached you, I said I had no doubt that you would get it in time."

"But you didn't know I was to be here."

He squinted at me under shaggy eyebrows. "True, but I had a feeling that you would. You have too deep an interest in that ship, Mr. Pettigrew, not to be here at this time."

"I understand she looks handsome," I said, trying to shift the subject.

"Aye, she's a trim little craft, as you'll see. Now will you accept the invitation?"

As I walked over to the Thorntons' afterward, I wondered whether MacNaughton had had any part in my being a member of the *Enrica*'s party. He loathed slavery, I knew. Yet the longer I thought about a possible role for him, the more I discounted it, unless he had been invited himself and had refused his invitation in favor of me. This I soon came also to doubt. It must simply be as Angus explained: by inviting me, the Lairds — really Bulloch himself — were returning a favor done for Bulloch.

But back in my mind the thought persisted that this was the

perfect way of dissembling, of throwing us off guard. By inviting a Northerner — a person moving freely in and out of the consular office in Liverpool and the legation in London — to the second trial run of the supposed Confederate raider, could not Bulloch and the Lairds be declaring their innocence of such an intended use of the ship and showing they had nothing to hide?

XIV

EARLY Tuesday, — a bright, clear morning, rather warm — I boarded a cab and drove at once to the waterfront. The day before, the *Enrica* had emerged from the docks and anchored in the river off Seacombe. We had not long to wait to cross over to her, for steamers left the Liverpool pier for Seacombe every half hour and charged a penny per passenger. I sat under the canopy in the afterpart of the ferry and was glad to avoid the spray thrown up by the huge paddle wheels forward, and the cinders dropping from the high black and white funnel.

As we neared the dock, the *Enrica* came clearly into view. She was decked with bunting. Her brightwork gleamed, and the summer dresses of ladies already aboard were a swirl of color. The sight of these ladies seemed to touch off a flurry of comment among a number of my fellow passengers. Evidently they, too, were among Captain Bulloch's guests.

We were no sooner off the ferry than a steam tug named the *Hercules* took us aboard, about a score in all, and brought us out to the *Enrica*. A railed gangway was lowered to the deck of the *Hercules*, and we mounted to the main deck of the *Enrica*. Seamen helped each passenger aboard. I couldn't help noticing how unlike the crewmen of a man-of-war they were in sloppiness of dress and manner. In fact, as I glanced along the deck, I saw no one in uniform except a man standing with Captain Bulloch and a group of people on the quarterdeck; he wore a blue jacket and visored cap and must be Matthew Butcher, captain of the *Enrica* — at least for the time being.

Then, as our group moved aft, Captain Bulloch came to greet each one of us with words of welcome and a warm smile. As on each occasion I had met him, I felt drawn to him and half regretted that I had worked, and would continue, to do everything I could to thwart his determination to make the *Enrica* a successful raider.

"Mr. Pettigrew, I wanted you to see this lovely ship close-at-hand," he said.

"I'm very grateful," I said.

If he was worried that the government might at last order the ship detained, one would never have detected it. He was unhurried and gracious. Then, as we cast off at nine o'clock and headed downriver for the sea, I received a distinct shock. I had been staring so intently, now at the shipping and now at Bulloch, that momentarily I had forgotten there might be others on hand to greet the visitors. That voice behind me, however, was unmistakable — deep and rich, edged with insolence yet slightly slurred, just enough to prevent it from sounding affected. Turning around, I found myself admiring Roger Clavering's appearance — his gray suit finely tailored, his crisp white shirt and dark blue cravat, his gray silk hat. He was a tall, striking figure, no doubt about it. Beside him stood Tamara Ravenel, wearing a robin's egg blue gown and bonnet, her hand resting lightly on his arm.

"How are you, Pettigrew?" he said, as I bowed. "After all you people have done to try to stop this ship, I didn't think you'd have the cheek to appear."

"You assume too much, Clavering," I said. "If my interest in the *Enrica* has been as great as you've remarked before this, you should have expected me here. What surprises me is to find you here."

"How's that?"

"Isn't it time you started back for Richmond? You haven't

[118]

been of much help to Captain Bulloch. You've even bid against him for supplies and equipment the South needs dearly. President Davis won't like that, Mr. Clavering. You'd do well to concentrate on buying your blockade runners and leave Bulloch alone."

Originally Clavering may have thought I favored the South or was at least neutral. If so, my association with Mr. Adams and the legation in London, and with Mr. Dudley and the consulate in Liverpool, had surely disillusioned him. Now there was something in what I said, or perhaps in how I said it, that had made him uncertain again — of this I was sure. Possibly he began to wonder, as he had at first, whether I was a Confederate agent myself, not necessarily an intelligence agent but one commissioned, like himself and Bulloch, to buy ships. Or did I have some special authoritative connection with the Richmond government, secret and superior to his.

"Are you giving me an order to return to America, Pettigrew?"

"By no means, Clavering. Just advice — simple, undiluted advice."

To tell the truth, I felt pleased with myself. I had meant to confuse Clavering; to a certain degree, I had succeeded.

Yet if my little ruse comforted me, I couldn't say that my visit aboard the *Enrica* cheered me. Quite the contrary. In the first place, the guests were blatantly pro-Southern. A number of the women in particular were so effusive to Captain Bulloch and his wife, a woman with a strong face but gentle eyes, that the Bullochs appeared almost embarrassed.

Secondly, the *Enrica* showed such speed and maneuverability that it would take a fast cruiser indeed to chase her down. We made several runs between the Bell Buoy, as it was called, and the northwest lightship. The sea was smooth, and the wind very light from the northwest. The *Enrica*'s speed under these favorable conditions was announced as 12.8 knots, and I heard a comment from a party of engineers and riggers whom Bulloch had taken along in the event they were needed, that the *Enrica* could make an additional knot or two.

The third reason for my gloom was that, as of early that morning, Maguire had found no one of the ship's complement yet recruited who would act as our agent. Most of the men had been kept aboard, so he had had little opportunity to talk with them over the weekend. Happily, he had learned that Bulloch had contracted with a shipping master to provide thirty or forty additional men the next morning, and Maguire had hopes of securing one of these. I began to wonder what would happen if he failed and the *Enrica* got to sea and, at some rendezvous, took aboard her guns and officers and cut loose on the high seas under the Confederate flag. The prospect was chilling.

At noon the guests trooped into the main saloon for a buffet luncheon. In the toasts that were drunk to the future of the *Enrica,* I could join almost without reservation, for there was no mention of a possible role for her as a destroyer of Union commerce. I thought that so far as most of the guests were concerned, they saw her as a blockade runner. Certainly I heard numerous allusions to the possibility of her running the blockade. Evidently they knew little of the demands for such a feat. The *Enrica* drew too much water and was probably not quite fast enough.

The women had welcomed the opportunity to go below; the breeze created by the *Enrica* at full speed had disarranged their hair even under bonnets. Tamara Ravenel's relief could not have lasted long, however, for we had no sooner finished our luncheon and the toasts than she joined me out on deck.

"Isn't this a wonderful day for the South!" she exclaimed.

"It'll be a more wonderful day for the South if Captain Bulloch gets the *Enrica* safely to sea," I said. And so it would.

"Do you doubt that he will?"

"That depends," I said, "on what the government decides to do."

"The government!" Tamara exclaimed. "Did you ever see

such a group of wishy-washy men? Why, they can't come to a decision any faster than a sewing circle. Talk, talk, talk! That's all they do. They won't help the South, but they can't make up their minds to detain this ship, either. Mark my word, Mr. Pettigrew: Captain Bulloch will get the *Enrica* to sea, and nothing Consul Dudley or old Mr. Adams can do will stop him. Nor you, sir!" She spoke with passion, and her voice rose so that people began to glance at us. "But maybe you're not trying to stop the *Enrica*. Perhaps you're working for both the North and the South. Perhaps you are more interested in profit than in honor."

About three o'clock, Captain Bulloch called all the guests aft.

"Ladies and gentlemen," he addressed us, "I hope you have enjoyed your outing today."

There was a marked murmur of approbation, followed by a clapping of hands.

"Is it over so soon, captain?" a woman asked.

"Oh, not quite," Bulloch laughed, "but there's not much time left. You see, I want the *Enrica* to complete her trials tonight, so I have directed Captain Butcher and Mr. George Bond, our Liverpool pilot, to keep the ship out until tomorrow. The sea is still smooth, so we shall run close to the bar, and all of you can go up to the city on the *Hercules*."

Thus it was that an hour later, we went down the gangway to the tug — the guests, the extra engineers and riggers, and Captain Bulloch himself.

Most of the way up the river Bulloch remained with the *Hercules*'s skipper in the pilothouse, but when he emerged to mingle with us just before the tug docked, I thanked him for his invitation and praised the *Enrica*.

"Like her, did you, Mr. Pettigrew? Do you think she'll be a good sea boat?"

"Undoubtedly, though today was no real test of that."

"You're right, of course. Yet she's bound to have many tests

[121]

before she's through — of different kinds, Mr. Pettigrew." Then he smiled and said he had enjoyed having me aboard, even if we were friendly enemies.

"I hope we are more friends than enemies, captain," I said.

"I hope so, too, sir," he said, and bowed.

There was a ferry for Liverpool waiting when the *Hercules* put into Seacombe. I decided to go directly from the ferry to the Thorntons', having promised Bruce a full account of the *Enrica* trials.

"You're just in time, Scott," Bruce greeted me at the door. "We have a special visitor."

It was Maguire, who sat on the horsehair sofa and smoked a foul-smelling pipe.

"We've trouble, Scott," Bruce said, fumbling with a button on his waistcoat. "Mr. Maguire has still not found anyone to give us reports on the *Enrica*'s locations and destinations."

"Not even from the group going aboard tomorrow morning?" I asked.

"Least of all from them, Mr. Pettigrew," Maguire said, gently tapping his pipe into an ashtray. "They're the sweepings of the Liverpool waterfront, about every nationality you can think of, and well liquored up. The sailing master is keeping them overnight at a warehouse, many of them have their women with them, and I tell you, sir, it's no meeting of gentlefolk. He is still short a few men, but he'll have them by morning, I'm sure. I wouldn't trust anyone there with the task you have in mind."

"You were confident you could find someone," I reminded him.

"That I was, and I was mistaken. If I could get one more crack at the crew Bulloch already has aboard, I might still prove myself right."

"I don't expect you'll have that chance, Mr. Maguire."

Both men looked at me.

"Captain Bulloch has ordered Butcher to keep the *Enrica* out all night to complete her trials. I strongly doubt that she'll ever

[122]

be brought back in. It's my guess that Bulloch will take the sailing master's crewmen out to the *Enrica* on the *Hercules* early in the morning, and that will be the last this part of the world will see of the *Enrica*. Bulloch has won."

"Do you have charts of the coast, Mr. Thornton, or even a map of the British Isles?" Maguire asked.

"A map, yes."

"My guess," Maguire went on, "is that Captain Butcher plans to spend the night somewhere down on the Welsh coast. He would never keep the *Enrica* running back and forth in the darkness off Liverpool."

The map was small-scale; I can't say that we learned very much from it. The rugged coast of Wales is broken up by many bays, and the more we studied the location of these, the more confused we became. We were certain only that the *Enrica's* hiding place would have to be within the coal capacity of the *Hercules* to reach it and return. We made a list of the possibilities, and Moelfre Bay appeared the most likely, though none of us had any feeling of certainty that this was it.

"If the *Enrica* will stay where she is long enough," Bruce said, looking up from the map and rubbing his eyes, "we may still catch her. Mr. Dudley wired Mr. Adams this morning that he'd better order the *Tuscarora* up into these waters without delay. If she left Southampton this afternoon or even this evening, there's a chance Bulloch may not win after all."

"A chance," I said, "but a pitifully slim one. It depends on how quickly Bulloch can get the *Enrica* out of wherever she'll be tonight, how long it will take the *Tuscarora* to come up into the Irish Channel, and how alert her commander is. I'm afraid I'd bet on Bulloch over Craven."

"And if the *Enrica* escapes, Scott, what becomes of your idea of having an agent aboard?"

"I'm sorry that I have failed you, Mr. Pettigrew," Maguire said. It was a statement of fact, rather than apology. Maguire had done his best in this respect, and had not succeeded. That was that. He was not a sentimentalist. "And yet, Mr. Petti-grew," he added, "you still may be able to put a crewman loyal to the North aboard the *Enrica*."

He had filled his pipe again and now held the match to the bowl while his shrewd, little eyes stared at me through the smoke. The silence seemed to grow heavier and longer with every puff.

"I'm not sure I follow you."

Maguire carefully blew out the match and placed it in the ashtray. "Yes, I think you do," he said, "though you may not like the drift of it."

I looked at Maguire, then at Bruce, who began to shake his head.

At last I nodded, glad to end the little drama then and there. Maguire would get me some seaman's clothing — nothing new — and take me to the shipping master Bulloch was relying on for his additional crewmen. I'd be just another down-at-the-heels tar ready for a hitch at sea if the pay was good enough. No one on the *Enrica* knew me, so there shouldn't be much trouble getting on the muster roll.

"Captain Bulloch knows you," Bruce said. "You'll never get by him."

"Captain Bulloch is the biggest obstacle," I admitted. "I suppose that, even in seaman's rig, I'd resemble myself too closely for him not to become suspicious."

"Why not shave your whiskers, Mr. Pettigrew?"

I looked at Maguire. Why not indeed?

"Bulloch is so pressed for time," Maguire said, "I don't expect he'll look too closely."

"How do you explain all this to Mr. Adams and Secretary Welles?" Bruce asked.

"That won't be easy," I admitted. "I'll write to each tonight and depend on you to mail the letters. I'll go back to my lodgings this evening and pay my board bill. For all my landlady will know, I'll be leaving on the last train for London, with every expectation of returning. Bruce, I'll be grateful if within three days you will pay my rent with money I will leave you, and tell Mrs. Washburn she need no longer hold the room for me. And please collect my clothes and send them on to my grandfather. Mr. Maguire, if you can get hold of some seaman's clothing, I'll be ready to go with you to the sailing master's before midnight."

There was a fury of arguments when I finished, as both Sally and Bruce Thornton sought to dissuade me. Maguire himself said nothing, then rose to go, declining Sally's invitation to supper. He said he would be back later with what I wanted.

At my lodgings, I wrote the letters, spent a few minutes with Angus MacNaughton recounting the day on the *Enrica*, and shaved (a painful task!). Afterward, I took a cab for the Thorntons, where I found Maguire with a duffle awaiting me, as promised.

Sally and Bruce were so reserved in greeting me that I thought I must be back in the State of Maine. And when I changed into the clothing Maguire had brought, none of it very clean, and stepped out to confront them, the silence was truly mournful.

Then Bruce began to laugh, and even Maguire, and Sally started to smile. "Who could believe it? Scott," she said, "you look almost depraved. There's just one trouble — you also look too clean."

"Too clean!" I said.

"Aye, she's right," Maguire said. "Too clean. Take soot from the stove and rub it about on your face and neck and arms."

"And too sober, Mr. Maguire," Bruce laughed. "Surely you would agree he is too sober."

"We must take care of that," Maguire said.

It was a happy moment. But it did not last. All too soon a heavy silence hung upon the room.

"Let's go, Maguire," I said.

"Good-bye to you." Bruce Thornton clasped one hand and

[125]

Sally clasped the other. "And for the love of God," he said, "be careful."

When Maguire and I reached the waterfront, we stood each other to several rounds of grog. It was raw stuff, but I found it helped to burn away the loneliness I felt.

XV

THE day might be the 30th of July, but the air was raw with wind and occasional light spurts of rain as we stood on the Woodside landing stage at six o'clock in the morning. All told, there appeared to be thirty or thirty-five men and nearly as many women. We were huddled together against the elements, and the fumes of gin and whisky were so strong, the landing stage smelled like a distillery. Numbly we watched the crew of the *Hercules* loading an anchor stock for the *Enrica*, also a large piece of scantling, and several brass castings obviously intended for her engines. Two or three of the tug's crew jeered us, but not for long. The curses that crackled about their heads, from the women especially, seemed to stun them into silence.

There was no doubt about the toughness of this crowd. After Maguire had parted with me, a block from the warehouse where the sailing master, one Fred Terrell, was putting up his men for the night, I stumbled into the warehouse and asked for him. A guard thumbed me to his office, a hole of a room with a cluttered desk, a broken-backed chair, and a cot where Terrell, an overblown man, lay snoring damply. He awoke the moment I opened the door, and signed me up so quickly, I gathered he had had trouble rounding up men. I said I was Dan Thomas from Halifax, Nova Scotia, but he put me down as being from Hull, England. When I asked why he did this, he said he had orders to sign no one from the North American continent who was not a Southerner. I was then taken upstairs to the second floor and given a pallet and a blanket for the night. But as I looked and listened to what was going on, I could see there wouldn't be much sleep for me.

The second floor of that warehouse with all those men and women was both slophouse and brothel. Fighting and screaming and loving all over the place, except in one corner where a half-dozen unattached men had a card game going.

"Mind if I join?" I asked.

The man nearest me merely grunted but hunched aside enough for me to sit down. No one asked my name; scarcely anyone said a word to anyone else. They were as intent and silent as the others were noisy. Only once, a straggle-haired harridan came over to us and asked us if we wanted any fun.

"With you?" the wiry little man beside me said. "Jesus!"

She screamed insults so vile, that, if I'd been he, I'd have knocked her flat. Instead, he looked at her without saying a word, then went back to his cards. Eventually she left, shrieking that she hadn't met a man, a real man, that night.

"A proper pig!" the little man said when she had gone, but that was all.

In the end, the room quieted and most people slept. I dozed myself, but the snoring and groaning were something to hear, and every so often someone would go over to a window that opened over the water and vomit with a sound between a whoop and a whine.

Sometime early, Terrell and a couple of men went around kicking us awake and herding us downstairs. There we were given a cup of tea, a slice of bread, and a chunk of cheese, and were then taken to the landing stage. We waited an hour in the rain, miserable and hungry — at least those who weren't sick from drink.

At seven o'clock, Captain Bulloch stepped out of a cab and strode briskly down to the landing stage. We must have been a hard sight, but he looked pleased and relieved to see us.

"Mr. Terrell," he said to the sailing master, "best get these men aboard the tug and we'll get under weigh."

[127]

But Terrell shook his head. "You won't get them aboard without their women, cap'n."

"But they can't go along, Terrell!"

"They'll have to," Terrell said. "You see, cap'n, some of these are their wives, an' some of them ain't, but none of them will leave their men unless they get a month's pay in advance, or thereabouts."

Bulloch's mouth opened and closed twice before an answer came. Then he shrugged. "Very well, Terrell, get them all aboard. This is not the time or place to bargain. We've got to hurry."

It was a foul trip. Throughout the morning, rain fell, wetting many of us who couldn't crowd under cover. In the afternoon, the sky was dull and cloudy, a distinct improvement over the morning, but hunger pangs began to tell on our dispositions. Fortunately, Bulloch shortened the trip by directing the *Hercules*'s captain, as we neared New Brighton, to cut down the Rock Channel. As soon as the tug swung toward the channel, I knew that our likeliest guess last night of a destination for the *Enrica* was correct: Moelfre Bay. We sighted the ship at three o'clock, and an hour later, drew alongside.

Once we were aboard, Bulloch told us we'd soon have a hot, substantial supper. In the meantime, we could look over the main deck and make ourselves comfortable. Other members of the crew would show us where the heads were. The women should go first. There was a great guffaw at the last remark, for both men and women had been relieving themselves publicly aboard the small tug. If Bulloch had recognized the necessity of informality before, that time had passed: he made this clear to all.

The mutton and potatoes served us for supper soon disappeared, washed down by an ample allowance of grog. Then, after the men — and a number of women — had finished their pipes, Bulloch called us all aft.

[128]

After complimenting us on being as splendid a collection of manhood as he had ever seen, he came directly to the point.

"We've been cruising in the Irish Channel to get this ship's engines in good working order. My engineer reports that they now are. That being the case, I propose to send the *Enrica* straight on its voyage without returning to Liverpool. That would simply be an unnecessary delay and expense. Now I want to ask if you men will ship for the run, say to Havana, touching at any port on the way."

He paused for a moment to let this sink in, but only for a moment. Then he went on.

"If the ship shouldn't return to England, every man would be sent back without expense to himself, or we could make some other satisfactory settlement with him. And I tell you men, all of you shall have one month's pay in advance, paid down on the capstan's head. Where could you find a better arrangement than this? The *Enrica* is a nice, comfortable ship, well found and well provisioned. Any man who serves aboard her can count himself lucky. Now I'll give you about five minutes to think it over."

The terms were reasonable, and most of the men found them so. The little man who had made room for me in the card game was a cockney named Mel Taylor. There were times when I could hardly understand him, and other times when he spoke a clear English that no one could misunderstand. This was one of the latter when he turned to where a small group of us were standing on the fringe of the crowd.

"Sounds good, don't it?" Then, as the men nodded, he added, "There's something stinks about it. He won't say anything straight out."

"Who cares?" one of the men muttered.

"What can we lose?" asked another. "We're out of a job anyway, right now."

"What are you going to do?" Mel asked me.

"I'm going to sign."

He scratched his head, which was nearly bald and therefore made him look years older than he was — I'd guess he was about in his mid-thirties. "I'll sign, too," he finally said.

When Bulloch again spoke to us, all but three agreed to go. Bulloch then announced that articles stipulating the terms of agreement were waiting in the cabin and that each of us should come down in turn and sign. Those whose "ladies" were with them should bring them along, and the "lady" of each would receive the one month's advance pay either in cash or in a note for the equivalent from Captain Butcher.

We now lined up in alphabetical order and waited our turn to sign. As men came up from the cabin, they said that Bulloch, Butcher, and the paymaster, a man named Clarence Yonge, were all present at the signing. I had no fear of being recognized by the last two, but Bulloch was another matter. On the other hand, if the Thorntons had been shocked by the change in my appearance, perhaps Bulloch would not recognize in the shabby, dirty sailor with his scraped chin and gravelly voice the full-bearded, black-suited visitor of the day before.

Then my name was called, and I went into the cabin and stood before the long table — really only a couple of planks resting on sawhorses — hat in hand. All three men looked me over thoroughly. I glanced at them, looked properly uneasy and awkward, I hoped, in the presence of such dignitaries, and kept turning my hat around in my hands. Finally Bulloch nodded, and Butcher asked me to read the articles.

"You can read, can't you?" he added.

"Aye, sir," I said.

I hurriedly read them and, taking the pen he passed me, signed my name in a crude, heavy hand.

"How do you want your advance," Butcher asked, "cash or a note from me?"

Most of the men, even those without women, had taken their advance in cash. I saw no reason to call attention to myself as an exception, so I chose cash, too. Yonge then paid me, I signed a receipt, and that was that. But when I reached the deck, I was sweating, and felt quite naked and exposed.

When all the arrangements were completed, it was close to midnight. The wind had moved into the southwest, raising a sea, and heavy rain squalls occasionally drenched us. Alongside the *Enrica*, the tug was beginning to ride uneasily. Her captain came aboard and spoke earnestly to Bulloch. The latter then called the crew together and told them the women would have to return to Liverpool at once on the *Hercules*. Though the cries of the women were shrill in protest, Bulloch remained firm. Soon, after kisses and tears, they gingerly picked their way down to the deck of the *Hercules*. The gangway was then hauled up, and the *Hercules* steamed away, the wind whipping away the cries of farewell, and smoke and darkness obscuring the tug.

By half-past two in the morning, we got under weigh, using steam alone. It was raining and blowing hard, and thus was no night to head into the Irish Sea with a new ship and a green crew. Bulloch, however, had no choice, any more than he had a choice as to direction. With the *Tuscarora* coming around from the south, he sailed northward. Had he lingered where he was, the *Tuscarora* would surely have caught us.

The *Enrica*'s speed must have pleased Bulloch. By eight in the morning, we were off the Calf of Man. With the sky clearing and the wind diminishing to a fresh breeze, we set all sails and tore along at a pace that Captain Butcher announced to the watch was 13.5 knots. They looked almost as pleased as Bulloch; it is always satisfying to a crew to know that they are on a fast ship.

This pace, however, was not maintained much beyond noon. The wind dropped away almost completely, so we furled sail and went back to steam alone.

All afternoon we steered along the coast of Ireland, finally, in the early evening, slowing our engines off the Giant's Causeway and hailing a fishing boat to take Bulloch and Bond, the pilot, ashore. They left in a driving rain, and we cheered them as the fishing boat headed toward land.

I joined heartily in the cheers. I admired Bulloch as a man and respected him as an enemy. He was resourceful, persistent, and honorable throughout. Large amounts of money must have passed through his hands, and I never heard a whisper questioning his honesty.

With Bulloch and Bond gone, Captain Butcher took the *Enrica* around the rugged north coast of Ireland. The sea was rough, and I knew again what it was to be seasick. Fortunately, with morning the sky cleared, the wind slackened to a steady breeze, and Butcher ordered the sails set. Steam was obviously to be used only as a necessity. Whether it was the steadier motion of the ship or simply getting my sea legs, my stomach settled down.

My hopes, meanwhile, that the *Tuscarora* might catch us vanished. We learned later that she looked into Moelfre Bay about twelve hours after we had left it. Mr. Adams then ordered Captain Craven to follow the *Enrica* across the Atlantic. This Craven said was futile, which, indeed, it was; instead, he followed Consul Dudley's advice to search every creek and bay along the north coast of Ireland — an even more futile quest.

While Craven hunted in vain, we were bearing away to the southwest, most of the time under sail. Where we were going no one among the crew seemed sure. Just what our purpose was, however, became increasingly clear with every day that passed.

There was no public announcement. Instead, Paymaster Yonge began to circulate among the warrant and petty officers, no doubt on Bulloch's order. He tried to excite their interest in the coming cruise of the *Enrica* and extolled the struggle of the Southern states for their liberty and independence. Every Englishman was wedded to the tradition of liberty, he pointed out, and the Confederacy was fighting against heavy odds. We could see Yonge talking with these officers, we often heard what was said, and soon the crew itself began to get interested and to discuss what the *Enrica* was supposed to do.

From the first, few men had doubts that the *Enrica* was to become a raider. Such a role meant that she had to have guns and ammunition, which she did not now possess, and commissioned officers in the Confederate Navy to command her. It would have taken a stupid sailor not to realize that we had a rendezvous somewhere with some ship that would supply us with what was needed. There was a great deal of speculation about that rendezvous but much more among the men as to whether they would go along on a raiding cruise. The prospect of prize money was excitedly discussed, though Mel Taylor had a way of dampening the excitement to a degree.

"We'll be lucky if we stay alive to collect it," he said. "The Yankees have got some fast cruisers. They'll have heavier guns than us, and I ain't looking forward to dying in a Yankee prison, either."

Several times I heard him talk like this, but before long, the men brushed his caution aside. The lure of gold was irresistible. Had he not been a good-natured man and a veteran seaman, they might have been rough on him. As it was, he was a fine topman, quick and surefooted, and deft with his hands. Alongside him, I was clumsy, though no worse than a number and better than many.

Eventually we sighted land, mountains that seemed to rise straight out of the sea. It was Terceira in the Azores, and we soon slid into the bay of Porto Praya, dropping anchor before the town, which lies in the northern curve of the bay.

Not far away, riding at anchor, lay a bark deep laden. Immediately after we moored, Captain Butcher broke out the white English ensign. Curious at this move, Mel and I watched the bark from our position high above the deck as our section clewed up the fore-topsail. The bark responded almost at once by hoisting a blue flag, and we saw the crew start to lower a boat.

"So that's it," Mel muttered.

"It looks that way," I said.

We soon found out that the bark, the *Agrippina*, skippered by an old Scot, Alexander McQueen, who liked his whisky and lots of it, contained all that we had guessed — and more. For days, we lay alongside her, transferring cargo. With Paymaster Yonge and his assistants checking the invoices, we first took aboard the slops, clothing, and other articles in the purser's department, placing them in the storerooms. Then we got the gun carriages aboard. Though the Lairds had made provision on the *Enrica*'s deck for twelve guns, only eight were to be mounted: six thirty-two-pounders — three to a side — and two pivot guns: an eight-inch smoothbore abaft the mainmast, throwing a sixty-eight-pound shot, and, forward of the bridge, a seven-inch Blakely rifled gun with a hundred-pound projectile. The guns we were ordered to leave alone until the officers arrived, but the carriages and carriage rings we installed. We opened the cases containing the shot and placed the shot on the racks. The shells we carried to the shell rooms, putting each shell in its proper box, the spherical shells in the starboard room, the elongated shells in the port room. The pistols, in four cases, went into the arms chests on the quarterdeck. Then there was the coal, all 350 tons of it, and a messy, filthy, stifling job it was to transfer this.

We were in the midst of our labors on the morning of the 20th of August, and having our troubles because of a heavy swell, when a lookout aboard the *Agrippina*, which was lashed to the *Enrica*, sighted a steamer bearing down on us. She was moving into the harbor at a fast clip, the water foaming at her bow and paddle wheels. Instantly everyone stopped work, and all kinds of fearful speculation rose. If the stranger was a Yankee cruiser, there was absolutely no defense that could be made. I dearly hoped to see the Stars and Stripes. Instead, she flew the British flag, and, as she rounded to, within voice range of us, and stopped her engines, it was clear that she was no man-of-war. The name *Bahama* was inscribed across her stern.

While we were still looking her over, a solidly built, broad-shouldered man mounted her rail and bellowed through a speaking trumpet, "Captain Butcher, this is Captain Raphael Semmes of the Confederate States Navy. The sea is too high to get the guns in place, so haul up your anchors and follow me around to Angra Bay until we find a lee and smooth water."

His voice had authority and carrying power. If this was not sufficient to convince Butcher that he was really Semmes and the *Enrica*'s future skipper, there was Captain Bulloch standing on the deck beside him. Near them clustered a group of officers under whose command we would presently pass. Butcher waved his hand in acknowledgment.

Semmes himself, with Bulloch, came aboard about four o'clock, just as soon as the transshipment began again. Semmes looked even more assured and masterful than when I had seen him leaving the Morley Hotel with Bulloch. His wax-tipped mustache and his piercing eyes made him look like a piratical Frenchman. Men stared at him covertly as he walked the deck with Bulloch and Butcher, but worked harder than ever when he approached them. His was not a winning presence, but it was certainly one that inspired respect.

What he thought of us I could only conjecture. Yet I was sure he must have deplored the condition of the *Enrica*'s decks and the appearance of her crew. Much of what we had trans-ferred from the *Agrippina* still lay helter-skelter on the decks, a forest of boxes and bales and barrels, an incredible jumble for a man-of-war. As for ourselves, we wore anything — red shirts, blue shirts, no shirts; caps, hats, or just hair, and pants of every description and condition. The only thing common to all of us was the coal dust that blackened our skin and clothes, not to mention the decks. Once I saw Semmes looking with such distaste, I thought he had in mind turning a hose on us.

With the approach of evening, Semmes had his baggage

brought aboard from the *Bahama* and, relieving Butcher of command, took possession of the stern cabin. His officers likewise came aboard, and thirty additional seamen Captain Bulloch had collected in Liverpool. "Jesus," one of them said, a burly man with a hat on the back of his head, "ain't you the pretty ones!"

The next morning, the Portuguese sent out a boat, demanding, so report had it, that, as a merchant ship, we should go at once into East Angra, the port of entry. Semmes, however, steamed out to sea, followed by the *Agrippina* and the *Bahama*. Once there, though the sea was not as smooth as it looked, we completed the task of bringing everything aboard, except for some of the coal. It was after nightfall when we ran into East Angra to anchor.

To our surprise, as we passed the fort, some officer hailed us sharply. When we made no reply, a puff of white and black smoke blossomed from the battlements and a heavy cannonball roared overhead. Glancing at Semmes standing on the lightly built bridge abaft amidships, I saw him shrug and say something to Bulloch. He ignored the Portuguese order and, running in with the *Agrippina*, dropped anchor. The *Bahama*, however, remained outside.

During the night, we were awakened by three cannon shots. Most of the crew scrambled to the main deck to see what was happening. Not far from us lay a small Portuguese armed schooner, and it was thought at first that she was firing at us. But this didn't seem to make sense, for she remained at anchor with only her riding light showing. Not until morning did we learn that the shots were fired from a mail steamer that ran into port to pick up mail and passengers. Warned by the shots, the passengers met her at the dock, and she left before sunup.

The British consul and several Portuguese customs officials came aboard the *Enrica* the next morning. Coaling stopped while they were present and until Semmes returned from a visit ashore. I suspected that according to maritime law, the Portuguese had insisted that Semmes suspend coaling operations until he had registered the coal as cargo at the customs house.

When coaling resumed, a number of us were called on to fit side and train tackles for the broadside guns, under the direction of the boatswain. The *Bahama*, meanwhile, had been called in. She had brought out two of the *Enrica*'s guns with her, and these were now transferred to our deck with block and tackle while the two steamers, lashed together, rolled gently in the swell. Luckily, although the harbor of East Angra was open, the wind was light and the sea smooth. But this was not the only activity. The carpenter, the gunner, and the chief engineer were busy laying the traverse circles for the Blakely and the smoothbore pivot gun.

Semmes and his officers drove us hard the rest of the week. Though Saturday was rainy, we worked without a letup, except for meals. Then, by evening, the guns were mounted, the shells, powder, and the stores stowed in their proper places, and the coal bunkers filled. The ship was no longer helpless.

The next morning, we were routed out of our hammocks early for a quick breakfast, followed by hours of cleaning the ship inside and out. Salt water, the holystone, and muscle presently wrought wonders. In addition, awnings were snugly spread, yards were squared, and the rigging was hauled taut. The last order for all cleaning details was to strip and clean ourselves. Men with spare clothing were to put it on; those without any — and I was one — were to wash their clothes and wring them as tightly as possible. Fortunately, they soon dried on us in the hot August sun.

With everything shipshape, the *Enrica* steamed slowly seaward. The *Agrippina* had left in the night, but the *Bahama* accompanied us out of the harbor. It was now late forenoon. Overhead the sky was cloudless, and around us the sea was an unbroken expanse of blue. Astern lay the island of Terceira, its slopes colorful with the light green of citrus groves and the white of the houses with their red-tiled roofs. In such a setting both ships hove to, and all hands on the *Enrica* were mustered aft on the quarterdeck.

Captain Semmes now mounted a gun carriage. He and his officers were splendid in new gray uniforms of the Confederate States Navy. It must have seemed odd to a number of them who had served in the old navy, as it certainly did to me, for navy officers to wear anything but dark blue. But there was no denying they made a very fine appearance.

Semmes stood for a moment looking at us in silence. Then, after removing his hat and waiting until all present had done the same, he read both the commission of President Jefferson Davis, appointing him a captain in the navy of the Confederacy, and the order from the Confederate Secretary of the Navy, Stephen R. Mallory, directing him to assume his command.

As he paused, our eyes left him and followed two small balls ascending: one to the peak, the other to the main-royal masthead. By the English flag which we still flew stood a quartermaster; beside the weather bow gun, a gunner with lockstring in hand; on the quarterdeck near us, our half-dozen bandsmen, their leader's eyes on Semmes.

"Until this moment," Semmes said, pride and excitement giving his voice a thrilling timbre, "this ship has been known as *Number 290* and *Enrica*. That is so no longer. I now christen her the *Alabama!*"

At a wave of Semmes's hand, the quartermaster struck the English Union Jack; seamen jerked the halyards, and the two balls burst open as the Stars and Bars and the pennant of the Confederacy were flung to the wind. The gun boomed in salute; the band broke into "Dixie," and a loud cheer went up from both men and officers. Unionist I may have been, yet I found the occasion so exciting I gave more than a perfunctory cheer. From the *Bahama* likewise came a cannon salute and three ringing cheers.

Then Semmes gave a short, energetic speech. He said that all of us were now released from the contracts we had signed and those of us who wanted to could return on the *Bahama* to be discharged at Liverpool, with our pay continuing until then. He wanted us to know, however, that the war he intended to support in the *Alabama* was a struggle against tyranny. He portrayed the Southern states as being sovereign and independent, having dissolved their league with the other states of the Union, and now fighting for their freedom against efforts by the North to subjugate them. As a Southern officer, he was determined to harass Northern shipping.

"If you will enlist as sailors of the Confederacy and come on this cruise with me," he said in ringing tones, "you will find excitement and adventure. We have a fine ship under us, a ship you may fall in love with as you would with your sweethearts in Wapping. We shall visit many ports of the world, and you shall have liberty in many foreign cities. We shall seize Northern merchantmen wherever we can find them, and if we should chance upon a Northern cruiser not too heavy for us, I will not hesitate to lay the *Alabama* alongside her and board her."

Again he paused. I could see the men were interested in what he was saying, and generally approving, though I heard one man mutter, "Hell, you could lose your life on this damned ship!"

Evidently sensing the men wanted to listen to more than rhetoric, Semmes smiled and said, "I realize you will want to hear about pay and prize money. I will not conceal from you the fact that you will be running certain risks on this cruise, but, as compensation, you will receive double wages. Ordinary seamen will be paid four pounds, ten shillings a month. Specialists will receive more, of course. And payment will be made in gold, and in advance."

At this, several men shouted, "Hear! Hear!" and most of them talked excitedly among themselves for a few moments.

"One more point," Semmes said, raising his hand to quiet

them. "If our fight for freedom is successful, the Confederate Congress will vote you prize money for the enemy ships that fall to the *Alabama*. Thank you."

As he stepped down to a burst of cheering, the boatswain and his mates piped us away. But even as we broke up, the boatswain passed the word among us that all who wanted to sign articles should report to the paymaster at once.

Again we lined up and went below in turn. What we had signed before as members of the *Enrica* for the cruise to a foreign port had no reference to our new status as Confederate seamen aboard the man-of-war *Alabama*. I had qualms, of course, about agreeing to serve the enemy, but loyalty to the Union made such deceit tolerable. Semmes, Bulloch, Paymaster Yonge, and the latter's clerk participated in the arrangements. Half-pay tickets were made out for wives and sweethearts; for those who wanted them, drafts were drawn for small amounts payable to relatives and dependents, and advance wages were paid to others, like myself, who had no paytickets to leave or remittances to make. This time, I had less fear of being recognized by Bulloch; and, indeed, he was so busy, he did not even glance at me as I passed. Yonge entered my name in his book and took my receipt for the advance. When I came out on deck, I had nothing like that feeling of sweating relief that I had experienced after the initial signing on in Moelfre Bay.

By eleven o'clock that night, the task was completed. Of ninety seamen, a total of eighty-five signed; those who refused were to return with Bulloch to England on the *Bahama*. We were a mixed bag: mostly English, with a fair number of Welsh and Irish, but also Dutch, French, Italian, Spanish, and Russian. Unless a man could prove he was a Southerner, Semmes would not accept a native of the North American continent; thus, this mission was consistent with the enlistment of the contingent at Moelfre Bay. The result was that not a single member of the crew was a Southerner, yet all were now enlisted in the Confederate States Navy aboard a ship built in England.

Only time would tell if Semmes could control them and if they would truly support him in a cause they knew little about.

It was near midnight before Captain Bulloch shook hands with Semmes and went down the gangway to the boat awaiting him from the *Bahama*. Aboard the *Alabama*, everyone was on deck and crowding to the rail to watch the brightly lighted *Bahama*. Her crew gave us three cheers; then, smoke blacker than the darkness pouring furiously from her funnel, she steamed away.

I think that momentarily many on the *Alabama* had a sense of aloneness. We were a silent group as we set the fore- and aft sails, Semmes now banking his fires and heading northeast.

Suddenly Mel Taylor drove an elbow into my ribs as the boatswain piped us below. "For Christ's sake, what's that?"

The men stopped and looked up. The sky was brilliant with stars, but there was one that blazed so brightly, the others shone dimly by comparison.

"That's Swift's Comet, sailor. It's a sign of good luck."

We turned and, in the light of one of the lanterns, recognized Lieutenant Kell, the *Alabama*'s first officer and a man we already knew as a firm disciplinarian.

"Aye, aye, sir. Thank'ee, sir," Mel said, and touching his forelock, he ducked quickly down the hatchway.

Good luck was exactly what I prayed the *Alabama* wouldn't have. At the same time, I realized, with a feeling of despair, that she was now so formidable that good luck was her likely prospect until a storm or Union guns could destroy her.

TWO

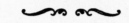

Service on the Alabama

XVI

THE next day was dismal. The *Alabama* rolled and tumbled. Spare shot cases came loose, guns strained dangerously at their new tackles, and the fire in the galley stove had to be extinguished. Water was leaking through the ship's upperworks. In fact, the ship had been partially built of green timber, and the seams, which had been caulked in winter, were parting under the tropical sun. There had been no time, moreover, to train the crew. All this meant that although we were close to the whaling grounds, so frequented by New Englanders, Semmes took the *Alabama* off the beaten track to finish conditioning her and get his crew in hand.

Largely under Lieutenant Kell's direction, the crew arrangements were effected. We were soon berthed, messed, quartered, and stationed. There were two assignments I hoped to avoid. One was at the guns, where I might one day be obliged to fire on a ship under the old flag; the other was in the fireroom, where the heat and filth were excessive, and stokers deserved their unheard-of pay of seven pounds sterling per month. Fortunately, there were not lacking volunteers to be stokers, and Kell must have become so used to seeing Mel Taylor and me handling canvas that that became our principal duty. It was an important one, too, as soon became evident, for Semmes rarely used steam to overhaul his prey.

For several days, Semmes worked us hard. He timed us

[145]

setting and furling sail, and if he didn't curse us for being slipshod and slow, one of his lieutenants did — Kell or Semmes's second, Richard F. Armstrong of Georgia, who had been at Annapolis and served with Semmes on the *Sumter*; the third, Joseph D. Wilson, also an Annapolis man and, like Armstrong, a shipmate of Semmes's on the *Sumter*; the fourth, Arthur Sinclair, of an old Virginia family, whose father and grandfather had been captains in the United States Navy; or the fifth, John Low of Georgia, a native-born Englishman and a first-rate seaman, as we soon discovered. Though young, Armstrong and Wilson had an especially fierce sense of discipline, almost as severe as Kell's.

The gun crews came in for hours of drill. Some of the men had served aboard men-of-war, and their experience now proved invaluable in breaking in neophytes. All of us turned to help recaulk the widening seams. All of us, too, were instructed in boarding and repelling boarders, should Semmes ever decide to fight it out at close quarters with a Union cruiser. I tried not to appear too adept with pistol, knife, pike, or cutlass. For that matter, I had no desire to be recognized as excelling at anything.

Finally, on the fifth day of September, Semmes turned back toward the whaling grounds, and he had a deadly instrument of destruction under his control.

I have rarely seen a more graceful ship than the *Alabama*. Just slightly more than a thousand tons, she had a fiddlehead cutwater, a high freeboard, a black hull that looked longer than its overall length of 235 feet, a beam of 32 feet, and an elliptical stern. She drew fifteen feet when provisioned and filled to her full bunker capacity of 375 tons. She was rigged as a barkentine, and her spars had a pleasing rake and were made of yellow pine. Her rigging was of the finest quality of Swedish iron wire. Her two horizontal steam engines were rated as giving her three hundred horsepower but actually provided a thousand. She was constructed in such a way that when she changed from sail to steam, her propeller could be detached from the shaft and drawn up into a well; it would thereby be no impediment to her speed, and the whole operation required only fifteen minutes to execute.

The *Alabama* was usually a ten-knot ship. While I was on her, she rarely went as fast as on her trials off Liverpool, but, of course, then she had neither guns nor ammunition aboard, and sea conditions were ideal. Semmes once logged her at 13.25 knots under both steam and sail, but only once. What made her so deadly was her flexibility. Rarely did she use steam in pursuit, but it was available whenever Semmes wanted it. He had to nurse his coal supply, however, for he had enough for only eighteen days, and not even that long at full speed.

On the morning of September 5, having arrived off Pico and Fayal the afternoon before, we were cruising under easy sail, the weather cloudy and the wind from the eastward. Suddenly the cry of "Sail, ho!" ripped down from the masthead. It was a brig, which took alarm immediately as we cracked on all sail in pursuit. I must admit to a feeling of satisfaction upon seeing Semmes pound his hands together in disgust as the brig presently left us behind.

But my satisfaction was short-lived. Our pursuit of the flying brig brought us to within two miles of a whaler lying to. As we ran down toward her, we saw that she had a whale alongside, partly hoisted out of the water by her yard tackles. Since we were flying United States colors, her crew evidently saw no reason to feel alarmed. When a cutter under Master's Mate George Fullam ran alongside and Fullam boarded the whaler, it looked for a few moments as if she would offer resistance. Evidently the captain at last recognized the danger, for we now flew the Stars and Bars. He surrendered.

By the time Semmes had stripped the whaler — the *Ocmulgee* of Edgartown, Martha's Vineyard — of her beef, pork, and small stores, darkness had fallen. He had permitted the captain and his crew of over thirty to load their six whaleboats with their baggage and miscellaneous supplies. The boats were moored near the *Alabama* while the men were imprisoned aboard. I wondered what Semmes would do with the whaler herself, whether he would send her into port or burn her. Actually, he let her alone during the night and sent a prize crew aboard under Lieutenant Sinclair. I was one of that crew, and none of us slept very soundly with the stink of whale oil all about us.

The next morning, Semmes sent word to burn the ship. Had he done so the night before, the fire would have probably scared off other vessels. Now the smoke would likely be mistaken as coming from some passing steamer.

Sinclair called us together and gave us the necessary instructions. "First, take the axes you brought with you and cut up the bunks in the cabin and the forecastle. They're probably of white pine — the Yankees like that — so you won't have any trouble smashing it up, and it'll burn nicely. The mattresses will be stuffed with straw. I want you to go to the cabin pantry and get a keg of butter and a keg of lard."

"Are we going to save that for supplies?" a stout man named Joe Larkin asked, innocently, I think.

Sinclair looked at him and smiled thinly. "If you'll wait a moment, I'll not only tell you what to do with those kegs — I'll also let you go get them yourself."

The reproof was unmistakable, but Sinclair was not an unkind man. He went on, "Make a foundation of the splinters and straw from the bunks, then pour the butter and lard on top of them. Put one pile in the cabin and another in the forecastle. I'll assign one man to light each pile. The rest of you get into the cutter and wait. The two firelighters must do their job quickly, but make sure the pile's really blazing before you leave it. Then get into the cutter as fast as you can. When I shout 'Fire!,' we'll shove off for the *Alabama*. Is all this clear?"

He assigned each of us places aboard the whaler, and we went to work with vigor, smashing the bunks to pieces, piling up the mattresses, and smearing the butter and lard over all. When this was done, he sent everyone to the boats, except Mel and me.

"I want you to light the forecastle pile, Taylor, and you to light the cabin pile, Thomas. Do it quickly, but do it!"

I went into the cabin, now a wreck of a place. A sense of guilt at my part in such destruction was momentarily overwhelming, and I stared around in helplessness and rage.

"Hurry up, Thomas!" Sinclair shouted.

My first match broke off, the second also. Then the third glowed brightly, and I held it to the straw.

The flame that leaped up caused me to pull back so quickly, I slipped on some lard and fell. For a moment I panicked, then scrambled for the deck above. When I reached it, the forecastle was already ablaze, and Sinclair was waving me to the cutter. After he leaped aboard, we shoved off, and rowed as hard as we could for the *Alabama*. But even before we arrived, the *Ocmulgee*, heavy with oil, practically exploded, and flame and black smoke towered skyward.

"You were slow, Thomas," Sinclair said.

"Yes, sir," I said humbly. "I slipped on some lard and fell."

He nodded. "You'll learn. All of you will learn. If we take enough prizes, we'll soon be incendiary experts."

"But there ain't no prize money from a burning ship, sir," Mel said.

"No, but we'll send enough ships into port so that you'll come in for a good share, I'm sure."

The next morning being Sunday and a lovely day, Semmes ordered a formal muster. First, the ship was cleaned, with the brass and ironwork soon agleam from polishing, and the deck spotless from our work with holystone and mop. The crew itself scarcely resembled the men who had left England aboard the *Enrica* or the *Bahama*. All were now clothed in duck frocks and trousers, highly polished black shoes, and straw sailor's hats. Our faces were red or brown from the tropical sun, and as a group we looked lean and fit. The officers, a truly large staff, were in their immaculate gray. To a man they wore sidearms. In fact, as long as I was aboard the *Alabama,* I don't remember seeing an officer, certainly a commissioned officer, without his pistol.

Ordinarily Sunday morning was the time for worship. It had been so on the *Tuscarora,* when we visited her in Southampton, and I half expected it to be so on the *Alabama.* It was common knowledge that Semmes was a devout Catholic and prayed on his knees before a little shrine in his cabin. But there was no church service this Sunday. Instead, it was the occasion for Semmes to read the Articles of War.

I had read these many times in the Union Navy, and the Confederate Articles of War were copied almost verbatim. But this was the first time it had ever occurred to me how frequently the word "death" was used. Death for exciting or causing or joining any mutiny or sedition. Death for striking or disobeying a superior officer. Death for deserting, or for advising or persuading anyone to desert. Death for sleeping on watch. Death for misbehaving before the enemy. Death for aiding the enemy in various ways. Death, in a number of other cases, at the discretion of a court-martial, which could be convoked without delay by the captain. In all honesty, there were some tough characters among our crew, despite how clean and well-turned-out they now looked. Furthermore, while we were only 85 in number, there was provision on the berth deck for 120. If Semmes enlisted men from some of the prizes we took, there would be more toughness to cope with. It wasn't hard to understand why the officers went armed.

As I listened to Semmes and observed his face and manner, I thought how different he was from the first time he had addressed us. Then he was firm but cheerful, almost good-humored. He was, of course, dependent on our enlisting for him to carry out his mission of destruction. He had been like a politician, possibly even a salesman. Now he wielded the autocratic, truly awful power of a regular navy captain, and he was fully conscious of it. His voice was harsh, his manner severe. He looked intently at us in the pauses between articles, and warning and menace were in his glance. Already he had confined men in irons for longer or shorter periods, according to their offenses. He was determined to have the most precise kind of discipline, and I began to feel that he wouldn't hesitate to enforce the Articles of War to the last extremity, if necessary. Though the day was warm and the beautiful, mountainous island of Flores, westernmost of the Azores, so near we could smell occasionally the fragrance of blossoms, there was something chilling in the whole ceremony. When we were dismissed, no one spoke at first; it was as if we had attended a funeral. I'm sure Semmes intended it this way.

Shortly after the muster, we ran close to the beach off the village of Lagens on the south side of the island. There we hove to, and after we brought alongside the *Ocmulgee*'s boats which we had been towing, Semmes released the whaler's crew and let them row ashore. This saved him the trouble of maintaining prisoners, but it meant, of course, that the United States consul on Fayal would shortly have word of Semmes's presence in these waters, if he did not already know, and word would be sent to Washington that much sooner. No one seemed to know where we were headed next, but I should have liked to ask one of the prisoners to tell the consul that we had just begun operations in the whaling grounds and would likely continue for a while. Unfortunately, they were kept under heavy guard, and no one was permitted to talk with them.

We had hardly rid ourselves of the *Ocmulgee*'s crew when the cry of "Sail, ho!" came again from the masthead, and the *Alabama* whirled off after a handsome, little whaling schooner approaching the island. Semmes ran up English colors to deceive her, but she refused to show her nationality. Instead, she set every stitch of canvas she could carry, clearly trying to get inside the three-mile limit. Whether Semmes would have recognized Portuguese sovereignty in those waters had the schooner's captain succeeded, I'd never know. Possibly. At any rate, the *Alabama* now unfurled the Stars and Bars and fired a blank cartridge for the schooner to heave to. She neither complied nor raised a flag. Semmes then waved his hand, and one of the bow guns sent a thirty-two-pound shot between the schooner's masts and just a few feet above her deck. At once, she luffed up into the wind, brailed up her foresail, and hauled her jib sheet to windward. And she finally raised the Stars and Stripes.

The schooner proved to be the *Starlight* of Boston. She was bound home from Fayal and was stopping at Flores to deliver a number of passengers, including several women.

Her master, who was about my age, was an angry man when he came aboard the *Alabama*. Unlike the *Ocmulgee*'s skipper, the *Starlight*'s captain protested bitterly Semmes's action.

Semmes's reply was firm and clear. "Every whale you strike will put money into the federal treasury, and strengthen the hands of your people to carry on the war. I am afraid I must burn your ship."

Semmes then ordered both the master and his crew of seven confined in irons. When they insisted that this was an indignity and an unjust procedure, Semmes turned on them and said, far less moderately than before, "You think this an indignity, do you? Well, you are right. But it is an act of retaliation against the action of your own government. Your consul at Tangier caused my former paymaster in the *Sumter*, Mr. Myers, to be taken from a French steamer with another Confederate citizen. Their heads were shaved, they were put in chains, and they were shipped across the ocean and imprisoned in Fort Warren in Boston. Do you call that humane, dignified, and just treatment? Master-at-arms, put these men in irons."

His voice echoed from the quarterdeck for all of us to hear. I could henceforth understand, if certainly not condone, why he should treat similarly the masters and crews of the next half-dozen ships we seized. Sometimes he interrogated them on

[152]

deck, sometimes in his cabin — increasingly the latter — but one could always hear, or imagine hearing, that harsh, inexorable voice, like that of a vengeful Fate, condemning a beautiful ship to flames and its crew to irons.

We landed the crew and passengers of the *Starlight* at Santa Cruz the next morning; then, running seaward, with the *Starlight* trailing along under a prize crew, we sighted a whaling brig. She proved to be Portuguese — the only non-American whaler we ever overhauled. Of course, we let her go.

Still, the day wasn't entirely lost for Semmes. Along toward sunset, a tremendous whaler ran right into our arms, beguiled, no doubt, by our flying American colors. She was the *Ocean Rover* of New Bedford, bound home after more than three years at sea.

"I thought I would stop by the Azores and pick up a little more oil," the master told Semmes. He looked a kindly man and was probably younger than he appeared — the beard made him a patriarch.

"That was your mistake," Semmes said.

"If you take my ship, it will be a dreadful loss to all of us at home. My children were babies when I left, and I hoped to be able to accumulate something for my family from this voyage."

"I am sorry for you," Semmes said, "but you have only your government to blame and the acts of your fellow New Englanders. They hate us and treat us like animals if we fall into their power. I will burn your ship, sir."

But he didn't, not that night, anyway. He put a prize crew aboard the ship and hove her to until morning. But, as with the *Starlight*'s master and crew, he caused the master and crew of the *Ocean Rover* to spend the night in irons.

Not everyone in the *Alabama*'s crew liked this policy of Semmes's. They didn't dare protest it formally, but I heard much sympathy for the Americans.

"Hell, they ain't nothin' but merchantmen," Joe Larkin said as we sat around the berth deck.

"Well, we can't go an' free 'em," Mel Taylor said.

"You're right," I said, "but why not let them know that Semmes allowed the *Ocmulgee* crew to load up their boats and go ashore?"

"You game to tell them, Joe?" Mel asked.

"I don't want no trouble with Old Beeswax."

"Old what?" Mel asked as the others started to laugh.

"I said, 'Old Beeswax.' Can't you see old Semmes waxin' up the points of that mustache he fancies? Ain't he just the cock-of-the-walk? Now I ask you!"

Thus Semmes became "Old Beeswax" to the crew. But not to me. It was too much like a term of affection.

Despite his fears, Joe Larkin must have done his work well that night, because the next morning, when the *Ocean Rover*'s master was released from his irons, he went straight to Semmes. A little while later, he and his crew were permitted to return to their ship, from which they filled their six whaleboats to overflowing with supplies and personal effects. In fact, the boats were so loaded down after two hours of work that when the skipper and his six boats, six men in each, rowed alongside the *Alabama* before setting out for shore, Semmes came out to stare down at him.

"Captain," said Semmes, a faint smile on his face, "those boats are riding pretty low. Aren't you afraid you'll ship some water?"

"No, sir! These boats will ride like ducks and won't ship a drop of water, you'll see."

"No, I'm afraid I shan't," Semmes said.

"Well, then, I want you to have this," the skipper said. And over the side he came once more, bearing a fruitcake that his wife had made and packed three years before. Semmes thanked him, bade the clerk take the crew's parole, and sent the boats on their way.

We had lain alongside the whaler all day and continued to lie there through the night. Most of us watched the *Ocean Rover*'s boats as they moved in a line through the moonlight to the shore. We actually heard the crew shouting out some sea chantey as they rowed. One would never have thought they had lost their ship.

The next morning, after a long chase and the use of a thirty-two pound shot to toss a shower of water over her stern, we overhauled the whaler *Alert*, sixteen days out of New London and bound for the South Indian Ocean. She had many items aboard that Semmes felt he could use: some choice beef and pork, ship's bread nicely put up, boxes of soap, a large stock of clothing for a whaling and sealing station, and a number of heavy oaken boxes filled with "Virginia twist," to the joy of all pipe smokers aboard the *Alabama*. Semmes sent the *Alert's* crew ashore, as he had the other crews, on this occasion not confining them in irons for any length of time.

We now put to sea with the *Starlight*, the *Ocean Rover*, and the *Alert*. Semmes had made inquiries, while we had touched at the Azores, if Portugal would receive prizes. He now told us she would not, nor were European nations very friendly to the idea, though he hoped they would become more receptive. We therefore burned the three prizes at considerable distance from each other.

But we had hardly taken our prize crews aboard before we sighted another ship and overhauled her without trouble. She was the *Weathergauge*, another whaler out of New Bedford. Like the *Alert*, she had a number of the latest Northern newspapers, which Semmes distributed to the crew after he and the officers had perused them. The North still had no idea, at the time they appeared, that the *Enrica* had escaped from Liverpool.

We chased a Danish ship, that night returned to Corvo to burn the *Weathergauge* in the morning, went two days without sighting an American ship, then overhauled and burned the *Altamaha*, also of New Bedford. Not long after that, we captured the *Benjamin Tucker* of New Bedford and the whaling schooner *Courser* of Provincetown. With eight whaleboats in tow, we sailed for Flores, where we put our seventy prisoners aboard the boats and sent them into port. Then we stood offshore and used the *Courser* for target practice.

And so it went, through that fine September weather — fine except for the 18th and 19th, when we bucked through a heavy gale. We captured the *Virginia* of New Bedford and, just before the gale broke, the *Elisha Dunbar* of the same port. During the storm the *Dunbar*, a mass of flame, madly rolled and tossed. Sails went flying off into the darkness like flaming birds; yards swung wildly, then dropped into the raging sea. Finally, the masts toppled, and a tremendous, foaming sea rolled over the doomed ship, extinguishing the fire but completely engulfing her.

The *Alabama* had now taken ten ships, and had put the crews of all but the last two ashore. A succession of gales from the 19th to the 23rd made it difficult to get rid of the men from the *Virginia* and the *Dunbar*. We were under reefed lowers, the wind from the north, and we drifted south to the thirty-fourth degree of latitude. Where we went, we found nothing, the equinoctial weather evidently having put an end to the whaling season. It was becoming obvious that Semmes must make a change of hunting grounds, and at the end of the month, he swung the ship's head to the northwest.

By this time, I felt my own role aboard the *Alabama* to have been a failure. While we were in the Azores, any reporting of our position would have been of little help; the crews we released would have given our consul at Fayal ample information on that count. What was really important was that the Union Navy learn where the *Alabama* might next go, and when the decision was made while we were at sea, there was nothing I could contribute. The first the navy would learn of Semmes's new destination would again probably be from the released crews of burned vessels.

On this occasion, it was not hard to guess where Semmes was

heading. His direction was toward the shipping lanes through which American ships passed on their way to and from Europe. He would inevitably find a rich harvest there. My only hope was that the navy, which surely knew by now that Semmes and the *Alabama* were loose upon the high seas, would anticipate his present move. A few cruisers in those waters could take care of the situation nicely.

Or could they? My respect for Semmes's seamanship and capacity for command had grown to the point where I realized it would take a smart captain indeed to best him. On the other hand, no man was above making mistakes, and it was possible that his evident pride in himself and his splendid ship might yet destroy him. And the more I saw of the devastation he already caused my country, the more earnestly I longed to help bring him crashing down.

XVII

"I tell you, men, there's something that ain't right about this cruise."

Alex Gill, a member of our watch, was a big, sandy-haired Scot, with powerful arms and shoulders and a large, knobby nose that gave him a mean look. He was a constant complainer. He found fault with the food. He derogated our two doctors, Francis Galt, a veteran of the *Sumter*, and David Llewellyn, his helper and a Welshman. Lieutenant Kell was a slave driver. Bartelli, Semmes's gentle Italian steward, was a sodomite. About Semmes himself he was not so explicit, but his hints were getting bolder.

"What ain't right about this cruise?" Mel Taylor asked, sucking on a capped pipe, the only kind we were permitted to smoke below decks.

Gill hitched up his pants and squatted down beside us, cursing the clothing he wore. While in the Azores, in the daytime we wore duck, but, at night, when the atmosphere was heavily damp, Semmes had us change to wool. We followed the same routine as we entered the foggy, rainy waters of the Gulf Stream where it nears the Newfoundland Banks. Gill favored sticking with the duck all the time.

"Well, it's like this," he said. "We're supposed to be a Confederate cruiser, ain't we?"

We nodded.

"There ain't any Southerners aboard outside the officers, are there?"

We agreed, of course.

"Have we touched at a Southern port yet?"

"We ain't had time," Larkin said. "We been too busy scoopin' up Yankees in the Azores."

"And do you think the admiral has any mind to run the blockade?"

"He might," I said.

Since the Azores, Semmes was known to the men not just as "Old Beeswax" but "the Admiral," too. Ordinarily when they used these terms, they meant them in good part. Gill sounded contemptuous.

"Might, hell!" Gill snorted. "He wouldn't risk the *Alabama* trying to get through to any of those ports."

Privately I agreed with him, but I said, "I don't see why not."

"You don't! Jesus, use your brain, Thomas. The *Alabama* might get damaged or captured trying to run the blockade. And what cargo have we got to run in? We're a cruiser, not a blockade runner. We're going to run Northern merchant ships right off the ocean."

"I still don't see what you're trying to say," Mel protested.

"I'm sayin' this. I'm sayin', as long as we don't touch at a Southern port, this cruise ain't legal. Semmes doesn't have any right — by the law — to do what he's doin'. So do you know what that makes him?"

He paused as we all looked at him. Evidently he expected some more positive kind of response, for an expression of disgust passed over his face and he got to his feet.

"Jesus, you're thick," he said. "Figure it out for yourselves."

He moved away, and, a moment later, Midshipman Bulloch walked by. He was Irvine Bulloch, the younger brother of Captain Bulloch, and the acting master. We scrambled to our feet, and he nodded pleasantly. Shortly afterward, our watch turned in without commenting on what Gill had said. There were raised eyebrows, but that was all. People aboard had been critical of the cruise before, but none that I had heard in such terms.

As for myself, I neither liked nor trusted Gill. He was a real troublemaker. At the same time, I didn't object at this point to the kind of trouble he might be brewing, if it would embarrass Semmes. In fact, the longer I thought of what might be contrived out of Gill's discontent, the more I began to think I should encourage him. I should have to be discreet, of course, for I could be useful only as long as I remained clear of trouble, or, at least, appeared to be clear.

Early on October 3, the *Alabama* opened the second round of activities. The fog suddenly cleared, and lookouts reported two ships coming toward us, one directly ahead of us, the other on the lee bow. They were fine, large ships which Master's Mate James Evans, who had an almost unerring eye for a ship's identity, pronounced to be American. The *Alabama* wheeled smartly, flung out the Stars and Bars, and fired a blank from one of the thirty-two-pounders. Though there was a lot of running around on the decks of the two ships, within two or three minutes both ships hove to.

Quarter boats at once boarded the prizes. They were the *Brilliant* and the *Emily Farnum*, both laden with grain and flour and bound from New York for England. The captain of the *Brilliant*, George Hager, had a long conference with Semmes in the latter's cabin, from which he finally emerged with tears in his eyes. The first people he met on coming out were Kell and Paymaster Yonge, and to them he said, as if having a compulsion to unburden himself, "Everything I own is in that vessel. I built her and I have a one-third interest in her, and now he'll burn her."

Kell, who occasionally sat with Semmes as a kind of admiralty court in such cases, remained impassive, but Yonge's lips tightened as he glanced at the *Brilliant*.

The *Farnum* fared better. Since her cargo was registered as neutral property, Semmes put her under a ransom bond and used her as a cartel, placing aboard her both the *Brilliant*'s crew and the prisoners we still carried from the Azores sweep. The *Farnum*'s master was pledged by Semmes to continue directly to his destination. Though we did not know it at the time, as soon as he was out of sight in the darkness, he came about and headed for Boston so that the North soon knew where Semmes was — or, to be correct, where he had been.

The next few days, while Kell was breaking in four volunteers from the two latest ships, we overhauled a number of neutrals, and Semmes was plainly becoming impatient as he walked his little bridge.

Then, on the afternoon of October 7, the *Alabama* caught and burned the bark *Wave Crest*, out of New York for Cardiff with grain, and, as the bark was blazing, we went after a hermaphrodite brig which had evidently been drawn to the burning ship and too late had realized its mistake. For nearly three hours, the chase went on through the moonlight. Finally the *Alabama*'s speed proved too much, and about midnight the roar of a thirty-two-pounder brought her to, and Master's Mate Fullam was dispatched with a quarter boat to secure her. She was the *Dunkirk*, out of New York with grain for Lisbon.

Semmes was as pleased over the *Alabama*'s being able to catch the brig with sail only as a husband is when his bride turns out to be a good cook. He met the *Dunkirk*'s captain as the latter came over the side.

"You made a fine run of it, captain. But you must have forgotten my little teakettle below. However, I outran you without using it."

Even in the darkness, illuminated only by the ship's lanterns, we could see the look of bewilderment on the man's face. "I'm afraid I don't recognize you."

Semmes stared at him, annoyance and pride struggling for dominance. "I'm Captain Semmes! And my ship, the *Alabama!*"

"Semmes! You, Raphael Semmes!"

"None other, captain." Quickly Semmes glanced through the *Dunkirk*'s papers and said, "I regret what seems to be indicated." Within minutes, the *Dunkirk* was afire.

Something rather extraordinary now happened. As Kell went down the line of prisoners on deck, checking identities, he halted before a tall, slender young sailor who looked unusually anxious. Suddenly he lowered the lantern he was carrying and said to the officer with him, "Put this man in irons and confine him in the brig immediately."

This was odd treatment, we thought, but Kell evidently recognized something dangerous in the man.

The next day, we learned more about him after he was tried by a court-martial in Semmes's cabin and, following his release, assigned to our watch. He was a Northerner named George Forest who had served with Semmes on the *Sumter* and deserted at Cadiz. The court could have sentenced him to hang but was lenient, possibly because Forest had once shared the dangers aboard Semmes's first raider and had served satisfactorily for a time. Actually, the sentence the court meted out jolted the crew almost as badly as a hanging: no pay and no prize money.

The second day after the *Dunkirk* fell to us, we took the *Tonawanda*, a packet ship from Philadelphia for Liverpool with sixty passengers aboard, half of whom were women and children. I was in the prize crew with which Master's Mate Fullam boarded the ship, and one would have thought from the terror on her decks that we were off the ship of Blackbeard himself. Actually, Semmes must have been perplexed as to what to do with the *Tonawanda*, for the *Alabama* was certainly no place for women and no fit nursery for children. He decided, therefore, to bond her, and ordered her to accompany the *Alabama*.

The ultimate solution was soon arrived at. The corn ship *Manchester*, out of New York, presently fell to us, and, after she was consigned to flames, Semmes transferred all the enemy crews to the *Tonawanda* and sent her on her way. Soon after the parting, we took the *Lamplighter*, out of Boston for Gibraltar. Her cargo was largely tobacco, and great was the rejoicing aboard the *Alabama* when this fact was learned. It can't be said that the ship's crew did not live well during these destructive raids.

Aboard the *Manchester* were copies of the latest newspapers. In fact, we kept up-to-date with what was happening in both Europe and America with newspapers from the prizes captured or the neutrals hailed. As in the Azores, Semmes read them first, then sent them to his officers, and eventually they came down to us. We read, among others, the New York *Times*, the *Herald*, the *Shipping Gazette*, the Liverpool *Mercury*, and *Gore's Advertiser*. To my surprise word of the *Alabama's* sweep through the Azores and our raid on North Atlantic shipping lanes had still not reached the United States. Americans knew that the *Number 290*, as she was still commonly referred to, had escaped from Liverpool, and there was a good deal of speculation as to where she had gone. Editorials expressed confidence that if she started a raiding career, she would soon be caught by some Union cruiser and destroyed.

Unfortunately for the North, catching the *Alabama* was not easy, and part of the reason was contained in the latest edition of the New York *Herald* captured in the *Manchester*, that of October 5. In their zeal to keep the public informed of the latest developments of the war, the editors printed the most recent information available on where United States Navy ships were and what they were doing. Ever since hostilities had broken out, one of the best sources of information Confederate political and military leaders possessed was the Northern newspaper press: they made no bones about acknowledging this, and freedom of the press probably cost many Northern lives.

Now the same source was proving valuable to Semmes. Aboard the *Alabama* we had kept posted on the misfortunes of the Union troops under General John Pope at the second battle of Bull Run, and General McClellan's miserable handling of the Army of the Potomac at the battle of Antietam. Whatever credit might be his for blunting Lee's drive into Maryland, his caution and poor leadership prevented Antietam, that dreadful September day, from becoming a catastrophic defeat for Lee's army. Now we learned in the papers the stations and identities of Union men-of-war and realized the *Alabama* had little to fear. Semmes could continue for at least a few days longer on his leisurely westward course, and despoil the shipping lanes.

Fortunately for Northern grain ships, Nature intervened within hours after our seizure of the *Lamplighter*. On that 16th of October, the barometer began to drop, and the wind rose ominously. We close-reefed the topsails, bent on the main storm-staysail, swung in the quarter boats, and rove lifelines over the decks.

Then winds of tremendous force struck us. We had already furled the fore-topsail; the fore-staysail now split into ribbons. Then the iron bolt on the weather quarter holding the standing part of the main brace gave way; the main yard broke; and the main-topsail split like the fore-staysail. Only the main storm-staysail kept us steady — if the ship's floundering drunkenly in mountainous seas could be called steady. Those of us holding desperately to the lifelines, knee-deep at times in water, ducked as a sea crashed aboard and smashed the lee quarter boat.

"God damn this storm! And God damn him!"

George Forest's words were whipped away so that only a few of us heard him. Then his feet slid out from under him, and he

[163]

catapulted across the deck. I leaped aside to avoid being knocked down, and, holding onto my life rope with one hand, caught him by an arm. A moment later, both Mel and Gill reached him; I could not have pulled him up alone.

"You all right?" Gill asked.

He nodded, then bent over and retched sea water. Straightening up, he looked more angry than frightened. "It's that bastard back there who's responsible," he gasped.

"He ain't God," Mel shouted.

"He's responsible for our being here — for me, anyway. Jesus, look at that!"

We looked up to see a gigantic wall of green water soaring over us and driving the ship nearly onto her beam ends. Then the *Alabama* righted, superb ship that she was, and struggled with another green monster. After that, we said nothing, just hung on and kept our heads down.

All at once, the wind and fierce rain ceased and a strange silence fell over the ship. But although the wind was calm, the sea in the storm's eye was more violent than ever. No longer were the waves running frightened before the wind. Instead, the sea rose in enormous, aimless cones that pounded the *Alabama* so irregularly, she slatted wildly back and forth while the storm-staysail, without a wind to fill it, jerked its tackles about as if to snap them. Above, the heavy clouds writhed like snakes.

Once, glancing aft, I saw Semmes standing near our double helm with his watch in hand. When the wind suddenly howled down upon us again, he returned the watch to his pocket. Like a scientist, he had been interested in the time we had been in the vortex of the storm. He subsequently announced to us that it had been thirty minutes.

Now, with the hurricane winds again assaulting us, we were no longer flung aimlessly about, yet, if anything, fared worse. Time and again, I thought we were going under. We could only

[164]

pray the storm-staysail held, duck our heads below the weather bulwarks, and hold on to keep from being swept overboard.

Eventually the storm passed. Though it took four and one-half hours from beginning to end, to most of us it seemed much longer. To George Forest, the time must have been like eternity.

The day following the storm, everyone was busy repairing the ship. Sails had to be mended, the main yard refitted, the battery put in order, debris and lifelines removed, and the ship readied again for a continuation of its cruise. Now, however, Semmes was more demanding than in the Azores; after all, we were fairly close to the American coast and within an area that home-based Union cruisers could reach by three days' steaming.

The storm had so thoroughly soaked us that our signal quartermaster dragged out half our trophies from his signal lockers to dry. These were the flags of our prizes, all seventeen of them, taken in six weeks of raiding. For a few hours, the *Alabama* looked quite un-Confederate in the massed display of the Stars and Stripes.

The other half of our trophies reposed safely in Semmes's cabin. These were the chronometers of the captured ships. For some reason which I could not fathom, Semmes seemed to take a special interest and pride in these, as if they were the swords of admirals he had defeated.

With the ship finally in condition, we started combing the seas again. For a while our luck seemed to have run out; although we overhauled and boarded nine vessels in the four days after the hurricane, every one was a neutral. Then, on October 21, in latitude 39° 35′ and longitude 63° 26′, we captured a truly beautiful ship, the *Lafayette*, bound from New York for Ireland with grain. Unlike many of the ships that had fallen to the *Alabama*, this ship's cargo was "covered," that is, placed under British consular seals specifying the cargo aboard was British. Semmes regarded this as simply a legal device to protect an American cargo, so burned the ship. Had the ship itself been British in registry, he would not have dared to destroy her.

[165]

The "covering" was clearly a response to the threat the *Alabama* posed for Northern shipping. From newspapers aboard the *Crenshaw*, a Glasgow-bound schooner taken three days after the *Lafayette* and having British certificates likewise, we learned that the United States was now fully awakened to the presence of Semmes in the shipping lanes. The *Alert*, with the crews of the *Brilliant* and *Emily Farnum* aboard, had reached port and spread the alarm. The New York Chamber of Commerce was seething with indignation, and sent resolutions to both Secretary of the Navy Welles and Secretary of State Seward, asking for action against Semmes. He was a "British pirate"; his ship, a "privateer"; his mission, "robbery" and "plunder." We also learned that Welles, responding to the pressure from commercial circles in all the Northern seaboard cities, was sending gunboats to the Grand Banks of Newfoundland, including a fast, converted cruiser which Commodore Vanderbilt, the New York merchant and transportation prince, had let the government have. It was named the *Vanderbilt*, and possessed more than the speed necessary to catch us, and could have outgunned the *Alabama*, too. In fact, there were at least a dozen cruisers now after the *Alabama*, from the Grand Banks to the Caribbean, that could have smashed her had they caught up with her. Semmes, however, seemed not at all disturbed. Forecastle gossip reported that he had said to Kell after reading of the dispatch that Union men-of-war were now after him, "While they are running from New York, I am running toward it."

We continued to do so, and, on the 28th and 29th of October, picked up two more prizes. The first was the bark *Lauretta*, which was skirting St. George's Bank on her way to Madeira and the Mediterranean with flour and staves. Semmes left her ablaze. The second prize, taken on a thick and rainy day, was the *Baron de Castine*, a brig bound from Bangor with lumber for the Cuban port of Cardenas.

A member of the prize crew under Fullam, who was fast

becoming the principal prize master aboard the *Alabama*, I hated to board that brig. I recognized no one, but it hurt to see the apprehension and despair in the faces of that Maine crew. In their anger they damned the United States Navy for the lack of protection in these waters almost as fiercely as they cursed Semmes for capturing the brig.

It was their good fortune that Semmes had other plans for the *Baron* than burning her. She was an ancient craft that could hardly have weathered the hurricane we had recently endured. Evidently regarding her as practically worthless, Semmes piled all his prisoners aboard her, exacted a ransom bond from her skipper, and sent her off to New York.

With the brig out of sight in the mist, Semmes went into the wardroom and spoke to his officers. What he said was passed on to us, as he no doubt intended. Curtly he informed the officers of his plan: he intended to strike terror into the very heartland of the enemy by raiding New York harbor, or the coast off Long Island or New Jersey.

"We will go in quickly, burn a ship or two, and slip away before the Yankees can catch their breath," he said. "I have charged the master of the *Baron de Castine* to convey my thanks to Mr. Low of the New York Chamber of Commerce for his resolutions concerning me: I am a 'pirate' and a 'robber,' of course. But, according to the newspapers, you are my 'hirelings' and the crew are 'scum' and 'Liverpool rats.' Tomorrow let us shove these epithets down the Yankees' throats."

Word of what Semmes said spread quickly among the crew. Moreover, we had only to read the newspapers from the *Crenshaw* and the *Lauretta* to note the fear and anger Semmes and the *Alabama* had excited. New York was already wary of a possible attack, while we read that in Boston the keeper of Minot's Light had given the city a terrible fright by reporting that the *Alabama* had tried to slip into the harbor under cover of darkness to burn shipping. Surely, I thought, with the whole coast apprehensive, the navy would have men-of-war ready to welcome the raider. Likewise, the numerous shore batteries guarding New York harbor would already be alerted. It was possible that Semmes's daring might cost him his ship, his own life, and the lives of many of his crew.

But if others had such thoughts, there was no evidence of it in anything I heard that night aboard the *Alabama*. We were issued an extra grog ration, and everyone talked about the great raid. Excitement ran high. Even after the men turned in, whispered bets were made on the berth deck on how many ships might be destroyed.

Long after most were asleep, I lay in my hammock listening to the throb of our engines and feeling something of the anger and despair I had witnessed among the State-of-Mainers on the *Baron de Castine*. Semmes was just daring and skillful enough to bring it off. If he succeeded, it might be all that was needed finally to persuade the governments of Britain and France that the North could not conquer the South and that they should recognize the independence and sovereignty of the Confederacy. I felt like uttering the prayer that the frightened coastal peoples of Europe used to offer against the raids of the Northmen, but I would change it and say: "From the fury of Raphael Semmes, good Lord, deliver us!"

XVIII

THE wind was high and a sea was running when our watch turned out after breakfast. Smoke whipped back from the *Alabama*'s funnel flat as a ribbon. Overside, we left a trail of yeasty foam threshed white by our propeller. Now and then we met a sea head on, and everyone on the forecastle ducked to escape the shower bath of spray. It was October 30, we couldn't have been more than two hundred miles from New York, and by late afternoon or early evening the *Alabama* would be in raiding position off the port, depending on how hard Semmes wanted to drive her through the day. At the moment, we were using both sail and steam.

Several of us had just come down from taking a reef in the fore-topsail when we saw Chief Engineer Miles Freeman, a stout, usually cheerful man, stride off toward the captain's cabin. Shortly a call went out for all officers to report to the captain.

The officers presently emerged from their conference looking as glum as Freeman, and word soon passed around officially that Freeman had reported only a four-day supply of coal left in the bunkers. This would be enough to carry us to New York but not enough to sustain a long chase. And chase us the United States Navy would — with any and every vessel it had available.

It was Master's Mate Fullam who gave us the details, and even while he was speaking, the *Alabama* began to swing southerly and shape a course away from the mainland.

"Now wouldn't you think someone, maybe Freeman, would have kept Semmes informed of how much coal we had before he got the idea of this raid?" Lieutenant Armstrong asked Sinclair within my earshot.

Sinclair nodded, the corners of his mouth drawn down in disappointment. "It would have been choice if we had overhauled a troopship."

"Hell, yes," Armstrong said. "But I would have preferred burning and sinking a half-dozen ships in New York harbor, where a million Yankees could see the flames."

The officers made little effort to conceal their disappointment, and the petty officers made even less. For the first time, I detected an undertone of criticism of Semmes. They felt that he should have known about the coal situation before announcing his New York raid. Even more outspoken were Forest and Gill. They not only said that Semmes should have made it his duty to know what went on in the engine room; they also

[169]

hinted that Captain James Maffitt of the *Florida*, an old friend of Semmes's, would still have taken the *Alabama* into New York.

Though disappointment cut deeply, hope and interest in the future quickly bloomed. Just where we were going no one really knew. In fact, I often heard the officers remarking to one another that even they never knew Semmes's precise destination. This made very difficult and problematic any hope of my being able to give such information to an American consul. All one could really tell from our present course was that we were bound to end up somewhere in the West Indies. And surely at some place there we would have to fill our coal bunkers.

Meanwhile, we began to relax to a degree from the eternal sighting, chasing, boarding, and burning. Then, in the first week of November, we took two prizes. One was the *Levi Starbuck*, captured on the 2nd, a Sunday, when the crew was mustered to listen to another reading of the Articles of War. She was a New Bedford whaler headed for the Pacific, and newspapers aboard her, only four days old, told of Union gunboats sent in pursuit of the *Alabama*.

The second prize fell to us almost by accident. At midnight of the 7th, we went off in pursuit of a very fast schooner. Shortly after dawn, a large vessel came over the horizon, heading northwest. Semmes let the schooner go and halted the oncoming ship, which proved to be the *T. B. Wales*, bound from Calcutta for Boston with jute, linseed, and saltpeter.

A number of contributions came to the *Alabama* from the *Wales*. One was the *Wales*'s main yard to replace ours. Another was a batch of eight volunteers, bringing our total up to 110 crewmen. A third was a group of passengers apart from the crew of the *Wales*. These were the wife and three small daughters of the *Wales*'s skipper, and a former United States consul, George H. Fairchild, with his wife and three daughters, also small. Though Semmes let the women bring aboard all their clothing and their children's, he refused to take any of the very fine

[170]

furniture the Fairchilds were bringing back from the East. He was otherwise very gracious to these people, turning two of his lieutenants out of their staterooms to make space for each couple and their children. All were invited to dine in the wardroom.

In the beautiful days that followed the burning of the *Wales*, the *Alabama* seemed almost like a pleasure craft. The ladies were often seated on the quarterdeck, where Semmes never sat, and even as Semmes used to gather his young officers about him after supper on the bridge, where he reclined in a chair smoking a cigar, so now the ladies attracted the officers as if by a magnet. Both women were pretty, soft-spoken, and well-educated, especially Mrs. Fairchild. One would have thought those officers had never seen women before. The crew, of course, watched from afar, and their comments on the tea party aft were impolite and ribald, to say the least.

The children, however, touched all hearts. They ran up and down the decks, playing their games. No place was sacred to them, and they were welcomed everywhere. Crewmen joined in some of their games, and even the tough little powder monkeys, who at first scorned them, soon were seen to banter with them.

During these days, Semmes was the soul of hospitality. He chatted frequently with his "guests"; he spoke to the children as if they were adults, and he and they discussed the operation of the ship very seriously. I saw him looking at them time and again with something more than amusement, something I would call benevolence. In the evenings, when his officers clustered about the ladies on the quarterdeck, Semmes would sit up on the little bridge, occasionally with Kell but more often alone, and smoke his cigar. He loved a good Havana, and once in a while I would catch a whiff of its fragrance and wonder what it was. Though I liked cigars myself, I was not half the connoisseur my Grandfather Pettigrew was. He would have been keenly interested in Semmes's brand of cigar.

I often wondered what Semmes thought about up there in

[171]

his lofty solitude. Presumably, with women and children aboard, he thought of his own wife and family. If so, he must have felt a little concerned about them. They were living with Mrs. Semmes's family in Cincinnati, which, though in many ways a Southern city, was actually in the North. Had they been in an Atlantic seaport, they might not have fared well as the dependents of the most devastating raider ever to scourge the American merchant marine. Even living in Cincinnati, they must have felt uncomfortable. In some ways a sensitive individual despite his harsh exterior, Semmes was surely aware of their situation. Possibly this was one reason he seemed to go out of his way to be kind to his present captives.

But it is also likely that, up on the bridge, Semmes was planning his next move. This move became evident when, after doubling the northeast tip of Dominica, we ran down the coast of Martinique, looked carefully into the harbor of St. Pierre, and slid on to find an anchorage at Fort de France. As we steamed into the harbor, we saw the object for which Semmes had evidently been hunting — the collier *Agrippina*, deeply laden with what the *Alabama* so sorely needed.

Once at anchor, Semmes sent an officer to report the *Alabama*'s arrival to Governor de Conde, and followed up the visit by making one himself as soon as possible. It was just about a year ago that the Union warship *Iroquois* had trapped Semmes, then in the *Sumter*, in the harbor of St. Pierre. The *Iroquois* had violated French neutrality by sailing into the harbor and daring the *Sumter* to fight. Though Semmes refused to be drawn into firing first, he had deeply resented this same governor's permitting the *Iroquois*'s violation. Whatever their relations at that time, Semmes and de Conde must have patched up their acquaintanceship, and de Conde must have disclosed something vital and distressing to Semmes, for Semmes returned to the *Alabama* with a dark and angry expression on his face. He sent at once for Captain McQueen of the *Agrippina* to come aboard.

Earlier we had discharged all our prisoners, including, of course, the women and children. Without the last, the *Alabama* seemed very quiet.

But not for long. Up the gangway stumbled Alexander McQueen, shouting a welcome to all within sound of his voice. Though it was scarcely noon, he had already been tippling. Kell met him at the head of the gangway and led him straightway to Semmes's cabin. McQueen refused to be intimidated by Kell.

"I been here eight days waitin' for you," he shouted. "Where the hell've you been?"

Later, we could hear him shouting at Semmes, but we couldn't hear what he said or Semmes's reply. When he appeared on deck again, however, his face was red and angry and sweating. He strode to the gangway without saying a word. It was only minutes later that the *Agrippina* began to break out sail and head for the open sea.

Mel turned to me. "Ain't there something funny about this?"

"Maybe the governor told the captain it's too dangerous to load our coal here," I ventured.

"Yankee cruisers are thick in these waters," George Forest said. "Could be we'll get out of here, too. It ain't any fun being aboard, but it would be worse in a Yankee prison."

"You'd be safe, George," Gill said. "You were captured and forced to serve."

Forest grunted, nodding toward Semmes. "You know, we ought to grab this vessel and go on our own cruise. By God, now there's a notion, Gill!"

That was a strange afternoon. Outwardly, all was as serene as the day was bright. Though Semmes permitted no one to go ashore, it seemed that the whole town came to see us. Bumboats surrounded us laden with fruits, vegetables, and tobacco. Little sloops brought a constant stream of visitors to our decks. The officers, dressed in their best, had a wonderful time, I'm sure, showing the numerous young women and their escorts about our tidy decks and directing their attention to Semmes, who made several appearances on his bridge.

"He does not look as I had thought he would, a bigger man with a great beard," one of the gentlemen visitors had observed with scarcely an accent.

"Do you mean you expected to see a Blackbeard or a Captain Kidd?" asked Lieutenant Sinclair with a disarming smile.

"But he ees not young!" a pretty young woman protested.

Semmes could not have helped hearing what was said. He shrugged and presently left the bridge. As a great raider who had successfully avoided capture by Union cruisers, he had a certain glamor in the eyes of neutrals. It was scarcely his fault that he was in his mid-fifties, with graying hair and mustaches. His appearance was plainly a disappointment to some of these romantic women, who thereafter became more attentive to their own escorts, and especially to the young officers who were their guides.

In all the excitement, with sailors trading with the bumboatmen and officers receiving the visitors, Mel Taylor came up to me. "Did you see what George Forest did?"

"Where is he now?"

Mel grinned. "Who knows? But I can tell you what he's done. Somehow he got himself to a bumboat and is full of Martinique rum."

"Semmes will like that!"

"Old Beeswax won't find out if George can help it."

Semmes permitted no one of the crew to have any liquor aboard in his own possession. To prevent any from being brought aboard from the bumboats, he had directed the quartermasters to examine every article traded to the crew. The quartermasters were old seamen themselves and could hardly be relied on to be as rigorous as Semmes had hoped. With the *Alabama* having no marines available as sentries, however, he had no choice. The result was that plenty of "oh-be-joyful" was being smuggled aboard and hastily concealed in lockers, bags, even the quarter boats. So while everything went smoothly and pleasantly with the visitors from Fort de France, a real potential for trouble was building up below on the berth deck. And when George Forest returned with five gallons of crude, powerful Martinique rum, it wasn't long before things began to happen to the normally obedient, almost docile crew of the *Alabama*.

The first thing that occurred was George's breaking out his rum. Instantly men went to find the liquor that they themselves had hidden. Between that and Forest's rum, they began to get unruly and talk loudly and fight. Nearly everyone was drinking now except Forest; he watched the loosening of discipline with an ironic twist of his lips, and kept pouring out his rum. For days, he and Gill had mentioned to the watch the possibility of seizing the ship. How it happened that, among such a garrulous lot as sailors are, no one babbled to the officers, I shall never know. Finally, when the noise became deafening and men were lighting lanterns and uncapped pipes — both against regulations — George suddenly jumped up.

"Let's take the ship!" he shouted.

"Aye, take the ship!" Gill echoed.

At that, men cheered and rushed for the main deck, some of the heavy imbibers cursing and tripping over their own feet.

I had been drinking, but only a few sips of George's rum — the worst I ever drank. George Forest was a clever man. Though he had his mutiny, I didn't really believe the mutineers could be successful. But, for a few moments, I considered challenging Forest for its leadership. The trouble was that the men had no real grievance and wouldn't follow a leader, regardless of the odds; the explosion had come too soon and was merely the matter of an excess of rum.

Still, for a brief period, the prospect must have looked serious to the ship's officers. As the mob of drink-crazed seamen came roaring on deck, the boatswain tried to stop them. He went down under a flying belaying pin. As Kell and a group of commissioned and petty officers rushed toward the forecastle, someone hurled a fid at Kell, too, and narrowly missed him.

"You over there," he shouted to those of us who were more sober, "grab these drunken fools and get them below!"

"To hell with you, Kell!" a man beside me called out.

And, with a cheer, many of the sober members leaped forward to aid their fellow crewmen. As they did so, a gunner's mate tried to block them. Instantly Gill lashed out with his fist, and the gunner, clutching his jaw and moaning, stumbled out of the fight. But Gill's triumph didn't last long. A quartermaster hit him over the head with a capstan bar, and he went down and out. A number of the crew now flashed sheath knives and began to surge forward. Kell ordered the officers, who were all armed with pistols, to stand fast, and, bidding Lieutenant Armstrong take over, he strode aft to Semmes's quarters.

Within moments, Semmes appeared, a navy Colt at his belt. Taking in the situation at a glance, he said crisply, "Mr. Kell, beat to quarters!"

There was a long pause until a quartermaster, who doubled as a drummer in the ship's band, and a sober crewman, who was a fifer, found their instruments. Meanwhile, Semmes stood with his hands on his hips, one hand never far from the Colt, and faced the crew down.

Then came the roll of the drum and the shrill notes of the fife.

The result was magical. Even in their drunken state the men responded to the discipline ingrained in them and went to their battle stations. Broken up into individual gun crews, they no longer presented the massed threat as before. The only weapons they had were belaying pins and their knives, since the cutlasses and small arms were locked up in the arms chests. On the other hand, the thirty officers — commissioned, warrant, and petty — were all armed with pistols and were easily a match for the 110 crewmen.

Semmes, accompanied by Kell, now strode along the gun

deck. He paused at each gun, and when he noticed a drunken sailor, he ordered the sober members to arrest him. If they hesitated, a group of petty officers following Semmes and Kell stood ready to do the job. In no instance, however, did the sober ones refuse. Often they had a rough time, too, because many victims fought and cursed their captors. The irons were soon clamped on them, however, and they were dragged to the head of the gangway. With at least twenty of the principal rioters, including the drunkest, weeded out, Semmes kept the crew at quarters for two hours while he used the water cure. Three quartermasters with draw-buckets dashed sea water over the mutineers in quick succession. This seemed harmless at first. The mutineers laughed and cursed and shouted, "You bloody quartermasters, come on with your water! We're not afraid of it!" But before long, they began to gasp for breath and shiver with cold. I never saw a more bedraggled or dispirited crowd of men when Semmes finally ordered the punishment to stop.

"Take their irons off," he said to the quartermasters. Then he turned to the mutineers. "Now you men get below and sleep off your drunk. Mr. Kell, beat the retreat."

The only man not to be freed was Forest. He was put into double irons and confined in the brig.

While the punishment had been going on under the ship's lanterns, the officers had looked on with faces the very masks of sternness, but the same could not be said of the rest of the crew. There were titters and guffaws as the culprits went from defiance to pleas for mercy. Now and then, when the laughter rose, an officer would glare at a gun crew, and they would freeze into silence. Actually many more were guilty than those undergoing punishment, and no one wanted to be observed enjoying the spectacle of the water cure lest he be given it, too.

"By God," Mel muttered as we went to our hammocks, "I'll bet we can't leave this port soon enough for those poor bastards."

But if Raphael Semmes thought he could put to sea at the

[177]

crack of dawn, he presently discovered he was mistaken. Steaming toward the mouth of the harbor came the powerful Union warship the *San Jacinto*. As at St. Pierre in the *Sumter,* so now at Fort de France in the *Alabama,* Semmes was trapped.

XIX

ALTHOUGH I am more responsive than people may credit me with being, I have learned to control, or at least conceal, most outward displays of my feelings. This may be in part the result of my heritage, in which the Maine influence was dominant over South Carolina's, and in part owing to what experience I had at sea and in law. Usually I am master of myself, but my first view of the *San Jacinto* very nearly undid me. Surely now, I thought, the severe losses our merchant marine had suffered would be avenged.

There was no question of the *San Jacinto*'s superiority if the two ships engaged in battle. She was a screw steam sloop mounting fourteen eleven-inch guns. She was twice as large, possessed twice the firepower, and carried twice as many men as the *Alabama*. She was also much more heavily constructed; her shot could easily shatter the scantling of the *Alabama,* which had been built primarily for raiding, not fighting. On the other hand, she was at least two to three knots slower than the *Alabama,* so that in any action she would have to keep the Confederate in range of those big guns or the raider might escape. She had been Captain Wilkes's ship when he had halted the British steamer *Trent* and removed the Confederate commissioners Mason and Slidell, thereby precipitating the famous crisis with England. If Wilkes hadn't been lying in wait for the *Trent,* the Englishman would probably have run away from the *San Jacinto*.

I wondered as I studied her — a slow, heavy wagon of a ship —whether her commander was up to his task. I had heard of him, William Ronckendorff; he had a reputation for being careful and methodical, but was not one of the brilliant or popular officers of the navy.

Off and on during the morning, practically everyone aboard the *Alabama* stared over the bulwarks at the powerful man-of-war. Even Semmes appeared on the bridge several times and studied her through his telescope. But a telescope wasn't needed to see what was going on. The *San Jacinto* cruised slowly back and forth, obviously making ready for the action her captain sought. Her tops swarmed with men slinging yards, stoppering topsail sheets, and readying preventer braces. She cruised very close to the harbor until a cutter, showing a French flag, put out from the government's dock and went to her. The cutter must have carried a dispatch from Governor Conde bidding her keep to the three-mile limit, for presently Ronckendorff moved farther out. Had he been reckless enough, he could have entered the harbor and destroyed the *Alabama*, but his own ship would have suffered from the guns of the coastal batteries and of a big French corvette lying nearby. More importantly, the action might well have brought France into the war against the Union. Ronckendorff, however, was a cautious man. He would pin the *Alabama* in the harbor until she chose to come out.

If Semmes was worried, he didn't act it. He gave a number of officers shore leave. He permitted the stewards from the various messes also to go ashore and buy necessities and the little extras in food and tobacco that help keep a sailor content.

Semmes's own steward, Bartelli, had served aboard the *Bahama* and had been so intimidated by her captain that when that ship brought Captain Bulloch and his crewmen to the Azores for the *Alabama*, Bartelli asked Semmes for permission to go with him. The *Bahama*'s skipper agreeing to let Bartelli go, Semmes took him on the cruise. From all reports, he made a superb steward. Aside from being easily hurt, however, he had a serious weakness for drink.

Personally, though I didn't see much of him, I liked Bartelli. He was soft-spoken and polite. He was always such an easy mark for rough humor that on a couple of occasions, I intervened to protect him when some of our pranksters tried to pull practical jokes on him. He didn't have many real friends aboard, though I knew of no one who actually disliked him. He sometimes talked with me as if I were an older brother.

Perhaps it was because he knew of the Italian's liking for me that Kell sent me ashore with the steward when he went to make some purchases for the captain's table. Kell apparently had another reason, too. When I reported to him in response to a messenger's call, his hard eyes looked me up and down as if I'd committed some offense.

"Thomas," he said curtly, "last night you were one of our few, real sober men aboard. Don't you like to drink?"

"I like only a little at a time, sir," I said.

"Well, good for you. Now I want you to go ashore with Bartelli and keep him away from the wineshops. Go wherever he goes. Understand?"

"Aye, aye, sir."

He dismissed me, and I went at once to find Bartelli and tell him I'd be going ashore with him.

"That is good, Dan, I am so pleased," he said, his olive face lighting up.

He looked over Semmes's larder and jotted down in Italian items to buy ashore. So preoccupied was he, humming as he worked, that he didn't seem to notice the sound of voices coming from the captain's cabin. Or perhaps he was so used to voices there that he paid no attention. But it was new to me; I strained to hear everything I could.

Of the two voices, one was Semmes's; the other, with a fairly strong French accent, I judged to belong to an officer from the French corvette moored to leeward of us. They were discussing a chart of the harbor, in particular the channels and soundings at mean low water. It appeared that the French had more information about the harbor than appeared on our charts.

"I am now ready, Dan," Bartelli said.

Three other stewards were leaving in the dinghy, which was manned by four sailors under a petty officer. We were allowed two hours to make our purchases.

I said little on our way to town. The more I turned over that conversation in my mind, the more indignant I became at the assistance the French were giving Semmes. Obviously, the captain of the corvette had sent his officer over to the *Alabama*. If Semmes had thought before that there was only one channel out, he now knew better. Furthermore, Semmes being the knowledgeable officer he was, the chances were that if he didn't know the harbor was deep enough at any point for the *Alabama* to reach the sea, Ronckendorff didn't know, either. Somehow, the Union captain had to be warned of this, else Semmes might slip by him in the darkness. As for how long Semmes would wait before making a dash for the open sea, I figured that, calculating gambler that he was, he would try it possibly that night or the next day. He couldn't afford to wait long; the Caribbean swarmed with Union cruisers, and one or more of them would be almost certain to look in on Fort de France and join the *San Jacinto* within one to three days. Semmes would then be locked up tight in the harbor.

As we neared the landing stage, I saw a schooner from Maine unloading lumber. Wherever we stopped at fruit or vegetable stalls, I could see that schooner and the piles of lumber on the dock — it was white pine — and for a moment I could smell the fragrance and coolness of the Maine woods and hear the breeze soughing through the treetops. I could even smell the lumber in the stall where Bartelli was dickering with the proprietor, but it was spoiled by the stench of fruit rotting in the tropical sun, fresh horse manure crawling with flies, and an open sewer nearby that emptied into the harbor. A light movement of the air seemed to carry the stench our way.

An idea struck me. There was no time to consider it judiciously, to deliberate about its feasibility or wisdom. Bartelli had been checking off the items on his list with a stub of his pencil. Almost every time the dewlapped proprietor of this particular fruit stall showed him his produce, he would lay the paper and pencil down and feel the fruit. I was just about to act when he picked up the list and checked off another item. Twice after that, I thought the moment favorable, but had to wait. Then the proprietor called him over to the side of his stall to look at some avocado pears.

Quickly I knocked pencil and list to the ground. Then, crouching to pick them up, I turned the list over, resting the paper on my knee, and scrawled the following: "A leaves night. Harbor deep everywhere. Warn US warship." I rolled the paper lengthwise between my palms and, standing up, placed the pencil where Bartelli had left it. Since he and the man were still discussing the merits of the pears, I wandered to the front of the stall and watched a half-dozen black boatmen rolling dice, each one chanting as he rolled.

In due course Bartelli discovered his list was missing, and we looked everywhere for it. After a time, the little dust whirls kicked up by the light breeze must have convinced him that the paper had blown away.

"Well, it doesn't matter," he finally said. "I think I remember everything on it."

As we left, laden down with packages, I told him I wanted to buy some cigars. We then went to a tobacconist, and I bought a dozen fine Havanas, but failed to find any chewing tobacco.

"You like to chew tobacco?"

Bartelli was horrified, as were so many Europeans, by the American custom of chewing tobacco. So, for that matter, were many Americans, including my Grandmother Pettigrew. She said that that was one of the numerous social criticisms made by Charles Dickens on his visit to America with which she agreed, and one of the few criticisms made by that English bluestocking traveler and writer Harriet Martineau with which she did not differ. Personally I disliked the custom. And Semmes, who would not tolerate having his decks dirtied, handed out rather severe punishments for any chewer not using a spit bucket. But for the moment, it was necessary to deceive Bartelli. And I knew where I was sure to find some chaw tobacco — and other things besides.

So after telling Bartelli I loved to chew tobacco and would be gone only a minute or two to get some, I left him with as little appearance of haste as I could manage. Semmes might query Bartelli about the afternoon, and I didn't want him to relate anything that seemed out of the ordinary. A fair number of people, moreover, were shopping or walking about, so I strolled almost casually along the waterfront to the schooner, the *Bertha* of Machias.

A half-dozen black stevedores were unloading her, and four of her crew were helping. I didn't see anyone who looked like her captain, but I guessed that the bushy-whiskered character with a dirty straw hat on the back of his head who was cursing out the men in the flattest of Maine accents, was one of the mates.

He looked up at me in my clean whites, took off his hat, and scratched a head that was amazingly bald for a young man. "What the hell do you want?"

His voice had a nasty edge, but I ignored it. "You wouldn't have any chewing tobacco, would you? I can't find any in town, and I'll swap three cigars for a plug."

"Get on with you," he growled. "I got no time to talk with any bastard off that pirate."

"Four cigars," I said.

He started to turn back to his men, who had stopped to stare at us.

"Five cigars," I said.

He shook his head, then stopped. "What kind of cigars?"

"They're good Havanas. Look!" I pulled five cigars out of my pocket, one by one, the rich, dark brown kind that the Spaniards in Cuba prefer.

He stared at me, and finally reached into a pocket and drew out a plug, already partly eaten off. Biting fiercely into it, he tore off a chaw which filled his right cheek. Only half the plug was left.

"Make it six cigars, an' it's a deal."

I extracted a sixth cigar from my pocket and the rolled-up grocery list which I stuffed into the middle of the handful. As I reached for the plug, he stretched out his hand for the cigars, and the exchange was effected simultaneously. At once I bit off a piece.

"Now this is something like it," I said. "Many thanks."

I left as he was thrusting the cigars into his shirt pocket. I could only hope that he would smoke one before the afternoon was over, and find the paper.

Two French sailors off the corvette had evidently witnessed the trade and had understood it, if not the language. They shook their heads and grinned as I passed. I suspected that, from their point of view, any man who would trade six cigars for a half-eaten plug of chewing tobacco had made a wretched bargain. I grinned back at them and worked the tobacco farther over into my right jaw.

When I reached Bartelli, he was just paying out the last of Semmes's money for a box of crystallized ginger. I wondered as I looked at his packages whether in my absence he had bought any liquor to take aboard. I hoped he would be true to his oath of abstinence aboard ship, because if he wasn't Kell would demand an accounting from me.

My walk with Bartelli to the landing stage was not a happy one. My arms were full of bundles, and the sting of the macerating tobacco in my cheek kept building up saliva. I spat repeatedly and with none of the unerring aim that old masters of the chaw possess. Bartelli looked disgusted as, after every expectoration, some of the remaining juice dribbled down my chin.

"How can you like that?" Bartelli asked.

"Oh, it's wonderful," I said, "just wonderful." But I was beginning to feel in my stomach that it was not so wonderful.

I was relieved when we reached the dinghy and I could put down my bundles and wipe my chin. It was an even greater relief to near the *Alabama*, where, before boarding her, I spat out my quid. But afterward, for at least a good half hour, I was far more concerned about the possibility of disgracing myself by being sick than about the *San Jacinto*'s receiving warning of our departure. Eventually the inner tumult subsided, leaving me grateful, to be sure, but also wondering if I hadn't played the fool this afternoon.

Around nightfall, however, there was a good deal of running about on the main deck. Anxious, those of us below poked our heads outside, only to see a great cluster of men gathered on the weather side, gazing at the Union cruiser. Spotting Mel Taylor there, I went up to him and asked what the excitement was all about.

"A boat from that Yankee lumber schooner has just run alongside that big brute out there."

"What difference does it make? We're goin' to have to fight our way past that Yankee anyway."

The voice was surly, and we turned to stare at Gill. He still looked sick from a hangover. Why he hadn't been punished like George Forest puzzled us, for he was just as guilty; George had been tied in the mizzen rigging all day — two hours up, two hours in the brig, then up again.

We strained to see the *San Jacinto* through the gathering gloom. Putting out from her side were two cutters, one moving toward one end of the harbor entrance, the second toward the other. The schooner's boat, meanwhile, was headed back to port.

"What did I tell you?" Gill boasted. "That Yankee's smart.

[185]

He's coverin' the whole harbor mouth. Those cutters will give him a signal wherever we go."

"He still ain't caught us," Mel said.

"It won't be long now."

Activity broke out very quickly after darkness set in, with rain falling. The first indication was smoke starting to pour from our funnel as our fires were lighted. Then up came the quarter boats to their davits. After that, verbal orders rather than drum and fife sent the crew to quarters, and the guns were loaded and cast loose. All lights were doused except for the lanterns in the engine and the fire rooms, and the carefully protected lantern for the powder magazine, where felt-shod men stood ready to load the powder bags for the guns. Even the binnacle light was shrouded. The final act was to raise the anchor, and hardly was it at short stay when we were full and by.

For a few minutes, it seemed that no one spoke above a whisper. Semmes had appeared on the bridge, a lonely, silent figure barely visible to us in the foretop. Up there, high above the deck, we stood ready to break out canvas once the *Alabama* was clear of the land. If the ship succeeded in reaching the open sea, then, between steam and sail, we should be able to run away from the *San Jacinto*. But first we had to slip by her and get out of the range of her powerful guns.

The ship was at nearly full speed, the rain stinging our faces like hailstones, when, from back in port, three rockets shot up into the air: the Maine schooner had warned the *San Jacinto* that the *Alabama* was on the way.

Semmes had chosen to leave the harbor by the most southerly route, perhaps because it permitted him to stay longer with the land as a background; in the darkness, the *Alabama* would blend with the mass of land and postpone her appearance as a discernible silhouette. Yet the particular signal from the schooner must have revealed the route the *Alabama* took, for we saw the *San Jacinto*'s lights come about. It required no great exercise of the imagination to see the man-of-war come rushing to intercept us, her cutwater plowing the water aside and her crew waiting to fire her huge guns.

I was hoping the *Alabama* as a ship wouldn't make it, but I hated the thought of seeing men I liked, even if in the enemy service, killed or wounded by bursting shells from the Union cruiser. To be completely honest, I didn't like to think of that as my own fate, either. On balance, however, I wanted us to be caught.

But gradually, to my dismay, I saw us begin to pull away from the *San Jacinto*, which suddenly hauled up before she even crossed the course we had taken. Did she even know where we had gone? Had she kept on her original course, she would at least have picked up our smoke, which had blown back toward the land, and she could have blasted away with her guns, possibly damaging us enough to slow us down. I could only conclude that Semmes must have passed so close to the land that not even the Union cutter had suspected his presence, else she would have signaled the *San Jacinto*. Semmes was smart — too smart, at any rate, for Ronckendorff.

How smart, we didn't learn until much later. The Union captain didn't really believe Semmes was gone until daylight showed the *Alabama* had flown. And Ronckendorff actually cruised off the harbor for another day or two until he was certain Semmes hadn't hidden the *Alabama* up some creek or inlet. By the time Ronckendorff finally acknowledged defeat, Semmes was nearly three hundred miles away, off the coast of Venezuela.

XX

ON the afternoon of November 21, the *Alabama* overhauled the *Agrippina*. At nightfall, both dropped anchor off the island of Blanquilla. Except for occasional fishermen or goatherds, who brought their animals over from the mainland of Venezuela to pasture on the coarse grass, the island was uninhabited. We saw neither fishermen nor goatherds when we arrived, but we did see something else — a whaling schooner, the *Clara L. Sparks*. She was lying close in, had a tent onshore, and her crew were on the beach, trying oil from a whale.

We had not even dropped anchor before the *Sparks's* skipper put a boat into the water and was rowed out to the *Alabama*. He was a puffy-faced man who started talking the moment he came over the gangway. We had come in flying the Stars and Stripes, so as far as he knew, we were one of Secretary Welles's latest cruisers.

"Lovely ship, here, by God, a lovely ship!" he exclaimed to Lieutenant Armstrong.

"Yes, and we've speed to burn," Armstrong said, taking the man's measure at once. "We can go like the wind."

"Just look at our battery — that Blakely and that smoothbore," Lieutenant Sinclair said, pointing to those two powerful guns.

"Wonderful, by God, wonderful!" the skipper said.

"Look at how versatile we are," Lieutenant Wilson said. "We chase with sail, and catch or run away with steam."

"I'll bet," the man said, and turned to Armstrong. "You said you had speed to burn."

"Oh, yes," Armstrong said, "and we've the men to man this ship, too." He pointed to the scores of seamen lounging about the deck, some of us quite openly listening to the conversation.

The skipper's face grew almost ecstatic. "By God, lieutenant, you've got just the ship here to give that pirate Semmes the fits."

Then Kell appeared, having observed what was going on, and curtly told the skipper the captain wanted to see him. As Kell and the man disappeared into the captain's cabin, the officers laughed like boys. They had a hard time looking sober when the *Sparks's* skipper emerged, white and shaken, and, as silent now as he had been garrulous before, quickly went down to his waiting boat. He must have suffered a great shock indeed when Semmes identified himself and told him he was aboard the *Alabama*.

Still, to give Semmes credit, he didn't destroy the schooner or its oil — out of respect for the neutrality of Venezuela. He did, however, put a guard aboard the schooner and over its crew ashore, while permitting them to continue their work. They were prisoners until Semmes chose to depart.

Meanwhile, for five days, the war receded. We filled our coal bunkers from the *Agrippina*'s cargo, whereupon the collier, with still another supply left, was sent off to some undisclosed rendezvous. We cleaned and whitewashed the hold. Semmes himself went off fishing in the gig, and his boat crew came back laden with fish, pelicans, plover, turtles, and specimens of coral. Officers took sailing cruises in the quarter boats in the afternoon, or fished. As for the crew, Semmes was surprisingly generous. We were issued rifles and went hunting. Fish fries were common, and most of us went swimming, armed guards standing by on the lookout for sharks. Several huge ones were sighted, but they did not attack.

There was one species of life on the island that attracted everyone: the flamingo, and large flocks waded and fed in the lagoons. Once a flock was drawn up in a line, and Semmes called Kell's attention to them.

"Look over there on the beach. Don't they remind you of red-coated soldiers on parade?"

Kell said something that I could not quite make out, but Semmes shook his head. "No, their plumage ranges from pink to scarlet."

Bartelli, with his Latin love of color, was ecstatic over the flamingos, and observing Semmes's admiration of them, asked me if I would go along with him and bring several aboard.

"What do you mean to do with them?" I asked. "You don't intend to take them with you, or to kill and stuff them, do you?"

He looked horrified and shook his head violently. "You will see when I have them aboard. I will not hurt them."

So Mel and I went rowing around in the lagoons while Bartelli, with a fishnet attached to a long pole, caught several of the beautiful birds. Once he had them aboard, the men were as apprehensive as I had been that he might harm them. He waved down the protests and presently showed us what he had in mind. Plucking a feather here and a feather there, without stripping a bird, he made several beautiful fans, one of which he gave to Semmes, and others to the officers. He also presented me with one, which I carefully stowed away in a duffle.

After five days at Blanquilla, everyone aboard the *Alabama* felt better. We had been three months at sea under severe man-of-war discipline, and now were more relaxed and tanned than ever. Even the engineers and firemen, who rarely saw the light of day when we were under steam, grew brown, and Chief Engineer Miles Freeman, already with ruffs of fat under his chin, put on more poundage from the game he shot and ate.

The exception in all this recreational activity was George Forest. He was given a quick court-martial and deposited on the beach at Blanquilla with a bag and hammock. A collection amounting to about eighty dollars was taken up for him among the crew and presented to him by Gill. Actually, as a mutineer, Forest got off lightly; the court might have ordered him shot or hanged. Though I didn't trust George, I liked him better than Gill and so contributed my portion to the collection. But as the boat left George on the beach, he cursed all of us and, above all, Semmes and the officers. Still, we weren't leaving him alone on a desert island. He joined the *Sparks*'s crew as soon as Semmes removed the guard over them, the schooner putting to sea only a short while before the *Alabama* departed.

Notwithstanding my mistrust of Forest, I'd have liked to give him a note to forward to the nearest United States consul, had I known or even been able to give an informed guess of Semmes's next destination. But Semmes kept his own counsel;

there was not even a convincing rumor circulating. And, of course, knowledge that we had been nearly a week at Blanquilla would be valueless. Forest and the *Sparks*'s captain would soon spread that news, but by the time the navy knew of it, we would be far away. I felt increasingly frustrated. The only time I had been able to do anything potentially helpful was when I had informed the Maine lumber schooner at Fort de France of the *Alabama*'s departure. Even then, Semmes's skill, the darkness and rain, and possibly a lack of alertness on the part of the *San Jacinto*'s commander had made a jest of my efforts.

Ironically, we were not long out of Blanquilla when Semmes let the information concerning our next objective seep down from the wardroom. When I first heard it from the lips of Fullam, our customary prize master, I thought at once of Sir Henry Morgan, the great buccaneer. The plan seemed more like one he would have contrived than Captain Raphael Semmes of the Confederate States Navy. Though the great California gold discoveries of 1849 and the 1850's were over, gold still flowed east in impressive quantities, much of it down the Pacific to the Isthmus of Panama, across the isthmus by railroad, and from Aspinwall (also called Colon) to New York by large passenger steamers owned by the famous Commodore Vanderbilt. According to reports, Semmes wanted to capture one of these steamers and use the gold to build additional *Alabamas* to raid Northern commerce. This might be a fine, lofty purpose for him, but what set the crew chattering and gibbering was the thought of the prize money. Every man Jack would be rich enough to buy his own house and spend the rest of his days as he chose.

According to Northern newspapers, one steamer was due to sail from Aspinwall in December, so Semmes, letting it be known that he would lay an ambush off the east end of Cuba — the usual route — slid along the south coast of Puerto Rico on November 29, entering the Mona Passage between the island and San Domingo after nightfall. I was amazed that we did not encounter at least one Union man-of-war, and so must Semmes have been. Union ships were probably too busy patrolling the Gulf coast or possibly chasing after the *Alabama* where she had been last reported. There was even one statement in several newspapers that the *Alabama* was now bound for Brazil and the East Indies. If the navy believed this, no wonder we had never sighted a warship since the *San Jacinto*.

The next morning, moving swiftly by sail along the coast of San Domingo, we halted a Spanish schooner out of Boston. She let us have a batch of the latest Boston newspapers, and within a couple of hours they had been passed down to the crew. It was a lovely Sunday. We had stood inspection and were chatting and reading in groups, while in the hazy distance towered the hills of that island so rich with memories of Columbus. The officers, having already read the papers, were smoking and staring at the shoreline.

Glancing through two of the Boston papers, I found most of the front page of each taken up with accounts of an expedition to be sent to Texas under the command of the Boston Republican politician General Nathaniel Banks, who so far had had his troubles in this war. One of the five generals of volunteers by the fall of 1861, he had seen action in early 1862 in the Shenandoah Valley against Stonewall Jackson and after an initial success, suffered a humiliating defeat. This he had redeemed in part, judging by the Northern newspapers, by a vigorous attack with his corps against Jackson at Cedar Mountain just before the second battle of Bull Run; Banks had even sent the famous Stonewall Brigade flying, though Jackson eventually checked him. Now Banks was to relieve his fellow Bay-Stater and a War Democrat, Major General Benjamin Butler, at New Orleans, occupy Galveston — which the navy had taken in October — and push up the Mississippi toward Baton Rouge and Port Hudson. According to the Boston papers, Banks was to have a force of thirty thousand men, to be sent directly from

Boston and New York into the Gulf of Mexico. The transports were to rendezvous at Galveston in early January, 1863.

We read more about the Banks expedition later that afternoon when we captured the *Parker Cooke* out of Boston, laden with so many provisions for San Domingo consumption that it took hours to transfer the crackers, shipbread, butter, cheese, salted beef and pork, and dried fruits to our depleted larder. Semmes burned the *Cooke* at nightfall. The next morning, we learned several interesting bits of news from the newspapers taken from the *Cooke*. The Banks expedition was to cooperate with Grant's forces north of Vicksburg in trying to squeeze the Confederates out of the Mississippi area by spring, and the transports were due to arrive off Galveston by January 10. A second item was concerned with the startling advance in marine insurance as a result of the destruction caused by the *Alabama*, the flight of American cargoes to foreign bottoms, and the shift of American ships to foreign, especially British, registry.

The next few days, we chased several ships but found them to be neutrals, largely Spanish. One night, we were ourselves surprised by a large man-of-war rushing toward us. We had no steam up, while she had both steam and sail. Our lookouts were probably lax that she should have been so long undiscovered. Semmes got us to the guns in time, but she could have blown us out of the water had she been a Union man-of-war instead of a Spanish steam frigate. After that, we were more alert but had no further cause for alarm. Again we chased ships, only to learn that they were anything but American.

One break in the succession of neutrals came on December 5, when a Baltimore schooner, the *Union*, flew into our arms. She was an old vessel with a neutral cargo, legitimately documented, destined for Porto Maria on the north coast of Jamaica. Semmes therefore spared her. He put the crew from the *Parker Cooke* aboard and sent her on her way under a ransom bond.

Much of this week we cruised off the east end of Cuba under

sail, closing in on Cape Maize at night and riding offshore until morning. The moon was near its full, and its light was so brilliant and the air so clear that the visibility was extremely good. Many of the crew posted themselves as assistants to the lookouts on duty. This was especially true the nights of the 5th and 6th of December. The Vanderbilt steamer was due on the 6th, but we saw not a sign of her — for that matter, not a trace of smoke all day. Although they were disappointed, the men were still confident we would catch the gold steamer.

That night, I had trouble falling asleep. What bothered me was not so much that we might capture one of Commodore Vanderbilt's treasure ships as the question of why the *Alabama* was in the Gulf, anyway. The Gulf was practically an American lake, though the Spanish and the French might dispute this. Semmes was a gambler, but a gambler who calculated the odds. He must have known from his experience in the *Sumter* that the Gulf could not compare with the Atlantic as a hunting ground. The blockaders, moreover, were thick off the Southern coast, and men-of-war were constantly changing station. Semmes had small chance of avoiding eventual discovery by Union cruisers. Sooner or later one of them would be fast enough to catch him, and strong enough to batter the *Alabama* to pieces. Why, then, was he here? Just to have a try at capturing a gold ship? It was possible, of course, but Semmes usually seemed to be one step beyond the immediate. He was endangering his ship and his crew where he now was. Was the capture of a cargo of gold worth the risk? Or did he have something additional in mind?

Somehow, I couldn't rid myself of the notion that his presence here in the Gulf had some connection with the Banks expedition. Did he propose to attack the transports? They would be escorted by men-of-war, of course, but even as in the War of 1812 American privateers would dash into a convoy and cut out a merchantman from under the guns of an armed escort, so Semmes might slip close to the transports and sink

[194]

several with the long-range Blakely rifled cannon. He could even reduce the risk to himself and use his shorter-range guns as well, if he attacked under cover of darkness. Still, it seemed a half-mad scheme, for all the fact that if it were even partially successful, it would buck up the spirits of the South and further depress those of the North, the year 1862 having been a year of near-calamity so far for the Union. But if Semmes really had such an idea, what would he do in the month between now and the time of the expedition's rendezvous off Galveston? If he continued his raiding career in these waters, the North would fill the Gulf with cruisers, and the Gulf was too small for him to escape eventual detection.

The next morning — Sunday, December 7 — was clear and bright, very balmy, with only a few fleecy clouds. The islands of Cuba, San Domingo, and Jamaica were all visible, Cuba especially. We had holystoned the decks, breakfasted, and were now hurriedly responding to the boatswain's order, "All hands clean yourselves, in white frocks and trousers, for muster!"

Suddenly from the masthead came the cry, "Sail, ho!"

"Where away?" asked the officer of the deck through his trumpet.

"Broad on the port bow, sir!"

"What does she look like?"

"She's a large steamer, brig-rigged, sir."

The officer then dashed to Semmes's quarters, while most of us crewmen rushed to the port side to see what we could — from our low perspective, only a trail of smoke.

Semmes appeared on the bridge almost at once and turned to Kell, who raised his trumpet. "All hands work ship!"

Instantly the engineers and firemen dashed below to get up steam. The propeller was lowered from its well into the water. The bow gun was cast loose. The topmen scurried up the rigging.

"Harbor furl!" Kell trumpeted to us.

And so we did, furling the sails tightly so that they would

[195]

catch as little wind as possible and not impede our pursuit. Had there been a stout breeze, we would probably have used both sail and steam, but since the wind was light, we would rely solely on steam. Within twenty minutes, we were ready, everything tight aloft and steam hissing from the gauge cocks.

The stranger was coming up very swiftly, a great paddle-wheeler with a huge funnel and sails furled as tightly as ours. When she was within three or four miles of us, we broke out the Stars and Stripes, and she responded with the same.

The ship was so fast that although Semmes tried to put the *Alabama* across her bow, as if to speak her, she swept by a couple of lengths ahead of us, and we had to be content with crossing her wake.

The steamer had her awnings set, and under these on her upper deck stood a crowd of passengers staring and waving at us. There were many women, gaily dressed, with streamers and ribbons from their bonnets flying in the breeze created by the ship's speed. A number had opera glasses trained on us. Among the male passengers were officers in uniform, while on the forward deck stood several groups of soldiers.

The people aboard the steamer must have thought the *Alabama* was a trim Union cruiser, but if so, they soon discovered their mistake. The *Alabama* wheeled, fired a blank from the bow gun, and, hauling down the American flag, ran up the Stars and Bars.

The effect aboard the steamer was dramatic. The women screamed and flew inside, the men at their heels. The soldiers fell into ranks. The steamer's captain obviously resolved to make a run for it, for black smoke suddenly billowed from the great funnel, and the huge ship swept ahead in a burst of speed.

Many reports were given of the *Alabama*'s speed; if their authors had been present now, they would have seen how exaggerated their reports really were when they observed how quickly she fell behind the Vanderbilt steamer. Fearing lest the steamer escape, Semmes ordered a shot thrown at her foremast, high enough above the deck not to hit anyone. The gunner obliged, Semmes yawing the ship a little to help him, and so accurate was the aim that the mast was nearly cut in two and was held in place largely by the rigging.

"Gallant shot!" Lieutenant Sinclair called out.

Even Kell cracked out a harsh, "Well done!"

Convinced now that safety lay in submission rather than flight, the steamer's captain ordered his engines stopped. The walking beam slowed its motion, and the great paddle wheels came to a halt.

Mel, Larkin, and I were among the boarding party sent to the steamer. We were all fully armed with pistol and cutlass, but the sight of the blue-coated soldiers drawn up as if to fight us made us wonder whether our weapons and small number would be effective. Luckily for us — or perhaps more so for them, in view of the *Alabama's* proximity — they did not oppose us as we went up the gangway.

Aboard the steamer, the *Ariel* of New York, the wildest confusion prevailed. The captain was calm and civil, and his crew resigned. The 140 soldiers, however, were sullen and angry; actually, they were part of a marine battalion assigned to men-of-war in the Pacific. We disarmed them and took their paroles. The male passengers looked worried. As for the women, I never heard such screaming and crying.

Our boarding officer, when he returned to the *Alabama* with the *Ariel's* captain, leaving Master's Mate Fullam in charge, must have borne a sad story of the women's behavior. Presently Semmes's own gig arrived, bright with new paint and scarlet cushions, Coxswain Freemantle at the tiller. In a few seconds, over the rail came our two handsomest lieutenants, Armstrong and Sinclair. Both wore their finest dress uniforms of gray and gold, and their swords. I recognized on Armstrong the most brilliant of Semmes's own sword knots.

Ordering Mel and me to accompany him, Armstrong went to the ladies' cabin. He stationed us at the open door and bade us let none of the *Ariel*'s male passengers or crew enter. Then he went inside, followed by Sinclair.

At the officers' appearance, fresh shrieks rose. I could see out of the corner of my eye the flush that gradually spread over Armstrong's long face. But for at least two minutes, he said nothing, and at his silence the frightened women gradually subsided.

"Ladies!" he finally said, and his voice was deep and sympathetic. "The captain of the *Alabama* has heard of your distress and sent me on board to calm your fears by assuring you that you have fallen into the hands of Southern gentlemen. In our protection you are entirely safe."

Many of the women still looked somewhat skeptical, and, evidently recognizing this, Armstrong, who clearly fancied himself a favorite with ladies, went on, his voice edged slightly with emotion. "We are by no means the ruffians and outlaws that we have been represented as being by your people. Let me assure you again: you have nothing whatever to fear."

He now began to walk among them, and, picking out the prettiest, he began to chat. Then he turned to another, and still another.

The result was that within a few minutes, he was surrounded by a chattering crowd of young women smiling their tears away. Soon one of them, bolder than the rest, touched one of the gold buttons on his coat and asked if she might have it as a memento of the occasion. Armstrong assented with a bow. Someone produced a pair of scissors, and the young woman carefully but quickly snipped off the button. At once, others clamored for a similar keepsake, to which Armstrong graciously assented. Soon he had scarcely a button on his coat, and Sinclair, who was now "discovered," fared scarcely better.

That evening, a party was held in the *Ariel*'s saloon. Armstrong had stationed guards at the various entrances to discourage possible troublemakers. If there were any, they never showed themselves. Instead, there was such festivity that one would not have guessed a state of war existed and the two young lieutenants were the captors of those who now honored them. At least, none would have guessed until the time for toasts arrived.

Then Armstrong, standing up and raising his glass of champagne, called out, "To Jefferson Davis, President of the Confederate States of America!"

People raised their glasses and drank, though there was a certain restraint in their cheers.

Hardly had the champagne been touched when a young woman, her black eyes flashing, stood up and cried, "To Abraham Lincoln, President of the United States of America!"

The uproar that ensued was tremendous, and all eyes were on Armstrong. But with a smile, albeit a weak one, he courteously drank to the toast.

In the morning, the two ships continued to lie close to each other. Everyone knew by this time that the *Ariel* carried no gold, and deep was the disappointment among the *Alabama*'s crew. Mel Taylor was philosophical about it, but Joe Larkin acted as though he had been dealt a personal hurt. Though Semmes removed the strongbox of the *Ariel*, he ordered all personal effects of the passengers and crew left untouched. Many of the male passengers had at first stripped off their watches and hidden them in their trunks; after all, we were pirates! They now looked sheepish.

The marines, I must confess, had not comported themselves very admirably. Stripped of their arms, which were collected for transfer to the *Alabama*, a number of them went hunting for liquor, evidently determined to bury their humiliation in drink. Fortunately, the *Ariel*'s wine steward threw most of his stock overboard.

With morning, Semmes sent Lieutenant John Low, our English-born fifth lieutenant, aboard to take charge of the *Ariel*. Mel, Larkin, and I were part of the prize crew of twenty. We were a small number indeed among the seven hundred souls

[199]

aboard the *Ariel,* so lest we be seized ourselves if he had to go dashing in pursuit of the cherished gold ship, Semmes ordered a steam valve removed; this action distinctly reduced the *Ariel's* chance of escape. But with no ship sighted this day, at nightfall Semmes ordered the valve restored. The two vessels headed together for Kingston, Jamaica.

While we were moving toward Kingston, Semmes halted a German brig. What he learned from her presently caused him to signal the *Ariel* to stop off Morant Point, Jamaica. He also sent over a boat ordering us to prepare to leave the *Ariel.*

"But why?" Low asked the quartermaster who had come over to deliver the order.

"Yellow fever, sir. The captain hoped to put everyone on the *Ariel* ashore and then take her out and burn her. He won't do that now because of the fever, sir."

"He's freeing her, then?"

"This very evening, sir. He's working out a ransom bond with Captain Jones now."

Word of the *Ariel's* impending release spread through the ship. Perhaps some passenger or crewman heard the quarter-master even as we did, or perhaps one of our men broke the news. Whatever the source of the information, passengers gathered around us, talking and laughing with us. Though they had taken our lieutenants into their favor the previous night, they had acted wary of us. Now even we were their very good friends.

It was while we were waiting for the return of the *Ariel's* Captain Jones, who had been kept on the *Alabama* ever since our boarding officer had left with him, that I came to a quick decision.

Slipping through the crowd to the ship's deserted saloon, I picked up two envelopes and two sheets of paper from a writing desk. Sitting down, I wrote on one sheet: "*Alabama* will probably attack Banks's transports. Notify Welles. Love, S." Hastily I folded the note and sealed the envelope, which I addressed to my Uncle Jonathan Dearborn, who had introduced me to Secretary Welles. I wrote the same on the other sheet, which I signed "Scott Pettigrew, Acting Volunteer Lieutenant, USN," and addressed the envelope, "U.S. Consul, Aspinwall."

Stuffing both notes into my pocket, I went out on deck. I could not be too particular about whom I gave them to, because there was so little time. But I refused to hand them to any of the women passengers — all I could see, even the older ones, appeared so taken with the *Alabama*'s people, I didn't trust them not to open the envelopes and give me away. Instead, as I brushed against a middle-aged male passenger and he turned with a startled face, I pressed the note to my uncle into his hand, along with a sovereign, and muttered, "Please mail this for me, sir." I was gone before he could bring his jaws together again.

A half-dozen steps farther, I stumbled in front of one of the *Ariel*'s officers — he had PURSER embroidered across his hat. As he reached to help me up, I closed his palm on the note to the consul, and held him for a moment. "Please deliver this," I said softly. Then, letting him go, I straightened up and said loudly, "Thank you, sir."

Without a glance at his face, I hurried through the crowd to join the prize crew forming at the gangway.

"Where have you been, Thomas?" Lieutenant Low snapped at me.

But it was more reprimand than question, so I merely saluted him and took my place without a word.

I was barely there before the boat bearing Captain Jones of the *Ariel* arrived. The passengers cheered him loudly when he came aboard and us even more loudly when we departed. They were in a truly cheering mood. When the brightly lighted *Ariel* began to draw away from us at about eleven o'clock, both ships and sea bathed in moonlight, handkerchiefs waved from the steamer, and across the widening space of water came a storm of cheers for Captain Semmes and the *Alabama*.

But if there was joy aboard the vanishing *Ariel*, there was little on the raider. Men swore viciously at the loss of the prize money on which they had built such hopes. Semmes, I was certain, was even more profoundly disappointed; there was no gold hoard with which to build other *Alabama*s to scourge his enemy's commerce from the seas.

I may have been the least depressed person aboard the *Alabama* that night, but that isn't saying much. I had passed on my notes, and this afforded me a little satisfaction. On the other hand, I was only too aware how speculative the information in them was. If I were mistaken and the navy took men-of-war away from protected areas of the ocean to convoy the transports, and Semmes struck into those areas, I could be the cause of ships and possibly lives being lost.

Even if the information I had sent was correct, the time in which the navy could act on it was short, probably much too short. The *Ariel* was due to return to New York within two or three days of her arrival in Aspinwall, but she couldn't fly. Whether he received the information through the consul or my uncle, Secretary Welles would have to act with the utmost speed. And, of course, he might not believe it, particularly when the news came from an officer who had left his post without permission and joined the ship commanded by a man whom Welles must now have hated more than any individual in the Confederacy.

On second thought, I think I was one of the most depressed members of the *Alabama*'s complement that December night.

XXI

"For God's sake, what's that?" Mel sat up in his hammock and bent his head, listening intently.

Others had heard it, too, and after a long moment of silence, men slid out of their hammocks and began to dress quickly.

What we had heard was an ominous clanking from the engine room, then a hissing, whistling sound as the ship blew off steam. Instantly our speed fell off.

"Jesus Christ, one of these days the tea kettle will blow up!" Gill growled.

"And you don't want to be on it when it does, do you?" Mel said.

Whatever Gill said in reply was lost in the boatswain's bellow, "All hands make sail!"

Up we scurried to the deck and aloft. All night, the *Alabama* had been coasting along on steam, the air being motionless. Now we threw to the morning breeze every stitch of canvas she had.

It wasn't long afterward that we learned that one of the steam-valve castings had given way. The ship was therefore entirely dependent on sail until repairs could be made. The accident made her so vulnerable, should any Union man-of-war happen along, that Semmes withdrew from the usual sea-lanes and ran in close to a beach on the north coast of Jamaica. The land was heavily forested and uninhabited, and the sea around deserted except for a fishing boat and a coastal sloop, neither of which put in close enough to observe us.

Fortunately for Semmes, Miles Freeman, the chief engineer, was a first-rate machinist, and the *Alabama* had been provided with the means to deal with just such a mishap. For forty-eight hours — by night as well as by day — the *Alabama* sounded like a foundry: bellows blowing, files rasping and screeching, and someone wielding a hammer so powerfully on an anvil he must have had the muscles of a giant. Few on the berth deck were able to get much sleep while this racket persisted, but if the cursing was loud at the unending uproar, it could hardly compare with the richness of the profanity that came up through the gratings from the engine room. Time and again, we saw Semmes descend the winding metal ladder to talk with the engineer.

[203]

"Damn it, Freeman, we can't waste much more time," he said.

"Doing our best, captain, doing our goddamned best," the engineer said, his voice sagging with fatigue.

"How much longer?"

"Maybe three hours."

"Get on with it, then."

And after Semmes went topside, the engine room burst into a wilder clamor than before.

It wasn't three, it was six hours, about nightfall on December 12, before Miles Freeman wearily climbed to the deck and rolled to the captain's quarters to announce that the repairs were completed. He emerged with a triumphant smile and a pocketful of cigars.

Within the hour, the *Alabama* was at sea again. We soon cleared the west end of Jamaica and entered the Gulf of Mexico, sighting nothing. Then a norther drew us into the Gulf of Honduras. Though the weather continued dismal, we clawed our way back up the coast of Yucatan, rounding Cape Catoche on the 20th as darkness set in. During the night, we reentered the Gulf of Mexico and, the next day, ran off to the westward with a free wind.

Before long, we sighted a large steamer, hull down, sailing in the direction of Havana. We could see her topsails and her smoke, and there was a great deal of speculation as to her identity. If she was a Union warship, she strangely ignored us. Personally I thought she might well be a French man-of-war or transport returning from Vera Cruz, Napoleon III having established his empire in Mexico under Maximilian some time before.

On the 23rd, we sighted a ship moving in the same direction as ourselves. The nearer we came to her, the more familiar she looked. It wasn't long before we recognized the stumpy topgallant masts and the bluff bows as belonging to the *Agrippina*.

She had taken all this time since leaving Blanquilla to reach this point, though we subsequently discovered that her skipper, Alex McQueen, his Scottish blood showing, had done a little favorable trading here and there on the way. There was nothing the matter with his navigation, however, for by late in the afternoon, both ships moved into the shelter of the Arcas Islands, which had evidently been the rendezvous specified by Semmes.

We spent a busy week in these three desolate, deserted coral islands. The islands formed a triangle, and Semmes anchored the ships in the center. All hands then went to work. Since the *Alabama*'s upper deck had again opened, it was recaulked. Sails were patched and rebent. With a view to having her as fast as possible, Semmes careened the ship, and we scrubbed her copper below the waterline. Then we loaded her with coal from the *Agrippina* and filled the empty collier with coral for ballast.

But, as on Blanquilla, all was not work — arduous as that was — on the Arcas Islands. The boats were put into the water and rigged for sailing. Parties went out fishing and turtling during the day to supply the crew, while in the evening there were sailing and swimming matches. Target-shooting was especially popular. Bartelli was greatly interested in the sponges on the ocean floor, which were visible fathoms down because of the unusual clarity of the water. He and I found one large sponge which he dried and cleaned, then presented to Semmes.

Christmas and New Year's Day passed with feasts and an extra ration of grog, but the crew was getting impatient. Everyone knew that the reconditioning of the ship in this particular spot must portend something unusual. Northern commerce was slight in the whole area.

"I'd say Old Beeswax wants to say hello to his old friends in New Orleans," Mel said. "That's where he got to sea with the *Sumter*."

"I'd say he wants to visit Mobile, where I've heard he's owned property for years," Larkin cut in.

Gill shook his head. "You're both wrong. The Yankees hold New Orleans and we'd have to run the blockade to get into Mobile — Semmes wouldn't risk the *Alabama* doin' that."

"Where do *you* think we're going, Dan?" Mel asked.

"Galveston," I said.

As all three looked at me, I went on, "According to the newspapers, there's an army of thirty thousand under General Banks sailing from Boston and New York. The bar at Galveston is so high that any transport that draws more than a dozen feet of water will have to anchor outside. That means a good many ships will be crowded together at anchor just waiting for a smart raider to pick them off."

"Jesus, if that ain't something!" Mel slapped his knee. "But what about cruisers protecting that convoy, Dan?"

"Of course, there'll be cruisers. That's why, if I were Old Beeswax, I'd attack at night. There'll be so much confusion, he could probably sink half a dozen transports, maybe more."

"Very clever, Thomas. I'll have to mention your plan to the captain."

We jumped to attention at the sound of Kell's voice. It was harsher than usual, and he was unsmiling.

"Thomas, come with me."

"Yes, sir."

I followed him at a respectful distance, and though I looked straight ahead, I was aware of the curious glances from seamen lounging on the deck. Kell knocked at Semmes's cabin, and, at Semmes's command, we entered.

"Captain Semmes, if you will be so kind, sir, will you repeat for my benefit when you plan to make the announcement you and I discussed this afternoon."

Semmes, who had been writing, put down his pen and stared at Kell, then at me. He began to frown, and Semmes's frown was not a pleasant expression to watch.

"I don't understand the meaning of this, Kell."

"Please, sir."

[206]

"Very well, though this is most unusual. At mess, tomorrow noon."

"Then you may be interested to learn that Thomas here just described to two of his shipmates what you propose to announce."

"Thomas, will you repeat, please, what Lieutenant Kell heard you say." It was politely phrased, but an order, and Semmes's voice was even rougher than Kell's.

Choosing my words and trying to be brief, I gave him my reasons why I would head for Galveston. "It was all in the newspapers, sir," I concluded. "All I had to do was to put the information together."

"I see. Thomas, what did you do before you signed aboard the *Alabama?*"

"I went to sea, sir."

He opened a drawer and brought out the muster roll. Meanwhile, I could hear Bartelli washing the supper dishes, and I wished I were off on one of the islands sponging with him rather than having to account for myself.

"Ah, here you are." His finger ran down the list to my name. "You're from Hull, I see."

"Yes, sir."

He turned to Kell. "What is Thomas's record like?"

"Clean, sir. He does his duty well. He's a foretopman."

"Did he have any part in the Forest mutiny?"

"Not that I know of, sir. In fact, he was one of the few sober men that night."

"How much education did you have, Thomas?"

"My grandfather taught me most of what I know, sir."

He shook his head. "That's not really answering my question, but let it go. Thomas" — he looked at Kell for a moment — "aboard the *Alabama* we don't ask many questions about a man's past or his opinions. We expect a faithful and efficient performance of duty, and this you have evidently rendered."

He paused, and I started to breathe more easily — too soon.

"But, Thomas, you are obviously an intelligent man, a man who can analyze news dispatches and read his commander's mind. Mr. Kell is correct: the plan you have described is one which the ship's crew will hear from me tomorrow noon. Thomas, if I hear that you have mentioned another word about that plan before the announcement, I will throw you into the brig for disobedience, and perhaps worse. Do you understand?"

"Yes, sir."

"One more thing. Whatever your education and your citizenship — and I will not press you further on these — if you are so clever as to discover both our destination and the reasons for it before most of my officers, I think you are also clever enough to make a shift from the foretop to one of the guns. Mr. Kell, do you think you could find a place for Thomas in one of the gun crews?"

"I'm sure I could, sir."

"Very good. You may go now, Thomas."

I left, realizing I had only myself to blame. I cursed the impulse that had ever prompted me to mention Galveston. Up to this point, I had succeeded in being inconspicuous; henceforth, I was a marked man. Semmes, moreover, appeared to sense I was not what I pretended to be, and his moving my assignment from aloft to a gun could not only be a penalty but a means of testing my loyalty. If I had any part in the discharge of a cannon against a vessel flying the United States flag, I would have demonstrated in his eyes that I was, in truth, a supporter of the Confederacy. Well, canny though he was, Semmes might be mistaken as to what I would or would not do. The number of my faults might be legion, but I did at least possess a sense of duty. I had risked much before this in the name of duty; I might risk even more.

It was as if my encounter with Semmes touched off a train of action. At the muster next day, Semmes told us that we would destroy as many Union transports as we could off Galveston, where they were to rendezvous on January 10. He sent the

[208]

Agrippina back to Liverpool, presumably to meet the *Alabama* again at some destination known only to Semmes and Mc-Queen, the collier's skipper. On the 5th, the *Alabama* left the Arcas Islands under sail, our coal being conserved for the action off Galveston and our escape. And on that day I was assigned to a gun crew manning one of the four thirty-two-pounders amidships under the command of Lieutenant Sinclair.

I had learned considerable about guns, but Sinclair, of course, did not know this; I was simply one of those who helped bear a hand on the tackles maneuvering the gun into position. On the way to Galveston, we held long drills every day, and the gun crews worked with a spirit and a smoothness that surprised me. One would have thought they were all Confederates. I don't think, however, that there was a man at the thirty-two's who wouldn't have preferred serving with the big Blakely rifled hundred-pounder mounted on the forecastle and commanded by Lieutenant Armstrong, or the smoothbore sixty-eight-pounder amidships under Lieutenant Wilson. Two thirty-two's were also under Wilson's command. With the Blakely and the smooth-bore alone, the *Alabama* was capable of sinking any wooden ship the Union had — provided, of course, she was not first sunk or disabled by even more powerful guns mounted by a ship of greater tonnage, like the *San Jacinto*, or one of comparable size, such as the *Tuscarora*.

As the *Alabama* neared her destination and the gun crews became more proficient and the ship's morale soared, I became increasingly anxious. Had either of my messages got through? If they hadn't, I dearly hoped the navy had furnished the transports with adequate protection. The thought of what the *Alabama* could accomplish in a night raid on undefended ships filled with troops was sickening.

The run to Galveston was made through consistently fair weather and on time, except for a day of calm, when Semmes, watching his coal, did not use his engines. By noon on Sunday, January 11 — a lovely day — the report spread through the ship that we were within thirty miles of Galveston. Semmes had explained that we would move cautiously toward the port until the lookout sighted the transports. After that, we would draw off until the moon came up at eleven-thirty, and then come about and steam in for the kill. Cautiously we edged shoreward. Both Semmes and Kell peered through their glasses but evidently saw nothing.

Then, at half-past three in the afternoon, the lookout at the masthead suddenly shouted, "Sail, ho! Land, ho!"

"How many ships do you see?" Kell asked.

"Five steamers, sir. They look like ships of war."

"Do you see a fleet of transports?" Semmes called out.

"No, sir."

This was startling news indeed, and the expressions of disappointment and disgust were numerous and vivid.

Then, as everyone squinted towards the shore, which was still too far away for us to see, a shell zoomed high over where the port lay and exploded in a burst of flame and smoke that was visible for miles.

"What's happening there?" Lieutenant Sinclair asked Wilson, who had joined him.

Wilson's mouth opened as if to reply, when Semmes turned to Kell, his voice carrying easily to us. "The enemy wouldn't be bombarding his own people. I tell you, Kell, Galveston must have been recaptured by our forces."

"I think you're right, sir."

"That means Banks's transports must have gone straight to New Orleans."

Kell shook his head somewhat dolefully. "I'm afraid what you say is correct, sir."

For a few moments, a strange silence settled over the *Alabama*. All eyes seemed to switch from Semmes to Galveston, over which more shells were bursting, and back to Semmes again. This time, unlike the *Ariel* affair, the men were looking for a fight, but as skillful and courageous as Semmes was, he could not take on five ships of war.

Suddenly from the masthead came the cry, "Officer of the deck, one of their steamers is coming out after us, sir!"

"Good," said Semmes, "let her come!"

"Then I assume we'll fight her?" Kell asked.

"We'll fight her."

Most of the men standing near him started to cheer, but he frowned everyone into silence again, and both he and Kell studied the faintly visible ship through their glasses.

"She doesn't look like any of the old steam frigates or one of the new sloops," Semmes said.

Kell lowered his glasses and smiled. "I can't say I'm sorry about that. If she were one of those classes, she'd be too heavy for us. She's probably an auxiliary of some sort, and we should be able to handle her."

"Exactly. Now, Mr. Kell, let's come about and go slowly. I want to decoy that steamer far enough away from the others so that we can fight her without interference from them. Tell Mr. Freeman to get the propeller into the water and work up a small head of steam — let the propeller turn over slowly now and again so that she doesn't gain on us too rapidly. When we're far enough out, we'll clear for action, furl sail, and fight her under steam alone."

For the next few minutes, the *Alabama* was a flurry of activity as men flew in response to Kell's trumpeted orders. Then we settled down to a long wait as the steamer came nearer and nearer to the *Alabama*, but dangerously far from fleet support. She looked as large as the *Alabama*, but she was a side-wheeler high out of the water, which meant that she was very vulnerable — a well-aimed shell or two into her paddle wheels, and that would be that.

Finally came Kell's order to furl sail, and the drums beat to quarters. Cleared for action, the *Alabama* came about once again and moved rapidly down on the Union warship. The latter was now about twenty miles from the fleet, though it was hard to be sure because darkness had set in. She was not a fast ship, but since both vessels were heading toward each other, the distance between them disappeared swiftly. Both cut their engines when they were about a hundred yards apart.

"What ship is that?" came out of the darkness.

Standing underneath a battle lantern, Kell trumpeted back, "This is Her Britannic Majesty's steamer *Petrel*. What ship are you?"

"This is the United States ship ——"

But the name was lost in the night, even after Kell repeated his question.

As the *Alabama* remained silent, the other ship spoke again. "If you please, I will send a boat on board of you."

"Certainly. We shall be happy to receive your boat," Kell called back.

We could hear a boatswain's mate call away a boat, hear the tackles creak as they lowered the boat to the water, even see the dim blotch on the water that was the boat moving toward us.

Beside the guns, meanwhile, the gun crews stood ready, the gunners with their lockstrings in hand. Anxious whispers sped down the row of cannon, chief of which was, "What the hell are we waiting for?"

Then Semmes turned to Kell. "I suppose you are all ready for action, Mr. Kell?"

"We are."

At Semmes's pause before replying, we could hear a conversation going on aboard the Union ship, so close were the two vessels. But when Semmes spoke again, the men had ears only for him.

"Tell the enemy who we are, Mr. Kell — we must not strike him in disguise. And when you have done that, give him the broadside."

"Aye, aye, sir," said Kell. Raising the trumpet to his mouth, he gave a clarion shout. "This is the Confederate States steamer *Alabama!*" Then he turned to the men and, in a fierce voice, cracked out, "Fire!"

The guns stabbed the night with reddish-white flame, and the crash was shattering. Rocked back by the blast, the *Alabama* righted herself in an acrid cloud of smoke that momentarily obscured the other vessel. The Union ship, however, returned the fire at once, and the two vessels, both under power again, fought side by side, the *Alabama* presenting her starboard broadside, the other firing her port broadside.

It was an amazing battle. The ships came within thirty yards, with the quarterdeck complements popping away at each other with small arms. At our opponent's rate and volume of fire, I fully expected the *Alabama's* light scantling would be crushed. Instead, the Northern aim was either high or wide of the mark. We were scarcely touched. Our shot, on the other hand, went crashing deep into the other ship's hull. We could hear the ring of our shells as they penetrated the thin, brittle, iron skin. Whole sheets of iron seemed to be shearing off. Suddenly one shell exploded inside her and started a fire. A second shell started another. Her walking beam was completely shot away — I was sure it was the gunner at the thirty-two-pounder whose crew I was with that took care of that. And finally a shell penetrated her engine room, which was above water, and a burst cylinder bathed the ship in steam. By now she was going down rapidly. Suddenly she fired a gun to leeward and ran up a lantern — the equivalent of a white flag in the daytime.

"Have you struck?" Kell trumpeted.

"I have."

"Cease fire!" Kell shouted as our men raised a loud cheer.

It had been only thirteen minutes since the guns had opened.

"We're going down! Will you help us?" an urgent voice called out.

At once Semmes ordered our boats lowered. This was the one

part of the battle that I could throw myself into, and, sitting next to Larkin, I put my back into rowing. When we reached the stricken vessel, which was sinking rapidly, bow foremost, men were jumping overboard and calling out frantically to us lest they be overlooked in the darkness. Actually, the flames lighted up the water for hundreds of feet, so there was little chance of their being missed. Quickly we hauled men aboard and rowed back to the *Alabama*. We deposited them at the gangway, then rowed back for more.

We were racing against time. Men near the sinking ship — the *Hatteras*, we found out — could be sucked under when she dived. These waters were shark-infested, and few of us believed the old saw that sharks would not attack at night. And, of course, by now other ships were on the way from the fleet.

Our boat was bringing in its last load, eight dripping survivors, when someone in another boat shouted, "There she goes!"

And in a great *whoomph!* of steam and fire, the *Hatteras* went down, our boat rocking wildly on the waves thrown up by her plunge. We then headed for the *Alabama*.

"Six minutes!" said Lieutenant Sinclair as our boat crew came up the gangway behind the captives. "Six minutes to pick up the *Hatteras*'s crew, and I think we've got everyone."

Lieutenant Wilson whistled in amazement. "Thirteen minutes for the fighting, six minutes to save that crew. By God, that must be close to a record!"

Certainly it was remarkable. True, the *Alabama* should have won, for though the *Hatteras* also carried eight guns, she had no gun heavier than a thirty-two-pounder, and only four of those. On the other hand, the Confederate fire was not only faster but devastatingly accurate, whereas Union marksmanship was so poor there was but one *Alabama* man wounded. No shot holes were dangerous enough to be plugged immediately, and not even a rope needed to be spliced. As against these results, the Northerners had not only lost their ship, but also suffered two dead and five wounded, and had all the rest of their men and officers, except for the boat crew which put out for the *Alabama* before the firing commenced, taken prisoner.

It was with a sore heart and humiliation that I saw the Union sailors ironed and placed on the berth deck. This action was necessary, of course, because there were so many of them (before the battle, the crews were almost even in number). But as I watched them led below and the officers' paroles taken, I wondered that the *Hatteras*'s skipper, Commander Homer Blake — who, it seems, was a friend of Lieutenant Kell's in the old navy — ever dared sail his converted merchantman into action with such poor gun training. The *Alabama*'s crew was good, but not that good, nor the *Alabama* herself so invulnerable.

Meanwhile, Semmes, before inviting Blake to his cabin where Bartelli said they drank a glass of wine together, ordered all lights on the *Alabama* extinguished. Still relying on steam, the raider now rapidly put miles between herself and the pursuing steamers. By the next morning, we were at least a hundred miles away, heading for the Yucatan passage out of the Gulf.

If the Union Navy was ever to catch up with the *Alabama*, it would have to change its tactics of pursuit or lie in wait for her when and if she ever returned to Europe. Of course, before the latter happened, much of the American merchant marine would have been destroyed or forced to change its registry — and not simply because of the *Alabama*. Two other raiders, for which Captain Bulloch was responsible, were also loose on the high seas: the *Georgia* and the *Florida*. The future looked bleak for the Union at sea, and when we heard from the *Hatteras*'s people of the horrible slaughter of the Army of the Potomac under General Burnside at Fredericksburg back in mid-December, I began to wonder if the North was really capable of defeating the South. The South's recovery of Galveston and the *Alabama*'s destruction of the *Hatteras* seemed almost symbolic of Southern skill and Northern ineptitude.

There was just one consolation in our foray toward the Texas coast, and that was so tremendous it helped ease the chagrin I felt at the *Alabama*'s victory over the *Hatteras*. By recapturing Galveston and forcing the Banks expedition to sail to New Orleans, the Confederate Army had frustrated Semmes in his determination to sink the Union transports. In so doing, the Confederates had inadvertently saved the Union hundreds, perhaps thousands, of lives. I had hoped, of course, that my information might have accomplished the same. I seriously doubted that it had arrived in time, and the growing sense of my futility disturbed me deeply. But, my own feelings aside, the North had achieved the equivalent of a victory of which it wasn't even aware, and had achieved it through no thanks to its own efforts. And I doubted that Raphael Semmes would have exchanged the satisfaction of destroying the transports for the sweet and convincing victory over the *Hatteras*.

XXII

THE *Alabama* entered the harbor at Kingston, Jamaica, about nightfall on January 21, and anchored off the naval station at Port Royal. For two or three days after leaving the Galveston area, we had gone entirely on steam, but we encountered such a succession of gales that there was fear the coal would be consumed. Hence Semmes put the ship under sail. Later, when we moved into the Yucatan passage, he went back to steam, aided by reefed topsails. Even so, the weather was adverse, and it took us nine days to sail from Galveston to the west end of Jamaica and a whole day, or at least until late in the afternoon, before we made the Plum Point lighthouse. Firing a gun, we unfurled the French flag and waited for a pilot. He soon boarded us and took the ship to its anchorage.

Just before we dropped our anchor, Semmes said to him,

"The flag up there may be French, but this ship you're taking in is the Confederate States ship *Alabama*."

The pilot, a model of coolness, replied, "I knew all along you were not a Frenchman."

There were three British warships in the harbor: the *Jason*, the *Challenger*, and the *Greyhound*. These ships, under Commodore Dunlap, were a squadron of the British West Indies fleet commanded by Admiral Milne. Hardly had we dropped anchor when a boat from the *Jason*, the flagship, arrived with a young lieutenant aboard. When Semmes identified himself and the *Alabama*, the lieutenant returned to his commodore. His information evidently stirred up the wildest curiosity, and although evening had come, boats arrived for hours from ship and shore, bringing officers to inspect the famous raider, meet her daring captain and his lieutenants, and stare at the blue-clad prisoners from the *Hatteras*. The presence of the prisoners was undeniable evidence that the *Alabama*, while a destroyer of commerce, was also a bona fide ship of war.

The next day, there was the same parade of visitors, this time with many of the officers' families. These English people naturally evinced a great deal of curiosity about the *Alabama*, which was, after all, English-built, English-gunned, and English-manned. They were lavish in their praise of the ship and its accomplishments. Personally I saw nothing laudatory in the *Alabama*'s having destroyed so many ships that were completely unable to reply with gunfire. She had been admirably handled, had successfully eluded pursuers, and had sunk the *Hatteras*, a weaker vessel. But by the remarks and attitude of the visitors, one would have thought we had won a succession of triumphs against heavy odds.

That morning, while Semmes went off in his scarlet-cushioned gig to pay his official visit to the commodore, Kell got working parties over the side to patch the timbers scarred or holed by the *Hatteras*'s shot. And, of course, a lot of cleaning and painting had to be done, with paint signs to be made for our visitors' benefit. Arrangements were effected for recoaling. The prisoners were also released and turned over to the United States consul.

In the afternoon and evening, liberty parties were permitted to go ashore, and on the next day as well. The officers likewise went ashore in shifts, though Kell remained aboard the ship. Semmes, shortly after returning from the commodore, had been rowed to Kingston, where an old friend was waiting in his carriage and drove him up into the mountains to his plantation. He could now relax, free of the undeniable pressures he had faced, and be confident that under the command of the stern, capable Kell the *Alabama* was in good hands.

But even Kell was not able — perhaps not even anxious — to control everything that went on ashore. Sailors on liberty from men-of-war can be a wild lot under ordinary circumstances, and circumstances now were hardly ordinary. Though the crews of the *Alabama* and the *Hatteras* were enemies, one would never have suspected it the way they went arm-in-arm, talking loudly and singing, along the streets of Kingston, turning in wherever they could for a drink, with the Confederates paying, since the Union men had lost everything when their ship went down. Of course, had the Confederates been Southerners instead of foreigners to a man, there might not have been such a display of good feeling. Often they were joined by men from the British cruisers, who, knowing the town better, led the others to the brothels. After the men had been a few hours ashore, the liberty patrols from the *Alabama* were busy picking their comrades out of the gutters and lugging them to the boats. Kell's face grew colder and harder with each boatload that arrived.

On the evening of the second day, Mel Taylor, Joe Larkin, and I went ashore. It was a relief to be off the ship and walking along Water Street. There were a few ships in the harbor, but trade seemed dull. The abolition of slavery in the British

Empire had seriously damaged the economy of Jamaica. As yet, neither the whites nor the blacks had completely adjusted to the change, economically or socially. There was the appearance of dilapidation about the waterfront section. Though the blacks were shy about speaking with strangers, the whites were not. They stood the Confederates to drinks, and some of them openly damned President Lincoln's Emancipation Proclamation, news of which had but recently reached the town.

I think part of the enormous popularity of the Confederates and the widespread interest in the *Alabama* came from the people of the island identifying themselves so closely with the cause of the South. They admitted the appalling poverty and living conditions of the blacks but attributed these to the black man's laziness, lack of resourcefulness, and general mental inferiority. I could imagine how my great-uncle Jonathan Dearborn would have scoffed at such assertions. A strong abolitionist, he had often told how he and Aunt India owed their lives to the skill and courage of a black man, Philip Adair. From some of these white men in Kingston I heard that the blacks might be planning an insurrection. The white men hoped that if this happened, Governor Eyre would stand firm and not hesitate to use troops. Every family they said, was stocking up with weapons against the day when the blacks might rise.

At one pub where we stopped, Paymaster Yonge was drinking alone. Near him were several of our watch who hailed us loudly and insisted we all lift a glass.

"Thomas," Yonge asked, "how'd you like shooting at Yankees that night we took the *Hatteras?*"

"I didn't do any shooting myself, Mr. Yonge. Just bore a hand on one of the tackles."

"That's still helping shoot up the Yankees," Yonge answered. He looked at me. If ever I saw a sad-eyed dog, it was Yonge, but I had the impression that behind his mournful countenance was a bright intelligence. He was a Southerner born and bred, and a veteran in sea service with Semmes. At the moment, he was deep in liquor, and this surprised me almost as much as when I observed him, on two or three occasions, talking rather freely aboard the *Alabama* with both officers and men from the *Hatteras*.

"You know, Thomas, why you lost your job aloft and were assigned to a gun?"

"No, do you, sir?"

"Semmes thinks you bear watching."

"I don't know why he thinks that."

"It's enough that he does."

His voice was thick, but his eyes were still those of a man in control of himself. When I made no reply, he said, "Thomas, watch out. Semmes has his eye on you, and Kell has, too. Kell 'specially."

"Why Kell especially?"

"Why?" He thrust his face close to mine. "I'll tell you why. Because he thinks he's seen you somewhere before."

"Oh, I think you must be mistaken, sir! I'm sure Mr. Kell never saw me before he came aboard the *Alabama*."

How was it possible? The only time Kell could have seen me that I knew of was when Henry Adams and I went to the Hotel Morley in London after Semmes and Kell had arrived from Gibraltar, where they had disposed of the *Sumter*. Shaven, I could scarcely resemble closely the bearded civilian he may then have seen. Yet Kell did have a remarkable memory for names — I had heard him call so many men on the *Alabama* by their names that I was sure he knew everyone aboard. Names and faces can be associated, as any army or navy officer in command of men knows, but he had seen me only fleetingly at the Morley. Still, if Yonge was correct — and there seemed no reason to believe that he was making this up out of whole cloth — I was a marked man and my usefulness, in the role I had envisaged for myself, was at an end.

"Thomas," Yonge laughed, "you're a sly one. Don't think I haven't had my eye on you just as Kell has."

[220]

"Why are you telling me this, Mr. Yonge?"

"I'm telling you it's time you quit the ship, Thomas. It's time everyone who believes in the Union quit the ship. Burning merchantmen is one thing. Sinking a man-of-war flying the old flag — that's another." His voice was passionate; saliva and rum dribbled down one corner of his mouth.

"Are *you* leaving the *Alabama*, Mr. Yonge?" I asked.

"Me? Why, I'm an officer!" He started to laugh, his shoulders shaking. Bibulous tears ran down his face. As I glanced at the group of sailors in the shop, Mel gave me a nod. Gratefully I left Yonge to his rum and laughter, and followed Mel and Joe Larkin outside.

That night was another experience in hammock-tossing as I tried to make up my mind what to do. In the end, convinced that my usefulness to the Union was over, I decided to remain in Kingston until the *Alabama* had gone, then report to the United States consul, and perhaps be sent home with the *Hatteras* crew.

The next morning, the *Alabama*'s complement witnessed an astounding sight. We soon noticed Armstrong in command of the ship, and to curious questions as to where Kell was, word flew around that he had gone ashore with an armed guard, looking for Paymaster Yonge. I must admit I felt apprehension on hearing this, though it presently disappeared as I reasoned that what concerned Yonge would not necessarily affect me. Presently one of our boats hailed us and drew alongside. A few moments later, Lieutenant Kell stepped aboard, his face the very picture of fury and disgust. Behind him came an armed sailor pulling Yonge by an arm, and behind Yonge another guard pushing the paymaster's fat rear.

"I can get up myself, damn you!" Yonge shouted to the men helping him. But he could hardly mouth the words, and he would have pitched forward had not the guard in front caught him.

"Master-at-arms, take this officer to his cabin and put two

[221]

guards at the door." Kell's voice was cold and contemptuous. For the first time since being commissioned, the *Alabama* had an officer under arrest and confined to his quarters.

The shore patrol soon let it be known what had happened. Yonge had helped himself to some of the gold kept aboard the *Alabama* for emergencies, having access to the strongbox as paymaster. With that, he had got a number of the *Alabama*'s crew drunk and taken them to the United States consul for "protection." Then, refusing to return to his duties, he went to a brothel. Kell found him there sleeping off his drunk.

"You should've heard Yonge curse Kell," one of the patrol said, shaking his head and grinning.

"What about Kell?" someone asked.

"Didn't say a word to Yonge. Just let him rant. When the madam asked for pay for letting Yonge stay overnight, Kell paid her what she asked. Didn't say a word to her, either. Then he turns to us and tells us to get Yonge to the boat and not be overgentle — that's how he said it — if Yonge gave us a fight."

"Did Yonge give you a hard time?" Joe Larkin asked.

"No, Kell scared him."

Word circulated that Kell was soon to send a message to Semmes that with coaling and repairs completed, the *Alabama* was ready to sail. The result was a great surge of men to go ashore for a last fling at the grogshops and the brothels. Since all could not go at once, they went in shifts, with two hours specified as the time each shift might spend ashore. I was relieved to learn that neither Mel nor Joe was in my shift, for I doubted that I would return to the *Alabama*.

As I dressed in my cleanest white ducks to go ashore, I found myself half-reluctant to leave the ship. I glanced around at the berth deck and later at the foretop and at the thirty-two-pounder where I had served. Mine was the last shift, and as I waited in line for the second to return and saw Mel and Joe come over the side, I wanted to shake their hands warmly and bid them good-bye. As it happened, both staggered aboard, deep in their cups along with many others. Then the line of waiting sailors filed down to take their places in the boats.

Once ashore, I dropped into a grogshop with several of the crew. We spent quite a while there, most of the men drinking heavily. A number of civilians were present, many of them seafaring men, to judge by their appearance and conversation. They smiled when we arrived, then went on with their talking. Soon we *Alabama* crewmen were all laughing and drinking, with everyone speculating as to where we were going next.

It was during one of those pauses, a silent period that sometimes occurs even in large gatherings, that my ears picked up the word "*Agrippina*."

"I talked with him only two days ago," said the voice. "Name's McQueen. By the Lord Harry, can't that man drink! Those lads from the *Alabama* wouldn't be in it with him. . . . But he talks too much."

"A lot of men do that," another speaker said.

"I don't mean that. He spills secrets. The *Agrippina's* the collier for the *Alabama*. He said she's on her way back to Liverpool for more coal. Damndest slowest scow I think I ever saw. My ship walked right up alongside of her without even trying, and McQueen came aboard to buy a case of whisky."

"Where's he bound for next?"

"Who, Semmes? How the hell should I know?"

"No, I mean your man McQueen."

"Oh, McQueen. Fernando de Noronha is what I'm told."

I had heard enough. My objective was the United States consulate. But breaking away from the *Alabama's* men wasn't so easy. When I started to stroll out of the shop, a sailor shouted, "Watch out for Thomas! He wants the choice piece for himself."

With that I was caught up in the rush of a half-dozen sailors who headed for a whorehouse highly recommended by the British seamen. Whooping and singing, they raced along, and I couldn't break away from them. Soon we dashed up to the door of a splendid mansion aglow with light. At the door we were met by a tall, tightly corseted female of uncertain age, with an air and voice of authority.

"Now you men quiet down, do you hear? You'll have your turn."

Kell or the boatswain couldn't have been more successful at subduing the group. Taking the numbered cards she passed out to them, they slipped inside like well-behaved schoolboys. Miss Hilda, as everyone called her, ran a taut ship.

The lower rooms of the place were filled with men from the British cruisers and the merchant ships in port. Some were playing cards. All were drinking, so far as I could see, and joking with the young women who were waiting on them. A fairly steady stream of men moved up and down the stairs, checking with the madam's assistant, a stocky, big-hipped woman, before going up, and with the madam herself on coming down.

The *Alabama* was well represented here when we entered, but the numbers were gradually thinning out, except for the group I was with. Several times I made as if to rise from the table where we were sitting, but was hauled down again with much laughter and assurance that I'd have my chance.

Finally the madam came over to us. "All right, boys, we're ready for you now. Who has the lowest number?"

"Thomas has it!" one of the men shouted, and another shouted, "Go to it, Dan! The *Alabama* has a hot reputation!"

So with a good deal of chaff and laughter they pushed me on, and I followed the madam, who nodded to her assistant. "Dark or light?"

"Light."

"Third down to the left. Lily's her name. Up with you."

I never climbed a flight of stairs more deliberately than I did those in that brothel in Kingston. When I knocked at the door, a shrill voice told me to come in. Even before I had closed the door, she said, "Christ, couldn't they send me a prettier one than you?"

[224]

But if she stared at me, I also stared at her. She might have been thirty, though with only a shift on and her hair down, she looked, at first glance, far younger. But even as she talked, an uproar broke out below, and a man bellowed, "Back to the *Alabama* with you and leave these boys alone!"

In two strides I brushed her aside and reached the window.

Below stood Lieutenant Sinclair and the quartermasters from the *Alabama*, while forming against them was a mass of British seamen and, behind them, a line of young women who had been waiting on the drinkers and cardplayers.

"You can't enter here, lieutenant," one Englishman said. "Your men are busy, and you can't have 'em."

"Say, Middy," a woman yelled, "the tickets to this ball are limited, and the company is select."

"Tell Old Beeswax to go to sea," another shouted. "Tell him to go burn some more Yankee ships and come back. We'll give up the boys then, and you'll have your turn."

But Sinclair merely smiled and bowed, asked to meet the hostess, and offered to buy drinks all around. At such politeness and generosity, the human wall parted and let him and his quartermasters inside. I knew that from being his playful opponents, the crowd would soon become Sinclair's supporters and that if I tried to break away once I came downstairs, I'd soon be overpowered.

"He's nice, ain't he?" said Lily. "Now, look here, let's get on with this."

"This is for you and the house for your services," I said, reaching for her hand and pressing a gold sovereign into it. "And here is another" — holding it up for her to see — "if you can get me out of here without being seen below."

She languidly brushed the hair from her eyes. "What if I scream and tell them about you, dearie? Maybe I'd get more than that."

I bore down. "You'd get nothing at all, Lily, nothing at all, do you understand? And you'd have lost the sovereign I've promised you."

"Only one sovereign?"

"Two, if you get me out of here right away!"

"Come along, then."

She reached for a wrap and, holding it closed, said, "Follow me just as though nothing was wrong. There'll be men in the hall, and maybe girls. If they see us sneaking along, we may run into trouble. Just be natural-like."

She opened the door and walked out, holding my arm. Down the hall we went as if we were promenading. Sailors who passed us grinned and made way. One civilian, straightening his stock, stopped and stared at us, then bowed and said, "The next time I will sign up for you, Lily."

"Do that," she said with a gracious smile.

"Lily, where do you think you're going with that Yankee rebel?"

Lily turned to the girl leaning against the doorjamb of her room. "He ain't eaten for two days, Moll. Just drunk. Thought I'd get Tess to fix him up something down in the kitchen."

We went down a back stairs into a basement kitchen, where two big black women were at work.

"Tess, will you make up some beef for the gentleman?" she asked one of the women, who wore a red cloth around her head like a turban.

"Now, Miss Lily, you know Miss Hilda don't want us to do things like that."

As Tess was speaking, Lily held a hand behind her back, palm open. I placed two shillings in it. She then held one up, and Tess sighed and quickly slapped two sandwiches together and gave them to us. After paying her, Lily took my arm and we walked out a back door.

"Now, look here," she said briskly, "you're on your own. Go through this yard and the one over there. If it's the Yankee consulate you want, it's down that street."

I gave her the two sovereigns I had promised. But as I started to leave, she caught my arm. "I don't even know your name, dearie."

"Dan — Dan Thomas."

"It's a good, strong name. Now get on with you — Dan."

I didn't see the *Alabama* put to sea, receiving and returning the salutes and cheers of the British squadron. Nor did I ever see Miss Hilda's ménage or Lily again. Instead, I was secreted in the United States consulate after having identified myself and explained to the consul that if Fernando de Noronha was the coal rendezvous with the *Agrippina*, Semmes was obviously planning a raid along the Brazilian coast. I further gave the consul my opinion that with our cruisers covering the areas which he had already raided, Semmes would probably move southeast from Brazil to catch our merchant traffic moving around the Cape of Good Hope.

This information passed on, I then relaxed, truly relaxed, for the first time since signing aboard the *Enrica* at Moelfre Bay. And in my new condition I had plenty of company among the refugees from the *Alabama*: the 120-odd officers and men of the *Hatteras*, a half-dozen deserters from the *Alabama*'s crew, and a gentleman who had been court-martialed and drummed over the side of the raider before she sailed — Paymaster Clarence Yonge.

THREE

Courier for the Navy

XXIII

"Young man, I don't know whether to treat you as insubordinate or recommend you for a medal of some kind."

I sat in Secretary Welles's office. The Secretary was considered grandfatherly by some, but he looked to me like a severe judge, and the gray afternoon light reflecting on his glasses gave an even colder expression to his face.

"Well, which should it be?"

There was not the slightest hint of humor in his face or voice. He expected a reply. "I hardly deserve the medal, sir," I said.

"Then you were insubordinate."

I sat even straighter. "Not intentionally, sir. When the *Alabama* went to sea, I considered my assignment at an end. Perhaps I should then have waited for orders instructing me when and how I should return. But there was so little time, sir. In a matter of a few hours, the *Alabama* would have been gone with none the wiser as to where she was bound. I made up my mind that it was my duty as an American and a volunteer officer in the navy to do what I could to disclose her destination to the nearest United States official. That meant enlisting aboard her and taking part in her activities — it is all in my report to you, sir. My chief regret is that I couldn't have been more effective, sir."

He looked at me for an uncomfortably long time before replying. "Mr. Pettigrew," he finally said, "both Mr. Fox and I

[231]

have read your report. I am not tale-bearing when I tell you that Mr. Fox thinks highly of it."

Gustavus Fox, the Assistant Secretary of the Navy, was the technical expert, the professional, in the department, so this was reassuring news.

"Your work, which you think ineffective, was scarcely so for lack of trying — this I will concede you. The department has checked with the officers of the Maine schooner in Fort de France Bay as to how they knew the *Alabama* intended to break out that night. It was no fault of yours or the schooner's master or mate that Captain Ronckendorff let the pirate escape. The *San Jacinto* should have blown the *Alabama* out of the water."

I realized, as he spoke, something of the depth of the Secretary's animosity toward Semmes. To Welles, Semmes was still a pirate, not just a rebel. And from the bitterness in Welles's voice as he mentioned Ronckendorff's name, I doubted that officer had any future in the navy.

"Now as to your warning about Semmes's raid on Galveston, the passenger and the purser on the *Ariel* to whom you gave the notes did their parts. Your note to your great-uncle arrived too late to be useful, though he telegraphed me immediately on receiving it. But your warning to our consul at Aspinwall was the one that counted. On her way back to New York, the *Ariel* sent word to our naval base at Key West. Our commander there got in touch with the admiral on the station, and he took appropriate measures to protect General Banks's transports. Unfortunately, the Rebel general, Magruder, recaptured Galveston, so the transports weren't there when Semmes arrived."

"Unfortunately, sir?"

"Yes, unfortunately, Pettigrew. If the army had held onto Galveston and Semmes had attacked the transports, we would have had men-of-war lying in wait for him. The *Alabama* would never have escaped. But there, as things turned out, it was probably fortunate for you as a sailor aboard her."

"Yes, sir." God knows I had no more desire to be killed than any man, least of all by my own side.

"Now the information on Semmes's next coaling destination should be helpful. The consul at Kingston communicated it to Admiral Wilkes, who will, I am sure, take the necessary action. As for your educated guess that Semmes will subsequently head for the Cape, you may be pleased to learn that that is also the opinion of most people in this department. But let's hope he never gets clear of the Brazilian coast."

"Yes, sir."

"So, sir, your record for trying is excellent, but you were still insubordinate. And don't think you can gull me with any of your legalistic reasoning. I had a hard enough time explaining to Mr. Adams and Secretary Seward that the State Department has no control over whatever course I may take in regard to you."

"Sir?"

"I don't mean to say Mr. Adams defended you. But he still has an excellent opinion of your merits. . . . Now, look here, Pettigrew, while I think of something appropriate to your case, consider yourself attached to this office and report tomorrow morning to Mr. Fox. In the meantime, why don't you find yourself a place to live other than the Willard Hotel? It's too expensive for a mere lieutenant. And, if I were you, I'd wire home for your uniforms. Mr. Adams had all your personal belongings packed and shipped to your grandfather."

People might make light of Secretary Welles and call him the "Old Man of the Sea" in derision, but Welles knew his job and wasn't going to let the mercantile interests pressure him into loosening the blockade in order to release ships to chase Semmes in the *Alabama* or John Newland Maffitt in the *Florida*. There were numerous cruisers after those raiders already, and if Welles issued some wild instructions to the cruisers, several of them had already had opportunities to deal with the raiders, and failed through no fault of the Secretary — the *Tuscarora* and *San Jacinto* with the *Alabama,* and the big frigate *Brooklyn,* which had let the *Florida* escape from Mobile under its very guns. Welles had a kind heart, too, though I could see that in my case, he really felt torn between approving and disapproving what I had done.

His advice about leaving the Willard was sound, though I was puzzled as to how he knew I was there. I had been lucky to find a room, but I couldn't afford to pay hotel rates on my salary. So I found — on the sixth try — a boardinghouse that was clean and not unreasonable in price. Afterward, I paid up my account at the Willard and wired my grandfather for my clothes.

That evening, with the boardinghouse redolent of the red snapper we had been served for supper, I stretched out on my bed to make a few mental notes. There are those who keep diaries and journals, and those who write long letters in which they express their thoughts and feelings. I am not a diarist, a keeper of journals, or an extensive correspondent. I flatter myself that I can write a good report and an effective brief, but there is something that inhibits me in expressing on paper what is truly inward. It is not a lawyer's reluctance to commit himself to paper — lawyers warn others of this, but indulge themselves incessantly in the practice. Rather, it is, first, a sense that what I might write would not truly represent how I thought or felt but, colored by my vanity either through exaggeration or understatement, would be a distortion; second, a desire to preserve a privacy even as I hope I would respect that of others; and third, a conviction that no one would really be interested, anyway. Instead, therefore, of turning to pen and paper, I often lie down and reflect. When I reach the point of contriving a plan of action, I like to walk.

So I let the reflections move across my consciousness without imposing on them any discipline of order. As far as the war was concerned, I considered myself lucky to have escaped with only the wound received from the shell from Fort Pulaski. My

[234]

service in England had been pleasant but frustrating, though not without excitement. My observation of Bulloch convinced me he was a very dangerous and gravely underestimated opponent of the North. The role of Roger Clavering still seemed unclear to me — other than that he was a Confederate commissioner for the purchase of raiders and the award of contracts to blockade runners. He moved with authority in both political and commercial circles in England. Yet he was a man whose orbit never appeared fixed, as Bulloch's generally was between Liverpool and London. Was he some kind of superagent for the Richmond government, who by now could have got back to the South by blockade runner or through Canada and the Middle West in disguise? Likewise, the precise relationship between him and Tamara Ravenel puzzled me. Judging by how she had repulsed him aboard the *Arcadia*, I suspected that if he now had his way with her, it was because he served her own purpose, whatever that was. That she was an agent collaborating professionally with him I had little doubt. That, as an agent, she might, on occasion, act independently of him I believed entirely possible. I hoped that Henry Adams, for whom I had conceived a genuine affection, or Bruce Thornton, who was now a good Maine friend, might be able to write me more about both Clavering and Tamara as soon as they knew I was home.

My cruise in the *Alabama* had convinced me that the United States merchant marine would continue to suffer dreadful losses until Semmes was beaten. He was ruthless, thorough, clever, and vindictive. Before I left Kingston in a Maine schooner that put into Philadelphia — from where I took the train to Washington — I heard Commander Blake of the *Hatteras* say that what was surprising about Semmes to those who had known him in the old navy was his energy. He had had a reputation for being able but rather indolent, with a taste for literature and a knowledge of law. But he was in no way the alert, vital commander that he had become since putting to sea in the *Sumter*, in early 1861. I don't think that the Navy Department realized how effective he really was, and I did not share Secretary Welles's confidence that he would be cornered off Brazil.

It came as a disappointment that for weeks after returning from Jamaica, I served as a kind of clerk and courier in the department, and companion to visiting civilian, naval, and military dignitaries in Washington. I came to know our muddy (or dusty) capital very well. The President was a familiar figure, driving or walking over to the War Department. He rarely came to the Navy Department, perhaps because he knew that in crusty Gideon Welles he had his stoutest and most consistent supporter and, for all the criticisms, perhaps his ablest cabinet member. More probable as a reason, however, is that it was the army that was bearing the brunt of the war and would win it if it was to be won — which still seemed doubtful as Vicksburg held out in the West; Admiral Du Pont's monitors, battered and half-sinking under Confederate gunfire, failed to destroy the Charleston forts; and Lee won his incredible victory at Chancellorsville with an army half the size of that of Fighting Joe Hooker.

Gloom was thick in Washington that spring of 1863, and with the gloom came an increase in bickering. I saw correspondence between Welles and Secretary of State Seward that was blistering in its mutual criticisms. Little Seward, brilliant but often rash, challenged Welles in jurisdictional questions and sought to extend control over the navy, particularly the navy's activities abroad. I heard Secretary of War Stanton, an enormously competent but domineering and unstable man, speak to Welles as if they were neighbors quarreling over a piece of property. Of course, our "Old Man of the Sea" could be just as abrasive in his retorts.

Welles was under heavy attack that spring, so it was no wonder his temper was edgy. Du Pont had failed at Charleston. Blockade runners continued in fairly large numbers to sift through the blockade both in the Gulf and on the Atlantic coast, though on the Atlantic side, Admiral S. E. Lee was tightening the navy's grip. And the commerce destroyers, particularly the *Alabama* and the *Florida*, were spreading a path of fire in the South Atlantic. Captain Maffitt of the *Florida* might be a jovial man, liked even by his foes, but his record for destruction was nearly as effective as the *Alabama*'s. The cries of anger from shipping circles were powerful, and carried through to Washington, to the White House as well as to the Navy Department. But how could Welles know that Admiral Wilkes in the West Indies retained probably the fastest ship in the Union Navy — the powerful converted *Vanderbilt* — for his own use, instead of sending her off, as instructed, after the *Alabama?* Or how could Welles foretell that, with Union manpower running out and Congress providing on March 3 for conscription to take place in the summer, with New York City to begin drafting in July, Secretary Stanton would propose to draft men out of the navy for the army? The "Old Man of the Sea" really had a storm going over that one.

Then again, in June, Lee began to assemble his forces for some undisclosed destination. Intelligence that came through indicated that he would presently move north, possibly invading Maryland or Pennsylvania, though this seemed a little far-fetched. At least, it did until one recalled the victories of his splendid army, the ineptness of Union leadership opposed to him, the impact that a victory on Northern soil would have on the militant peace groups in the North, and the still strong Southern hopes for European recognition. By late June, Washington was deeply worried.

But those of us in and out of the Navy Department found Secretary Welles more concerned, at least superficially, over two other developments than the mysterious movements of Lee's army. One of these was the fatal illness of his old friend from school days, Rear Admiral Andrew H. Foote, who had worked so well with General Grant in the early victories in the West. The other was the activities of the Rebel raider *Tacony* off the Atlantic coast. In fact, Admiral Foote, who was to replace Du

Pont, came on from New Haven to New York, expecting to sail to Port Royal aboard the *Tuscarora*, which had returned from European waters. That vessel, however, had been ordered out after the *Tacony*, and Foote remained at the Astor House, where he was stricken. Under some pressure from the President, Welles then appointed Rear Admiral John A. Dahlgren to command the South Atlantic Squadron in Foote's place. He also issued orders to more men-of-war to join the hunt for the *Tacony*.

It was in the midst of the command crisis brought on by Foote's illness and the alarm over the *Tacony* that he sent a runner for me over in Operations.

"Pettigrew," he said crisply, his lips barely visible through the thick white beard, "I haven't forgotten you. I want you to go to New York, then to Portsmouth, and finally to Portland. You won't have a long time at home, but I think you will be able to manage work and pleasure. First of all, go to New York and convey my heartfelt good wishes to Admiral Foote personally. As you may know, he's an old friend of mine and a valued officer in the navy. I am unable to leave this post, and letters and telegrams are never too satisfactory at a time like this. Incidentally, I introduced your Uncle Jonathan to him at my home in Hartford, years ago."

"I'll be glad to, sir."

"Good," he nodded. "Then I want you to deliver a package of ships' plans and specifications from Mr. Fox to the commandant of the Portsmouth Navy Yard. After that, go on to Portland and check on the progress of two double-ended gunboats being built there. Mr. Fox feels there is an unaccountable delay in their construction. And, of course, you will want to see your family."

"Thank you, sir."

"Wherever you go, find out everything you can about the *Tacony* if she is still at large. I have over twenty men-of-war trying to find her and not one has, as yet. At the moment, there is but one available armed ship left north of Portsmouth, and that's the revenue cutter *Caleb Cushing* in Portland. If you hear anything definite about the *Tacony* — definite, mind you! — wire me at once. Vice-President Hamlin and the entire Maine delegation in Congress have been pestering me. The pity is, you Maine people build and sail so many ships, the Rebels are bound to capture a lot of them all over the world, or wherever those pirates go. Now I'll give you three weeks for combined official business and leave."

I thanked him warmly, but he brushed me off. "Remember me to Jonathan," he said.

Thus it was that with a leave paper signed by Welles himself, I took the earliest train for New York. It was a slow trip. Twice we had to pull off on sidings and let troop trains by. Once we drew off to give the main track to a long, double-engined freight train with six of its flatcars jammed with artillery. The weather was hot, and cinders and soot blew in through the open windows. A youngster in the seat ahead of mine, with his mother and two baby sisters, complained for a long time about having something in his eye until I finally asked the woman if I could try and get the cinder out for him. She said she would be grateful, so I took a spare handkerchief from my pocket and, using the corner of it, extracted the black speck. I don't think anyone was sorry to reach New York that evening.

Since it was late, I took a room at the Astor but was unable to see Admiral Foote until the next morning. He was so ill that his doctor gave me only a couple of minutes with him, but he seemed pleased that I had come as a special representative from his old friend. At least, he smiled, and his lips formed the words "Thank you," though I heard no sound. I soon left.

As I entered the station to take the train for Boston, intending to go first to buy my ticket and then to the telegraph office to wire Welles about Foote's condition, I ran into a crowd of people who had just got off an incoming train. Quickly I stepped to the right to slide by them, or, rather, to let them pass me.

It was then I saw Roger Clavering, a valise in one hand and a cane in the other, moving along in the midst of the crowd. I could not stop; there were people behind me pushing to get inside. But I looked around and saw him emerge from the station and turn up the street. I wanted to rush out and see where he went, but there was no time to follow him.

On the train to Boston I kept wondering where he had come from and what he could be doing in New York. He must have been supremely confident that he would not be recognized. Of course, he would also have papers on his person supporting another identity. I wondered, too, whether Tamara Ravenel was with him in New York. She hadn't got off the train with him, but this didn't mean much. They may already have taken up residence in the city and she not have accompanied him this time to wherever he had come from. The train had originated in Boston, but there were numerous places along the line where he might have been, among them New Haven, New London, Westerly, and Providence.

After staying that night at the Parker House in Boston, I went on to Portsmouth, and took a cab from there across the bridge to Kittery and down to the navy yard. It was a busy place, with carpenters and riggers swarming over several men-of-war on the ways and others being equipped and armed. Soon, with the commandant's receipt for the package from Welles in my pocket, I returned to Portsmouth, and after a long, impatient wait, I caught a train for Portland.

I delighted in the sights and smells of Maine. There were stretches of sandy beaches at Wells and York and Old Orchard, with its too-numerous summer hotels. Every now and then, I could get glimpses of the sea and whiffs of its aroma. There is something magical about the sea air and the scent of pines on the coast of Maine. I saw to my dismay, however, how many of the wooded areas around the towns were being leveled and how houses were rising as people crowded into busy little mill cities like Biddeford and Saco.

As for Portland, it was clearly visible in the late afternoon from the pall of smoke hanging over it from locomotives, steamers, and factories. Yet, as my cabbie drove his horse leisurely over the cobblestones of Congress Street and up Bramhall Hill to our home on State Street, it felt wonderful to be back again. Returning home, for me, was a restorative like water to a thirsty plant.

And when, in response to the sounding of the brass knocker, appropriately shaped like a gavel, my grandmother herself — an ample figure with brown eyes that crinkled at the corners when she smiled — came to the door, I experienced an overwhelming rush of emotion.

Then my grandfather was driven up to the front of the house from his chambers by Pat, his Irish handyman, and we welcomed him at the door. Though his hair was grayer and sparser than I had last seen it, his step was firm, his mustache neatly trimmed, and he himself as fashionable as ever, with his dark gray suit and his silver-headed cane.

"Scott, my boy, you're home at last."

We clasped hands, and the strength of his grip and the light in his eye told me much about my welcome.

XXIV

THAT evening, we talked long about many things. When I had been ordered north by Welles, I had telegraphed home for my folks to expect me, so they had invited Uncle Jonathan to come to supper. He had declined, saying he thought my grandparents should have me to themselves my first evening home.

"That was thoughtful of Jonathan," my grandmother said, "but it means you will probably have to answer many questions twice. He'll want to know much the same information as we."

When I said that I didn't mind, my grandfather smiled, produced a box of fine Havanas that I had brought him, and said we might as well get started on both the cigars and the questions. And so we went on after our neighbors had gone to bed and until the mosquitoes became altogether too daring. As Chief Justice of the State of Maine, Grandfather was especially interested in Semmes's court of admiralty law that he conducted in his cabin.

"A mere façade," he said.

"I always did think he was a pirate," Grandmother said, "and now I'm surer than ever."

"And you're just as mistaken as ever, my dear," he said with a smile. "What he does is nasty work but only what Jonathan and I helped Captain Vail accomplish back in the War of 1812. Yankees capturing British ships were patriots then; Confederates doing the same to our ships are pirates now."

"But Semmes is burning those ships, Brad," she protested. "He isn't sending them into port where they could be sold and possibly recovered."

"He's doing that only because neutral ports will not accept those ships as prizes. And, of course, he is no privateersman, as we were. He is a Confederate navy captain aboard a duly commissioned man-of-war. That's right, isn't it, Scott?"

"Yes, sir. But Secretary Welles agrees with Grandmother; to him, Semmes is still a pirate."

"Welles is a man of strong convictions, and his emotions are never far from the surface. I suppose it's superfluous to ask how he feels about the *Tacony*."

"He's furious, of course." I told them what I had learned about the *Tacony*, although we in the Navy Department knew only what we had gleaned from the crews of the ships the *Tacony* had destroyed.

When one talks about daring among the Rebel naval officers, the palm must surely go to Lieutenant Charles W. Read, twenty-three years old (three years younger than myself). In

May, the *Florida* captured the brig *Clarence* off Brazil. She was bound for Baltimore, and Read, who had been a bold fighter in several Mississippi River engagements, told Captain Maffitt of the *Florida* that he would like to take the *Clarence* into Chesapeake Bay and burn Union shipping. Maffitt gave him four petty officers, twenty men, and a boat howitzer. Read captured the Maine-built bark *Whistling Wind* on June 6, burning her as Maffitt and Semmes might have. Then he captured two other ships and learned from newspapers aboard that Chesapeake Bay was too well protected. So he decided to concentrate on coastal raiding instead. It was after he made this decision that he seized the bark *Tacony* off Cape Henry on June 12, and, seeing that she was a better sailor than the *Clarence*, he resolved to move to the *Tacony*. He had barely started the transfer when a schooner, the *M. A. Shindler*, sailed within range of the *Clarence*'s howitzer and was captured. Then, when the howitzer was being conveyed to the *Tacony*, the schooner *Kate Stewart* appeared. Not at all disturbed, apparently, Read used a wooden cannon he had built aboard the *Clarence* to frighten the *Stewart* into surrendering, too. After that, he burned the *Clarence* and the *Shindler*, put the prisoners aboard the *Stewart*, sent her to shore, and swept northward in the *Tacony*.

"It was from these prisoners when they reached land that we first heard what was going on," I said. "The skipper of the *Tacony* caught a train to Philadelphia and told the owners of the *Shindler* what had happened. They sent off a telegram to Mr. Welles."

"I suppose Mr. Welles kept the telegraph wires warm when he heard," my grandfather said.

"As a matter of fact, he wasn't on duty at the time. It was a Saturday, and Mr. Fox was in charge. But he quickly wrote out a telegram over Mr. Welles's name and had it sent to the navy yards at Philadelphia, New York, and Boston. At least two dozen ships are still out hunting."

"But the *Tacony* is still capturing prizes, according to the newspapers, and most of them off the Maine coast," my grandmother said. "That lieutenant must be a brave and skillful young man."

"Oh, he's that for sure," I conceded. "He captured a dozen more ships by the time I left Washington, and bonded two big steamers. One was the *Isaac Webb*, bound from Liverpool to New York with 750 passengers aboard. Can you imagine his doing all this with just one small cannon mounted?"

"I don't quite understand why our ships can't find him," my grandfather said.

"Well, of course, there is a great deal of shipping along the coast, and I presume the *Tacony* resembles so many vessels that she would be hard to identify."

"Is Portland safe?" my grandmother asked.

"It should be," Grandfather laughed. "Yes, my dear, I think you can sleep peacefully at night."

The next morning I accompanied Grandfather downtown in the carriage. He offered to let me have it for the day, but I declined, not knowing how long I'd be. He insisted, however, that Pat drive me down to Franklin Wharf, where the gunboats were being outfitted. Before I left the city hall, he introduced me to the mayor of Portland, Captain Jacob McLellan, and to the collector of the port, Jedidiah Jewett.

"I hear a lot about you from the judge," said McLellan, a vigorous man with a staccato voice. "When's that devil Semmes going to leave our Maine ships alone?"

"When he's caught, sir." A silly question and an obvious answer, but McLellan, I realized, was only being pleasant.

"Foxed us, that's what he's done, foxed us every time. Just what that young buck Read has done. Heard the latest on the *Tacony*?" As Grandfather and I looked at him, his mustached lip tightened. "Yesterday, he took the fishing schooner *Archer* off Southport, transferred to her, and burned the *Tacony*. Put the *Archer*'s crew ashore, and the captain hied himself to a

[244]

telegraph office first thing. Now where's our navy, I ask you, where in hell's our navy?"

I had no answer, despite what I had said to Grandfather last night. The coast is a long one to cover, but I often wondered myself how these raiders consistently eluded our cruisers and gunboats.

Later, after I had made an inspection of the two gunboats *Agawam* and *Pontoosuc*, and talked at length with their contractor, I returned uptown and looked up my Uncle Jonathan. He crushed my hand, then shouldered through the noonday crowd to a restaurant. We ordered swordfish steak, and delicious it was, with a lemon and butter sauce.

Uncle Jonathan opened with questions. We covered pretty thoroughly my stay in England, the *Alabama* experience, and what I had done since. He was uneasy about the war. While he thought Secretary Welles right in maintaining the blockade rather than weakening it by sending more ships after the raider, he considered the navy ill served by some of its captains. The army's performance made him nearly apoplectic. He liked what he knew of Grant, though admittedly he knew little. But he was fiercely antagonistic toward McClellan, and contemptuous of Burnside and Hooker.

"We'll never beat Lee until we get someone as tough and dogged as himself — not brighter, because there isn't a smarter officer in either army than Lee. But we've got more men and more material, and if we can get hold of someone with lots of guts and at least half a brain, we'll beat the Rebels someday!"

"But manpower is something we're starting to run short of," I said.

"I know," he said, blowing on his coffee to cool it, " and the way that draft act is set up, it won't really work. If you've got three hundred dollars, you can buy a substitute. Why, that's iniquitous! Do you know what the average workman in the city — not the country, mind you — earns a year?"

As I shook my head, he said, "Between five and six hundred

dollars! Now, Scott, tell me, boy, how many city workmen could muster three hundred dollars? Damn few, I tell you. And no one who works on a farm. That means only the well-to-do and the rich can buy out."

"The Washington and New York papers are saying this makes it a rich man's war and a poor man's fight."

"Don't tell me what the papers are saying, boy. I get them from all over the country, and most are critical of the draft. I heard Lincoln himself doesn't like that three–hundred-dollar loophole — I surely hope he doesn't."

"What do you think is likely to happen when the draft starts?"

"Hell, that's easy. Protests. We're a protesting people, Scott. There have been protests in every war in our history. I'm not against a draft as such, you understand. But it was a badly written law, and my sympathy goes out to those who will be the victims of it."

He was silent for a moment, then, smiling, he said, "Let's forget the war for the time being."

The next day, Friday, June 26, I went down again to the gunboats and had the feeling that work was going forward a little more swiftly as a result of my visit the day before. I also took the ferry across to Cape Elizabeth and looked at some shipbuilding going on there. Later, I walked out to Fort Preble and chatted with a few of the officers. I found them to a man impatient with garrison life and eager to be with Hooker.

About six o'clock that evening, my grandparents and I drove up past the observatory to the eastern promontory from which we had an unsurpassed view of the island-studded harbor. A number of sailing ships were moored at the wharves, and several rode at anchor in the bay. The *Forest City*, a seven hundred-ton side-wheeler of the Boston line, was at her dock, likewise the screw steamer *Chesapeake* of the New York line. A small steamer, the *Casco*, could also be seen, and at her dock the sailing cutter *Caleb Cushing*. Busy as the port had been a few hours before, it was now almost breathlessly quiet, the silence broken only by a gun from Fort Preble and the sweet notes of a bugle.

We stared at the *Caleb Cushing*, at the harbor, and at a fishing schooner slowly making her way past the forts. Apart from a couple of small boats down near the wharves, she was the only moving object in the harbor. Other carriages stood near ours, and people were watching the schooner. Well handled — almost smartly, I thought — she finally dropped anchor near Pomeroy's Rock off Fish Point.

"Well, that's that," my grandfather said, "another day gone. I wonder where General Lee is this evening. Wherever he is, I'll wager it's not as quiet as it is here."

"Don't you like it calm and peaceful, Brad?"

"Yes, my dear," he said to my grandmother, "but it seems almost offensively peaceful when I think of what is likely to happen down in Pennsylvania or Maryland in the next few days."

"Well, nothing is ever offensively peaceful to me."

We deliberately avoided anything that touched on the war the rest of the evening — not an easy thing to do, I discovered.

The next morning, about half-past eight, while we were at the breakfast table, church bells started clanging away in a most unchurchly manner, while whistles began to blow wildly down on the waterfront.

All of us looked at one another, then I dashed for the window. There wasn't much to be seen, and, when I said so, Grandfather called for Pat to hitch up the carriage. Even before Pat was ready, Uncle Jonathan arrived. After a thundering knock, he plunged into the house, a strong, vital man for all his being nearly seventy-five years old.

"Scott, go get your pistol! Brad, Liza, get your field glasses and have Pat drive you to Munjoy Hill as fast as he can. I'm taking Scott to the docks."

"Jonathan, for Heaven's sake, what's happened?" my grandmother asked.

"The *Caleb Cushing*'s gone! Her second-in-command, Lieutenant Davenport, ran off to sea with her to join the *Tacony*, or the *Archer*, or whatever vessel Read has now. Jake McLellan and Jed Jewett are organizing a chase."

Off we drove to the docks, where we saw the *Casco* arriving from Fort Preble with troops from the Seventeenth United States Infantry under command of Major George Andrews. These immediately headed for the *Forest City* and dragged two fieldpieces aboard. A big steam tug, the *Tyger*, puffed in from the upper bridge in the harbor, crowded with men from the Seventh Maine Infantry under Colonel Mason. About thirty of these, with Mason himself, left the tug and went aboard the *Chesapeake*, which was getting up steam, thanks to the mayor's persuading the agent of the line to charter her. Meanwhile, the *Forest City*, under Captain Liscomb, and the tug went off in chase. Just before the *Forest City* drew up her gangplank, a revenue officer leaped aboard. Someone identified him as Lieutenant Merryman, who had arrived at four o'clock that morning to assume command of the *Cushing*.

Since the volunteers were now boarding the *Chesapeake*, I thanked my uncle for bringing me down and went aboard, too. There were about fifty of us, and so many lent a hand in dragging two brass six-pounders from the state arsenal into position, that we got in one another's way. Others were ordered by Captain Isaac Willett, the *Chesapeake*'s commander, to pile bales of cotton from the cargo around the ship's engines and sides.

I gravitated toward the guns. The Seventh was an infantry outfit, and, except for one crewman, no one seemed to know much about their operation. Fortunately there was a sergeant in charge who knew his job. At my suggestion, we tripped the wheels so they wouldn't move with the ship, and rove ropes to check the guns on the recoil.

"Good for you, Scott. Give 'em hell!"

It was Mayor McLellan, who was about to depart. The words were barely out of his mouth when Captain Willett came up, a large, brisk man, followed by Colonel Mason, who looked very earnest and very important and wore a sword much too long for him.

"Have you any final instructions, sir?" Willett asked the mayor.

"Just these," McLellan barked. "Catch the scoundrels and hang every one of them!"

With that, he strode down the gangplank, which was drawn up immediately. The *Chesapeake*'s pilot held onto the whistle cord, and, our propeller thrashing the water white, we backed out into the Fore River to the cheers of the swarms of people on the docks. Soon we were throwing a tremendous billow of black smoke over the stern as the ship vibrated strongly and we leaped forward to the chase.

The excitement aboard was like that at a racetrack. No one seemed to know for sure whether Davenport had sailed off in the *Cushing* to join the Rebels, or the Rebels had somehow slipped into port and cut out the *Cushing*. Most seemed inclined to blame Davenport, but when I recalled the fishing schooner that had anchored not far away from her dock, and how the schooner's sails had been harbor-furled with a swiftness and neatness that was unlike the more deliberate movements and casual flaking of our Maine coast fishermen, I thought the chances better than even that men from the schooner had boarded the cutter in the night.

Hearing my name called, I went up to the pilothouse and climbed the ladder to its top where Willett, Mason, and several officers were standing and taking turns looking through Captain Willett's glasses.

"Lieutenant, I'm glad to see you keeping an eye on those guns," Willett said. "If they broke loose, they could play hell with my deck."

[249]

He introduced me to Colonel Mason, who said my uncle had published in the *Eastern Courier* an account of my early blockading duties and something of my experience with the *Alabama*. Willet then passed the glasses to me. "I'd appreciate your opinion as to what we should do, lieutenant. You can see the cutter now — there isn't enough of a breeze for her to make much headway."

I stared through the glasses. The *Caleb Cushing* was plainly in sight, bearing south-southeast from Portland Head Light. The *Forest City* was about three miles from her, the *Chesapeake* about six miles from Portland Head and seven from the *Cushing*.

I turned to Willett. "I don't think we have any real choice but to come up on her and find out what she intends to do. With steam, we have the advantage of maneuverability, but she has heavy cannon compared with our popguns, so let's not get too close."

"My idea exactly," said Willett.

We watched the scene for a few minutes longer. The *Forest City* was almost up to the *Cushing*. The *Tyger* we had long since passed, and we were now closing the distance rapidly.

Suddenly from the *Cushing*'s side came a flash and a puff of smoke.

"That means business," Captain Willett said. "Pilot, steer for her, and we'll run her down."

Not liking the thought of what the *Cushing*'s guns could do to us while we approached, I went forward to the brass field-pieces.

"Load both guns," I said, and when this was completed, I ordered the gunner to stand ready to fire the port gun.

"I think I could hit her, sir."

"Not at this distance."

"No, but pretty soon I think I could scare her."

"Let's wait for a while."

Again the cutter fired, then a third shot. This last brought the *Forest City* to a slowdown very quickly, and she lay to, evidently waiting for us to come up.

Once more, the *Cushing* fired. It was a ricochet that fortunately fell short of us, and a great laugh went up aboard the *Chesapeake*.

"There's a good man on that gun," our gunner admitted. "He had the right direction."

"He's too good," the sergeant growled. "Them fools can laugh, but if the next shot hits, they'll laugh out of their arseholes."

Once again, the cutter fired, with no better results.

Then Willett called out, "Pettigrew, give them a shot!"

The gunner and I bent over the port gun. "Take your time," I said. "When you're ready, stand clear and let her have it."

An eager young man, the gunner fired almost at once. He leaped upon the carriage, clapping his hands in delight, then groaned. Though a splendid line shot, it lacked distance. We were still too far away.

The *Forest City* now moving toward us, we slackened speed and let her come close enough so the officers aboard both steamers could decide on a course of action. I thought it strange the cutter didn't give both ships a broadside — she could have sunk us or damaged us severely. Finally, the officers agreed that the *Chesapeake* should ram the *Cushing*. Willett trumpeted to the *Forest City*, "We'll steer straight for her and run into her any way we can, and you can take what's left."

Colonel Mason then told everyone to keep cool and obey orders. The men cheered him, and from the *Forest City* three cheers came booming over the water.

The *Chesapeake* now picked up speed again, heading directly toward the *Cushing*. It looked to me as if we would hit her amidships. Then, to our astonishment, her deck suddenly swarmed with men. She dropped a boat crammed with them over the side, followed by another. Immediately afterward, she fired, and the grapeshot whistled all around us.

"Stand ready!" Mason ordered. "They intend to board us. No, by God, they've set the *Cushing* afire. Sink the devils!"

"There's a white flag in the near boat!" I shouted to Captain Willett.

He grabbed his trumpet. "Hold your fire! I'm not a pirate, to fire on a flag of truce!"

It was a close call. Someone in the first boat was waving a white handkerchief, and waving it frantically.

The *Chesapeake* rode in silence as the boats drew alongside, but it must have seemed ominous as their men looked up into a bristling array of muskets and pistols aimed at them. To us, however, there was nothing ominous about them, rather, something startling: they were Union sailors — the original crew of the *Cushing* — unarmed, some of them in irons, and all of them looking cast down. They scarcely said anything as we helped them aboard.

Davenport himself looked angry and hurt. "It's hard," he said, staring at us reproachfully, "after a man has been taken prisoner, ironed, and his life threatened by pirates, to be shot at by his own friends."

"Lieutenant," Willett said, "we didn't know if you were friends or enemies. Where are the Rebels?"

Davenport waved toward the *Forest City*, and, to a man, we followed his arm and watched the boats creeping toward the steamer.

"We'd better get over there and help," Mason said.

Davenport shook his head. "There's no need — they left their arms on the *Cushing*."

"Then let's try to save the cutter."

"Oh, no, sir, don't try that," one of the men said. "They set the fire to blow her up. They'd have sunk you if we'd told 'em how to get to the powder magazine, but no one did."

"Good for you," Willett said. "Now why don't you men go down to the galley and get something to eat?"

As they went below, we stared now at the burning cutter and now at the *Forest City* moving over toward us.

"We've got them all tied up," Lieutenant Merryman, Davenport's new superior officer, shouted. "It was Read and his crowd from the *Tacony*. Maybe we can save the cutter."

"The fire's got too big a start," Willett shouted back. "We'd better stay away from her."

So we stood off for a while until a few volunteers insisted that Willett let them have a boat to go put the fire out. Though he refused, Mr. Fox, the agent for the New York line, finally relented, and off they went on a fool's errand. When they saw it was hopeless, they tried to bring back the cutter's boat. The people on both steamers and the tug were now pleading with them to get out of the way of the blazing *Cushing*. At last they cut the boat loose and rowed mightily to reach the *Chesapeake*.

Suddenly there was a tremendous flash and a shattering roar, and the *Caleb Cushing* was blotted out in one great, swirling, black smoke cloud. Fragments of masts, spars, timbers, and shells blew hundreds of feet into the air and peppered the water in a wide radius, miraculously sparing the boat crew. The cutter's bow went under, then what was left of her lurched forward, and she went down in a violent hiss of steam.

No one said a word until Captain Willett, looking at his watch, remarked, "It's half-past two. Time we were getting back to town."

As a fleet of small craft sailed into the area, picking up debris from the explosion, both steamers headed for port.

On the way, the *Forest City* headed toward a strange schooner, which I recognized as the one that had entered Portland harbor last evening. When I mentioned this to Captain Willett, he swung the *Chesapeake* over toward the schooner. It proved to be the *Archer*, with three of the Confederates aboard, according to the *Forest City*; the schooner was ordered into Portland, with the *Tyger* to see that she got there. The *Forest City* and the *Chesapeake* then steamed for Portland.

[253]

As we entered the harbor, the forts fired salutes to which our six-pounders responded, church bells rang, and waves of cheering rolled up from the wharves and the eastern promontory, which were alive with people. One would have thought we had accomplished a tremendous feat. Well, we had, so far as swift organization of the pursuit was concerned, and the cooperation of the civilian and the military authorities. But the real credit for accomplishment, even though we couldn't concede it, belonged to Read, who attempted such a daring venture, cutting out the *Cushing* and taking her to sea past the guns of several forts. He had managed to get into the harbor, we learned, by capturing two Falmouth fishermen, Albert Bibber and Elbridge Titcomb, and forcing them to act as pilots. But he had released them before the fight, and the *Forest City* picked them up.

As soon as we landed, I went over to the *Forest City*'s wharf and watched the prisoners being herded together there by soldiers from the Seventeenth Infantry before being transferred to the *Casco* for imprisonment in Fort Preble. Read himself was a spirited young man, of medium height and spare build, who didn't appear too depressed. An officer of swift speech and energetic movement, he answered questions from Major Andrews of the Seventeenth, and Mayor McLellan, with promptness and courtesy. He rarely smiled, but who would, in his circumstances?

After I saw Collector Jewett speak with one of the fishermen Read had seized, Elbridge Titcomb, I drifted over to Titcomb, introduced myself, and remarked that he must feel relieved that his experience with Read was over.

Titcomb grinned, in a lopsided way. "I sure am, lieutenant. But he was decent to us, I've got to say that. We were off Damariscove Island in a dory. We'd left our trawls when this schooner came up, put a boat overside, and brought us on board. They looked like fishermen themselves, except for Read in his blue coat and pants, so we thought they were jokin' when

[254]

they said we were prisoners. They laughed a lot, you know, so we thought they were out for a good time. When they asked us to pilot them into Portland, Bibber and I didn't know just what to do. Still, they might just be what they said they were, so we felt we better do what they wanted."

"When were you certain they were Rebels?"

"When they armed themselves after the sun went down and locked us in the cabin."

"When did they let you out?"

"Right after they took the *Cushing*. They rowed over to her about half-past one, surprised the watch, and ordered everyone into the hold. Then they got us aboard to pilot them out of the harbor. There wasn't much wind for a while, so they had two boats towin' the *Cushing*. It was almost sunup when we cleared the forts, the tide was comin' in and the wind blowin' light. I still don't know how we got clear without bein' seen."

"Well, now you've got quite a story to tell your grandchildren, Mr. Titcomb."

He scratched his head. "I guess you're right, lieutenant, but I'd rather take home a doryful of fish than a story like this."

We laughed, and I turned away, but my good humor vanished when I heard the jeers and catcalls from the gathering crowd directed at the Rebels and the cries of "Hang the pirates!" They weren't pirates, and I was glad the troops had them under guard. Still, I could understand how the people felt, for word had quickly spread that Read had also intended, had there been time, to seize or destroy the steamers and set fire to the wharves and shipping. The whole city might have been consumed. Even so, the cries disturbed me, and I stared at the angry faces, particularly of the men, many of whom, I thought, for all Maine's sturdy contribution to the war, should be in uniform.

Then, to my amazement, I saw, back in the middle ranks of the crowd, a woman I instantly recognized as Tamara Ravenel.

XXV

I was about to cross over to meet Tamara when the prisoners were marched off between us, headed, flanked, and followed by soldiers from the Seventeenth Infantry. By the time the column had passed, she had disappeared. Questions as to where the lady with the blonde hair had gone earned me nothing but stares and shrugs.

I walked along Commercial Street but could see no one resembling her. After a long spell of waiting, I finally caught a cab and drove to each of the principal hotels, where I inquired of the desk clerk if a Miss Ravenel had registered. Though I had no real hope that she would be there under such a name, I used the question as an excuse to describe her. Two of the clerks I knew, and they tried to be helpful. Others gave me as little assistance as they could get away with. In the end, I returned home frustrated, annoyed, and curious.

That evening Uncle Jonathan came to dinner, and we talked long and late. But, when I went to bed, my thoughts touched only lightly on the principal events of the day. Instead, I kept asking myself what Tamara Ravenel could be doing in Portland. Though a busy little port, it was far removed from the war. Could she have had some connection with Read's raid? The longer I thought about this possibility, the less persuaded I was that any connection existed. The circumstances of his sweep up the coast and of his raid into the harbor were such that I could not envisage a role for her. But if her presence in Portland at the time of the raid was purely fortuitous, what brought her here? Where had she disappeared to?

I missed being able to discuss the problem of Tamara. Most of the generation I had grown up with in Portland were off to war, had moved to the West, or had married and were involved in their own domestic problems. I suppose I might have been able to talk about her with Uncle Jonathan, who would have been reasonably objective, I'm sure, but I hesitated to develop a subject that could be construed as more personal than I was willing to concede. It might have been more to the point, and easier, too, to go to the army's provost marshal in Portland or the sheriff or the mayor. She was, after all, an enemy. On the other hand, I could produce no evidence that could stand up in court. And if I did have such, I should probably have hesitated to use it until or unless I was convinced that what she was doing was of a life-or-death nature to the country and its citizens. Even in a sentimental country like our own, conviction on an espionage charge might mean death for a woman, though up to this point the Lincoln Administration had been lenient, as with young Belle Boyd and the reputedly beautiful Washington hostess Rose Greenhow, both of whom were conveyed from prison in Washington to the Confederate lines in the summer of 1862. But with feelings deepening as the war went on and bloodshed increased, there was no depending on the continuance of leniency.

For whatever purpose Tamara Ravenel was in Maine, I would have to be certain of the evidence and of the purpose and significance of her mission before I could take any action against her. But, admittedly, my bump of curiosity was as large about her presence here as about Roger Clavering's presence in New York City.

The next day, the minister at our church expressed in his pastoral prayer preceding the sermon his gratitude and thanks to the Deity for having spared the city from the fury of the raiders whose "criminal" efforts had been foiled by the patriotism, courage, and efficiency of the citizens of Portland. Had his parishioners been a "sanctioning" congregation, I am sure the church would have rung with fervent amens. Though I did not differ with the gist of the sentiment, I could not but reflect that what was criminal in the State of Maine would have been considered patriotic in Mississippi where Read was born.

That afternoon, Uncle Jonathan and I drove to Cape Elizabeth to spend a couple of days with Bradford and Ruth Dearborn, his son and daughter-in-law. The younger Dearborn, my Uncle Brad, farmed the old Dearborn property which still belonged to Grandmother Pettigrew. He was an earnest man who was a better reader than a farmer, and Aunt Ruth was a worrier, particularly over finances. Their daughter Clara, who taught school in Portland, was spending the summer with them. I was looking forward to seeing all of them again, but I would miss my cousin Jed, with whom I had spent many happy hours. Jed had enlisted in the army back in January.

My visit was not exactly a joyful reunion. All were glad enough to see me again, I think, especially Clara, who was tall and dark and thin enough to slip through a keyhole — I remember my grandmother saying to the Chief Justice years ago that it was probably the result of Aunt Ruth's poor cooking. But when Uncle Brad said, "I wish Jed had your luck to be home," what could I say in return? I hadn't been home for going on a year and a half, and Jed had been away for less than six months. On the other hand, Jed was in the army, and that was unquestionably a more dangerous service than the navy in this war: he was in the Fifth Maine, which was part of General Sedgewick's Sixth Corps in the Army of the Potomac.

My aunt kissed me and said she was happy I had recovered from my wound so nicely. She also told me she had prayed that that awful Semmes would spare me, when she had learned I was on the *Alabama.* "Someone ought to hang that man. He's a pirate."

"Oh, come, Mother," Clara said with an impatient shake of her head, "Semmes is no more a pirate than Grandpa was. And Lieutenant Read isn't a pirate, either."

"By golly, we had a pretty good view of that fight yesterday," Uncle Brad said. "You should've heard the dishes in Ruth's pantry rattle when the *Cushing* blew up. How about that, Ruth?"

"Oh, my, yes. Why, I had to take down the kitchen dishes in the pantry and every dish from my good set in the dining room to see if any were broken. Praise be, none were. We just couldn't afford another set now, what with Jed away and no money coming in from crops and Bradford still bringing home books."

"What's the latest, Brad?" Uncle Jonathan asked.

"A first edition of Adam Smith's *Wealth of Nations*. I bought it at a house auction a week ago. No one there seemed to know its value. Let me get it for you."

My uncle brought out the calfbound copy, which Uncle Jonathan and I admired, much to his pleasure. He had, in truth, a quite extraordinary library, which he enjoyed both collecting and reading. Where other men might spend their money on drink, he spent his on books, with the same result — his family often suffered. It was this sort of extravagance which made my aunt so money-conscious, which caused her to hide in several places known only to herself and Clara such money from the sale of butter, eggs, and milk as he left lying around the house or in his pants pockets.

After two days in the old farmhouse with its untroubled vista of the sea and surf-crested reefs and clumps of pines running down to rocks and sand, Uncle Jonathan said to me, "Scott, we're leaving today for Portland." The finality in his voice left no room for argument. Nor was I sorry to leave. Though I loved the house, the countryside, and the seascape, the tensions in the family made every meal a clashing of little daggers. Uncle Jonathan took refuge in silence and rested his hopes in Jed.

So, on Wednesday morning, we returned to Portland. Uncle Jonathan was silent for several miles, then he sighed deeply and said, "Scott, see if you can't get this sack of bones to go a little faster. I've a feeling General Lee and General Hooker are close to being rough with each other."

Before we returned to my grandfather's home, we stopped at the office of the *Eastern Courier*, Uncle Jonathan's paper. It was there we heard that General George Meade had replaced Hooker as commander of the Army of the Potomac and that elements of the two armies had tangled that very day at a cross-roads town in south central Pennsylvania called Gettysburg.

Those were exciting days. Reports were constantly coming over the telegraph wires, but were never full enough to satisfy the need for information. Crowds clustered around the newspaper offices and the railroad station, and papers were snapped up as soon as the newsboys appeared on the streets. The initial reports from Gettysburg alarmed everyone, since it appeared that, once again, the Army of the Potomac, in which were numerous Maine regiments, was doomed to defeat. Yet, somehow, Lee couldn't seem to get his way with Meade. At first people walked the streets as if to a funeral, depressed by the early battle accounts and the first fragmentary casualty lists. Then reports came through that though Sickles's Third Corps was cut to pieces, Vincent's brigade of Sykes's Fifth had stemmed Longstreet's attempt to take Little Round Top, with the Twentieth Maine and Colonel Joshua L. Chamberlain covering themselves with glory in saving the extreme left wing of the Union Army. The news was like an elixir to the people in the streets. And when we learned eventually that Pickett's great charge had been repulsed, cheers rippled through the city.

"We've got him, we've got Lee!" Uncle Jonathan exulted as he sat in his shirtsleeves at his office desk, bent over the telegram his operator had just brought him. "If only Meade will advance."

"Don't count Lee out," Grandfather said, sitting in a rocker and, despite the heat, looking immaculate and unrumpled in his dark gray suit. He could smoke a cigar with more grace than any man I ever saw, and he now pointed it delicately at Uncle Jonathan. "If Meade attacks, Lee may do to him what Meade did to Pickett. You don't realize that Meade's army is probably as badly cut up and disorganized as Lee's."

[260]

The Fourth of July passed with the usual accompaniment of firecrackers, parades, and speeches, but the celebration seemed restrained, and crowds again clustered, waiting for news from Pennsylvania.

When word arrived the next day that Lee was retreating, people began to realize that, though the Army of the Potomac had fought a defensive battle, it had won a great victory. But the mood for cheering vanished as reports came through of the enormous casualties. Even the news that Vicksburg had fallen and a Confederate army of thirty thousand had surrendered to Grant failed to touch off any wild rejoicing.

On the other hand, Vicksburg's surrender strongly affected Grandfather and Uncle Jonathan. When the telegram reached his desk, Uncle Jonathan read it quickly and passed it to Grandfather.

"This frees the Mississippi except for Port Hudson," Grandfather said.

"And that's bound to fall in a week or two at most. Brad, that'll mean the Confederacy will be cut in half."

"And, with Lee defeated, I think the South will have to go on the defensive everywhere. They'll be hard to beat, Jonathan, but I think the end has started."

A pleasant bit of news arrived for me that afternoon, in the form of a letter from Bruce Thornton's father inviting me to visit them whenever I could and stay as long as I cared. With my leave slipping away, I decided to go early the next morning on the cars, and I wired the Thorntons when I would arrive. Pat drove me to the station, my grandfather's last words as I stepped into the carriage being to be sure to look over the battlefield in Hampden where he and Uncle Jonathan had vainly tried with the local militia and sailors from the *John Adams* to stem the redcoat charge back in 1814.

I arrived in Hampden in the late afternoon. I did not know just what to expect, but I thought of a small farm and of a prototype of so many of our Maine farmers — a lean, rather silent man who had torn a living from the soil and probably showed it in his face and walk. Instead, a vigorous, stocky man of medium height, wearing a dark suit and hat met me, shook my hand warmly, and boomed me a welcome. We climbed into his freshly painted black carriage drawn by a beautifully curried gray horse.

"By George, Kate and I have hoped to meet you ever since Bruce and Sal wrote to say you'd gone off on the *Alabama*. I said to Kate, 'He'll be lucky to get off that ship alive!' She agreed, of course. Why shouldn't she? I'm sure it was true."

And so it went, the fierce flow of speech, the asking and the answering of his own questions. Surprisingly, Noah Thornton was not at all boring. When I mentioned that Grandfather and Uncle Jonathan had been present at the battle of Hampden, he plunged into an account of that encounter as seen through his own eyes as a small boy. The road we were on went straight through a portion of the battlefield, and he had a glorious time pointing out where this and that incident occurred.

When we drove up to his house, what rose before me was a great, sprawling mansion of the early Federal period, all white paint and green shutters; a huge barn, tidily kept, and men working in the fields in back of the house and on the sides of the driveway. It was haying season, and one rack was piled high with sweet-smelling clover and timothy, while another, having discharged its load, headed down toward the fields. This, then, was an estate, but I began to suspect that even these extensive holdings, at least for Maine, could not begin to support such evidence of success. Mr. Thornton must have other sources of income, I decided, and I recalled Uncle Jonathan's mention of timberlands.

Mrs. Thornton was slightly taller than her husband and considerably less ample. But she was no shrinking female. She had firm opinions which she did not hesitate to express; she would watch and listen, her brown eyes lively and interested, but with a word here and there, she gave one the impression of being a full participant in a conversation. For all his voluble confidence, Noah Thornton turned, time and again, for support and confirmation to his Kate.

We talked of many things during supper and the long evening when we walked around part of the farm. Foremost, of course, was their children.

"Bruce is doing work he wanted to," Mr. Thornton said, "but I think he realizes it's not easy to move from the consular to the diplomatic services. A man needs to know the right people."

"Mr. Adams is impressed with him," I said.

"But is Seward? Is Lincoln?"

"Noah, how could they know of someone like Bruce?" his wife protested. "Now, I ask you!"

"Give them time," Mr. Thornton said. "Just give them time."

He smiled, and we turned to the war, then to what I would like to do the next day. Before I could even say that I had nothing particular in mind except to visit with them, he asked, "Would you like to go down to Castine? I've an absentee neighbor there who has stalled on selling me a field. We could catch the cars to Belfast and take the ferry over. While I'm talking with my man, you could look around and see where your ancestors fought."

I said I'd like that. He didn't ask if I had been there before, and I didn't tell him I had, for it had been years ago, and I'd enjoy walking around the town again.

So it happened that the next morning, we were up early and caught the southbound train, getting off at Belfast. It was a busy little port, with two or three ships being built. The ferry to Castine was scarcely more than a small tub, and there were fewer than a dozen passengers aboard, including ourselves. The skipper — an old man with tobacco juice staining his whiskers, whom people addressed as "Captain Jenkins" — was cheerful as

[263]

he threaded his way through incredibly thick river traffic. Most of this consisted of schooners in ballast going up the Penobscot to Bangor, and others, almost awash with the lumber stacked on their decks, heading downriver for the open sea.

"Castine's a quiet place nowadays," Captain Jenkins said. "She's been goin' downhill for years before the war. Bad idea when they moved the courts away, back about 'forty. Built a lot of ships up to 'fifty, an' had 'round two thousand people. Now they drift away every year. Nothin' to do, you see. Oh, a little shippin' an' shipbuildin', but not much. Not much business at all. Bangor gets all of that, or most — what's left over goes to Bucksport an' Brewer on this side of the river."

"When I was a boy, it used to be a mighty busy place," Mr. Thornton said. "During the British occupation, its customs house was the busiest in Maine."

Captain Jenkins laughed, and the sound came through the gaps in his teeth like a wet hiss. "Those were the days! No one was supposed to trade with the British in Castine, but they sure did. They used to run a stage from clear over in Hallowell in the Kennebec country every day. Cargoes came across the river at night. Castine's goin' down, I tell you, way down, an' with Semmes an' all them pirates loose, there ain't goin' to be much left."

When we drew into the Bagaduce River and headed for the main dock, just a handful of ships could be seen. One was a little white sloop, the *Swallow*, out of Portland, according to the legend on its stern.

"That's a handsome little craft," Mr. Thornton said, nodding toward the *Swallow*.

"Sure is," Captain Jenkins said. "She come in here late yesterday an' goes out today. To the east'ard."

"How do you know?"

"Lord sake's alive, I asked its skipper when I was leavin' here this morning. Won't know nothin' if you don't ask."

As we made for our dock, we passed a brig unloading salt that was so like the Maine brig whose mate I had warned of Semmes's escape from Fort de France that I had to give her a long second look before realizing she wasn't the same.

Ashore, Mr. Thornton went his way and I, mine, both of us agreeing we should meet down at the little restaurant on the pier. It didn't look promising, but we had resisted Mrs. Thornton's urging to take a dinner basket along.

I strolled around the few streets, gazing at the many splendid houses, a number of which were beginning to look dilapidated. I inspected the ruins of Fort George, from which my Uncle Jonathan escaped with the great privateersman Captain Vail in 1814. Then I cut down close to the water to see the house where Grandmother's mother, Betsy Morris, had hidden a privateer captain, Tom Dearborn, her future husband, who had led a storming party against the British during the siege in the Revolution. Afterward, I worked my way along the shore to the point on the bay from where Tom had swum out to the American fleet. I admired the view down the bay between Cape Rosier and Long Island, across the wide reach to Belfast, and down to the southwest where rose the high, misty hills of Camden. It was a beautiful vista, and the white sails of the ships in the bay and river and the trailing smoke of several steamers, one of which was headed up toward Castine, provided a certain animation which added to my appreciation of the view.

"I didn't know that you were such a devotee of nature, Mr. Pettigrew."

I turned sharply to the right where I had started to go even before I heard the voice. Then I saw her, seated at an easel, the sun bright on the blonde hair that escaped the blue bonnet. She was half hidden by a roll of the land, but in another moment, I should have discovered her, anyway. In fact, as I approached her, I had a feeling that I had surprised her almost as soon as she had surprised me, that she had spoken in order to cover a momentary confusion.

[265]

"Oh, I admire nature, Miss Ravenel. But I wasn't aware that landscape painting was among your accomplishments."

"I have no great talent at it, I must confess."

She gave me her hand, and I sat down beside her as she wiped her brushes and prepared to put her materials away.

"Please don't stop now that I'm here," I said. "Just ignore me and keep right on."

She flashed me an odd sort of glance from under her long eyelashes. "Would you like to see what I've painted?"

I already had. Though with no true appreciation of art, I could see that she had painted a rather accurate reproduction of the immediate coastline. What struck me, however, was that the view was toward the land rather than toward the sea, that the topography of the land was remarkably clear, and that the painting represented more than what could be seen from this particular vantage point.

"Very pretty," I said.

"Pretty! That's a damning adjective."

"Then let me say I am impressed by your eye for accuracy and your use of color."

"That's better."

"I'm glad. I hardly expected ever to see you this far north, Miss Ravenel. Isn't this dangerous country for a Rebel like yourself?"

She was silent for a moment. "You might think so, of course," she finally admitted. "It might indeed be dangerous if I were. Now let me ask you what you are doing in this forsaken little place."

"I'm visiting friends," I said, "and looking over this town where my ancestors fought. Now, Miss Ravenel, are you here because you are entranced by the beauty of the area? And weren't you in Portland when Read and his crew were captured?"

She shook her head. "I wasn't even in Maine then. But what a blessing to Maine shipping that he was captured."

"Yes, it was, and it will be a greater blessing when Semmes and the *Alabama* are captured, too."

"I doubt that will be so easy — you should know from your service on the *Alabama*. . . . Oh, dear, my escorts are coming, so I must hurry and leave you."

Her voice had grown light and gay again, and I followed her gaze toward the water. Two men in a small boat were nearing the shore. I helped her collapse her easel and carried it and her paintbox to the beach.

As one of the men took the materials, Tamara turned to me. "You'll carry me through all these nasty rocks and wet sand, won't you, Mr. Pettigrew?"

She seemed almost weightless, and was fragrant with an elusive perfume. Once I slipped, and she clasped me close, and at her touch I felt warmer than the heat of the day warranted. When I was about to place her in the boat, she kissed me on the lips. As the boat headed back into the harbor, she waved, and I waved back. Then I started on the long return walk to the pier. I had gone but a short distance when I saw the sloop *Swallow* pick up Tamara and the oarsmen and, trailing the boat from the stern, steer down to the East Passage between Long Island and Cape Rosier.

After lunch, as Noah Thornton and I waited for the ferry back to Belfast and watched the little Rockland steamer leave, I told him much of what I knew about Tamara Ravenel and Roger Clavering.

"Then you do believe that she's a Rebel spy?"

"She was hardly a spy in England," I said. "She was an agent, rather, helping procure ships and arms for the South. What she was before that on this side of the Atlantic I don't know. What she is right now baffles me, but her painting certainly revealed a good deal about the Castine coastline. If you want a straight-forward answer to your question, it's no. But I am suspicious."

Mr. Thornton scuffed his feet. "But, Scott, there must be

enough charts of the Maine coast available in the South. The Richmond government must surely have a number."

"Of course, but the charts are of the approaches and the water levels, not of the land itself."

"And you think the *Swallow* may be headed down the coast for Miss Ravenel to do some more painting?"

"We have only Captain Jenkins's statement that someone on the *Swallow* said they were going down east. If that is true, and we have no way of confirming it, it's likely Miss Ravenel will, as you say, do some more painting."

"But to be afraid of a young woman painting the land and the sea and the sky!" Mr. Thornton laughed heartily.

"I know it sounds ridiculous, but it's thanks, in part, to people like her that the South is able to find the means to continue fighting."

"But why, Scott, why in Heaven's name should the Richmond people want this done? Are they thinking of invading the State of Maine when they have practically no navy to speak of — no oceangoing navy — and we have hundreds of ships?"

"It doesn't make sense to me, either, not at the moment, anyway."

"No, it certainly doesn't. I think your imagination is working overtime, Scott."

At this, I became stubborn. "Mr. Thornton, my experience in war hasn't been extraordinarily extensive, but I've already learned that a lot of things are accomplished that appear to make no sense at first and may indeed look impossible. It appeared most unlikely that Semmes could take the *Alabama* out of Fort de France with the *San Jacinto* cruising off the harbor entrance. It seemed to make no sense for Semmes to put his head into the lion's mouth by going so near Galveston to sink the Union transports, but if the Rebels hadn't recaptured the city, General Banks's transports would have been there and Semmes would certainly have sunk a number of them. And would you have thought that Lieutenant Read with twenty sailors and one popgun could have sailed the *Tacony* up the Atlantic seaboard, capturing as many merchant ships as he did, with over two dozen Union men-of-war trying to find him? Would you have believed beforehand that he could have entered Portland harbor, captured the cutter *Caleb Cushing* from under the guns of the forts, and got her to sea?"

"What's to be done, if all you say is true?"

"Do you have friends in any of the towns down on the coast?"

When he said that he had friends in many towns but especially in Bar Harbor, Winter Harbor, Steuben, Jonesport, and Machias, I said, "I'd be grateful if you would get in touch with them as soon as you can and ask them to keep an eye open for the *Swallow* and any artists painting along the coast."

"They'll think me a fool," he frowned, "but I'll chance it. I'll get telegrams off to some as soon as we reach Belfast, and I'll write to others this evening. . . . Well, here comes Jenkins and his ferry. Let's compose that damned telegram on the way over to Belfast, and the letter on the train home."

XXVI

DESPITE the substantial difference in views between Noah Thornton and myself, my visit to the Thorntons went off nicely. To my surprise, I found Kate Thornton on my side. The more I told her of Tamara, the more she bristled. Though no shrinking violet herself, she seemed mistrustful of aggressive women, and she considered Tamara aggressive. His wife's support of my suspicions clearly relieved Noah, and when she helped recast the model letter to his friends that he and I had contrived, in order to give it a more personal and less apologetic note, he began to evince a real interest in what the replies would contain.

After two more days following the Castine trip, I left for

Portland, Mr. Thornton agreeing to write me at my Washington address as to the results of his queries. I parted with a conviction that I left two good friends behind.

In Portland, I made a final check on the gunboats, paid my respects to Mayor McLellan and Collector Jewett, and arranged my plans for passage to New York on the *Chesapeake*. Though I had enjoyed my leave, I was looking forward to a return to duty. The fact that my cousin Jed had been present at Gettysburg, even if his regiment took no significant part, made me yearn for something more active than a desk routine.

Before the *Chesapeake* sailed for New York on Sunday evening, accounts were coming in over the telegraph wire of bad feeling developing among crowds of men in New York City, where the draft had started on Saturday and was to get under way in earnest on Monday morning.

"I don't know what we'll be getting into when we land," Captain Willett of the *Chesapeake* said to me while we were waiting for other passengers to come aboard. "Maybe you passengers won't want to go ashore right away." As he turned to his duties, I realized that the situation in New York might become very serious.

The trip was uneventful. Double lookouts were posted for raiders, but there was no knowledge at the time, not even a rumor, that any were off the coast. The captain, however, was taking no chances. I presumed that because of my part in the capture of Read, the *Chesapeake*'s officers and such members of the crew as I encountered went out of their way to be cordial, Captain Willett asking me to have a nightcap with him before I turned in. The result was that the run to New York, which I hadn't looked forward to, was surprisingly enjoyable.

But as we drew near the North River docks on Tuesday afternoon, one could feel the tension growing among both passengers and crew. Smoke from fires was rising from several parts of the city. We could clearly hear the distant clangor of fire bells. Ferryboats were crowded with people leaving Manhattan. Gunboats were patrolling the waterfront; one had anchored off the Battery, its guns trained shoreward. When we docked, people shouted to us not to land, and waved bills in an effort to get the *Chesapeake*'s captain to take them to the Jersey shore. Most of our passengers remained aboard, but I thought I could at least try to get to a hotel for the night; I was very curious as to what was happening.

Once ashore, I found it impossible to find a cab. I saw none of the horsecars running, and I had just about decided to try to get back aboard the *Chesapeake* when a van filled with police and sailors stopped and a voice sang out, "Want a ride, lieutenant?" As I ran toward the van with my valises, a naval officer stepped down and proffered his hand.

"Scott Pettigrew!" he said.

I recognized Jim Hunt, who had been in training with me in Newport and was now on Admiral Paulding's staff in New York. A sailor quickly handed my valises into the van, while Jim, also a lieutenant, drew me inside.

"We're in something of a hurry," he said. "Where are you bound?"

"As a matter of fact, I don't know," I said. "Wherever I can find a hotel room."

"We're headed for the St. Nicholas. It's Governor Seymour's headquarters, and there have been reports it may be attacked, so we've been sent to reinforce the guards there. Why don't you get a room there if you can, stow your bags, and join us? We can use every man we can get."

He introduced me to the police sergeant, a burly man named Winters. The sergeant told me I'd better arm myself with a pistol and a police club. I said I'd take the club and leave the pistol in my valise.

"You'd better change your mind, lieutenant," Winters said. "That mob has plenty of snipers."

At the St. Nicholas I found a room on one of the lower

[271]

floors. I also found the place swarming with guards, most of them civilians who had volunteered to help the police.

"It looks peaceful enough here," I said.

Jim nodded. "At the moment, but attacking that mob is like trying to pick up quicksilver."

The hotel management sent sandwiches and coffee out to us as we patrolled the streets, and while waiting for whatever might happen, Jim told me something of what had occurred.

In New York there had been increasing resentment against the influx of Negroes on the part of the foreign population, especially the Irish, who comprised about one quarter of the eight hundred thousand or so people in Manhattan. Labor troubles had been breaking out ever since the start of the year, when longshoremen's daily wages were reduced from $1.50 to $1.12. There had been several strikes, and in each case — the last as recent as June — Negroes under police guard had been brought in to take the strikers' jobs. Most of these longshoremen were Irish, and the Negroes suffered severely whenever the strikers could lay their hands on them. The Draft Act seemed to the Irish a policy designed to force them to fight for the freedom of Negroes who would simply take the bread out of their mouths.

"You have to remember, too," said Hunt, "that Governor Seymour is a Democrat and opposed to the draft as unconstitutional. He tried to quiet the rioters by telling them he thought the draft ought to be suspended. Congressman Fernando Wood is a real rabble-rouser. Most of his constituents are Irish. Then there's been the copperhead press, especially the *Daily News*, thumping away at the draft. Granted, the draft has that money-exemption clause, but the protests from many come pretty close to treason. And, if you ask me, there's some Rebel money in this somehow and Rebel leaders, too."

"Rebel leaders?"

"I'm certain. Damn it, there's a Virginian named John Andrews, an avowed Secessionist, who's been riding around on a gray horse, egging the rioters on. He did it before they started rioting, and he's been doing it since. I saw him once at it."

"Anyone else?"

"They've found one dead man, a leader, who was obviously disguised. He was quite young and definitely no longshoreman."

"Is that all, just two?"

"Well, there's been talk of others, of course," Jim said. "Good God, Scott, you know how rumors can fly at a time like this. But, for what it's worth, some police detective told Sergeant Winters he saw a tall man in a black suit talking with John Andrews in the lobby of the United States Hotel last week, and just yesterday after the rioters burned the Colored Orphan Asylum. The odd thing was, according to the detective, the man in black was really mad that the rioters were concentrating on the Negroes instead of the draft officers and the police."

"Haven't they been after the draft officers and the police at any time?"

"At first. You see, last Saturday morning Provost Marshal Jenkins in the Ninth District stood up in his office at Forty-sixth Street and Third Avenue and started the draft rolling. There was a drum with thousands of little papers in it, and his assistant was blindfolded and ordered to draw out the names. The first was that of one William Jones. Everyone laughed when the name was read, and some smart aleck pulled out a bandanna, wiped his eyes, and said, 'Poor Willie!' Of course, everyone howled all the louder. Eventually the name of an alderman was called, and someone shouted, 'There's three hundred dollars for sure!' It was all good fun, you know. But over the weekend, hundreds of men learned they were drafted. They got to thinking and drinking, and started listening to Andrews and others, and it didn't seem so funny. Result? When Jenkins read a number of names on Monday, someone shot off a pistol, others threw bricks and stones into the room, and soon the draft officials and the police were fighting for their

[273]

lives. They got out just before someone poured kerosene on the floor and set the place afire. When the fire department arrived, the mob wouldn't let them near until it was too late."

"Was it like this all over the city?"

"Not everywhere, but in enough places so that the police had to call on the army and navy for help. The Superintendent of Police, Kennedy, was beaten and dragged through filth, and is barely living now. The police at Forty-third Street and Third Avenue were badly handled by the mob, and a company of the army's Invalid Corps was mauled coming up Third Avenue. They were hunted down like dogs. Several hundred sailors came in last night at midnight from their ships and the Brooklyn Navy Yard, and General Harvey Brown, who has taken over the defense of the city, has sent all over the East for help. Trouble is, many of the New York regiments are off with Meade's army."

"How large is the mob?"

"Commissioner Acton, who took over from Kennedy, estimates over fifty thousand, but he said it may range as high as seventy thousand. They've sacked mansions, they've hanged and burned Negroes, they've fought soldiers on Delancey Street and marines on Pitt Street. Colonel O'Brien of the Eleventh New York Volunteers was beaten to death today near Thirty-fourth and Second Avenue. Right now there's terrific fighting on Eighth Avenue north from Forty-third for several blocks, and on First Avenue, from Eleventh to Fourteenth streets."

"How many men with the law?"

"Maybe a couple of thousand. Plus civilian volunteers. Even so, those regiments better get here in a hurry, or this city won't be worth looking at by the end of the week."

But by morning we learned that though Meade was sending thousands of troops north, with some already en route from Pennsylvania and the railroad tracks cleared all the way for their trains, none had arrived. We heard, too, that on Wednesday the aldermen and the city council passed a bill authorizing funds from which the city would grant three hundred dollars to each man drafted, to enable him to avoid service in the army. Mayor George Opdyke vetoed it, and I heard many citizens speak warmly of him for doing so and for his explanation that he felt he would be buying the peace of the city at too dear a price to submit this way to the dictates of the mob.

Meanwhile, controlling most of his precincts through telegraphic connection from police headquarters, Commissioner Acton, thanks to the cooperation of General Brown, sent detachments of police wherever they were needed. Along with them went troops, marines, and sailors if necessary. The group I was with was suddenly detached late on Wednesday afternoon and sent along with many others to Nineteenth Street and First Avenue. In the morning, a mob of thousands had been dispersed at Thirty-second and Seventh Avenue by artillery. They had gathered again, with reinforcements at Nineteenth and First.

Unfortunately — or perhaps fortunately — we didn't get there in time. The main force sent to drive them off was a small infantry detail under Colonel Cleveland Winslow, supported by two howitzers under Colonel Edward Jardine. As we hurried up from a distance, we heard the crash of the howitzers and the unceasing crack of musketry. Flashes from the rooftops revealed the rioters firing down on the soldiers. Evidently considering the battle hopeless with not enough men to enter the houses and rout the rioters from the roofs, Winslow must have ordered a retreat. It may have been a wise move, but it was the signal for the rioters to swarm out of the buildings by the hundreds and drive the soldiers in flight down Nineteenth Street. Though there were uniformed dead and wounded left on the street, we had no recourse but to pull back ourselves to avoid being overrun. But as we did so, a mounted man appeared where Nineteenth crosses First Avenue, and waved an arm imperiously. At once another wave of rioters, brandishing clubs and muskets, set off toward us. The light was not very bright among the buildings, and I was not close enough to be certain, but I could have sworn the mounted man was Roger Clavering.

"Is he your man in black?" I shouted to Jim Hunt as we turned and ran.

"I don't know. I only heard about him from Sergeant Winters."

We made it back to safety, Hunt reported the result to police and army headquarters, and we sat down to wait until reinforcements arrived. Meanwhile, the mob, we heard, was busy chasing down Negroes and burning their houses.

Halfway through the evening, a young man named Leonard raced to the St. Nicholas and, between gasps, told us how his sister Ellen had hidden Colonel Jardine, a wounded soldier, and the regimental surgeon who had assisted Jardine and the soldier in the Leonard house. Leonard himself had managed to reach the St. Nicholas by climbing over the rooftops of several houses until he was far enough away from the action to go down to the street and run. The mob, however, was searching the houses, one by one, for the fugitives, so it was only a question of time before the men would be discovered.

Hunt sent off this information, too, and received word that a large police detail and a company of regulars with two pieces of artillery were on the way. A mixed force from the St. Nicholas then marched out to join them.

This time, when the mob heard us approaching and took to the buildings as before, the army commander turned the guns on the buildings, sending the rioters flying down to the street. The small force of infantry then cleared the street with the bayonet and released the prisoners. The surgeon had been badly beaten and Jardine had escaped death by telling rioters who had threatened to shoot him that he was dying, anyway, from the loss of blood. While our group carried the survivors back to the St. Nicholas, the troops remained on guard.

It was after midnight when we returned to the hotel. We then learned that while we were on this foray, the Seventy-fourth Regiment had arrived, with the Sixty-fifth, a Buffalo regiment, shortly afterward. This was reassuring, but it raised our numbers only by a thousand at most.

That night, when word reached us that the rioters were organizing more efficiently so that they could attack simultaneously in different places of the city, we found out that the police and the army had also reorganized. Separate headquarters and reserves were set up in Harlem and in the Eighteenth, Twenty-sixth, and Twenty-ninth Precincts, instead of all forces being sent out from the common headquarters on Mulberry Street. This would save long marches and expedite action. But for emergencies a general reserve was stationed in Mulberry Street. Though the cars had started again on Third and Eighth avenues and stores had reopened, thanks to action already taken and to the new organization, terrific fighting broke out during the night on Greenwich Street near a government warehouse which contained twenty thousand muskets. Had not police and troops arrived in time, the result could have been a disaster for the city. As it was, fires still raged through the night.

Few of us had much sleep that night, expecting emergency summons at almost any hour. Then, when I was dozing off, Hunt shook me awake.

"Come outside and listen."

"Where do we go this time?"

It was still early, but the sky was beginning to look less dark as I went outdoors. The sentries, usually patrolling, were standing and listening. So now did I.

"Jesus, ain't that a sweet sound!" one of them said. It was. From the distant waterfront came the thunderous beat of many drums and an occasional bugle call. Soon an officer, a young lieutenant, galloped up, flung himself off his horse, and dashed for the hotel.

"Where's the governor?" he demanded.

"He's probably sleeping," Hunt replied, "but he won't be for long."

The officer, who at first seemed offended, finally smiled. "I've got good news. The Tenth and Fifty-sixth New York are on Broadway, the Seventh is due here in a few minutes, and there are eight more regiments on the way. General Brown sent me to inform the governor."

"He'll be glad to hear this," Jim replied. "So are we. We'll need all the troops you have."

Soon they arrived, a long serried column of blue infantry marching in perfect step to the throbbing, urgent beat of their drums — the Seventh New York. By the time they grounded arms in front of the St. Nicholas, the hotel was ablaze with lights and the windows filled with cheering people, almost hysterical in their relief. Yet I wondered whether this regiment, containing so many dandies from New York society, could deal effectively with street fighting in their own city.

Neither I nor anyone who may have wondered as I did was long in finding out. For if anyone thought the arrival of so many troops would immediately intimidate the rioters, he was mistaken. Even before their arrival, a small force had been sent to disperse a group of rioters who, greatly reinforced, drove the soldiers into Jackson's Foundry at Second Avenue and Twenty-eighth Street. When the besieged called for assistance, more troops were dispatched, but these could not disperse the mob, either. Then the Seventh Regiment moved in force, and the rioters fled. But when the Seventh returned, the rioters reassembled on Twenty-ninth Street. The force that General Brown now ordered against them ran into a killing fire from rioters in the street and on the rooftops, armed with muskets and pistols. Losing several of their number, including a sergeant who was left dead on the street, the soldiers fell back.

It was at this point that orders came from General Brown and Commissioner Acton for all available men to move into the area. It was close to midmorning before Hunt's and Winters's group joined the powerful force of police and soldiers. But we

[278]

wasted no time once we arrived. The military commander announced to the mob that he intended to remove the sergeant's body. They made no attempt to interfere until his men had placed the body in a wagon. Then they surged forward, shouting and shooting.

With great coolness the soldiers unlimbered their battery of field artillery and swept the streets with a blast of grapeshot. The rioters, however, darted into the buildings to join many of their comrades already there, and fired down from the windows and the rooftops. At first, the military opened up on the buildings with the artillery. When this failed to check the rioters, police and soldiers were ordered into the buildings on both sides of the street while other troops held the street clear.

The men with Hunt and Winters dashed up the stairs of a house on the right side of the street. Instead of opposing us in the rooms, the rioters sought to check us on the landings. Several shots sent them scurrying for the roof. In fact, it was on the rooftops that much of the hand-to-hand fighting occurred. Men would fight, flee to the next roof, and turn and fire at anyone trying to jump the narrow space between buildings, then flee again. It was dangerous, exhausting work, pursuing them, let alone struggling with them. In the hand-to-hand encounters the police were much more skillful with their truncheons than the sailors.

My one personal contribution came when Sergeant Winters and I had three men pressed into the corner of a rooftop. The man I swung at eluded me and ran. The sergeant, on the other hand, was struggling with a big rioter who was trying to wrench his club from him. The third rioter, evidently not noticing that my own antagonist had fled, raised a massive club to bring it down on Winters's head. Had he succeeded, Winters's skull would have broken like a melon, as had happened to a poor Negro we had seen dead in the street. But luckily I brought my own truncheon down on the man's arm with all my force. His weapon dropped to the street, and, clutching his arm, he leaped across to the adjoining building.

Many of the police and soldiers, having cleared the roofs, turned back down into the buildings, catching rioters on the stairways and in the narrow halls. Here it was a case of the clubbed musket of the soldier against the clubbed musket of the rioter, pistol against pistol, and police truncheon against club. The rioters fought so ferociously, it seemed they preferred to die — and many of them did die — rather than surrender. In the end, they were forced to yield or flee, if they could, numbers later being found hiding in closets and under beds. As I saw the houses they lived in, dark filthy lodgings for which they paid an exorbitant rent to absentee landlords, I experienced a feeling of horror at the life they had been forced to endure.

When I finally reached the street again, I was practically sobbing for breath. I had a lump on the back of my head, and my jacket was nearly torn from my back.

Hunt appeared but a moment or two later and looked even worse, with blood streaming from a cut over his eye. As I helped him bind a handkerchief around his forehead, he said with a grimace of pain, "I think I'd rather fight the Rebs than these birds again. Just look at that street."

It certainly looked like a battleground, with the bodies of soldiers and rioters littering its surface, the piles of bricks and masonry brought down by the cannon fire, the glass from broken bottles and windowpanes glittering in the light, smoke rising from burning buildings, and swarms of rioters being rounded up. The battle itself — for it was scarcely less than that, with fifteen soldiers killed and many wounded, and larger casualties among the mob — appeared about over in this area. The mob seemed to realize that they had at last met a force capable of dealing with them. Suddenly they began to break up.

But they did not do so before a man in a black suit on a black horse rode through them and pointed them toward another street. Just then a twelve-pounder went off near us, and its smoke obscured our view. By the time the smoke had cleared, the column of rioters was running down the street like a swiftly flowing river, and horse and rider had disappeared.

XXVII

WHEN I returned to Washington, I found the city bathed in humidity and Secretary Welles suffering from a summer cold, with occasional spells of chills and fever, and feeling generally at a low ebb. I was back at my multifarious and inconsequential duties again for several days before Mr. Welles, accompanied by one of his bureau chiefs, Mr. Faxon, passed down a row of desks one afternoon and stopped at mine, a makeshift affair of cracker boxes, like many of the others.

"Pettigrew, I see you're back on the job," he said pleasantly. "Make an appointment to see me tomorrow, won't you? But not in the morning, please."

When I entered Mr. Welles's office late the next afternoon, he was busy signing a batch of letters. After his secretary removed these for mailing, Welles turned to me.

"That was a good report on the gunboats, Pettigrew. Now tell me about the *Cushing* affair."

I told him about that experience, bringing out details that I assumed the official reports would not have mentioned. I noted especially the cooperation among military and naval personnel and civilians.

He sighed when I finished. "I wish there were more evidence of such cooperation right here in Washington." He was silent for a moment, his head cupped in his hands as if he were half asleep, and I knew he was alluding to the constant strain between the Navy Department and the War Department, not to mention the State Department. "Pettigrew," he finally said, "how's your Uncle Jonathan's health?"

"He's fine, sir, thank you. He sent his best wishes to you and wanted me to assure you that he and many others in Maine appreciate what you're going through." I handed him an editorial from Uncle Jonathan's paper.

Welles grunted and leaned back in his chair while he read. "I'm grateful," he said when he finished. "You have no idea the pressure I've been under from New Englanders and New Yorkers to station a warship of some sort, especially a monitor, in every port. The *Tacony* really scared the shipping interests. Your Vice President from Maine — Hannibal Hamlin — your Maine senators, Senator Wilson from Massachusetts, Governor Andrew of Massachusetts — these and others have been after me. If I did that, or if I sent squadrons all over the world after the *Alabama* and the *Florida*, I'd be criticized for not stiffening the blockade. As it is, I'm always criticized for letting so many blockade runners through. I should be immune to criticism now, but I suppose I'm not. Of course, I criticize, too. Do you realize what an opportunity General Meade lost in not pursuing Lee? He listened to his generals and took their advice. After the cabinet meeting a week ago, the President caught up with me as I was returning to the department. 'What does it mean, Mr. Welles?' he asked. 'Great God! what does it mean?' He was all for a vigorous pursuit by Meade. Didn't your Uncle Jonathan know Meade's father?"

"Yes, sir, he first met him in Spain."

"Well, Meade has stout virtues, but the command of an army may be too much for him. I asked the President if General Halleck shouldn't have been up to the front to advise and encourage Meade. After all, Halleck was only four hours from Meade. You've seen Halleck, haven't you?"

"Yes, sir. I believe they call him 'Old Brains.' "

"Rubbish! He's general-in-chief, but he is so inferior to the President in both judgment and will that I advised Mr. Lincoln to issue orders to Meade himself. But the President respects Halleck's knowledge, so always defers to him. I tell you, Pettigrew, Halleck originates nothing and anticipates nothing. He takes no responsibility, plans nothing, suggests nothing, is good for nothing. His being here in Washington is a national misfortune."

He stopped suddenly, as if aware he had said too much, and went to a window and stared out, pounding his hands together.

I felt sorry for him. Everyone in the department knew he was trying to get the War Department to send reinforcements to General Gillmore, who was attempting to take Battery Wagner on Morris Island down in Charleston harbor. Under cover of a heavy fire from Admiral Dahlgren's monitors, Gillmore had assaulted Wagner on the 18th of July but had been repulsed. Among the dead was Colonel Robert Gould Shaw who led the 54th Massachusetts in a charge, the first Negro regiment from a free state to see action. Halleck now had doubts about sending reinforcements and didn't know where he could get them.

Still, that Welles should say so much to me, a very junior officer, was startling. I could only attribute it to the obvious fact that he had to confide in someone or explode, so numerous and exasperating were his frustrations.

"Pettigrew," he said, walking back to his desk, "when you were in Maine, did you hear that the *Florida* was taking prizes off New York while Read was cutting out the *Cushing?*"

"And you know, of course, that she exchanged shots with the gunboat *Ericsson* off Nantucket on July eighth?"

"I read about it, sir."

"Well, luckily for the *Ericsson*, which was outgunned, a fogbank appeared, and contact was broken off. The last we heard of the *Florida*, she was received by the governor of Bermuda with a national gun salute. The nerve of the man! The *Florida* may still be there. Now, have you also heard that Alexander Stephens tried to come to Washington?" Stephens, the Vice-President of the Confederacy, was reputed to have been an old friend of Abrahan Lincoln's.

[283]

"I've heard rumors, but that's all."

"He got in touch with Admiral Lee of the North Atlantic Squadron, and Lee sent word to us. Of all the presumption! The military channels are always available for whatever Stephens wants without a special trip to Washington, which would only encourage the peace groups here in the North. . . . You were in New York City last week when the draft riots occurred?"

"Yes, sir."

"Is it simply fanciful of me to imagine a design in all that has happened?"

"I'm not sure I follow you, sir."

His lips twisted in impatience, and he gnawed the corners of them. "I mean that all these separate events form a design. I'm becoming convinced that Lee's invasion of Pennsylvania, the appearance of Rebel raiders off the coast, and Stephens's mission were all parts of one movement, had one origin, were all concerted schemes between the Rebel leaders and Southern sympathizers in the North — the whole put in operation when the government is enforcing conscription. I don't for a moment believe those riots, not only in New York but elsewhere, were simply the accidental and impulsive outbreak of mobs."

"I don't believe it either, sir."

"What's that? You agree with me?"

"About the New York riots — yes, sir. About a design for the whole — I don't know. I hadn't given it serious thought."

"I could be mistaken, of course. But if there had been an understanding between the mob conspirators, the Rebels, and some of our own people, the combination of incidents could not have been more advantageous to the Rebels. No, I still think these developments were all part of a plan. Now tell me why you think the New York riots were not purely accidental."

At that moment, a knock sounded at the door, and Welles's secretary put his head inside to announce that a courier had arrived from Admiral Dahlgren.

I was relieved that we had been interrupted. It was becoming

[284]

something of a burden to be the repository of so much confidence; even had I been prepared for it, the role would have been awkward for me as a junior officer. Nor, after his disclosure of opinions about momentous developments, did I feel the occasion appropriate for revealing the little I knew about Andrews, Clavering, and the riots, or my suspicions with respect to Tamara Ravenel's activities along the Maine coast. I hoped that Secretary Welles would forget about any continuation of our conversation.

That evening, in the company of Lee Judson, a lieutenant who had served with Admiral Porter at Vicksburg, I went down to listen to the marine band playing on the White House lawn. The program was a mixture of martial and operatic music of the lighter variety. Judson said that a fortnight ago, Secretary Welles had instructed the marine commandant to have the band play more martial and national airs. When the band complied, one of the President's secretaries, John Nicolay, came to Welles and protested, urging that the band had a responsibility to cultivate and refine the public taste with German and Italian airs. According to Judson, our "Old Man of the Sea" told Nicolay such music was all right for the refined and effeminate but that it was insipid to most of our fighting men in garrisons, or on furlough in Washington.

Judson, who had a face like a poet's and a tongue like vinegar pickle, laughed. "Nicolay told Welles, 'But I like such music, and there are many in Washington who share my tastes.' And old Gid said to him, 'Mr. Nicolay, I'm glad I'm not responsible for your tastes. Operatic music may be fine in time of peace, but it inspires no zeal or purpose in our soldiers in time of war. We'll have more martial music for a while, sir.'"

"I'm afraid Mr. Welles isn't very popular these days, with Charleston likely to hold out, blockade runners still slipping through, and the *Alabama* active in the Indian and the Pacific."

"Tell me a cabinet member who is popular. Certainly not

[285]

Stanton or Seward or Blair. Possibly Chase at the Treasury, but, my God, he is so pompous!"

"Stanton may be liked by the more radical Republicans — and, of course, he's enormously able, and probably incorruptible."

"No one's disputing that," Lee said. "He's also insufferably arrogant and power-hungry. Makes old Gid look like a shy little laddie from the hills who doesn't know what he wants in the big city."

"By comparison, perhaps," I laughed. "And, in fact, he may be shy under his crustiness. But he knows what he wants, and it's to make the Navy Department as efficient as possible and keep it from being clawed by the War Department or the State Department."

"He also wants something else," Lee said.

"What's that?"

"He wants Raphael Semmes, dead or alive."

"Yes, he does seem to take Semmes personally."

"Whoever sinks the *Alabama* — if anyone ever does — will go shooting up in rank. But he'd better not let Semmes escape."

"I don't think anyone's likely to catch up with the *Alabama* for a while. We don't have the men-of-war in those seas to run her down."

We turned away from the music, walking slowly along the dusty streets. Carriages and cabs were endlessly passing, and a convoy of quartermaster carts creaked down toward the riverfront. From the Potomac itself came the occasional blast of a steamer's whistle, while one could hear the constant tooting and chuffing of locomotives in the railroad yards. On the sidewalks both civilians and soldiers, with a few sailors to be seen, strolled along, many pushing into the bars or to the music houses where the gay girls held out. I noticed that a shocking number of the soldiers were ambulatory wounded — a grim reminder that the capital was a city of hospitals. The air was redolent with dust, horse manure, whisky, and tobacco. Washington was far removed indeed from the sleepy town of prewar days. I doubted that it would ever be the same again, or anywhere near the same, when the war was over.

That night, before falling asleep, the spell of the city still with me, I wondered if I would ever plead a maritime law case before the Supreme Court. The country probably had too many lawyers, and Washington had an unusually large concentration of them. Yet competition in itself was something that rarely troubled me. What was disturbing was the extent to which influence and friends counted in getting cases. I had to admit, however, that even more than being able to plead a case, I should like to be a member of the Court itself. To be a governor, a congressman, or a senator exercised for me no appeal comparable to that of being a Justice. Unfortunately, too often one had to be a political figure first to be appointed. It was rumored that Stanton had never lost his hope of many years' standing, of becoming a member of the Court, and it was fairly common knowledge that Salmon Portland Chase at the Treasury hoped to become the next Chief Justice if he couldn't be President. How such a rancorous man as Stanton could exercise judicial impartiality or how the pompous, fuzzily liberal Chase could be clear and precise, eluded me. My grandfather was a better lawyer and a greater judge, I was certain, than any on the present Court. But he had not been a politician or done any President a personal favor or come from a populous state with a large number of electoral votes, so he had never received through the years a kindly nod from the White House. Well, I could get along without being a politician. I would rather spend my life differently.

Two days later, Welles sent for me. When I took a chair at his nod, he turned to face me and folded his hands over his waistcoat front.

"Pettigrew, I'm sorry we were interrupted the other day. As

you know, I have an idea that Lee's invasion of Pennsylvania, the coastal raiders, Stephens's mission to Washington, and the draft riots were all part of the same package. I think you agreed with me that the riots had some leadership. They've been breaking out in a number of Northern cities, you may know."

"Sir," I said, "I cannot account for what may have occurred in other cities, but I think there is a little evidence that the New York riots didn't just happen. Perhaps to begin with, yes, but in their later phases, there seemed to be something of a coordination of efforts — all designed to keep the police and others spread thinly and to cause a distraction of effort."

"I know of John Andrews, who was a Virginian and a Southern sympathizer, and I know that the corpses of one or two men indicated they were men of refinement — certainly not men who earned their living by their hands as did most of the rioters. There were reports of Southern voices heard, too. Still, it's all very vague and insubstantial."

"I realize that, sir, but among the leaders — and definitely there were leaders — was a man I could almost swear was the same man who was active in England buying up ships and supplies for the South and working closely with Captain Bulloch. His name is Roger Clavering, and I mentioned him in several of my reports."

I told him about my seeing Clavering as I was about to leave New York after paying Mr. Welles's respects to Admiral Foote, and my glimpses of the strange rider in New York during the riots.

He looked thoughtful for a few moments after I finished. "The man you saw may or may not have been acting under instructions from Richmond, but if I were a betting man, I know where I would place my money. The situation was made to order for Rebel agents. Stanton doesn't deny this possibility, but he doubts that all these events were part of a deliberate plan. The President had his doubts, too, and I'm not as sure as

I was the other day. It seems to me, though, that we can easily underestimate the malevolence of Jeff Davis. He's a dictator, as the South will eventually find out if they don't know already. He and Semmes are cut from the same bolt of cloth."

He paused, breathing heavily. For him the war had become increasingly personalized in terms of those two men. Mr. Welles was not a cruel man, ordinarily not vindictive at all, but his hatred of Davis and Semmes was unbounded.

"One of these days, Pettigrew," he went on, "Raphael Semmes will have to take the *Alabama* back to Europe for refitting, and when he does, the United States Navy will be waiting for him. One of these days, too, the British government will have reason to rue letting the *Alabama* and the *Florida* out of port."

"I certainly hope the government won't permit the Laird rams to escape, sir."

His brows drew together in a worried expression. "Mr. Seward assures me that Palmerston and Russell will be cooperative and that we have little to worry about."

"I have a friend, sir," I said carefully, thinking of a letter I had just received from Bruce Thornton, "who writes that the rams are nearing completion and that Captain Bulloch has been observed aboard both of them."

His lips tightened. "You're telling me nothing that I don't already know, Pettigrew. Consul Dudley, I need scarcely tell you, keeps me informed as well as Mr. Seward. So do other consuls. All agree that so far as they can determine, the government evinces no intention of detaining the ironclads."

"The government finally did act in the case of the *Alabama*, sir," I reminded him, "but, by that time, Captain Bulloch had taken her to sea."

"Palmerston and Russell must never let that happen again. Mr. Adams must make it clear to them that if they let those ships go to sea, they will be guilty of a hostile act against this country. . . . Now, look here, Pettigrew," he continued, "I know you are probably itching to see action somewhere, with Dahlgren off Charleston or possibly with the blockaders."

"Yes, sir, I am."

"Well, I am going to disappoint you. You will be an official courier. You will be sent to the various squadrons, to the navy yards, possibly to Europe. You will do something else, too, a duty not expected of other couriers, or only a few at most, and I won't tell you for the present who they are. I want you to make a written report to me personally whenever you come across anything that awakens your suspicions — something you've heard, someone you've seen, some event you've witnessed. Don't consider anything of this nature too insignificant to bring to my notice. I realize we have a Secret Service under Colonel Baker, but that is under Mr. Stanton's department. I have no intention whatever of creating a rival agency. I simply want to keep better informed of whatever the Rebels' intentions may be, particularly where they may affect this department, and I'll be interested in knowing whether there are groups in the North whom they may be persuading to give them assistance. Is all this clear?"

It was, and I told Welles that I appreciated his trust. I then asked him if there was anything he had specifically in mind that I should be alert for.

He shook his head. "No, Pettigrew, there is not. But I have a feeling — and it's only a feeling as yet — that as the Rebels get increasingly hemmed in, as they will, they'll try by devious ways to divide us and attack our resolution to crush them. I suspect we may be approaching a period when wild schemes will flourish. If any of these even remotely involves the navy, I'd like to know about it."

"Yes, sir," I said.

I realized, of course, as I walked back to my desk, that I had said nothing about Tamara Ravenel and her painting. I couldn't. For the moment, my suspicions at Castine now

seemed as ridiculous to me as they must then have seemed to
Noah Thornton. I wondered, though, if his friends had observed the *Swallow* in any of the little harbors down the Maine
coast.

XXVIII

MY assignment as a courier in the department involved numerous trips by train and steamer — now to one of the blockading
squadrons, now to the navy yards in Boston and Brooklyn,
several times to St. Louis, once to New Orleans by train and
riverboat, where bushwackers fired on us from the west bank of
the lower Mississippi. Always I went in uniform; this was
Welles's stipulation to all his couriers, especially to those
moving through the border states or in occupied territory. With
the war having moved away from the Ohio-Mississippi system,
naval uniforms were not as common a sight as they once had
been, and I found myself the recipient of many bad cigars and
worse whisky, all proffered with the best of will.

Wherever I went, I kept eyes and ears open for anything
clandestine. There were, reputedly, hosts of copperheads in the
Middle West — those Democrats committed to peace whatever
the price. There were also numerous Southern sympathizers,
who, while ostensibly pursuing their innocent ways, passed on
information to raiding bands of Confederate cavalrymen and to
earthbound Confederate guerrillas. From conversations with
people on trains and steamers while passing through Ohio River
country, I learned that the great cavalry leader General John
Hunt Morgan, who had been captured with many of his officers
and men in late July, was now securely imprisoned in the Ohio
State Penitentiary at Columbus. Some people worried that the
copperheads and Southern sympathizers might try to release the
prisoners, while others scoffed at the possibility.

A real shiver went through this part of the country just past mid-September, when General Rosecrans's army was barely saved from humiliating defeat by General Thomas's great stand at Chickamauga. People didn't feel easy until Grant, Sherman, Thomas, and Hooker let Braxton Bragg learn the full strength of Union arms at Chattanooga the last of November, roundly defeated him, and opened the door to an invasion of the eastern South.

Throughout the fall, a near-panic about the ironclads began to develop in the big city newspapers on the seaboard. The *New York Times* appeared especially alarmed. Secretary Welles seemed to feel that the editor, Henry Raymond, was controlled by the prominent Republican boss Thurlow Weed and influenced by Secretary Seward. If Mr. Adams should contain the panic by admonition or threat to Lord Russell, then the greater the glory that would accrue to the State Department and, above all, to Seward himself, whose political ambitions had by no means died. Whatever the explanation for the *Times's* apprehensions, sometimes I thought Mr. Welles did not fully appreciate the ironclad danger. I was sure that he was aware of the danger and that it worried him, but he disliked Seward so intensely that when Seward said, in cabinet meetings or in correspondence, that England would not let the ships get away, as had the *Alabama*, he took Seward grimly at his word. It was as if he held the little gamecock personally responsible for whatever damage the ironclads might do, rather than take sufficient precautions himself.

Luckily for the Union, Consul Dudley and his office kept on the trail. Bruce Thornton wrote that the consul often came to his apartment. Affidavits were being procured from engineers, shipwrights, boilermakers, and others, testifying that Captain Bulloch was constantly examining the rams, both the first one launched in early July and the other still on the stocks. Bruce said, too, that Paymaster Yonge, late of the *Alabama*, showed up in Liverpool, left his mulatto wife, and went to London. His wife then appeared at the consulate with letters from Bulloch concerning the *Alabama*. Dudley dashed to London and found Yonge divulging the details of his career to Benjamin Moran. Dudley then gathered up Yonge and a solicitor, and obtained a complete deposition from Yonge that would convict the Lairds and Bulloch under the Foreign Enlistment Act. When the government showed no disposition to act, he secured another affidavit from Yonge, who said that he was convinced the two ironclads were those he had seen in the plans made by the Lairds which were now in Bulloch's possession.

"The government at last gave in," Bruce wrote, "but I doubt that the affidavits from Mr. Dudley and Mr. Adams were solely responsible. The victories at Gettysburg and Vicksburg have stunned the pro-Southern people over here, and editorials now predict the North will win the war. With the *Alabama* and the *Florida* having taken many of our ships, Palmerston and Russell must have realized that we would reach the end of our patience if the ironclads also got to sea. Indeed, Mr. Adams told Lord Russell bluntly that this would mean war. As of yesterday, October 10, the government has taken custody of the rams. If I were Deacon Littlejohn back home, I'd shout, 'Hallelujah!' "

If Secretary Welles was a little skeptical about ironclads that year, he could hardly be blamed, in view of the experience with them at Charleston. In the great April attack on Sumter and the other forts, the monitors had had bolts sheared off, plates weakened, and turrets jammed, and one monitor went down the night after the battle. They were more wisely handled after Admiral Dahlgren took over from Du Pont. But even Dahlgren, with army assistance, was unable to crack the port's defenses decisively, though Fort Wagner on the northern tip of Morris Island was finally evacuated by the Southerners in September, and Charleston lost its great place as a terminus for blockade runners.

I saw Charleston for the first time during the war when I brought a message to Dahlgren on the 6th of October. My dispatch boat ran alongside Dahlgren's flagship, the *New Iron-*

sides, a high-sided ironclad and the most powerful ship in the navy. Boats and floats hung about her stern and divers were at work. Aboard there was much excitement, though never a word about it from Dahlgren, a stern-looking officer with a short mustache and long sideburns but no beard. He was curt in his greeting, promised me an acknowledgment to take back the next morning, and dismissed me.

"What happened here?" I asked one of the deck officers.

"Those goddamned Rebs," he said, and he sounded as admiring as he was indignant. "They came out last night with something that looked like a cigar and rammed a torpedo at the end of a spar into our stern. Wrecked us down below, though not too badly, I guess. At least, we're still afloat."

"Didn't you see them coming?"

"Not until they were about fifty yards away. That craft had almost no silhouette. Then we hailed her, and her captain fired a shotgun at us. Hit Ensign Howard, and no one knows if he'll live or not."

"Did the 'cigar' go down?"

"No, though even the Rebs thought it would when the torpedo went off. We captured their skipper, a lieutenant named Glassell, and a fireman. The others stayed aboard and got that damned thing back to Charleston for all the fact that the whole fleet was firing at it with rifles, pistols, and cannon. According to the Reb officer, they call the craft 'David.' I suppose that means we're 'Goliath.'" He laughed, but rather uncertainly, I thought. "You know, all they need to do now is to build a craft that'll run completely underwater. Then we won't sleep at all at night."

That evening, I looked at Charleston from the deck of the flagship. Sumter was an utter wreck but still defiant, the officers said. All the forts had taken a severe beating, and both the fleet and the army under Gillmore had thrown shells into the city. Still, Charleston held out, and I had to admit that, down deep, I admired the courage and tenacity of my mother's people.

[294]

Though they couldn't disperse the fleet, they could prevent the fleet from entering the harbor. It looked like an indefinite standoff.

I wondered, as I gazed at the city, whether Tamara Ravenel or Clavering had been this far south recently. Through an army captain, Richard Benton, who worked for Colonel Baker in the Secret Service, I learned that there was a file on both of them. Lee Judson and Benton had gone to the same academy, and it was through Lee I met Richard — as Lee called him — a stocky man with a marvelous control over his facial expressions. Benton was the soul of caution until he felt sure of me; then he checked the files. He divulged little about their contents, but enough for me to realize nothing was there about Clavering's possible role in the New York riots and nothing about Tamara's trip to Maine. In fact, the last two items on both was a confirmed report, of the previous fall, of their return from England to Wilmington via a blockade runner that stopped at Nassau, and the suspicion reported by an agent that he had seen them in Cincinnati in the spring. I decided that, for the present, I'd keep to myself what I suspected about Clavering's riot role. And, if it were possible, I'd be even more closemouthed about Tamara off the Maine coast.

On Tamara I had finally received a report from Noah Thornton that indicated he was again embarrassed to have taken me so seriously. Of all the dozen letters or telegrans he had sent, only one recipient, a native of Winter Harbor, had indicated that he thought he had seen a sloop resembling the description of the *Swallow*, but he had hastily added that many craft were constructed similarly so this meant nothing. Mr. Thornton wrote me that to a man his correspondents had joshed him, wondered if he had taken up a new hobby, or expressed concern about his mental health.

It bothered me deeply that the yield of the letters and telegrams was so small. If only one man had thought he might have seen the sloop, was the *Swallow* really from Portland? I decided to write Uncle Jonathan to ask if he would find out her home port and who her owner was.

Uncle Jonathan's reply, after extensive inquiry, was that the *Swallow* belonged to a local merchant named Jason Carter who was a respected Republican and a heavy contributor to the party. He had taken a trip along the Maine coast with family and friends the past summer.

This was at least progress of a sort. It tended to confirm the impression of Noah Thornton's Winter Harbor friend. But, for the time being, I decided to let Noah think of me as he pleased. I wanted to know more about Jason Carter before I said anything else. I wrote to Uncle Jonathan requesting that he compile a dossier as soon as possible on Carter. I knew he would be both discreet and thorough.

My suspicions were increased by a conversation I had with Richard Benton. Lee Judson and I drifted over to the Willard's bar one evening and met Benton there. The Willard was the whispering gallery of wartime Washington. I felt reasonably sure that much of the important information the South did not learn from Northern newspapers, it learned from agents who hung around the Willard. Army and navy officers, government clerks and government contractors, when well liquored, were prime sources of information. Secret Service operatives kept eyes and ears open not just to identify indiscreet persons and traitors, but also to listen to whatever might be whispered of Southern plans. Such operatives often liked company at the Willard in order not to be identified themselves for what they were by appearing too often alone. So when Benton invited us to join him at the Willard, we went.

It was the day after Thanksgiving, many people were home for the holidays, and the bar was thinly populated. We chatted about many things, but the main topic, as it was of the men around us, was the reported escape of General Morgan and his officers on Thanksgiving night from the Columbus penitentiary. They allegedly escaped by tunneling.

"Don't tell me they got out on their own!" exclaimed a burly civilian with cigar ashes on his paunch.

"Do you think they had help from the inside?" another civilian asked, a pouch-eyed man with a voice so soft I found myself straining to hear.

"Yes, and maybe from the outside, too. There are a lot of secret Rebs out there who would put up money for bribes."

"That may be so," said he of the soft voice, "but the Morgan crowd are clever men. They've showed it on many of their raids. They might have managed the escape by themselves."

"Hell, I don't believe it. Reb officers are supposed to be gentlemen, and that sort wouldn't know how to use their hands to dig through a cement floor and tunnel out."

"Either you underestimate gentlemen, or you don't know Southerners, sir. That's been part of our trouble right along. We never figured they'd be able to put up the resistance they have. And that mistake goes right up to Lincoln himself. Remember his call for seventy-five thousand volunteers after Sumter fell? Why, we've got nearly a million in the army right now."

"I'm afraid you're right. Lincoln's made so many mistakes I don't see how he can get elected again. Why, I heard —"

We never did find out what he had heard because they put their heads together, and shortly afterward, Benton nodded to us, and we left.

"Do you think that man was right about Morgan's getting help in escaping, Richard?" Lee asked as we walked through the dark streets.

Benton was silent for so long, I thought he wasn't going to answer. Then he said, "Of course."

"Why 'of course'?"

"For any number of reasons. I'll give you just one: because there were at least a half dozen who escaped, and they certainly weren't all in the same cell. Someone had to be bribed not to notice the absence of the men digging. That takes nothing away from the cleverness, as that fellow called it, of Morgan and his officers — it increases it, if anything. The man was also right about the many Southern sympathizers out there. I don't mean the Democrats or the plain old copperheads, who'd like peace and who hate abolition, the President's use of habeas corpus, the loss of Southern markets and ports, and, of course, the slaughter. I mean there are those who actively support the South."

"The Knights of the Golden Circle?" I asked.

"I think the pro-Administration politicians in the Middle West exaggerate the importance of that crowd. They don't distinguish between being anti-Administration and being pro-South."

"I've an idea," I said, "that active Southern sympathizers in the North are careful about calling attention to themselves by joining organizations."

"But aren't most of those organizations secret? What man would know another is a member unless he's one himself?" Lee asked.

"Membership has a way of becoming known, just the same," Benton said, "in spite of threats of dire consequences. But as for active Southern sympathizers, they do exist, I assure you, and not just in the Middle West."

He said no more on the subject. But what I had heard at the Willard and from Benton made me increasingly curious and suspicious about the *Swallow*'s trip and her owner.

The Administration received a boost that fall from an unusual quarter, and Secretary Welles became euphoric. This was the arrival of a small Russian fleet at New York in September, under Admiral Lisovskii, and one at San Francisco in October, under Admiral Popov. It required no scholar of European history to realize that anticipating possible war with England, France, and Austria over her internal and territorial problems involving Poland, Russia had ordered her ships out of harm's way. Most people, however, looked at the visits as goodwill gestures toward the United States, and they received the Russians with wild enthusiasm. Inviting Admiral Lisovskii to make use of the Brooklyn Navy Yard, Mr. Welles could not do enough for the Russians. He hoped that the squadron would visit Washington, anchoring in the lower Potomac. When the admiral signified his wish to do so in early December, the Secretary called a number of us to his office and bade us draw up plans with Baron de Stoeckl, the Russian ambassador, for entertaining the officers. He also wanted us to work out a schedule of visits to the fleet by dignitaries of the foreign governments represented in Washington, important members of our own government, and members of Congress. He put two steamers at our disposal. "God bless the Russians," he had said when they arrived in New York. Now he told us, "The Russians are rendering us a great service. We must not forget it."

I was looking forward with growing curiosity to the visit of the Russians. Lee Judson, however, was cynical about the goodwill being displayed; he thought it excessive and unwarranted. Yet even he was curious about the Russians and their ships, which he believed would be dirty and poorly constructed.

"Remember, Scott, those crews are serfs, or were until the Czar freed them two years ago. Can you imagine what our ships would look like if they were manned by ex-slaves?"

There were so many holes in whatever he was trying to prove that I merely said, "Well, many of their officers are aristocrats. I don't think they'd tolerate dirty ships."

"Hell, they're probably too lazy to be concerned. I doubt if they even know how to pull on their own pants."

I never had a chance to find out by personal inspection whether the Russian ships were dirty or their officers reluctant to dress themselves. Secretary Welles sent me to New York with a bundle of dispatches for Admiral Paulding. These had to reach Paulding at the Brooklyn Navy Yard as soon as possible.

He wanted me then to go on to the Portsmouth Navy Yard and pick up dispatches and copies of ship designs from Commodore Pearson, the commandant.

"There's not any urgency for these last," he said, "so why don't you take the *Chesapeake* to Portland, spend a day or two with your folks, stop off at Portsmouth on your way back by train, and return here next weekend?"

I thanked him for his kindness, but he bade me brusquely to get on with my assignment.

After delivering the dispatches to Admiral Paulding, I took a ferry to Manhattan and bought a ticket for the trip to Portland.

The *Chesapeake* was loading cargo at her North River dock, and Captain Willett was anxious to be on his way. It was Saturday afternoon, December 5, and the stevedores seemed to be showing their fatigue.

Willett greeted me like an old friend when I went up to join him at the wheelhouse after leaving my valise in my stateroom. I found him annoyed at the delay in loading. "You'd think they'd want to get home to their families."

I suppose there isn't a ship captain who isn't anxious to get to sea when his company holds him responsible for keeping a schedule.

Finally, at five o'clock, the *Chesapeake* cast off her lines, backed out into the river, and threaded her way through the harbor, busy with merchant traffic even this late in the day, and crossed and recrossed by ferries and tugs. The *Chesapeake* was a fairly large propeller steamer for the coasting trade, not of great speed but a good, steady vessel. On this run north she was carrying flour, sugar, wine, and sundries. Though these were not a heavy cargo, they gave her a desirable weight and stability as we began to pick up a sea, once clear of the coast.

I remained out on deck largely by myself until supper. Though darkness had set in early, the lights in the city and aboard the sailing ships, steamers, tugs and ferries were pleasing to watch. Our own lights seemed even more cheerful as we shook clear of the harbor and pursued our way to the northeast. I noticed two six-pounders forward, and wondered if the owners had bought these from the State of Maine after they had been brought aboard during the chase of the *Caleb Cushing*. At last, chilled by the breeze, which was partially created by our own passage, I went to my narrow stateroom, threw my coat and hat on the bed, washed up, and went to supper.

As a coasting steamer, the *Chesapeake* lacked the refinements of a transoceanic steamer, but her cook could prepare plain food in a very satisfactory manner. Tonight the supper was baked cod, and while I am not overly partial to fish, except shellfish, this tasted delicious, perhaps, indeed, because of a good appetite from so much fresh air.

The passengers were about twenty-five in number, all male. Only two of them seemed at all remarkable; these were tall, spare men, one with a beard, the other mustached, both of whom had a certain air of authority. They talked much together, occasionally looked at the others in the dining saloon, then would fall silent. As a matter of fact, few of the passengers said much.

The next day, I encountered the first mate, Charles Johnson, when I was walking around the deck. Though it was the Sabbath, no one appeared to be aware of it except the cook, who served us a roast of beef for dinner, with apple pie that was thick in the top crust but otherwise very tasty. Feeling a little sluggish afterward, I walked around and around the deck. The sky was gray and threatening, the air sharp, and the sea rising in the brisk wind. By this time, after the *Caleb Cushing* affair and my return trip at the time of the New York draft riots, I recognized a number of the crew and they, me. Johnson was a sturdy man, possibly in his forties, with a drooping mustache. He brightened when I held out my hand to him on the lee side opposite the forward hatch.

"I saw you come aboard last night," he said, shaking my hand vigorously. "I'm sorry I didn't get a chance to speak with you."

"Has anything exciting happened aboard since the draft riots, Mr. Johnson?"

He shook his head. "Very quiet. We're grateful."

"I don't suppose you'll have any cause for alarm unless another raider comes up the coast."

"No, and that's not likely this winter, is it? The blockade must be pretty tight by now."

"Oh, there's always a chance of someone slipping out of Mobile or Wilmington, particularly Wilmington, but otherwise, no."

"Not even Charleston?"

"Anything is possible, of course, and runners still go in and out, but it's unlikely that a real raider will get loose from there anymore."

"Well, that's a blessing," he said, rubbing his hands together for warmth.

"You've a light passenger list this trip," I said, glancing around at the few passengers I could see.

"As a matter of fact, there are more than usual this time of year. . . . You know, that brings up a point, lieutenant. Seems crazy even to mention this, but most of these passengers came aboard without any baggage, and four of them brought a mighty heavy trunk with them. I don't know why, but I'm kind of curious about some of these men. Have you noticed that most of them don't talk much?"

"Two of them do, but just with each other," I said, and I described them. I thought it interesting that Johnson should have been impressed enough by what he had seen to mention it to me. The rest of the day I tried to be as observant as he had been. I wanted to ask him later whether he had found out who the two men were, but I never had a chance to speak with him privately. Just before supper, however, I saw the bearded character near the stern, watching our wake.

"Looks like it's building up for a storm," I said.

He turned like a flash, then relaxed and looked back again at the sea. "Could be," he said.

"I'm glad the *Chesapeake* has good sea qualities," I persisted. "We can get some bad weather off this coast."

"I wouldn't know, lieutenant, but you're probably right."

Just then, the supper bell rang, and as he turned to leave, I thrust out my hand. "My name's Pettigrew."

He hesitated for a moment. "Mine's Braine," he said. "John C. Braine."

I wondered at the full announcement as I ate my supper. It was as if he expected me to know who he was or wanted me to be sure to remember his name, which I had never heard before.

That evening, I felt that something wasn't quite right aboard the *Chesapeake*. I could not put my finger on anything definite. It was only a sense of uneasiness that had nothing to do with the storm that was so long brewing. Later, after I had latched my stateroom door for the night, I removed only my jacket and shoes, and loosened my collar. I also placed my revolver on the little washstand. As I lay there, listening to the creak of timbers as the steamer met the seas, I wished that she were faster and that we were nearer Portland than just off Cape Cod.

I could not have been asleep long when a fusillade of shots brought me to my feet. I slipped into my shoes and jacket, grabbed my revolver and dashed for the door. After waiting just a second before I opened it, I stepped into the corridor.

Instantly someone fired at me. I fired back, but the man had ducked away as I pulled the trigger. Then men caught me from the rear. They were upon me before I could aim, and after a blow from a pistol butt had stunned me and started the blood pouring down over my face, my hands were wrenched behind me and handcuffs clamped on my wrists. I was tossed back into my stateroom. As I tried to shake the haziness from my brain, I heard other shots, followed by a long silence which was broken only by a groaning man being brought down the corridor. I now must have lost consciousness.

Some time later, I was jerked to my feet and pushed and dragged to the main cabin aft. When I entered, I saw Captain Willett and several of the crew in irons. Both the chief engineer, James Johnson, and the first mate, Charles Johnson, were wounded. Johnson the engineer had a pistol ball in the hollow of his chin; Johnson the mate, one in the left arm and one in the knee. Charlie was in a great deal of pain, and lay on one of the cabin lounges. Five of our passengers had no weapons and were apparently bona fide passengers. There were six others in the cabin, two with rifles and four with pistols.

Suddenly the door opened, and Braine stepped inside, accompanied by his table mate of the voyage.

"You men, pay attention! I am Lieutenant Braine and this is Lieutenant Parr. I have seized this ship in the name of the Southern Confederacy, and you are my prisoners. Some of you were foolish enough to resist, and were wounded. The second engineer, Owen Shaffer, fired at us and died when we shot back. Lieutenant Parr here will do what he can for the mate and the chief engineer. In a little while, Captain Willett, I'll want from you your coasting license from the New York Customs House, the permits for the cargo, and whatever you collected from us in passage money."

"Are you making this ship a raider?" Willett asked.

"I am."

"You're not taking us to sea with you, are you?" The passenger looked as fearful as his voice sounded.

Braine's hard face cracked slightly. "Hell, no, we'll drop you off somewhere near land. Can you swim?"

"Oh, no!"

"Huh. All right, lieutenant," he turned to Parr, "see if you can't dig out those bullets."

He left, while Parr went to work with his knife. He extracted the ball from the engineer's chin and the one from the mate's arm, but couldn't reach the ball in the knee. "You'll have to wait until you're on shore for that," he told Charlie Johnson.

Then he looked at the rest of us. "I'm leaving you men alone with a rifleman outside each door." He nodded to his followers, and they trooped out after him.

For a while, nothing was said. We heard only the soft groans of Charlie Johnson as his knee wound throbbed.

"First thing I knew," Captain Willett said, "Charlie came to my stateroom and told me someone had shot Owen. I went out, saw him lying on the deck, then got up to see who had done it. Was just going into the pilothouse when Parr put a pistol to my ear and slipped the irons onto me. Kept me in my room an hour or so, then brought me here."

"Where they headed for, cap'n?" the nervous passenger asked.

"Grand Manan, they said."

"Do they have their own navigator?" I asked.

"Yes, a fellow named Osburn. He was one of the six passengers who bought a ticket in New York before coming on board. He's one of them. There must be about sixteen in all."

Morning came. They brought us food and removed the irons to let us eat. Captain Willett was ordered forward for a few minutes, then returned after a conference with Braine. In the afternoon, he went forward again and turned all the ship's papers, cargo permits, and money over to Braine and Parr.

Finally, we stopped at Seal Cove on Grand Manan. A boat was lowered and four men went ashore. What they did there we never knew, but when they came back, the steamer moved toward St. John. When we were nearly there, a pilot boat came out and ordered us to stop. It was now too dark to see clearly, but even from inside the cabin we could hear shouting between the boat and the steamer. Then the pilot boat swung alongside the *Chesapeake*, and a line was thrown to her.

"Someone's coming aboard," James Johnson said.

It was Roger Clavering, brisk and businesslike and, as usual, self-possessed. Braine must have given him a list, for he glanced at all of us, then stopped at my name and stared at me.

"In trouble again, eh, Mr. Pettigrew?"

"You may be in greater trouble than I am, Mr. Clavering," I said. "This is piracy."

"You think so? Not with a letter of marque authorizing me to operate a privateer against federal shipping."

"Then it had to be for a ship you already possessed, not this ship which you hadn't yet acquired."

He smiled. "Well, this is mere legal quibbling, and I have no intention of arguing the case with you. Let the courts fight it out, if they must, while Lieutenant Braine captures prizes for the Confederacy." He turned to the others. "I am going to send most of you ashore in the pilot boat, including Captain Willett. I'll keep a couple of engineers and three firemen to work the ship. And you will also continue as our guest, Mr. Pettigrew."

He named fourteen, besides Willett and the black stewardess, who were to go back in the pilot boat. Charlie Johnson was carefully lowered into the boat. James Johnson was forced to remain behind. As he passed me, Captain Willett squeezed my shoulder. I realized it was not only an expression of sympathy, but also a gesture of reassurance; he would still do what he could.

While I remained behind, now locked in my stateroom, with a bar across the door, the *Chesapeake* took the pilot boat in tow for a half-dozen miles before casting it loose. The steamer then bore away for Nova Scotia, presumably for coal. Whether the *Chesapeake* entered immediately on a privateering career or headed for Wilmington — as an overconfident guard who brought me supper indicated she would — she would need fuel.

I can't say I viewed my captivity with enthusiasm. If the *Chesapeake* slipped through the blockade and Clavering handed me over to the Confederate authorities, incarceration in a prison camp was not a welcome fate. Moreover, there was always the chance that Union guns would sink us, or, to avoid capture, Clavering or Braine — whoever was actually skipper, probably Braine — would run the ship ashore, and the surf that often ran high on the Carolina coast could mean death for all of us. However I looked at my prospects, they didn't appear encouraging.

Yet there were two factors that buoyed me up somewhat. One was that shipping the quantity of coal the *Chesapeake* would require for sea would take a little negotiating and time for loading.

The other factor was the incredible self-confidence of Clavering in sending Willett and the others ashore. Had I been in his place, I'd have kept them aboard until I had finished coaling. Surely by now, Tuesday night, our failure to arrive in Portland would be causing the steamship line considerable worry, but Clavering must have been certain of completing his arrangements before Union pursuit could be organized; otherwise, he must have realized that Willett would spread the alarm, as indeed he did. From the pilot boat, Willett managed to get a small boat from a ship near Partridge Island, and with four of his men and two passengers, rowed to town, landing in St. John at four o'clock Wednesday morning, December 9. He went at once to the United States consul, J. Q. Howard, who wired American authorities.

I could well imagine the activity in the States once word arrived of the seizure. From Gideon Welles would go a flurry of telegrams to the navy yards in Portsmouth, Boston, and New York. All available gunboats and cruisers would be ordered to sea. Actually not many would be immediately available, because of repair work, refueling, taking on powder, and the like, and few would be at full strength. The result would be a mixed pursuit fleet: a few regular warships, perhaps, and other ships that were merely merchant ships, possibly even prizes, with cannon hastily put aboard and scratch crews mustered. All this could not be accomplished at once; in the meantime, the *Chesapeake* would be on her way to safety.

As it happened, the steamer didn't find the quantity of coal at Shelburne in Nova Scotia that was needed. She did take aboard a few tons, but a violent storm kept her in port for two days. Though we tossed and rolled so wildly at anchor that I was in a constant fight against seasickness, I took no cheer from the delay caused by the gale; I realized that Union ships, bucking the wind, high seas, and driving snow, would make little progress.

Nor did I take much encouragement when I saw Clavering rowed ashore. While he was probably going to try to arrange for a coal supply further east, I felt that it was unlikely that he would come back aboard. If he had to go south immediately, he may have felt that there were safer ways of getting there than with John C. Braine.

In fact, when we sailed out of Shelburne and into Lahave, where Braine found little coal but stayed for two days, selling bits and pieces of the *Chesapeake*'s cargo, I became increasingly convinced the man was a pirate. I suspected that he had done some of this kind of merchandising at Shelburne, too. As long as Clavering was aboard, there seemed to be a kind of official connection with the Confederacy. Braine, however, must have been acting on his own; I could not believe Clavering would have condoned these sales. Clavering might line his own pockets, but scarcely with such small change and at such risk to a prize like the *Chesapeake*. Of course, I could have been mistaken.

At last, Braine took the ship farther eastward to the harbor of Sambro, about fifteen miles from Halifax, which he entered in the late afternoon of the 16th. Here a Canadian coal schooner awaited him, no doubt the result of Clavering's negotiations, and the *Chesapeake* started shipping coal aboard. Once she completed this operation, she could be on her way to Wilmington.

During these days, I had seen nothing of Braine or Parr, and after the pilot boat left us in the Bay of Fundy, I was confined most of the time in my stateroom with a guard outside the door. When I was permitted on deck a few minutes each day, I was put in irons. No communication was permitted between me and the members of the crew. I wondered, as I listened to the coaling going on through the night, whether James Johnson and the others were being forced to assist. I realized that time was running out for those of us who were Union men aboard the *Chesapeake* — or the *Jane,* as she had been rechristened. Eventually, when Braine and his men broke off work for the rest of the night, I fell asleep.

What woke me was the sound of feet racing along the corridor, then an uproar of voices, and a scrambling down the gangway. Although I jumped out of bed and went to the door, I could now hear nothing in the corridor. I tried the door, but it was still barred from the outside. Glancing out my cabin window, I saw two boats jammed with men, rowing ashore.

Even before I could put on my jacket, James Johnson came running to my door, shouting, "Lieutenant Pettigrew!" He lifted the bar and threw open my door. "They're gone! Our boys are coming in!"

As we reached the deck, I noticed the schooner still alongside. She had nothing to fear, since she was Canadian, anyway. For that matter, even if the steamer coming toward us was an American, she couldn't make a hostile move because the *Chesapeake* was in Canadian territorial waters. What she could do was to rescue us if we flew the flag union down, the maritime sign of distress. Quickly we hoisted the flag, and our little group of men on the *Chesapeake* cheered as the American steamer, guns on her starboard side trained on us, swept down toward the *Chesapeake*.

Then, with relief, came astonishment. Instead of drawing up, taking us aboard, and departing, leaving the fate of the *Chesapeake* to the courts, she struck us on the port side, and a boarding crew swarmed over both the steamer and the schooner. All this by eight o'clock. By one o'clock, the warship and her prize, the *Chesapeake,* left the harbor.

Grateful? I was deeply grateful.

I was also appalled. The commander of the warship had committed a grave infraction of international law, and I could just hear the abrasive disgust in Gideon Welles's voice when he learned how the success of discovery had been compromised by blunder.

XXIX

THE recapture of the *Chesapeake* on the morning of the 17th of December was but a continuation of the irregular proceedings that had started when Braine seized the steamer twenty miles off Cape Cod a little after one o'clock on the morning of the 7th.

To begin with, our rescuer was the U.S.S. *Ella and Annie,* a captured blockade runner which was rechristened the U.S.S. *Malvern* even before she returned from this cruise to the Boston Navy Yard. As the *Ella and Annie,* she was hastily armed, manned, and dispatched by Commodore Montgomery, the commandant, shortly after noon on December 10. Though not the first warship to leave in pursuit of the *Chesapeake,* she was the most aggressive and persistent, and might have caught us sooner had she not had to put into Halifax for coal. Furthermore, her officers and crew had had no experience working together, every officer had volunteered for the cruise, and a number had just returned from two years at sea on other warships. Her commander, Frederick Nickels, was an acting volunteer lieutenant, not regular navy, which may have explained, in part, his ignorance of international protocol or his rashness in ignoring it. Probably the latter.

"By God, did we ever show up the regular navy!" he exclaimed when I introduced myself to him and thanked him for my release.

"But isn't this a risky procedure?" I pointed toward the *Chesapeake,* where Union sailors had found two of the Confederates in hiding. They had also discovered one on the Canadian schooner and were bringing all of them to the *Ella and Annie*.

"You mean I should turn them over to the British authorities?"

"Yes, and the *Chesapeake,* too."

"I will, like hell! I'm going to finish loading the *Chesapeake* with coal from the schooner and get out of here fast."

I shrugged. I was too relieved at what he had done to stress the illegality of it all; his superiors would see to that.

When the *Chesapeake* was coaled, he put a prize crew aboard her with orders for Boston, and, with the *Chesapeake* following, the *Ella and Annie* headed out of Mud Cove for the mouth of Sambro harbor. Before we had even left the harbor mouth, we fell in with the steam sloop of war *Dacotah,* under Captain Albert G. Clary, which Nickels had beaten in the quest for the *Chesapeake.* We slowed our engines as the big man-of-war drew near. After we had identified ourselves and the *Chesapeake,* Clary spoke through his trumpet. "Where do you proceed with your prize?"

"To Boston," Nickels replied.

"Did you catch the pirates?"

"Only three — two on the *Chesapeake* and one on the coal schooner back there. The others saw me coming and fled in boats."

"You'd better report aboard at once, lieutenant."

In a few minutes, Nickels was back on board. There was no need to ask what had happened. He looked angry and disappointed, and he came directly toward me.

"You were right, Pettigrew, too damned right. Clary has ordered me to proceed to Halifax with the *Chesapeake* for adjudication."

But all this was but a beginning. Once we had arrived at Halifax in company with the *Dacotah,* a delay occurred at the United States consulate, where an official neglected to introduce Clary's lieutenant to Charles Tupper, the Provincial Secretary, and to General Hastings Doyle, the Governor of the Province. Both Tupper and Doyle were annoyed, and Clary found himself engaged in an apologetic correspondence.

When the British interpreted as defiance the breakdown in protocol and American reluctance to surrender the three prisoners until assurance was given that they would be tried as pirates and murderers, the authorities became threatening and refused to permit any of the five United States men-of-war which had now arrived, to leave the harbor. Even after the *Chesapeake* was delivered to the authorities, and the three prisoners as well — one of whom was helped to escape by sympathetic citizens — hard feelings persisted. At last Commodore Thomas T. Craven of the frigate *Niagara*, just in, went ashore and conferred with General Doyle. Whether it was owing to the commodore's illness or to his straightforward manner or whatever, he and General Doyle hit it off smoothly, and Doyle promised to try to apprehend all the pirates and have them tried, as the consulate was pressing, for murder and piracy. The unpleasantness passing, the British garrison could now stop manning their batteries and our ships could sail for home.

Having been instructed by the commodore to remain behind as a witness to the seizure of the *Chesapeake* and to give what testimony I could at the hearing, I watched our ships depart with nothing of the relief and pleasure that clearly animated the people of Halifax. Both the Confederates and the United States consulate were amassing provincial legal talent, and the hearings were likely to go on for a long time. But though I had to obey Commodore Craven's order, I decided to get in touch directly with Secretary Welles, whose instructions I had been originally following when the *Chesapeake* was taken.

Welles's reply was terse and brief: I was to make a complete deposition, have it properly witnessed, deposit it with Consul White or Vice-Consul Gunnison, and report to Washington as soon as I could.

I left Halifax by steamer for St. John, where I spent a few hours with Captain Willett, whose company had instructed him to remain at St. John and give testimony to the magistrates there on the seizure of the vessel, and hold himself available to go to Halifax for the hearings. He was still angry over what had happened to his ship, and foresaw endless legal wrangles before the *Chesapeake* was released.

While I was in St. John, he introduced me to Consul J. Q. Howard, who accorded me a long interview after I produced my credentials and informed him that my grandfather was the Chief Justice of Maine. Howard was a pleasant, if reserved man who admired the people of St. John and the Province of New Brunswick despite the frequent criticisms of him in the provincial press. He received me kindly. He said that his own investigations revealed that the plan for the capture of the *Chesapeake* had been contrived in St. John by Clavering and that, of all the men with Braine, only Lieutenant Parr was a native Southerner; the others were Canadians. Braine himself was a Canadian, had served as an officer with the Confederate infantry, and, when captured, was imprisoned for six months at Fort Warren in Boston, possibly less because of his military connection than because he was believed a Knight of the Golden Circle, a pro-Southern organization. He was at Warren the same time that the Confederate commissioners Mason and Slidell were there, after Captain Wilkes had seized them aboard the *Trent*, and was released only by the intercession of Lord Lyons, the British ambassador to Washington.

"If Braine is so determined to help the South," I said, "I don't believe any trial will prevent his continuing to assist them."

"First, he must be apprehended," Howard said. "As you know, warrants have been issued for the arrest of Braine and his men, but I think it unlikely that Braine will be found."

"How did Clavering secure his letter of marque, sir?"

"The letter was for a privateer named the *Retribution*. She was condemned as unseaworthy and sold at Nassau months ago. The letter was then transferred to Clavering, possibly at the Charleston customs house. Braine had no commission, but simply the order from Clavering authorizing him to capture the *Chesapeake*. The transferred letter of marque to Braine could only be validated by his taking the *Chesapeake* to the Southern port which he had the best chance of entering."

"That would be Wilmington."

"Right, and that is why he changed the name of the *Chesapeake* to the *Jane* with the port designation Wilmington, North Carolina."

Consul Howard was obviously a man well posted on what was going on. I decided to press him. "Sir, what is the feeling here in St. John about the war?"

"Mixed. No one approves of slavery, but there is considerable sentiment in support of the South's right to secede from the Union. And you must not forget that many people in the maritime provinces are descendants of the Tories who migrated here after the Revolution. There is constant rivalry with Americans over fishing and lumber rights — not all the people in New Brunswick were in favor of the boundary settlement under the Webster-Ashburton Treaty of 1842. I wouldn't discount, either, the fear of United States economic domination and the sometimes high-handed attitude of our naval captains in halting Canadian merchant ships. The seizure of the *Chesapeake* in Canadian waters by young Nickels is a flagrant instance of violation of Canadian rights. It will gain us no friends."

"But Canada is a base for Southern plotting against us," I said. "Braine's capturing the *Chesapeake* is just the most recent example."

"Granted. And it's not likely to be the last, which scarcely makes life easier for United States consular officials like myself."

"Is it presumptuous of me to ask if you anticipate any increase in anti-American activity?"

"I think it very likely, not necessarily by many Canadians, though by some, and certainly not by any provincial government. But many Southerners and pro-Southern United States citizens are already in Canada and will continue to test the composure of British and United States authorities."

"Mr. Howard, Roger Clavering is a Confederate agent. I've encountered him several times, beginning in early 1862 on a liner bound for England. Do you know if he was in St. John before the *Chesapeake* affair?"

Howard smiled. "I think you must be more than a volunteer officer in the navy, Lieutenant Pettigrew."

"Not so. But Clavering and I do seem to have a penchant for getting in each other's way. I consider him a very dangerous enemy of the Union."

"I think you are right. But he is also a charming man — at least when he wants to be — he knows everyone important in the maritimes, or seems to, and he has helped a number of individuals of note to increase their fortunes by sending cargoes through the blockade and disposing of them very profitably. So in answer to your question — yes, he has been in St. John several times that I know of and perhaps more that I don't. The ladies appear especially pleased to have him on their dinner lists."

"Is he ever seen in the company of a blonde woman of medium height by the name of Tamara Ravenel?"

"Oh, come, lieutenant, you're not serious?"

"I couldn't be more serious, Mr. Howard. She is a Confederate who often works with Clavering, and if you have any doubt, I refer you to Colonel Baker of the Secret Service, who has a dossier on her as well as Clavering."

After an appropriate pause, Howard shook his head. "Lieutenant, I have never seen or heard of such a person. If you'd like, I will make some discreet inquiries."

"Thank you, sir. And if in the future you should hear of such a person in this area, I should appreciate your sending word to

[315]

me. I realize you report directly to the State Department, but there need be nothing official about your notice to me, and I shall be most grateful."

Howard was a hospitable man, and invited me to spend Christmas with him. But I declined. I took a steamer for Boston, arriving there Christmas night. The next morning, I boarded a train for New York and thence to Washington.

Once back in the capital, I submitted a report to Secretary Welles, who later questioned me at length about Braine's seizure of the *Chesapeake* and the ship's recapture by the *Ella and Annie*. I now told him about both Clavering and Tamara, and, to my surprise, he suggested that I relate everything I knew about them to Colonel Baker. "I don't like Lafayette Baker," Welles added. "Baker has no powers of discrimination and little regard for truth. He believes everything bad, he suspects everybody, and he has no regard for the character and rights of any man."

"Then, if I may say so, sir, I am surprised that you should wish me to confide this information to him."

"Because we need a miserable specimen like Baker, a human bloodhound, to run men like Clavering to earth. We can't have a repetition of anything like the *Chesapeake* affair, Pettigrew. Do you realize what it cost to send a dozen ships to sea after that vessel? And then that fool Nickels loses his head. Well, let the State Department fight it out now."

"With all deference, sir, I can't feel too annoyed at Nickels personally — quite the reverse, sir. If he hadn't come into Sambro harbor, I might still be aboard the *Chesapeake*."

Welles shrugged. "Of course. For that matter, if the *Dacotah*, the *Ella and Annie*, and the others had set up a blockade of the harbor, a storm might have dispersed them and your John C. Braine have taken the *Chesapeake* into the open sea. No, I can't feel that Nickels's act was too dreadful, though I shall have to reprimand him. But, to go back, we can't permit Clavering to remain loose. If Baker can get him — and the woman,

[316]

too, for that matter — then the sooner the better. I'll set up an appointment with Baker for you right away."

Baker, however, was evidently out of Washington at the time and for some while afterward. When he returned, he was busy investigating the Navy Department itself in behalf of the Senate Naval Affairs Committee, whose chairman, John P. Hale of New Hampshire, had been engaged in a continuous feud with Secretary Welles since early in the war, when an altercation developed over ship procurement. The two men loathed each other personally, but their differences were also expressive of a contest of authority, with Welles determined not to be told by a Senate committee chairman how to run his department. Hale's having the department investigated and his listening to Baker raise questions about the loyalty of hardworking, respected personnel, including the principal clerk, Mr. Faxon, and Welles's great assistant, Gustavus Fox, infuriated all of us in the department. Yet perhaps not all of us, for surely a few clerks or officers had vented their dissatisfaction and spleen to Baker or Hale. This sort of suspicion made us all wary of one another and was hardly conducive to the development of a cooperative atmosphere so desirable for the faithful and efficient performance of duty. We came to regard the arrogant, argumentative Hale as much an enemy as Jefferson Davis, while for Baker, the dominant feeling in the department seemed to be contempt, edged with a certain apprehension. I could now understand Secretary Welles's opinion of him.

Although I tried to restrain my feelings when with Richard Benton, Lee Judson was less guarded in his comments on Baker, who, in Lee's opinion, was a miserable, filth-eating bastard.

Benton smiled and shook his head as he watched from our table at the Willard the coming and going of officers and their guests. "Baker may seem to be all that, and God knows he's not an easy man to work for. But he's an enormously able, courageous man, too — suspicious, perhaps, but it's his business to be suspicious. And, Lee, if you can show me a department in

[317]

this government where there isn't a certain amount of disaffection and corruption, I'd like to hear what it is."

"But to impugn the character of such a man as Fox!"

"Well, Baker is suspicious, as I said, and I suppose there's something in every man's conduct that could lead to a challenge of character. He didn't get far with either Fox or Faxon, you'll note."

"I still don't know just what Baker's job entails," I said.

"Nor will you in every respect," Benton laughed, "not until the war is over. Of course, there are some things that are more or less common knowledge. He's really the head of a detective bureau, largely civilian, under the War Department. He was a New Yorker who migrated to California, where he distinguished himself on the Vigilance Committee during some stormy days in 1856. He came back east with the outbreak of war, and, on the basis of his California experience, Secretary Seward hired him as a detective for the State Department. When the army wanted information in the summer of 'sixty-one on Southern military movements, he volunteered. He was captured but so convinced the Rebs of his Southern sympathies that they made him an agent in the North. Naturally, he fed a lot of information to Washington."

"Does he still do that sort of thing?" Lee asked.

"Not any more himself, though his agents supplement the work of the army's own spies. Incidentally, after Stanton became Secretary of War, he brought Baker under his wing. But Baker moves widely. He helps the Treasury Department against counterfeiters. He investigates the practices of contractors, which, I suppose, is why Senator Hale turned him loose on the Navy Department. He runs bounty jumpers to earth for the War Department."

"I gather he also keeps an eye on Confederate activities in Canada," I said.

"Yes, along with the adjutant general in the War Department, and the *Chesapeake* affair that you were involved in has interested him mightily."

"Then that's one plot that he evidently knew nothing about," I said.

Benton merely shrugged.

"Is his commission real?" Lee asked.

"Oh, yes. Originally he received a colonel's commission, District of Columbia Cavalry. Many of the troopers actually came from Maine, Scott. Before this war is over, he will probably be a general — and I'm completely serious."

I had the feeling from what Benton said that Baker was far more active than was evident from any general description of his activities. I also wondered how effective he was in each of the areas mentioned, especially in catching up with bounty jumpers. But I was truly curious about my interview with this controversial Argus of the Union, whose virile reputation as a splendid horseman and a crack shot with both pistol and rifle was somewhat qualified, in the opinion of many men, by his abstention from profanity and his long-standing membership in the Sons of Temperance. In fact, he was hated by many for his opposition to the liquor-selling establishments in Washington, of which there were reputed to be 3,700, and for his raids on the infamous gambling halls and the numerous brothels.

When I finally received a note from the Detective Bureau that Colonel Baker would like to see me, I was both gratified and relieved. A sloppily dressed clerk conducted me to his office, which was small, contained no books, no rug, only a reproduction of Lincoln's most recent portrait on the wall, three chairs, and a table-desk with but a small pad of paper on its top. Baker put out his hand, then asked me to sit down. For a long moment, he stared at me, and I, in turn, studied this brown-bearded, compactly built man who moved with catlike grace.

"You were on the *Chesapeake* when Braine captured her."

"Yes, sir."

"Tell me about that affair, please."

Of course, he knew all about it, and I was certain that he knew all about me, too. I therefore chose my words carefully, greatly condensing the account.

"Did you know any of the pirates who seized the ship?" he asked me when I finished.

"No, sir."

"Did you know Roger Clavering?"

When I said that I did, he asked me to tell him when I had first met Clavering and the circumstances of our acquaintance-ship.

"And don't hesitate to go into more detail than in your account of the *Chesapeake* affair, lieutenant. I like details."

He smiled, ever so slightly, for the first time, and I realized that from now on, the details would be new to him. I therefore related everything of any significance that had marked the course of my relationship with Clavering — and, indeed, Tamara Ravenel. From time to time, as I spoke, Baker jotted notes on the pad of paper, eventually filling several pages. Occasionally he would nod, as if in encouragement, or grunt, which I didn't know how to interpret. But he said nothing, and his face remained expressionless. When I finished, he sat back in his chair and laced his fingers across his vest. He glanced at the clock on the mantel, and I was shocked to see that it was already four in the afternoon. I had been with Baker an hour and a half.

"Now, Lieutenant Pettigrew," he said in a tone as emotion-less as his face, "I understand you came to see me because Mr. Welles thought you should do so."

"Yes, sir. Mr. Welles seemed to think you might be inter-ested in a man who could make the navy send out a dozen ships to capture the *Chesapeake* and who might contrive other plans against the United States."

"Oh, indeed, I am interested. Clavering and Miss Ravenel are people to watch. Of course, we already know something

[320]

about them, but you have added to our store of knowledge.
. . . You are a lawyer in civilian life, Pettigrew?"

"Yes, sir."

"And your grandfather is some kind of judge?"

My beloved grandfather would have acknowledged this and
let it go with a wry smile, perhaps, but I couldn't.

"My grandfather is Chief Justice of the Supreme Court of
the State of Maine, sir!"

"Have you traveled in the South, Lieutenant Pettigrew?"

I replied that, except for navy duty, I had not been there
since I was a small boy.

"How well do you know the West?"

I mentioned my limited firsthand knowledge derived only
from my trips as a courier.

By the time he inquired if I was familiar with our northern
border and I had to tell him that I knew only that between
Maine and New Brunswick, I realized that I was poorly acquainted with my own country.

"I think I know parts of England and the Orient better than
much of the United States," I said.

"You have traveled more than many Americans," he said.
"Now . . . you may be wondering why I have been asking
these questions."

"Yes, sir, I am."

He continued to study me for a moment, then began to speak
in a voice that was somewhat louder and perceptibly harder.

"Lieutenant, the war is about to enter a new phase from the
South's point of view. I don't refer to the appointment of
General Grant to the command of our armies and to the spring
offensive he will undoubtedly open against the South. I think
the military pressure will become so strong against the Rebels
that they will try all kinds of diversionary tactics against us."

In the pause that followed I asked if he was alluding to
encouragement of the various peace organizations in the
country.

"Yes, and perhaps the arming of the more militant pro-Southern and anti-Administration groups. But I am speaking of something else, too, and this you have already been a victim of: Rebel activities in Canada for raids across the border or on our shipping."

"But haven't these developments already been in progress for some time, sir?"

"True, but the new element I look for is a more careful coordination and intensification of them."

How often, it now seemed to me, had I heard this apprehension expressed of what the year 1864 might entail. But this time it was coming from the most prominent detective chief in the country, not even excepting Allan Pinkerton, whose principal work during the war was with the army in the field.

"Now, Pettigrew," he went on, "to meet these moves by the South, we must coordinate all items of intelligence we can obtain, and plan counteraction on the basis of such intelligence. This is where, in your way, you can help us. I know all about your background and what you have been doing since you entered the war. It's my business to know, particularly if I intend to ask you, or anyone, to assist my office. This includes not only your tour of duty in England and your *Alabama* experience, but also your friendship with Henry Adams and with Bruce Thornton and his wife."

I am afraid my face became quite hard as he spoke, for he shook his head. "Do not take offense, lieutenant, or be surprised at the information available to me. . . . I am aware that Secretary Welles has asked you to submit reports to him. He asks this now of a number of his officers. But, lieutenant, what I want from you is detailed reports. Remember, Pettigrew, details! Even as to how men — and women — look when they talk, what they do with their hands, what clothes they wear. Do they wear spectacles? Do they smoke? Nothing is too small for my interest. I won't ask for your reassignment to this office. I won't ask for reports on your colleagues. But wherever the navy sends you as a courier, at home or abroad, keep your eyes and ears open and send me reports. It is through such reports from my own professionals and other detective agencies, from military and civilian police officials, that we can obtain the information that will enable us to counter the Rebels acting behind our lines or beyond our borders this spring and summer."

When I told him that I'd be glad to assist him so long as there was no conflict with my primary duty to the navy, he said, "I'm grateful to have your help, lieutenant. There are three points I wish you to bear in mind. One is that, if you have occasion to speak with me again, never wear your uniform."

"I'll remember that, sir."

"The second is that I do not want you to think I underestimate the importance of Roger Clavering or Tamara Ravenel, particularly Clavering. I am ordering an increase in our surveillance of them effective at once, and I shall make available to you whatever information we may gather about them. You will understand, I am sure, that we may have to let known enemy agents continue to operate for a time in order to see if what they are doing is part of a larger plan that eventually we must move to counter.

"Finally, I know it is unnecessary to remind you, though I will do so, that no one apart from Secretary Welles should know of your connection with this office — not your colleagues, not your friends, not your relatives — not even, unless absolutely necessary, the Chief Justice of the Supreme Court of the State of Maine!"

XXX

WASHINGTON in the early spring of 1864 had less of gaiety and more of business in its attitude than I had sensed before. Most of it had to do with the massing of troops and supplies for the great campaign to come in Virginia. For fifteen miles along the

Potomac stretched the army camps and training grounds, and everywhere one went, one heard the voice of the drill sergeant and passed columns of blue infantry marching south. Near Twenty-second and G streets was the headquarters of the depot quartermaster, and here one saw for blocks the government warehouses, storehouses, workshops, factories, and corrals, employing upwards of ten thousand men. From this area came the long convoys of canvas-topped wagons which, like the endless batteries of artillery and troops of cavalry, moved south. Brothels and gambling houses seemed to do less and less business, though in the few gambling houses I entered, the politicians appeared to take up some of the slack caused by the officers leaving for the front.

I heard innumerable serious discussions among members of Congress and others about the coming campaign. At first, I thought they were alluding only to Grant's great offensive until, by more careful listening, I realized they were giving at least as much attention to another campaign — the Congressional and Presidential elections. The Congressional elections of 1862 had been so disastrous for the Republican party that it barely retained power. Though victories at Gettysburg and Vicksburg had been helpful, Meade's failure to pursue Lee after Gettysburg had bitterly disappointed people, and conscription and the widespread abridgment of habeas corpus caused deep anger. A boom developed in late 1863 and the winter of 1864 in behalf of the Secretary of the Treasury, Salmon Portland Chase, whom Welles disliked and Seward loathed. Though it didn't last long, many people seemed to feel that almost anyone was preferable to Lincoln, who, according to his critics, picked bad generals, kept a cabinet that would not work together, lacked determination, issued an Emancipation Proclamation that had no meaning to it, and, in the outline of his emerging reconstruction policy, was too conciliatory to the South. I heard numerous predictions that Lincoln might not win the nomination of his party and that if he succeeded, he was sure to lose the election.

Members of Congress appeared to be anxious to disassociate themselves from the Administration in order to gain support in the fall elections.

The obvious hope for an Administration victory lay in Ulysses S. Grant and the western generals he had brought east with him, and in General Sherman, who was to synchronize his offensive toward Atlanta with Grant's thrust against Lee's army. With military victory, the Administration was sure to win; without victory, it was doomed.

Sick of the inconstancy and shortsightedness of politicians, I stared at the stubby Grant with frank curiosity whenever I saw him, which was frequently. He was hardly impressive to look at, a quiet, bearded man who cared nothing about his appearance, muddy or dusty, and who usually had a cigar clamped in his jaws, whether walking or riding. There was a no-nonsense air about him that encouraged one, but he was certainly not a man to lift his soldiers to wild enthusiasm, as did the dashing, elegant McClellan. But whereas McClellan had won no great victories, Grant had.

My opportunities to observe what was going on in Washington that spring were somewhat broken up by courier trips. One was to General Banks's Red River expedition which, with assistance from Admiral Porter, was aimed at Louisiana and east Texas. Banks was a better Massachusetts politician than a Union General, and Porter nearly lost part of his fleet in the swamp and the narrow river when the water fell. I never saw an angrier or more quarrelsome group of men than Banks's officers at their repulse. I wondered how many would now be alive to quarrel if Raphael Semmes had succeeded in his original plan to sink the Union transports bearing the troops for that expedition.

As for Semmes's most recent whereabouts, the *Alabama* had burned her way off Java Head and up Sunda Strait near the coast of Sumatra. The U.S.S. *Wyoming* was on the search for her on that station but kept missing her, once by only forty-eight hours. The *Alabama* worked her way down the China Sea to Singapore, where she spent Christmas Day of 1863. Her catch must have been disappointingly small, owing to the flight of American merchant ships to the safety of ports or to the greater safety of foreign, particularly British, registry. The last news reaching the Navy Department in April, 1864, was that she had called for three days at Cape Town in late March before heading west into the South Atlantic.

"Do you suppose she'll go directly for Europe or raid the South American coast?" Lee Judson asked when the consul's report from Cape Town reached us by a fast steamer.

"From what I know of Semmes," I said, "he'll go where he thinks there's a better chance of finding more of our ships. That'll be off the South American coast. But, of course, a lot depends on the *Alabama* herself."

"What do you mean?"

"She must be in pretty bad shape by now after such a cruise — I'll bet her bottom needs scraping and her engines overhauling. I doubt if she's the fast, trim lady she once was."

I wondered, too, if Mel Taylor and Joe Larkin were still with her and, for that matter, Gill. My service on the raider seemed a long, long time ago.

"If she returns to Europe, she's asking for trouble," Lee said, "particularly if she puts in at an English or a French port. The *Kearsarge* has been waiting for her for quite a while."

I looked down the long row of desks in the department. "The *Kearsarge* doesn't have exactly what you might call a remarkable record against Confederate raiders."

"That's for certain. The *Georgia* got away from her at Bordeaux and the *Florida* at Brest, and, while there were extenuating circumstances in each case, those escapes don't make John Ancrum Winslow or the *Kearsarge* look good."

He lowered his voice as he mentioned Winslow's name. Captain Winslow was no favorite with Secretary Welles or the department. Like Admiral Farragut, he was Southern-born, a

North Carolinian (Farragut was a Virginian), and, like Farragut, he had remained loyal to the Union. But, unlike Farragut, the equally blunt Winslow couldn't hold his tongue where political matters were concerned. At home when General John Pope was defeated at Second Bull Run in the summer of 1862, he was quoted by a Baltimore newspaper as having said, "I'm glad of it. I wish they would bag Old Abe." Secretary Welles, though aware that the remark, if true, originated with Winslow's annoyance at the President's ever having appointed Pope, wasted no time in sending the officer to Europe as a kind of exile. While in Europe, Winslow had become involved in an incident with England over his enlistment of a number of Irishmen for his crew, contrary to England's Foreign Enlistment Act. It was common knowledge in the department that while Welles hated Semmes, he could barely stand to hear Winslow's name mentioned.

"The *Kearsarge* may have failed with the *Georgia* and the *Florida*," I said, "but if, somehow, she can get rid of the *Alabama*, Winslow will be forgiven for everything he has said and done — or not done."

"Maybe," Judson sounded dubious. "Old Gideon isn't quick to forgive or forget. Remember: of all the cabinet, he and Postmaster General Blair are the only men who've been true to Lincoln throughout."

I realized that Welles must be having a rough spring, with the political campaign gathering momentum and the Republican convention due to meet in June and the Democratic convention, in August. This may have accounted in part for his ill humor. He was also concerned about France's building ironclads for the Confederacy, Bulloch's continuing machinations, and the ability of blockade runners still to slip in and out of Galveston, Mobile, Wilmington, and, occasionally, Charleston.

My own life at the time was uneventful: a series of duty trips, reports to Welles and Colonel Baker, and occasional visits to bars and gambling houses with Judson or Benton. All this was hardly exciting fare compared with any previous year of the war. Then, the last day in April, Mr. Welles called me into his office and bade me pack for Europe.

"I want a complete report from you on the *Sea King*. I hear that Bulloch's dickering to take her over when she comes back from Bombay, and refit her for another *Alabama* cruise. There's another raider being refitted in Calais — the *Rappahannock*. Matthew Maury, who used to have charge of the Naval Observatory here, was responsible for buying both the *Rappahannock* and the *Georgia* for the Rebels. He's not in the same class as Bulloch, and his ships are inferior, but I don't want that vessel to get out of Calais. Find out what you can about her. Talk with Mr. Adams, Consul Dudley, Mr. Dayton, and Consul Bigelow. I want you to take a letter to Captain Winslow of the *Kearsarge*, too." Dayton was our Minister in Paris; Bigelow, the consul general there.

So just when I had resigned myself to a routine existence based in Washington, I was ordered to be up and away. If I wasn't to be present when the great land campaigns opened in the first week of May, or as the fleets tightened their hold over the Confederate ports, I was at least to do some fast traveling.

Hence, within a fortnight or so after Grant had crossed the Rapidan and entered upon the bloody experience of the Wilderness, and Sherman had moved out of Chattanooga on the road to Atlanta, I was on the high seas headed for Liverpool.

On arrival, I went at once to the consulate, where I found Mr. Dudley in conference with Bruce Thornton and Maguire. When the conference ended, they soon emerged from Consul Dudley's office. The greetings we exchanged were those of old friends.

Later, in his office, Dudley paced back and forth as he read the letter I handed him from Secretary Welles.

"Look," he said, "I'll have a summary drawn up tomorrow of what we know, which isn't much, not even as much as we knew

[328]

about the *Alabama*. We know Bulloch has his eye on the *Sea King*, but he'll have to move much more secretly and adroitly to get her to sea. He also faces the same problem that he did with the *Alabama:* he will have to put guns on her somewhere outside the British Isles. I couldn't guarantee that, whatever the difficulties, he won't succeed — he's that able. I can't tell you the number of times I've wished that man were on our side."

Mr. Dudley then asked me many questions about the political situation at home. He was sorely disturbed at the growing opposition to the Lincoln Administration. Finally he said, "Be sure to stop by tomorrow afternoon for that summary."

Passing up Mrs. Washburn's boardinghouse this time, I registered at a hotel. Tomorrow I would have to get on to London, or the day following at the latest. Once in my room, I took a nap. Not that I needed sleep, for I had slept out of boredom a good part of my way across the Atlantic, a slow, stormy voyage that required more than two weeks to complete. The trouble now was that ever since coming ashore, I had found the ground rocking and myself getting dizzy, after having avoided seasickness on the trip across.

At supper with the Thorntons, Sally and Bruce kept me recounting what had happened on the *Alabama*, in Portland with the chase of the *Caleb Cushing*, and on the *Chesapeake* when Braine seized her.

"Whatever happened to the *Chesapeake?*" Bruce asked.

"The vice-admiralty court in Halifax gave its decision in mid-February, restoring the ship to her original owners but declaring Braine's seizure not an ordinary piratical act and possibly not an act of piracy at all. So no penal action was taken against him or his crew."

"What of Clavering?"

"For the moment, we've lost sight of him, but he'll turn up, I'm sure, in some trouble spot."

"And Tamara Ravenel?" Sally asked.

"I don't know where she is, either. But last summer she

wasn't far from Hampden." At their exclamations of surprise, I asked, "Didn't your father write you that I met her when he and I went to Castine?"

"He wrote that the two of you were in Castine, but he said nothing about her," Bruce said. "Did you ask him to keep it a secret?"

"Yes. The incident struck me as a little odd," I said, and I told them about it.

Bruce slowly shook his head. "It doesn't make any sense to me."

"I have a feeling," Sally said, "that Miss Ravenel does very little on sheer impulse. I admit I can't think of a reasonable explanation for her painting in Castine, but I'm certain there was a motive of some kind behind it."

When they asked what I proposed to do after leaving Liverpool, I told them that, among other things, I would visit the *Kearsarge*.

"Be sure to meet our cousin James Thornton, Winslow's right arm," Bruce said. "He's a lieutenant commander, and by all reports a very able officer."

James Thornton was indeed an able officer. Before leaving Washington, I had checked over the list of officers and crew of the *Kearsarge*. The ship had the reputation of having an especially well-drilled crew in seamanship and gunnery, and, without taking anything from Winslow, who was an excellent skipper, a lot of the credit was due to James Thornton. But I had never suspected he was related to my friends. I promised to give him their regards.

When I arrived in London, it was the Liverpool reception all over again, but more surprising because the legation office was not remarkable for its cheer. Wilson was effusive and loud, but meant well. Moran, cantankerous Moran, shook my hand warmly and said he considered it a genuine pleasure to see me again. Coming from Moran, such a statement, commonplace as it was, meant something. Henry Adams was out of the office when I entered, but when he returned, he moved quickly to take my hand.

"This is splendid, Scott," he said. "Come in and pay your respects to Father."

Mr. Adams received me with a touch of frost. I suspect he had never quite forgotten my suggestion of bribing a member of the *Alabama's* crew. Yet when he had read the letter I gave him from Mr. Welles, he said that he and Henry might be able to talk with me that very evening. He was remaining close to home these days because his daughter Mary was very ill with some affliction of the lungs.

Supper was a sober affair. Mary was sick, Mrs. Adams was suffering from one of her headaches, and Brooks was away visiting a friend. Henry and I tried to carry on a conversation, but Mr. Adams's problems seemed to weigh on him so heavily that his conversation lacked zest entirely. Though Henry and I talked, there were long silences when the three of us made a serious business of eating. Fortunately, Mr. Adams became more attentive, even charming, later on.

We talked of many things that evening — of English hostility and English friendship, of raiders, of the terrible death grapple in Virginia, of politics and peace.

"This war cannot continue much longer without ruining the structure of our government and our society, and shattering the ideals on which they are based," Mr. Adams said.

"Isn't this result inevitable, sir?" I asked. "By destroying the system of slavery, we are bound to force a change in the structure of Southern society, and the new industrial wealth that is being created by the war is already modifying society in the North."

"All this may be inevitable, given the long duration of the war, but not all of it is desirable. The elimination of slavery? Yes. It has been a foul blot. But the economic changes, so numerous and radical, the centralization of political power, the use of executive power, however necessary, to abridge civil

[331]

liberties — these are developments to be viewed with the profoundest concern."

"In my opinion," Henry said, "the rise of industrial power has made all of us victims of the machine. Why, even slavery was clearly on its way out when the cotton gin appeared and strengthened it. We fight for raw materials to feed the machine, and fight for markets to distribute its products. We wear the cheap clothing it makes, ride in trains that it creates, and buy the foods that it is producing in the new forms of food processing. I understand our army is now being provided with 'dessicated' potatoes — at least I believe that's the dreadful term. Our whole life is becoming synthetic, artificial, determined by monstrous forces that we have called into existence."

"But we can't go back to a rural society, Henry," I said.

"True, but there are ideals, particularly of the worth and dignity of the individual and his work, that we should fight to preserve and that are being lost, and hastened in the losing by the war."

"You must see now," and Mr. Adams smiled, "that Henry and I have had some long and increasingly frequent conversations about the war."

"Yes," Henry said, "and Father manages to remain cool when he reads the criticisms of the North in the papers, while I get angry and show it all too often. When we learn what's happening at home, this upsets us, too, so we vent our impotence by discussing its causation. And I assure you, Scott, that's a fascinating but futile exercise. I envy my brother Charles in the cavalry, who looks after his horse and his men and thinks only of what's going to happen next."

Mr. Adams now changed the subject. "What do you do after leaving here?" he asked me.

"I shall go directly to Captain Winslow of the *Kearsarge* with a message from Secretary Welles, then to Paris to see Mr. Dayton and Mr. Bigelow. I hope to leave tomorrow."

"The *Kearsarge* is now off Flushing at the mouth of the

Scheldt," Henry said. "You'd better take a ferry across to the Hook of Holland, then a train to Flushing. Have you heard anything new about the *Alabama*? The last we heard, she was at Cape Town."

"She's had time to raid in the South Atlantic," I said, "but the pickings were probably so very poor that my guess is she is bound for Europe right now and shouldn't be far away."

"Captain Winslow could extend Raphael Semmes an interesting welcome back to Europe," Mr. Adams said.

"What wouldn't I give to watch that welcome!" Henry exclaimed.

"From philosophers we have indeed turned warriors," Mr. Adams said, laughing slightly. And slightly is all that I ever heard him laugh.

XXXI

WHEN I boarded the *Kearsarge* at Flushing, where she had only recently gone from Dover, Captain Winslow received me courteously but with a certain unmistakable reserve which I suspect had its origin in suspicion of any courier bearing a special dispatch from Secretary Welles. I had no knowledge of what the letter contained, but I presume Mr. Welles reminded Winslow of his duty to bring the *Alabama*, of all raiders, under his guns as soon as possible and if she put into any European port, never to let her escape. If this was the purport of the message, I could surely understand Winslow's attitude; nor did his attitude change after he signed a receipt indicating he had both received and read what I had brought. He had been assigned to the European station in part because of his criticism of the Administration. Moreover, whether it was his fault directly or not, he was held responsible for failing to intercept the *Georgia* and the *Florida* in their flight from French ports. I was sure he did not need to be reminded of his duty. I was also sure that Secretary Welles, with his hatred of Semmes, was making absolutely certain that Winslow did not forget.

But whatever his personal feelings, Winslow was too shrewd to dismiss me immediately. It wasn't every day that a courier arrived in Europe from the Secretary of the Navy with a message for the commander of one of the navy's smaller men-of-war. He extended me an invitation to stay aboard for the night, before going on to Paris in the morning. I gladly accepted.

Later that evening, with supper over and his officers about him smoking their cigars, Winslow warmed up. A stocky, cherubic-cheeked man with a stubbly brush of black beard, he spoke with the energy with which he walked, and retained only a touch of Southern accent. As he introduced me to his officers before the meal, I thought he was already more cordial than when I had first appeared. This may have been because he had had time to get over his initial resentment. It may also have been owing in part to my having changed from civilian clothes into uniform; my status may thus have been more acceptable to him.

I was much taken with James Thornton, his executive officer. He was a tall, quiet, rather serious man, bearded like most of the others. When he spoke, which was not often, he had an air of kind authority. In some ways he reminded me of Semmes's executive, Lieutenant Kell. I suppose I was drawn to Thornton because of his kinship with Sally and Bruce; when I gave him their greetings, he seemed pleased. It had been several months since he had last seen them.

I found among the officers an eagerness to have the *Alabama* return. To a man they were certain that the *Kearsarge* could win a battle with her; Acting Masters Wheeler and Stoddard were plainspokenly convinced, while Thornton was quietly confident. For a year, the *Kearsarge* had been on the Channel station, and both officers and crew were restive, Acting Master Sumner to the point of having asked to be relieved from duty and Wheeler considering it. The only honorable way of bringing the steamer's assignment to an end appeared to be in destroying the *Alabama.*

They asked me many questions about Semmes, his officers, his crew, the *Alabama's* armament, her gunnery, and her sailing qualities, and I gave them all the information I could.

"Semmes and I were shipmates a long time ago," Winslow said, squinting in the candlelight, "but I have forgotten much of what I knew about him, or never learned what I'm now looking for. Can you tell us if he plays a touch-and-go situation cautiously or does he take a chance?"

I was silent, with all eyes on me, as I recalled when the *San Jacinto* nearly trapped the *Alabama* in Fort de France, when Semmes broke off his raid on New York rather than run out of coal, when he swept up the Gulf to Galveston and, finding no transports, lured the *Hatteras* into a fight.

"I think, sir," I said at last, "that it's not necessarily a case of either one way or the other. I don't mean to split hairs, but in a tight situation, he will often take a risk, the odds of which he has calculated very finely. So far, his calculations have paid off. On the other hand, I'm convinced he has real weaknesses."

"Yes? What are they?"

"He is a man of enormous pride — in the South, in his ship, in himself. He is also a man with a consuming hatred of the North, particularly of New England, which he damns as the home of abolitionists and factory owners. Of all the officers on the *Alabama,* I think he was the only one who took a real pleasure in burning ships, many of them, of course, from New England. At the same time, I think he finds it a little humiliating personally, as well as for his ship and the South, to have his reputation based largely on destroying merchant ships. I doubt that Captain Bulloch would have approved his proposed raid on our transports in the Gulf when they might have been protected by warships. And I'm sure Bulloch wouldn't have approved Semmes's taking on the *Hatteras.* The *Alabama* was

[335]

constructed primarily as a commerce raider, not a man-of-war. It is when his pride and hatred fuse that his judgment, in my opinion, becomes questionable."

Winslow looked at his long cigar ash, and his officers looked at him.

"Pettigrew, my conclusion from what you have said is that under proper provocation, Semmes might not be able to resist standing up and fighting if I should meet him at sea, or coming out of some port and fighting if I could lure him beyond the three-mile limit. Is my conclusion correct?"

"It is, sir."

"Well, Thornton, what do you make of it?"

"From all I have heard of Semmes, sir, I would say that Mr. Pettigrew's reasoning is sound."

The other officers nodded, and Captain Winslow said, "This will bear thinking on. But, of course, we can't act until that damned ship arrives in these waters."

The next day, I went on to Paris. The French capital in early June was a lovely place. The construction of the magnificent tree-lined boulevards, parks, and public buildings under Baron Haussman's direction was still going on, giving the visitor an impression of affluence. I never saw so many well-dressed people on the streets; even the poor wore their clothes with an air, while many officers and enlisted men cocked their caps at a jaunty angle that would have horrified the English military and amused our own. As for the women of Paris, I saw more hard faces among them in a few blocks than I ever saw in London or New York.

Mr. Dayton, our Minister, received me with the utmost graciousness. He was a man in his middle fifties, a Princeton graduate, formerly a member of the Supreme Court of New Jersey and a United States senator. Tall, courtly, and dignified, he appeared well fitted for the Paris post. It was perhaps appropriate, too, that he had something of a reputation while in Europe for being a bon vivant in both dining saloon and boudoir. Though I doubt that he possessed the ability of Mr. Adams, he had performed quite effectively in discouraging Napoleon III from recognizing the South and in keeping down the number of ships delivered by French builders to the Confederacy. If he had failed to dissuade the Emperor from attempting a conquest of Mexico, it was less because of any deficiency of skill or tact than because the United States, torn by the war, lacked the strength to enforce the doctrine originally proposed by President Monroe.

Dayton glanced through Mr. Welles's letter and murmured, "Ah, yes, the ironclads. I doubt, Lieutenant Pettigrew, that France will construct any more ironclads or wooden ships for the Confederacy."

"That is good news, sir, but one can't forget that the Emperor encouraged the South to place orders in France."

"True, but that is probably in the past. The two ironclads that were being built are presumably to be sold by the Emperor's order — at least, that is my understanding. It happened like this. Last fall, some clerk in the shipyard office at Nantes came to Consul Bigelow and offered to sell him letters revealing the Southerners' plans to have the French build ships for them. Actually six were already under construction: two ironclads and four wooden ships. Mr. Bigelow notified me, and I spoke with the Emperor. The Emperor has about decided that all must be sold. Whether negotiations have been entirely completed is difficult to be sure of. I believe, however, that one ironclad goes to Prussia, as do two of the wooden ships, the other ironclad to Denmark, and the remaining two wooden ships to Peru."

"Is there any chance that the Emperor might change his mind and make other ships available to the South?"

"I doubt it, lieutenant. After all, we are very close to triumphing over the South, and His Majesty would not want to

[337]

have been caught backing the wrong horse. Whatever Captain Bulloch may now do, his efforts to obtain ironclads for the Confederacy are finally and irrevocably defeated."

Mr. Dayton's manner was suave and his voice confident. I felt reasonably certain he was right, too; I would have felt more reassured, however, had Mr. Adams told me what he had. In fact, there was something about Dayton that, to one who had known Mr. Adams, was a little too omniscient and — perhaps I did him an injustice — oleaginous. I wondered, moreover, if Dayton realized how resourceful Bulloch could be. Mr. Adams was never one to underestimate a worthy opponent.

But I would be unfair to Mr. Dayton if I did not acknowledge his hospitality and kindness. He introduced me to his family, and revealed an unmistakable pride in his son William, Junior, who had recently been to London on some kind of secret business, according to Moran at the legation. Moran had been put out because young Dayton had visited the Adamses several times but had never stopped in at the legation office to pay his respects. I found the son a bright, agreeable person, somewhat too self-assured. Mr. Dayton also arranged for me to be shown around the new Paris and offered to have the legation provide me with tickets to social events, or letters of introduction. For the moment, I declined until I had sent off letters to Secretary Welles and had seen Mr. Bigelow.

Consul General John Bigelow I liked at once. He had a fine carriage and a splendid, rather leonine head. More important, he possessed warmth and genuineness of manner. In his late forties, he had earlier studied law but had achieved his reputation with the *New York Evening Post*, which he owned and edited on a partnership basis with the celebrated William Cullen Bryant, whose poem, "Thanatopsis" I had recited in a declamation contest as a schoolboy of twelve — though not well enough to win the prize of two dollars.

He was less confident about the French-built ships than Dayton. "The Emperor may indeed have given instructions to dispose of those ships, lieutenant, but he can be quite fickle. I will admit, of course, that he has not permitted the *Rappahannock* to leave Calais."

"Surely he's not likely to change his mind with the great campaigns going on under Grant and Sherman."

Bigelow shrugged. "Who can tell? If it appears that they are winning, no. But the latest information is that Grant is having a hard time and suffering enormous casualties, while Sherman seems unable to bring General Johnston to battle. How long will our people put up with the death toll and the indecisiveness? If Napoleon senses that our resolution is weakening, he may change his mind on the whole question of letting ships be built for the South."

"Is there anything we can do, apart from beating Lee and Johnston, to influence the French?"

"There is," and Bigelow's fist came down on his desk. "If our government means to prevent any vessels from entering Confederate service, it has got to make its determination known on this side of the water promptly. We need several ships over here besides the *Kearsarge*. They should be instructed to appear in the different ports, and disappear, then reappear frequently."

"Why do you think that, sir?"

"Because their arrivals and departures will be telegraphed. They will awaken surmises and speculations and spread the idea that we are alive and a naval power."

"But won't people realize there are only a few of them?"

"Nonsense! People forget the names of the vessels that are announced, and with active, dashing commanders, two or three vessels would soon be multiplied in the mind of the public to twenty. The psychological effect of all this — and I don't exaggerate when I say it — would be worth more just now than anything Mr. Dayton can say to the Emperor's ministers, which the public will never know about, anyway, since nothing written in English ever reaches the French people unless, occasionally, it's a popular novel. Write that to Secretary Welles, if you wish — I'm going to write it to the Secretary of State. Maybe, between the two of us, we can get some action."

"Do you think there is anything more to fear from Bulloch even if the Emperor orders these six ships sold?"

"Bulloch is always to be feared — that you should know, lieutenant, from your own experience. He will never stop trying to put the Confederate flag on the ocean, not until the Confederacy collapses, in any case."

"Have you any indication, sir, that if the *Alabama* puts into a French port, the government will accord it protection?"

"There's an enormous interest and sympathy, partly romantic, in Semmes and his ship contending alone on the high seas, but I trust that the government will observe the usages of international law very carefully. This means, among other things, that the *Alabama* will not be able to remain indefinitely in port. If Winslow really is eager to meet the *Alabama*, I think he may get his chance."

There was a down-to-earth practicality about Consul Bigelow that I liked. He might lack something of the polish of Mr. Dayton in manner and rhetoric, but he had a sense of realism. His suggestion of how we might convince the French we were really the naval power we claimed to be, had in it an element of imagination that was appealing, and wholly feasible, too, so far as I could see.

Yet it was Mr. Dayton who kindly put me up at his home and found a nurse to look after me when I came down for several days with a bout of malaria that occasionally recurred from the time I had originally contracted it, in the Orient with Captain Nathan Cummings and the *Grace Stone*. Fortunately, I had sent off reports to Secretary Welles prior to becoming ill, though before I had completed a summary of Mr. Bigelow's views. I could scarcely hold a pen in my hand, my teeth chattered, and I was nauseatingly giddy with chills and fever.

When I was finally able to keep on my feet unassisted and walk in the garden, I was shocked to realize how weak I was and how much time had passed. I thought of the *Alabama* and wondered whether that graceful, deadly ship was still on the high seas or safe within a French port. When I asked Mr. Dayton, he said that she was still at large but must be getting close to the Continent by this time. He told me that I must not think of her in my condition but should concentrate on getting well. Luckily, I have a swift recuperative system, but it was not that alone which made me feel energetic again.

I had just dropped into the legation office after dinner on Saturday, June 11, and found both Dayton and his son greatly excited, for all their reputation for calmness. In fact, it was unusual to find Mr. Dayton there at all on a Saturday afternoon.

"She's here in France," Mr. Dayton said. "At least, we think she is."

"What's this?" I asked.

"I have just received a telegram from Edouard Liais, our vice-consul at Cherbourg, that a Confederate steamer has anchored in the harbor. Liais thinks it is the *Florida*."

I had forgotten that the *Florida*, as well as the *Alabama*, had been much on their minds, and that the *Florida* had earlier slipped out of a French port.

Then, in the late afternoon, while everyone waited for further details, came the tremendous news from Liais: "The rebel steamer is the *Alabama* with thirty-seven federal prisoners."

Instantly Mr. Dayton sent off a wire to Captain Winslow at Flushing. He also informed the Minister of Foreign Affairs, Drouyn de Lhuys, and protested the *Alabama*'s use of a French port. Even Mr. Adams could not have been more prompt, for all Dayton's reputation for indolence.

That weekend and the first part of the next week, we followed, through the telegraph wire and the newspapers, the rising crescendo of developments. Winslow received Dayton's telegram on Sunday, the 12th. He immediately wired Consul Eggleston at Cadiz, who forwarded the message to Horatio

[341]

Sprague, the United States consul at Gibraltar, ordering Commander Preble of the steam sloop of war *St. Louis* to take on provisions immediately and proceed with all possible haste to Cherbourg. The *Kearsarge* herself left Flushing at once for Dover, where she received a new trysail and topsail on the 13th, and arrived off Cherbourg at noon on Tuesday the 14th. At the legation someone rounded up a chart of the French coast, and we studied the harbor with magnifying glasses. There were two entrances — or exits — an eastern and a western. It thus became clearer why Winslow should want the *St. Louis* to join him: both passages had to be covered in case the French should order the *Alabama* out of port and Semmes made a run for the open sea.

But Winslow did not wait for the *St. Louis*. Steaming toward the Cherbourg breakwater, he stopped his engines off the eastern entrance and sent a boat inside to communicate with Vice-Consul Liais with a view to obtaining for his crew some of the prisoners released by Semmes. The request denied by the French, the *Kearsarge* moved closer to the *Alabama*, which was anchored in the roads, and the crews of both ships stared eagerly at each other. Yet there was scarcely a sound as the *Kearsarge* swung away toward the western passage and took up her station off the harbor, cruising back and forth.

As we learned of this action by Winslow, it certainly looked like one champion throwing down the gage to another. I recalled at once the conversation I had had with Winslow and his officers, and Winslow's interest in what I had to say about Semmes's pride. There was soon no doubt that whether Winslow had deliberately lured the *Alabama* or not, Semmes could not ignore the gesture. The telegraph key began presently to tap out a message from Cherbourg that Semmes had sent the following to the Confederate agent, M. Boufils, for transmission by Vice-Consul Liais to Winslow:

"I desire to say to the U.S. consul that my intention is to fight the *Kearsarge* as soon as I can make the necessary arrangements. I hope these will not detain me more than until tomorrow evening, or after the morning of the next day at furthest. I beg she will not depart before I am ready to go out."

News of the coming duel soon spread through Paris. The newspapers were full of it, and there was a rush of the curious to the trains for Cherbourg. Sympathy was largely pro-*Alabama*.

Meanwhile, the *Alabama* was denied repairs at Cherbourg because the yards there belonged to the French Navy and what she needed to have done was not indispensable to her going to sea again; furthermore, she had not had to enter Cherbourg by any accident of the sea. She should have stopped at one of the great commercial ports, in the view of the French government, or at a commercial port of Spain, Portugal, England, Belgium, or Holland. If she chose to remain at Cherbourg, she would be interned. The more we thought of this judgment of the Minister of the Marine and the Colonies, the better we could understand Semmes's decision; it was compounded of pride and necessity — necessary if the *Alabama* was to remain on active duty. Semmes therefore withdrew his application for repairs and was coaling rapidly.

The impending fight between the two ships was one that I was determined to witness. Though I still did not feel entirely fit, I had improved since learning of the *Alabama*'s arrival and the *Kearsarge*'s moving into position offshore. I informed Mr. Dayton that I intended to buy a ticket for Cherbourg and leave on the morning of the 16th.

"Then I will save you the trouble of paying for that ticket yourself, lieutenant, and I will assure you of a chance to see at least the *Kearsarge* before the battle. It is my pleasure to give you an official assignment from this legation as a courier to Captain Winslow."

He waved my thanks aside. "In view of your service on the *Alabama*, I believe this is due you. And should anything happen to the message en route, I will give you the gist of its contents to disclose to Captain Winslow. The three-mile limit, as you

[343]

well know, was accepted at a time when that was the maximum range of cannon. With the increased range of cannon today, the French government, through its Minister for Foreign Affairs, has expressed concern that the battle may occur so close to the French coast. They would like to forbid it altogether, but I have told the minister that no other rule than the three-mile rule is known or recognized as a principle of international law. I have instructed Captain Winslow that no battle must occur within the three-mile limit and that if he will lose nothing by fighting six or seven miles off the coast, he should try to do so. All unnecessary trouble with France must be avoided."

"Very good, sir."

"Then you'd best leave on the early morning train, lieutenant. I would suggest, too, that you remain for the battle and bring back a copy of Captain Winslow's report with you. I will have the legation reserve a passage for you on a Channel steamer at Calais. I have correspondence for you to deliver at the legation in London and more for you to carry to Washington. Since you have indicated your desire to return to the United States as soon as possible, I wired London, and Mr. Moran has reserved a cabin for you on the *Britannic* sailing Wednesday next."

Again I expressed my thanks to Mr. Dayton, and, on the morrow, could scarcely reach Cherbourg soon enough, so great was my impatience.

That morning, I had taken the suggestion of Consul Bigelow and dressed in civilian clothes. I was glad that I did; it saved me from a number of useless altercations. Not only was the train filled with Southern sympathizers among the French and a number of English aboard, but there were at least a half-dozen Confederate naval officers in their gray uniforms trimmed with gold lace and buttons. They were a gay lot and hopeful of a chance to serve on the *Alabama* in the coming battle. So had I been eager to serve on the *Kearsarge* until Mr.

Dayton informed me that the French would not permit me to fight any more than they would allow Winslow to take aboard the released prisoners from the *Alabama*. The Confederate officers were therefore doomed to know disappointment even as I had. In fact, it was only my official capacity as a courier from Mr. Dayton to Captain Winslow that would persuade the French to allow me to leave the waterfront for the *Kearsarge*.

Fortunately, I had little difficulty in getting out to the *Kearsarge*; Vice-Consul Liais had chartered a steam launch to take me out to the sloop of war. After checking my credentials, a French naval officer waved me aboard. I found the *Kearsarge* cruising rather close to the three-mile limit, where, for all any of us knew, Winslow might have decided to fight had not Dayton sent me to Cherbourg with the cautionary instructions.

Captain Winslow was tense, laconic, but fairly cheerful. "Is Semmes finished taking on coal?" were his first words to me after I delivered Mr. Dayton's letter to him in his cabin.

"Yes, sir. The report from the vice-consul is that the *Alabama* will be coming out tomorrow."

"We'll be ready for her. Has Semmes recruited any more crew?"

"No, sir. The French refused him officer volunteers from Paris even as they denied you permission to enlist the *Alabama*'s prisoners."

"Well, at least they're playing no favorites for a change."

We talked for a minute or two longer, I told him about the battle report I was to bring back with me, and then he dismissed me. When I reached the deck, I stood by the gangway with James Thornton, chatting. As I glanced along the black hull amidships, I noticed a very slight but unmistakable bulge projecting at right angles.

To my question, Commander Thornton said, "A year ago, we adopted a device Admiral Farragut's wooden ships had to use on the Mississippi River against Rebel shore batteries and ironclads. We draped anchor chain over our sides to protect the engines, secured the chains to the hull, and cased them in with one-inch deal boards."

"If you beat the *Alabama*, Semmes will claim he lost to an ironclad."

Thornton shrugged. "He has the same privilege. I'm sure he's got enough spare anchor chain in his lockers, and he has enough time to do everything but box the chain in."

"Does he know about this?"

"I'm not sure. The marine prefect of Cherbourg sent an officer out to inspect us just before you arrived. He noticed the anchor chain bulge, too, and asked what it was. I wouldn't be surprised if his office has already passed the information on to Semmes."

I wished Thornton the best and left for shore, my thought now being to find a place on some craft that would go out and observe the battle. With a note from Vice-Consul Liais as support, I managed to find a French pilot-boat captain who was not averse to accepting an additional passenger for an outrageous sum, despite his already being crowded, or so he said.

That Saturday night, in the long twilight, I strolled through Cherbourg. French naval vessels rode at anchor in the harbor; one of them near the breakwater, an ironclad named *La Couronne*, was to act as a policeman of the three-mile limit. The *Alabama* looked trim and ready, her standing rigging stoppered, her light spars sent down, and the top-hamper disposed of. In the distance I could see the *Kearsarge* cruising slowly back and forth. Inshore or at the wharves lay a number of pleasure craft, one of them a lovely steam yacht, the *Deerhound*, belonging, I heard, to a rich English manufacturer named John Lancaster, who was here with his family.

A number of the *Alabama*'s crew had been given a few hours' liberty, and wherever they went, people invited them into wineshops and toasted them. Though I kept a sharp eye for Mel Taylor and Joe Larkin, I saw neither. I recognized a number of the crew, but there were many new faces. No one recognized me, I was sure. I thought it significant of the trust between Semmes and his crew that he could let so many of them go ashore the night before the battle. As I watched them gather at the landing stage very early in the evening, to be taken to the *Alabama*, I doubted that any had deserted.

Among the officers, I identified Sinclair and Wilson — and Semmes. The first two were with a group of fellow officers down from Paris who were feasting them royally in one of the cafés. Semmes was a severe, aloof figure who walked to a church on the top of the hill, where undoubtedly he prayed for success; he was ever a faithful, devout Catholic. Crowds stared at him, but he ignored them completely. I was torn between dislike and admiration of the man. He would need all his courage and skill when he faced the *Kearsarge* on the morrow.

The next morning was the Sabbath, and all the lowering clouds and rainy, blustery weather of the previous week had passed. It was a day of bright sun and blue sky, obscured only by a very slight haze which the breeze from the westward was too light to dissipate. Church bells were ringing for masses, but far more people seemed to be heading for the docksides than for the churches. Others lined the hill, and as I headed for the waterfront from the consulate, I noticed the upper-story windows of houses crowded with observers. The *Alabama*, judging by the smoke trailing from her funnel, was getting steam up. So was *La Couronne*. So, too, was the English yacht *Deerhound*.

With binoculars borrowed from Mr. Dayton, I went aboard the pilot boat, one of at least two French luggers that were going out to witness the contest. My French, though only passable, was adequate for me to realize that I was alone among a group of possibly twenty-five intensely Confederate partisans. They included officers of the French Navy, a number of town officials, and citizens who evidently had influence and money enough to obtain passage.

When, at nine forty-five A.M., the *Alabama* headed from her

[347]

anchorage toward the western entrance, the French ironclad fell in behind her and the *Deerhound* behind the ironclad, while the luggers brought up the rear.

As the *Alabama* passed the big man-of-war *Napoleon*, the French crew cheered the raider, and the *Napoleon's* band played "Dixie." The luggers likewise cheered, and we could also hear the distant roar of applause from shore. If popular support could win a battle, there was no doubt of the *Alabama's* victory.

Actually, as I watched the raider steam toward the *Kearsarge*, which had taken up a waiting station six or seven miles offshore, I wasn't so confident as I felt yesterday. The two ships were pretty evenly matched. In tonnage they were about the same: the *Kearsarge*, 1,031 tons; the *Alabama*, 1,016 tons. The crews numbered 163 for the *Kearsarge*, 149 for the *Alabama* — no significant difference. In guns the raider had eight as against the Union ship's seven. For the *Alabama*: one hundred-pound Blakely rifle, one sixty-eight-pound smoothbore, and six broadside thirty-two-pounders. For the *Kearsarge*: two eleven-inch Dahlgren smoothbores, one twenty-eight-pound rifle, and four broadside thirty-two-pounders. If the *Alabama* kept the *Kearsarge* at a distance, the long-range hundred-pounder could knock the *Kearsarge* to pieces. On the other hand, if Winslow moved to within four hundred to five hundred yards, the massive Dahlgren pivot guns, one forward and one aft, each firing a shot weighing 135½ pounds, could tear the *Alabama* apart. Because she had been so long at sea without overhaul, the *Alabama* was probably a little slower than her rival, and through the glass I used, I could see no chains draped down the raider's hull to protect her engines. Semmes's crew, however, had long worked well together and had fought the *Hatteras*. Many of the *Kearsarge's* men would be under fire for the first time. This was so even a match that the favorite was largely picked on sentiment.

"You look worried, my friend."

I turned at the amused tone and saw a very young man with a

formidable brown beard and bright blue eyes. He wore a business suit but a workman's cap, and held a sketchbook under his arm.

"My thoughts are not pleasant," I said.

"You are a Southern American, monsieur?"

Although he spoke in clear French, I had never heard a Confederate so alluded to, and I hesitated. "No," I said at last, "I am not. I am a citizen of the United States. My name is Scott Pettigrew."

He bowed. "I am Jean Soult, an art student of Edouard Manet." As I had little knowledge of art or artists, the name Manet meant nothing to me. "There are critics who deplore that Manet exists," he said. "Someday I hope he will have the pleasure of laughing in their faces."

"Perhaps he will, monsieur. Do you live in Cherbourg?"

"Cherbourg!" If I had said the North Pole, he could not have been more incredulous or disdainful. "I am from Paris, monsieur, and I have come to this provincial port to sketch the sea fight for Manet."

"Do you know anything about ships?"

"No, but does that matter to an artist? . . . My God, what was that?"

We stared seaward. Black and white smoke billowed up from the *Alabama*, which had fired her starboard broadside at the *Kearsarge* rushing toward her with foam at her bow. I glanced at my watch; it was not quite eleven o'clock.

"Ah, those two begin," Soult said, as he opened his sketchbook.

"Not yet, monsieur," I remarked. "At least, not the *Kearsarge*."

The two ships had been about twelve hundred yards apart when the *Alabama* fired. Then she fired another, and yet another broadside before the *Kearsarge* sheered and replied with a broadside of her own. But Winslow was still too far away, possibly nine hundred yards. I could see the splashes made by the Dahlgrens, far short of their mark. Still the *Kearsarge* drove on in the face of a rapid and withering fire, trying to close the range. When it appeared that she might pass under the stern of the *Alabama* and rake her, Semmes sheered, presenting his broadside and firing.

And thus the two ships began to describe a circle, and then another — in fact, seven full circles in all. The distance between the ships progressively narrowed. At first, this was clearly Winslow's desire in order for his eleven-inch Dahlgren smoothbores to become effective. Then, when their fire became intolerable, Semmes tried to close the range entirely in order to board, but was frustrated by Winslow.

The firing itself followed an interesting pattern. That of the *Alabama* was at first rapid and high, then slowed and became more effective. The *Kearsarge* fired more slowly throughout and much more accurately, to judge from how the *Alabama* began to come to pieces when the *Kearsarge*'s big pivot guns, firing with the bulwarks removed, came within range. I could easily see in my mind's eye the crews of both ships ramming home the gun charges, bringing the guns into position, aiming, standing away, and the gunners pulling the lanyards. Then, with some men holding their hands over their ears, would come the blast, the recoil, and the swabbing and loading of the guns again. Down in the engine rooms the engineers and firemen would be drenched with sweat and black with soot and oil. They lived close to a terrible death if ever a shell penetrated the boilers. In the powder magazines all would be dim and silent and everyone desperately careful. But there was other work, grim work — that done by the surgeons, particularly on the *Alabama*. Through my binoculars I saw an entire gun crew almost wiped out, and the details of the screaming survivors and the chunks of flesh being shoveled into the sea by one cold-nerved crewman were fortunately something I learned about later rather than observed.

"These Southern Americans are losing, I fear," Soult said, as a shot smashed the *Alabama*'s gaff and the ensign came down.

"Not yet," I said, as Semmes sent it up again at the mizzen masthead. But the battle couldn't last much longer. The Dahlgrens had obviously gutted the *Alabama,* for she began to list.

"Why doesn't she make for shore?" Soult asked, his eyes alternating between the ships and his sketch.

"She's trying to," I replied, and on the seventh circle, Semmes set his fore-trysail and two jibs and headed inshore.

Semmes now presented his port broadside, which had only two guns, the other two having earlier been shifted to increase the weight of his starboard broadside. Though he was frantically trying to shift the other two broadside guns back to port, the maneuver was futile. The *Kearsarge* moved ahead to lay herself across the *Alabama*'s escape route.

Down fluttered the *Alabama*'s ensign from the masthead, and from the men on the lugger came expressions of sympathy which quickly changed to anger as the *Kearsarge* fired again.

"Why are your countrymen doing that?" Soult demanded.

"I don't know. There must be a misunderstanding. They may think the flag was shot away rather than lowered."

He gave me a look of outraged disbelief and turned to his sketch. In reality, I was as puzzled as he, but if anyone on the *Kearsarge* had misinterpreted the lowering of the ensign, none could make a mistake about the white flag that the *Alabama* now displayed over her stern. The firing ceased altogether, the billowing smoke clouds drifted away, and in the oppressive silence, the screaming of gulls nearby sounded thin and eerie.

With the *Alabama* sinking rapidly by the stern, I saw a boat loaded with wounded row over to the *Kearsarge.* The *Alabama*'s other boats appeared to be smashed. Men were jumping into the water.

Higher and higher climbed the bow of the great raider as she began now to slide under. Her mainmast, evidently partly shot away, broke near the head as she settled. Her funnel, spouting smoke, likewise broke away, and in a great cloud of steam and smoke, the *Alabama,* her bow pausing momentarily in a near-vertical position, sank out of sight in seventy fathoms. I looked at my watch: the time was 12:24, exactly ninety-seven minutes since the *Alabama* had opened the battle.

For a few minutes, it seemed that no one would rescue the men struggling in the water. I saw only one boat put out from the *Kearsarge*; like the *Alabama's* most of her boats must have been shattered, too.

"Captain, let's save some of those drowning men!" I called to our lugger skipper.

He looked at me stupidly, then, as the others aboard took up the cry, he nodded, and we started to sail toward the area. Instantly the other lugger followed us.

But our pace was agonizingly slow. Fortunately, the *Deerhound* steamed under the stern of the *Kearsarge*, asked or was asked to pick up survivors, and headed right in among them, dropping her boats and throwing lifelines. Eventually the *Kearsarge* managed to get two more boats patched up and into the water.

Grabbing a boathook, I fished two crewmen alongside, and willing hands dragged them aboard. One was insensible, the other throwing up the sea water he had swallowed. Then a wounded quartermaster caught my hook, and I pulled him aboard. By this time, there were very few survivors left in our vicinity. We were just turning away when I heard a faint cry for help. At once I pointed to a man thrashing water, though feebly, and the captain brought the lugger around. I caught the man with the hook as he was going under. Soult and I hauled him aboard, and I recognized him at once as Mel Taylor. His belly and right leg were dripping blood, and I did not think he had long to live.

As I carefully laid him down, holding his head on my knees, he opened his eyes. At first they were vacant, then he started to smile, ever so slightly, and his lips moved.

As I leaned close to hear, he said, in barely a whisper, "It's Dan, ain't it?"

"Yes," I said.

"Where were you, Dan?" He closed his eyes, said something that I couldn't hear, and died.

Cradling him, I stared across the waters at the *Deerhound* steaming rapidly toward England with the survivors she had recovered, at the boats of the *Kearsarge* still combing the area, at the shore with the bright sun sparkling on the red roofs and the docks crowded with silent watchers. And I shook my head at the utter misery that had occurred.

"Did you get your sketch?" I asked Jean Soult.

If my voice was harsh, he ignored the tone. "Yes, my friend," he replied, resting his hand lightly and briefly on my shoulder. "But, alas, it is only of the ships, not of men like these who fought them and suffered and died."

XXXII

THE next day I took to Paris copies of the preliminary reports of Captain Winslow to Gideon Welles, the originals going through regular channels. In Paris, Mr. Dayton gave me other correspondence to deliver to both Mr. Welles and Secretary of State Seward in Washington, and to Mr. Adams in London. I then boarded the train for Calais and a Channel steamer for Dover.

In London I found the legation besieged by Americans and Englishmen friendly to the North, congratulating Mr. Adams on the sinking of the *Alabama*. They seemed not at all disturbed by the accounts in the papers containing Semmes's allegation that the *Alabama* had lost to a ship that was virtually an ironclad. The accounts also mentioned that the *Alabama*'s powder had lost some of its efficacy. What they did not say was how poor the gunnery was on the raider, compared with the precision of that on the *Kearsarge*, thanks to Commander Thornton's training. Much, of course, was made of the fact that if a

[353]

hundred-pound projectile from the *Alabama* which lodged in the sternpost of the *Kearsarge* early in the contest had exploded, the ship would have become unmanageable and the *Alabama* would have won. Although this was a possibility, the shell didn't explode, and that was that. Only about a tenth of the *Alabama*'s 370 shots hit the *Kearsarge*, which suffered three men wounded, of whom one later died. Firing 173 shots, the *Kearsarge* not only sank her opponent but inflicted casualties that included at least nine deaths and thirty wounded, not to mention twelve subsequent deaths from drowning — of whom Bartelli was one — and prisoners taken.

One incident of the battle, about which Mr. Adams and Henry asked me many questions, concerned the departure for England of the *Deerhound* with *Alabama* survivors. She had picked up Semmes, thirteen of his officers, and twenty-seven of his men. Aboard the *Kearsarge* there had been many angry men when the yacht left, and officers had begged Winslow to fire a shot at her to make her heave to. This he had wisely declined to do, though he, too, was indignant. After all, the *Deerhound* had stood by until Winslow himself had asked her to help save the men in the water, and there was legally nothing binding on her to return the men to the *Kearsarge*. For that matter, Winslow landed in France the prisoners his boats had picked up, and paroled them. What rankled was that Semmes had escaped. Even Englishmen, including two correspondents from the *London Times*, took the view that the *Deerhound* had assisted the *Alabama* by not turning the Confederates over to Winslow. John Lancaster himself, however, protested that the men had never been Winslow's prisoners in the first place, that he had not intervened until requested, and that an English yacht on the high seas was English territory. What he had done for the *Alabama*'s people he would also have done for those of the *Kearsarge*, had the situation been reversed. Though both the Adamses regretted that Semmes had not been captured, they recognized, I am sure, that Lancaster was on firm ground.

Before I sailed for New York, Henry told me that he had seen Tamara Ravenel twice recently, in London. He understood that she was about to appear in print with a book she had written on the role played by female Confederate spies, including Rose Greenhow, Belle Boyd, and herself. She was also active in interesting shipping firms in chartering and building specially designed ships to run the blockade.

"She is an enterprising woman," Henry said.

I asked him to keep me informed, and left for Liverpool, where, after a very brief look-in on Bruce and Consul Dudley, I boarded the propeller liner *Britannic* for New York.

The passage was swift and uneventful, much faster than the eastward passage, and I landed in New York late on July 5. At once I wired Secretary Welles news of the *Kearsarge's* victory.

That evening, I looked up my friend Lieutenant Jim Hunt, whom I had last seen during the draft riots of a year ago. Over a dinner at the Astor we chatted about many things. He told me that the draft in the city, while continuing, was not very successful, owing to the three-hundred-dollar loophole and the bounty jumping. He also said the peace elements were very strong and included Republicans as well as Democrats, especially the influential editor of the *Tribune*, Horace Greeley. Nationally, a motley collection of factions at Cleveland had nominated the "Pathfinder," General John Frémont, for President. This move threatened to split the regular Republican party, which, at its convention in Baltimore in early June, renominated Lincoln. Secretary Chase had resigned from the Treasury, to be succeeded by William Pitt Fessenden of Maine.

"This war is a mess," Jim Hunt said. "Grant has failed to destroy Lee's army and has lost almost as many men as Lee had in his own army to start with. Grant slipped across the James River and might have come in on Lee and Richmond from the rear at Petersburg if his generals hadn't fouled up their attack. Now it has turned into a long siege."

[355]

"What about Sherman?"

"Fighting it out in the woods and mountains of western Georgia and not getting very far. . . . I tell you, the news you've brought will cheer all of us up."

I found even greater gloom in Washington. In fact, though Mr. Welles was delighted with the *Kearsarge* victory, he was annoyed that the dispatches I brought him on the 6th contained only bald accounts of the triumph, and he said he would write Winslow at once and demand a supplementary report.

"I'm sure Captain Winslow did not intend to send only this preliminary report, sir," I said.

"He should have known better than to have sent the brief report he did," Welles snapped. "He also made a grave error in paroling his prisoners. The *Alabama's* career was such that it did not entitle those of her crew who were captured to be paroled. She was a pirate, a British pirate at that!" And at this point, he denounced the *Deerhound's* owner, John Lancaster, and, above all, Raphael Semmes. "Why, that wretched man," he said of Semmes, "actually threw his sword overboard after he surrendered. It no longer belonged to him to throw away."

He was so vindictive in his rage at Semmes and the British and so annoyed at Winslow that I could only conclude that he was becoming a victim of the strain produced by the war. This strain was evidently increased by word received this very day of a great drive down the Shenandoah Valley by the Confederates, and their capture of Harper's Ferry.

"This is just the sort of diversion a smart man like Lee would contrive," he said. "But does Grant do anything about it? He does not. He sits in front of Petersburg showing little strategy and less invention. Perhaps he doesn't know much about this Rebel drive."

"But the War Department must know, sir."

"They're dunderheads over there, Pettigrew. Halleck is, as usual, confused, and Stanton ignorant. The Rebels are heading for Washington, and Stanton, Halleck, and Grant are asleep or

[356]

dumb. What started out as a minor movement may become a major push, thanks to the War Department and its neglect, ignorance, folly and imbecility in the last degree. Such mismanagement! I tell you, Pettigrew, it's impossible for the country to bear up indefinitely under these monstrous errors and wrongs."

The next day, I received a letter from a most unexpected source — Consul Howard of St. John, New Brunswick. After reminding me that I had asked if he would notify me if he ever learned of Roger Clavering's being in St. John, he said that Clavering was there now, evidently one of several leaders of a sizable body of Confederate civilians or pro-Confederate Canadians circulating in the city. He further said that he had written a full account of what he knew to Secretary Seward. Since he also observed that there was wild talk of ships cooperating with some military venture of these strangers in the city, I went immediately to Secretary Welles.

"Pettigrew, I already know about this."

His remark truly deflated me when I told him of Howard's letter, and he interpreted my ensuing silence correctly. "It's no mystery," he explained. "Seward got in touch with me about this yesterday and informed both me and Stanton. You are to see Baker at once."

So off I went to see the chief of the War Department's detectives. Though more often than not he was grilling suspected persons on their loyalty in Carroll Prison, the annex to the Old Capitol Prison, his principal office was still in the basement of the Treasury Building, and it was there that I found him.

"Pettigrew," he said, after nodding me to a chair, "I have spoken with Secretary Stanton about these strange doings in New Brunswick." He paused, and, as he studied me, I thought it probably typical of the man's vanity that he should say that he had discussed the matter with the Secretary of War rather than the reverse. "I want you to go to St. John at once, speak with

[357]

Howard, and mix with those Rebels up there. I'm sure they're working in connection with the Confederate commission in Canada. Get up there fast. Send me reports."

I set out, within hours, by train for Bangor. On the way north I ran over the material I had quickly gathered, principally from Richard Benton but also from Lee Judson in the Navy Department, about the Canadian commission. In the spring, Jefferson Davis had appointed three dignitaries to Canada, obviously to further the interests of the Confederacy. According to suspicion, they were to encourage dissidents in the North to make trouble for the Lincoln Administration and thereby, it was hoped, help secure the election of a peace candidate for the Presidency. These three emissaries were President Buchanan's former Secretary of the Interior, Jacob Thompson of Mississippi, who was chairman; Clement Clay, a former senator from Alabama, and a sick man; and James P. Holcombe, a scholarly former professor of law at the University of Virginia. Holcombe was already in Montreal when the other two left Wilmington by blockade runner for Bermuda in May. They then sailed on a British steamer for Halifax, crossed to St. John, went up the St. John River and overland to Riviere du Loup, where they hastened by rail to Montreal.

Associated with them was George N. Sanders, a former United States consul in London, affluent, a lavish host, a man who knew everybody, but whose influence had still been unable to secure the release of his officer son from Fort Warren in Boston. There were rumors that this commission was actively involved in all kinds of treasonous activities in the Middle West and that it was to members of the commission — now in Toronto, now in Montreal or Niagara Falls — that Confederate agents in the United States, particularly former officers from Morgan's raiders, reported. When in England, I had heard Clavering's name linked with that of George Sanders in procuring ships and supplies to run the blockade or raid Northern commerce, so it came as no effort to suspect that the two were associated in some other enterprise nearer home.

Leaving Washington at this time, with General Jubal Early and his Confederates moving closer to the capital and government people beginning to take alarm, was a wrench. It seemed to me almost as if I were fleeing from the greatest danger the city would face since the first battle of Bull Run. To be sent to St. John was a far less exciting prospect. Only the fact that Clavering was there gave the trip any real point so far as the war was concerned.

I found Consul Howard deeply concerned by recent events. These men in St. John, he said, had been gathering for several weeks. It was a little difficult to discover their leaders, but one was a Captain William Collins, formerly on the staff of the Confederate general Leonidas Polk. "He's a thoroughly bad man, a desperate character, lieutenant, who carries a Colt on a low-slung cartridge belt. Rumor has it that he has already killed two men since he arrived here. This I doubt. But the other men appear afraid of him."

"If men are pushed too far in their fear, they often turn against such a leader."

"Not here, lieutenant. He has a Man Friday always near him, an Irishman named Phillips, who's the next thing to being feebleminded and who is a huge, powerful brute. Phillips could kill a man with his fists alone."

"Anyone else worth knowing about?"

"Yes, there's a young man, in his mid-twenties, I'd say. His name is Francis Jones and he's a handsome fellow, fair-haired and blue-eyed, with considerable education. He's often seen in the company of Collins and Phillips, though what he could have in common with them baffles me."

"What about Clavering?"

Howard shook his head slightly. "He comes and goes. In my judgment he's more of an organizer than one of the actual

[359]

leaders. As such, he is, of course, far more dangerous. Again, unlike the others, he keeps his mouth shut. If you go out among them, you'll hear a lot of loose talk. But even making allowance for the liberating effects of alcohol on a man's tongue, I heard enough to warrant my informing Washington."

I soon heard it, too. I bought some workman's clothes and a hat, shifted my residence to a cheap lodging house, then strolled into the nearest saloon and ordered a whisky.

All that evening, as I drifted around, I listened to enough talk to remove any doubt, if I ever had had any, that this was a Confederate gathering of considerable size. How large was not easy to determine, because the men had evidently received orders not to bunch up and thereby attract attention and suspicion. It wasn't until the next afternoon, however, as I wandered into another of the innumerable saloons in this little Canadian port, that I heard anything of specific value.

"By God, we'll run them clear to the Penobscot the way old Jube's pushin' them into the Potomac!"

Fortunately, another man entered when I did. We went to the bar and quietly ordered, while listening to the speaker.

"If those bastards over in Calais knew what was goin' to happen, they'd start runnin' now." At the grunts of approval, the speaker added, "When Bill Collins hits that bank on Saturday, I'd hate to be a Yankee inside it."

There was a fierce "Shh!" from someone sitting near the door. No one needed to explain that the two men who now entered were Bill Collins and his faithful shadow Phillips. The latter was a big, heavy-faced man with staring eyes. Collins, however, had a swaggering air about him. I thought him probably capable of almost anything.

He ordered a whisky, then turned to the group. "Did I hear someone mention my name?"

Not a man spoke.

"Who was it?"

It was no question but an order. After a long silence, the tall man who had been holding forth stood up.

"It was me, cap'n."

"What's your name?"

"Sam Henry, sir."

"I won't ask you to repeat what you said, Henry, because I heard it, but, by God, if anyone talks that way again, I'll kill him. Do all of you understand? . . . And just to show you I mean what I say, I want you to step up here, Henry."

I give Henry his due. He walked straight up to Collins, half-drunk though he was, and gave the officer the semblance of a salute.

Collins did not return it, but looked over his shoulder at Phillips. "Cuff him!"

With two long, shambling steps forward, the Irishman drew back his arm and struck Henry on the side of the head with his palm. It didn't look like a hard blow. Yet Henry was thrown to one side and lay unconscious.

Without another word Collins strode out, followed by the giant Phillips.

We watched in silence as he stopped outside, hitched up his trousers, and was joined at once by a man who crossed the street — Roger Clavering.

"I've been looking for you, Collins," he said, a trace of annoyance in his voice.

Collins's chin came up. "I've been available, Mr. Clavering."

"I'm sure you have. Now please come with me."

As the two men walked away, with Phillips trailing behind, the saloon came to life.

"God damn him!" I heard one man mutter.

Others picked up Henry and poured whisky between his lips. Henry presently came to.

As soon as I could do so without making myself conspicuous, I left, walked along the streets, and came in at the back door of the consulate. I told Howard what I had seen and heard.

[361]

"I'll notify the State Department at once," he said. "Secretary Seward will tell Stanton, and Stanton will alert the military in Maine."

"And I'll leave for Calais."

"Then you'd better speak with Sheriff Brown of Washington County in Maine. If you can't find him, notify the officials of the Calais National Bank."

We shook hands, and I went to my lodgings. Next morning, I boarded the stage for Calais.

Though by no means new, Calais had some of the rawness in appearance of a frontier town. A number of houses and buildings were under construction, most of the streets were still uncobbled and dusty, and there were as many men riding horses as driving wagons and buggies. What I didn't see was guns, and I'd have felt better if some had been evident.

Washington County was not small, and though the county jail was at Machias, Sheriff Brown could have been in almost any town on the day that I arrived. Fortunately, he was in Calais, and answers to inquiries sent me to the local jail, which happened to have no inmates at the time. When I asked him if we could speak in private, he nodded to one of the constables, who let us into a cell back of the office. There I identified myself, told him what I had told Consul Howard, and added that Howard was sending the alarm to Washington.

My opinion of sheriffs, as political appointments, is not high, but Brown struck me rather favorably. Though a large man, somewhat placid in appearance and deliberate in speech, he could move very quickly, and his questions revealed a searching mind.

"How many of these men, in your estimation, have assembled in St. John?"

"At least scores and possibly several hundred, but it is hard to be sure."

"Are they planning to cross the border as a unit?"

"I don't know. I had the impression that a few might be coming, with the bank as their objective. I suppose that's one way they maintain their force in St. John — robbing banks."

"Then all you can be sure of is this Collins?"

"And probably his bodyguard, Phillips."

"Well, that's enough to cause trouble. I tell you what I'll do, lieutenant. I'll inform the bank people, and I'll get a posse together. If there are just a few raiders, we'll take care of them. If five hundred or a thousand men cross the river, we'll have to evacuate the town and wait for our soldiers to get here. They could be a long time arriving, and there might not be enough of them available in this part of the state. We'll just have to trust to luck it'll be a small party."

Two days later, on orders from Secretary of War Stanton, all military units in the county, including the Home Guard, were alerted. On application from Governor Cony, the government was reportedly making two gunboats available. The police in neighboring towns were warned, and the citizens of Calais were ordered to clear the streets on signal in the vicinity of the bank on Saturday, which was a full banking day.

The little town of Calais thus made ready to meet the invasion.

XXXIII

"HERE they come, sheriff!"

"How many?"

"Three, sheriff. Three riders."

"Let 'em come, then. Let 'em go right into the bank. Nick," he said to one of his deputies, "you take your men around the bank and across the street. I'll cover this side and the front. Lieutenant, will you keep your eye on the horse guard?"

"Right."

"Jim!" he called to a young lad, freckle-faced and excited.

"Go tell the Home Guard to fall back toward the bridge once those men have entered the bank — they mustn't escape back to Canada. We want to catch them all."

Away he scampered, while the rest of us watched the three horsemen riding slowly up the street. There were people moving along the sidewalks, and wagons in the street, so the men couldn't have noticed anything out of the ordinary. What the raiders didn't know was that once they reached the bank, everyone was to clear the surrounding streets entirely. Nor did they realize that whoever entered the bank would find no helpless and submissive clerks. Both the bank president and his principal clerk were armed with shotguns and waiting.

I looked at the sheriff standing in the driveway of a store and acting with such coolness that I thought the army had lost a fine officer because of his age. He had a dozen of his deputies on foot, a half-dozen others already mounted, and guards holding the horses of those afoot. Most admirable of all, in my opinion, was his order to everyone, including the bank men, not to kill any of the raiders, if possible, and not to let the townspeople get their hands on them afterward.

"We'll try them according to law," he explained. But privately he said to me, "Unless we take them alive, we'll never find what all this mess is about. Three highwaymen today and maybe a thousand next week."

As the riders drew up to the bank, I pointed out Collins and Phillips. The third I had never seen before, but remembering Consul Howard's description, I identified him as probably Francis Jones. All three dismounted and tied their horses to the hitching rail. While Jones remained outside, the other two sauntered into the bank.

"This is it, boys. Let's go!" the sheriff said.

Instantly a line of men started moving around the bank. The shoppers simply evaporated from the streets. Toward the river bridge, the escape route to Canada, I could see a file of blue as the Home Guard moved into position, closing off the street. Meanwhile, the sheriff, three men, and I walked swiftly toward the bank front, and fanned out.

Jones now took alarm, his head turning this way and that. He shouted to his companions, but his cry was drowned out by a shotgun blast from inside the bank, followed quickly by another. Instantly Collins and Phillips plunged outside, pistols in hand, but before they could aim, a half-dozen rifles and pistols were leveled at them, and the sheriff fired a warning shot from his pistol, over their heads.

"You men lay down those pistols!"

The voice of this calm, pleasant man fairly crackled with authority; the raiders paused. "I'll count five — just five! — and you're all dead men. Drop those pistols and get your hands in the air!"

Jones let his pistol fall, then slowly Collins dropped his, and his cartridge belt as well. I think Phillips might have been stupid enough to shoot it out, but Collins muttered something to him; the big man tossed his pistol to the ground, too. The deputies then closed in, and the sheriff slipped handcuffs on each Confederate.

The surrender of the raiders was the signal for the townspeople to pour into the streets and surround them, shouting and shaking their fists. The sheriff's men were so hard-pressed that it was only when the Home Guard unit marched up from the bridge and shouldered a path through the crowd that Sheriff Brown was able to escort the men to the town jail. Then he dismissed his posse, while the guard officers posted a cordon around the jail.

Toward evening, with the sheriff, the bank president, and the bank clerk being cheered as heroes, hundreds of the curious crowded close to the jail. Many had been drinking and were growing more threatening in their demands that the prisoners be hanged.

Brown, who seemed to feel that I was at least partially responsible for the day's excitement, stared at the crowd through the open window, then turned and said, "Lieutenant, I can't keep these men here in Calais. I'm going to take them to the county jail at Machias. They'll be safer there."

"But you can't remove them now," I said. "You'll have to wait until these people go home."

"Oh, I've no intention of taking them away now. I'll wait until our people are home asleep."

"Who will be going along with you?"

"A mounted detail of the Home Guard. And if you want to come, I'd be glad to have you. I'll get a horse for you."

Brown didn't leave the little jail himself but sent men off on errands. Whenever the crowd became too demanding, he would go outdoors and speak with them. They would cheer him, but insist that, at least, he show them the prisoners, to make sure they were still on hand.

"You haven't seen them escape, have you?" Brown laughed. "How could they do so with you people out here?"

With the blazing torches and the torch smoke, the shouting and occasional scream of a girl who came too close to a venturesome boy, the scene reminded me of what I had read of peasants during the French Revolution threatening to burn down a chateau.

Still, toward midnight, people went home. After all, the near-robbery had not succeeded, their life's savings were still secure, and there was church to attend on the morrow. By three o'clock, a small cavalcade of horses and a wagon drew up to the jail. The prisoners were placed in the wagon along with supplies, six of us mounted horses, and off we went to Machias.

Though the sheriff had forbidden anyone to talk until we were clear of the town, the sound of the hooves and the jingling of bits, not to mention the creaking of the wagon wheels, would almost surely have awakened people on most nights. The emotional surge of the previous day, however, must have exhausted them. Had this been a town on the Indian frontier in the West, the Indians would have had matters entirely their own way in any predawn attack.

Machias was a good fifty miles from Calais. Our pace was so slow that not until Monday morning did we reach the county jail. Once the prisoners were locked up in that larger, stronger building, Brown said he had been truly afraid that the citizens of Calais might storm the local jail and that he might have to fire at them to save the prisoners' lives.

The sheriff began to pay Jones a good deal of attention the next few days, chatting with him, playing chess, treating him in a kindly fashion. Though designed to elicit information from him, this method was bound to take time to secure results, so, with Brown's assurance that he would get in touch with me if Jones began to talk, I returned to St. John.

Once back in that port city, I reported my presence to Consul Howard and again took up residence in a cheap lodging house — a different one this time, to avoid having to answer the landlady's questions as to where I had been.

Again, as I circulated among the numerous groups hanging around the waterfront, I found plenty of Southern sentiment. I also saw several sailing vessels, mostly schooners and brigs, lying together near shore and out of the stream of regular harbor traffic. Several times I observed men who were obviously in some kind of leadership capacity among the Confederates, go aboard these ships.

Yet the saloons seemed less exuberant than they did before the attempted bank robbery. I heard bitter remarks that Collins had acted on his own and, by being captured, damaged Confederate chances. Just what the chances alluded to were, I wasn't sure, but when word reached St. John that a Confederate warship, the *Tallahassee*, had burst out of Wilmington on August 6 and was leaving a trail of burning ships from Sandy

Hook along the New England coast as she raided northward, I began to wonder if there wasn't some connection between her and what the men here in St. John were planning.

It seemed to me that everyone in St. John was following the *Tallahassee*'s progress, judging by the conversations in public places. Of course, we were always behind in the news, for we were dependent for whatever we learned on her release of prisoners from the ships she destroyed, or on reports of sightings. At the consulate we were constantly requesting and receiving information, sketchy as it was, by telegraph.

Though many of the ships she was taking were small fry, I was certain the alarm along the seaboard would be so great that the navy would have many men-of-war trying to find her, as the department had tried to do with Read and the *Tacony*. At the same time, as reports of her size and armament came in, I was also certain that she would be a formidable antagonist. She was a seven-hundred-ton, iron, twin-screw steamer, two hundred feet long, with two funnels. A former blockade runner and very fast, she was painted a light lead color and mounted three guns: a long Parrot aft, a hundred-pound rifled cannon amidships, and a rifled thirty-two-pounder forward. Reports gave her the appearance and elusiveness of a ghost ship and credited her commander, John Taylor Wood, who had served on the *Merrimac* against the *Monitor*, with ruthless efficiency. That Wood was shrewd became amply clear, for though he burned two schooners just off Friendship, Maine, and looked into the Penobscot, he avoided repeating Read's mistake of entering a port where Union men-of-war might have cornered him.

Meanwhile, those of us who were Northerners had little to cheer us in the general war news that reached us. The most encouraging word was that Admiral Farragut had run the gauntlet of the Mobile forts on August 5, and had captured or destroyed the Confederate fleet. The great prize was the powerful ironclad *Tennessee*, which had taken on the entire Union fleet before she surrendered. But the monitor *Tecumseh* had struck a mine and went down, carrying with her the captain, T. A. Craven, who had missed capturing the *Alabama* when in command of the *Tuscarora* two years before. But Craven would be remembered for permitting the pilot of the monitor to precede him to the escape hatch when there was room for only one at a time. Balancing the Mobile victory was the failure of General Burnside's mine to break the siege of Petersburg and Sherman's futile efforts to crash through the Atlanta lines. To cap it all, the *Tallahassee* was devastating our coastal shipping like a wolf in a sheepfold.

With excitement running high about the *Tallahassee*, I received word from Sheriff Brown to come at once to Machias. When I arrived, Brown took me into his office at the county jail and, making sure the doors were closed, told me that he wanted me to listen to a strange and incredible tale.

"I can't imagine your telling anything strange or incredible, sheriff," I said. Nor could I, and I was eager to hear what he had to say.

But Brown did not reply as I had expected. "I'm not going to tell you this myself. I want you to listen to it from Francis Jones."

"Are you the only one who knows about this, sheriff?"

"No, I was so doubtful about it all that I asked Jones to repeat his story for a lawyer in town who's a friend of mine. Well, my friend was so angry he said he wished we had shot all three men during the robbery attempt."

"Did he suggest anything you might do?"

"I told him I thought I ought to write to Washington, and he urged me to go right ahead. But first I wanted to get one more opinion. No one likes to make a fool of himself by believing just anything he's been told. I'll ask you to be frank with me after you've heard Jones out."

"But will he talk with *me*?"

"I've prepared him for you. He knows you're an officer in government service."

When I asked Brown if he knew anything about Jones's background, he nodded. "Something. His father was a college president in St. Louis, and at some time a superintendent of the toll collections and of the poor. Jones himself is well-educated and knows several languages. He was married, but his wife and baby died. Since the war began, he served as a guerrilla fighter, was wounded, and, since 'sixty-three, has been a courier. He's had thirty-two missions through the Union lines, three times to Canada via Bermuda and Halifax. He knows the Rebel commissioners in Canada and most — maybe all — of the biggest Rebel agents in the Union. Now I'd like you to listen to him after dinner, lieutenant. He'll speak freely because of his mother's influence and because he holds a grudge against some of the men he's been working for. Ask him any question you want to. He'll talk."

I went to a boardinghouse for dinner, one recommended by the sheriff for the culinary and housecleaning skills of the woman who ran it, rather than for her disposition. In the afternoon, I reported to the jail at half-past one, the time agreed upon for our meeting with Jones. The sheriff took down his ring of keys and personally went to the cellblock and brought Jones into his office. The prisoner, slim and rather handsome, with long planes to his face, blue eyes, and wavy blond hair, acted very self-possessed to begin with, then showed evidence of anxiety and, occasionally, indignation in voice and manner. He shook hands with a firm grip and accepted gratefully the cigar the sheriff offered him. So did I, though I could testify more to the sheriff's generosity than to his taste.

When the early-afternoon light in the office was dim with cigar smoke, the sheriff quietly informed Jones of what he had told me about his career.

Jones nodded, was silent for a few moments, as if putting his thoughts in order, then began to talk. His voice was mellow; his speaking pace at first slow but gradually accelerating; his face at times frozen, and at others, lively and amazingly revealing of his feelings. He told of a great conspiracy forming throughout the North, though with its focus in the Middle West. "On or about the time of the Presidential election, an inroad will be made into the free states, and that will be the signal for a general uprising of powerful disloyal societies in the North."

"Do you know in what states in particular?" I asked.

"Oh, yes. They are Maine, Michigan, Ohio, Indiana, Illinois, Iowa, and Missouri."

"Do you know the names of these societies you mentioned?"

"The Sons of Liberty, the Order of American Knights, the Knights of the Golden Circle, the Knights of the Southern Cross, the Independent Order of National Guards, and the Knights of Bethlehem. There may be others."

"Can you tell me the objective of this uprising?"

"The main objective is the overthrow of the present government, so the insurgents will try to burn, pillage, and destroy all public property such as government warehouses and stores, banks, railroads, and public buildings."

"But why include Maine in your activities? There aren't many copperheads here, and not all of these societies you speak of."

"That may be true, but what secret organizations there are, have pledged themselves to help in the invasion of Maine."

"I don't understand what you mean by an 'invasion of Maine,' Jones."

I observed him closely as he drew deeply on his cigar and slowly blew a streamer of smoke toward the ceiling. I had the impression that Sheriff Brown was even more watchful, though he had heard the story before; he would soon be putting his reputation on the line when he wrote to Washington.

"It's like this, Mr. Pettigrew. In order to divert attention from the main effort in the Middle West, we decided to create a diversion in the Northeast, beginning in Maine and, perhaps, spreading as far as Boston. It will take the form of an actual invasion from two sources. The principal demonstration against the State of Maine will be made by about five thousand men, with a large park of field artillery. Many of the men and their leaders will be experienced raiders from the cavalry commands of General Morgan, General Wheeler, and General Stuart."

"How, in God's name, will an army like that ever get here?" I asked.

"They will be brought from the South by eight blockade runners, armed with four guns each. The expedition will consist of five columns landed at five different points, but within supporting distance of one another. They will scour the countryside for horses, mules, and transportation, concentrate at a designated spot, organize for a general destruction of public property, and subsist upon the country."

"How can they be sure of where they'll land?"

"That's been taken care of. About fifty experienced engineers and draftsmen left Halifax in May and have since been exploring, surveying, and making charts of the coast. They were brought to Canada originally by blockade runners and pretended to be artists while they worked. I saw several of the charts when I was acting as private secretary to our General Carroll in Canada."

Threads were certainly being tied, so, in hopes of seeing the process continued, I said, "You've mentioned that the invasion is to have two sources, and you have described what you termed the 'principal demonstration.' What is the other?"

"The other is an expedition out of New Brunswick consisting of, I guess, twelve to fifteen hundred men. Some are escaped prisoners, but many are seamen sent to Canada last spring. They are to embark in sailing vessels and will be convoyed by two men-of-war. I have heard the *Florida* and the *Tallahassee* mentioned."

"The *Tallahassee!*"

"Yes, I understand she is powerful and fast," he said.

"Are these men to sail from St. John?"

"Yes. At first, it was planned that this expedition would be two thousand strong, but it was finally decided that five hundred men should be used in an attack on Johnson's Island." For a moment I couldn't place it. Then, even as I did so, Jones explained. "That's in Lake Erie, not far from Sandusky, Ohio. The leaders hoped to release the Southern officers in prison there, and by this movement draw off the attention of the federal government from the real point of attack, the coast of Maine. The attack on Johnson's Island is to be made in September."

"But I thought you said the main focus of the conspiracy is in the Middle West."

"It is. But when Washington starts concentrating on the Middle West, the invasion of Maine will take place, and when the government rushes to defend this state, then will come the uprising in the Middle West. This will be supported by raids into Iowa and Illinois by guerrillas from Missouri and Arkansas who are to seize the prison camps and release all Southern officers and soldiers. These will then join in the attacks."

"Tell me, Jones, do these conspirators really expect to receive much help from within Maine?"

"Of course not. But the secret organizations in Maine, such as they are, have pledged themselves to support the invasion and thereby swell the entire force to twelve or fifteen thousand men. With so many Union troops away in the South, that will be a formidable army for any Union force in Maine or all New England to handle."

It would, indeed, and as he then proceeded to name the generals, the colonels, and the majors of this invasion force, I began to realize how carefully these plans had been formulated. I realized, too, how widespread were the Confederate sources of information, as Jones listed the names of more than a score of Southern agents in Northern cities, as well as those at Quebec, Montreal, Halifax, and Bermuda. For Portland he named a Major Dudley Harris — alias Spencer, alias Barbour.

When I asked Jones what Harris looked like, he said, "Harris is about thirty-five to forty years old and has a bulldog look. He takes snuff and squints with his left eye when looking intently at one. He has dark hair and eyes and a slight scar under the right eye."

This was a description of no one I could remember having seen, so I had no comment.

By this time, the afternoon was well along, and Jones was growing tired. I therefore told him I had but one more question, and that was why he was revealing all this information.

It was now that he became excited. "It's like this, sir, and Sheriff Brown has heard it before. My mother is a good Union woman and has begged me repeatedly to leave the Rebels. I thought about it a long time and, while in Halifax, wrote to President Lincoln, asking the privilege of taking the oath of allegiance under the Amnesty Proclamation. I was refused, since I had also asked exemption from military service. I sent this answer to my mother to satisfy her that I had tried to get out of the Rebel service. Then the Southern agents in Halifax found out, somehow, that I had written to the President, and I was ordered to report to Captain Collins in St. John. This was my reward after risking my life time and again for the South."

He said again he thought he had been misused by the people he had served, he was sick of the war, and he wanted to take the oath of allegiance.

We let him go at this point, though before Brown returned him to the cellblock, I asked him if he knew Jason Carter, a merchant of Portland. He shook his head and said he had never heard of the man. I felt increasingly certain, however, that Carter, in whose yacht Tamara Ravenel had reconnoitered the Maine coast the previous year, was a member of one of the traitorous secret organizations Jones had mentioned.

When Brown returned from the cellblock, he sat down wearily. "Well, lieutenant, what do you think of that?"

"I thought you were exaggerating when you described

Jones's story as strange and incredible. I apologize, sir. I think you should write Washington at once and ask for an official investigation. I will write the Navy Department supporting your request."

Shortly afterward, we parted, Sheriff Brown to return to his home to write his letter that evening, I to my boardinghouse to write two letters: one to Secretary Welles, another to Colonel Baker.

The next morning, I went down to Machiasport and boarded a little steamer for Eastport, where I bought a ticket on another for St. John. After listening to Francis Jones, I was now more interested than ever to find out both what was happening with the Confederate force in St. John and the latest information on the *Tallahassee*.

XXXIV

WHEN I returned to St. John, I had a long talk with Consul Howard. I gave him few details of the great conspiracy, but I told him considerable about the Confederate plans for the invasion of Maine, especially the proposed use of men-of-war, including the *Tallahassee*, to convoy troops from St. John to the Maine coast.

"There's no cause to worry about that at the moment," he said. "The consulate at Halifax reported by telegraph that the *Tallahassee* has just put into Halifax to take on coal. The bank-robbery attempt has probably killed any idea of an invasion."

"Let's hope so. I don't think our government had any idea how extensive the invasion plans were, and I suspect the Confederates decided we learned about their plans sooner than we did. I remember when I came back here after the robbery attempt that many of the men along the waterfront felt discouraged. Collins must have taken matters into his own hands or acted on some higher authority than Clavering, possibly one of the commissioners in Montreal or Toronto. Clavering didn't want that bank raid to come off."

"Do you think the *Tallahassee* has any troops aboard?"

"I doubt it, sir. But I'll bet that she has plenty of small arms, field artillery, and ammunition aboard for these men here in St. John. If she didn't plan to escort these ships in the harbor" — and I pointed to the covey of brigs and schooners — "at the moment, she might return later. She's fast and strong enough to run the blockade off Wilmington again without much difficulty."

"Well, we can only wait and hope our cruisers are closing in on Halifax."

Those were anxious hours, particularly after we heard that the *Tallahassee* got safely away from Halifax on the night of August 19, only four hours before the first Union man-of-war arrived at the port. While our apprehensions rose hourly, and consular officials kept glasses trained seaward, I mixed with the Confederates in the port, trying to get some hint of plans through what might be said. I heard nothing, however, to lead me to think that these men expected the raider to appear off St. John. There was intense and sympathetic interest, but that was all, so far as I could gather. Then came a reassuring word from Halifax that the port authorities there had so limited the amount of coal permitted the *Tallahassee* that further extensive raiding was out of the question. She had aboard only enough coal to enable her to reach Wilmington and, even then, not sufficient for full steaming. In the end, we learned that she reached Wilmington safely, after engaging in a running battle at night with blockaders and then coming under the guns of Fort Fisher guarding the entrance of the Cape Fear River. In her cruise of twenty days, she had burned or scuttled twenty-six ships and eluded a score of Union men-of-war in search of her.

With the end of an invasion threat, at least as far as any assistance by the *Tallahassee* was concerned, I was eager to return to Washington. I might have been interested in remaining in St. John had not Clavering disappeared from the city. He was like a number of other Confederate agents, always stirring up mischief, now here, now there. Secretary Welles, however, ordered me to remain until further notice.

In the meantime, the North was excited by several peace maneuvers and the meeting of the Democratic convention. The press in St. John, notably the *Morning Freeman* and the *Daily Evening Globe*, gave rather more coverage to these events than I expected, though hardly enough to satisfy the intense curiosity of those of us who were United States citizens. Fortunately, the consulate subscribed to a number of newspapers in Boston, New York, Philadelphia, and Washington, so though we were behind the actual developments, we generally kept up.

The most interesting peace project, while it was only one of several, had begun in July and went on for a considerable time. This involved Horace Greeley, the editor of the *New York Tribune*, who subsequently published some but not all of the correspondence between himself and Mr. Lincoln. What he didn't publish, the President read to the cabinet, and I eventually learned about it from Secretary Welles.

Greeley hated slavery, but hated war almost as much. He became so excited when someone told him a fish story which he believed — namely, that the Confederate commission in Canada had powers to negotiate peace — that he decided to act. My Uncle Jonathan always thought Greeley unstable and inclined to go off half-cocked.

At any rate, when the Rebel General Early was at Washington's very gates, Greeley wrote Lincoln that "our bleeding, bankrupt, almost dying country — longs for peace; shudders at the prospect of fresh conscriptions, of further wholesale devastations, and of new rivers of human blood. And a widespread

[377]

conviction that the government and its . . . supporters are not anxious for peace . . . is doing great harm."

To this, the President retorted that he would meet "any person anywhere professing to have any proposition of Jefferson Davis in writing, for peace, embracing the restoration of the Union and abandonment of slavery." He then designated Greeley himself to bear the government's statement to the negotiators, and offered to give the Confederate commission a safe-conduct to Washington. Greeley took off for Niagara Falls and soon discovered that the commission had no such peace powers as he had believed. While Greeley was deeply embarrassed and published only that part of his correspondence with the President which showed himself as an honest advocate of peace, the Lincoln Administration let it be known through a public announcement that it would still seriously consider any proposition which entailed the restoration of peace, the integrity of the whole original Union, and the elimination of slavery. The South was clearly not interested. Welles thought Greeley a scheming busybody, my Uncle Jonathan agreed with him, and from the little I knew of Greeley, I saw no reason to differ with them.

The most effective peace maneuver that late summer was summed up in the news that reached our consulate at St. John on September 3. Two days before, advance elements of Sherman's army had picked their way into Atlanta through the smoke and debris of blazing supplies and buildings. Hood, who had replaced Johnston earlier, had been no more successful in holding off Sherman, and had evacuated the city. This was the best news all summer, and when I slipped in through the back door of the consulate, a glass was thrust into my hand, and I was happy to join in a toast to that fierce warrior, William Tecumseh Sherman.

I was now extremely impatient to be away from St. John. I therefore welcomed an order from Washington which sent me back to Machias the first week of September to confer with Major Levi C. Turner, the army's Judge Advocate for the District of Columbia, who had been dispatched to Maine, among other reasons, to take down the testimony of Francis Jones.

I found Turner a brisk, efficient man with a friendly face, until I noticed that his eyes never joined his lips and cheeks in smiling. Under the Judge Advocate General — a courteous, gray-haired Kentucky War Democrat, Joseph Holt, who was energetic and ruthless — Turner was charged with making political arrests. None, in fact, could be made except on his warrant. Draft dogers who fled to Canada lived in fear of Turner as well as Baker, as did Democratic newspaper editors critical of the Administration.

When I appeared at Sheriff Brown's home, the sheriff introduced me to Turner, who said, "Pettigrew, I read your letter to Secretary Welles with much interest. He forwarded it, the day he received it, to Mr. Stanton, who turned it over to Mr. Holt and me. Yours, sir," he said to the sheriff, "was sent by Mr. Seward to Mr. Stanton. Now, Pettigrew, as a former lawyer, you must have given Jones a thorough interrogation. I have completed my sessions with him, and I'd like to compare notes with you. Sheriff, you can check us both."

Turner then asked me, point by point, what Jones had said to me. He didn't tell me what Jones had said to him, but I doubted that Jones had mentioned anything new, though he may have amplified what he had told me. Now and then, Turner jotted down notes as I spoke.

"Did he say anything about caches of medical supplies and ammunition?" Turner asked.

"Yes, he mentioned there were some in New York, Cincinnati, and Indianapolis."

"Not St. Louis?"

"He said 'other places' but did not specify St. Louis."

"Did he disclose where these caches were or where they had been stolen from?"

"He said that seventeen thousand of the new Henry repeating rifles had been stolen from the New York quartermaster and hidden in a Brooklyn warehouse."

Turner wrote in a small, precise hand, and managed to cram an enormous amount of wordage onto a single page. Looking up from his notes, he asked me if I thought Jones was telling the truth throughout his confession.

"I think he was," I said. "And certainly you are in a position, sir, to have some of his statements checked for their veracity."

He sat motionless, staring at me, quite unseeing, I was sure. "If all this is true or even a portion of it —"

He left the sentence unfinished, shook his head, and got briskly to his feet. "Are you going to Portland, Pettigrew?"

"I am, unless you have further need of me."

"Good. Then perhaps we can take the steamer from Eastport together. There are other questions I should like to ask you, but they can wait until we're aboard."

After he had gone, Sheriff Brown told me that Turner had insisted on being alone with Jones. "I did not tell him that I was present when you questioned him."

"I saw no reason why you shouldn't have been present with me. Of course, I can understand why he'd want to speak with Jones privately." I said further that the sheriff was to be warmly commended for his patriotism. I didn't add that I thought he was to be complimented on his intelligence in conducting himself so effectively in his office.

The trip from Eastport, some thirty miles from Machias, to Portland was wretched because of a severe storm. We rolled and pitched constantly. Whenever anyone left his stateroom, he had to rush from doorknob to doorknob, or to anything that he could grab onto. On deck, it was a case of withstanding a booming wind and driving rain, getting wet instantly without oilskins, and having to shout to be heard. The result was that I saw little of Turner until we were near Portland. With the rain passing and the wind subsiding, he came on deck for air, his face pinched and pale from seasickness.

"How you people can actually choose the navy over the army when you know you'll be sick is something I'll never understand," he said, as the steamer slipped in a kind of corkscrew motion.

Then he asked me what I knew about the so-called artists on the coast this past spring and early summer that Jones had mentioned. I told him about what I had seen the previous summer. I mentioned Jason Carter, the Republican merchant of Portland, in whose yacht Tamara Ravenel had made her reconnaissance of the Maine coast. Turner said that he would have one of his agents check into this matter. He wouldn't have time to pursue the case himself on this trip. Not only had he investigated, while at Machias, the official transaction of the Board of Enrollment for the Fifth District of Maine, but he would still have to go to Lewiston to make a similar investigation for the Second District. He hoped that when I returned to Washington, I would make myself available for corroborating testimony, if necessary. I said I would be glad to do so.

When we landed in Portland, Turner was annoyed that it was too late for the train to Lewiston. He said he planned to spend the evening at a hotel working, and take the cars north in the morning. He might be detained in Lewiston for a couple of days, but hoped to return to Washington as soon after that as possible.

As for myself, I spent the night with my grandparents, who sent at once for Uncle Jonathan to come to dinner. They were about to return to Augusta for the court sessions, and my uncle was to accompany them as far as Lewiston, where he was to confer with a group of Maine newspaper editors.

"Who knows? You may meet Major Turner in Lewiston," I said.

Uncle Jonathan frowned. "I'm not sure I want to. I don't approve of these arbitrary political arrests made by him and his

[381]

department nor of the shutting down of newspapers critical of the Administration. If I do meet him, I'll tell him what I think of his policies."

"Now, Jonathan, don't you do anything rash," my grandmother cautioned.

We talked about the November election coming up. Grandmother was so fervently pro-Lincoln, she would not admit the possibility of a defeat despite Uncle Jonathan's frankly expressed doubts of a Republican victory.

"Oh, you Democrat!" she exclaimed. "Don't tell me you're going to vote for General McClellan!"

"You know Jonathan, my dear," my grandfather said. "He talks Democratic, is registered Democratic, and votes Republican. What worries me is that Lincoln may not be given a chance to run again."

Uncle Jonathan nodded. "The movement within the Republican party to get Lincoln to retire in behalf of someone else is strong."

"This is something I'd like to know more about," I said.

"There's a movement inside the party to unseat the President, and a special convention has been called for September twenty-eighth," Grandfather said, drawing delicately on his thin, pale cigar. "The movement has been confidential, but it embraces some influential people. Men like Senator Ben Wade of Ohio and Henry Winter Davis of Maryland are extremists and think the President not aggressive enough. Greeley has said Lincoln is already beaten and we must have another ticket. Whitelaw Reid is claiming credit for getting the *Cincinnati Gazette* to come out for Lincoln's withdrawal. You know that, Jonathan."

"Yes, the *Gazette* has declared that people regard Lincoln's candidacy as a 'misfortune' — that's the word Richard Smith of the *Gazette* used."

"More than that," Grandfather said, "Greeley of the *Tribune*, Theodore Tilton of the *Independent* in New York, and

Parke Goodwin of the *New York Evening Post* wrote to all the governors in the North on September second, supporting the drive to remove Lincoln as a candidate."

"Why, it's a betrayal of a great President!" my grandmother wailed, close to tears.

"A desertion, at any rate," I said. "But since that letter you refer to, Grandfather, the country has heard that Sherman has taken Atlanta. Surely that will make a difference."

"I think it will — that and the elections in this state and Vermont."

"And don't forget Farragut's victory at Mobile," I said.

"Yes, all these are factors, and there may be others before November."

Back in Washington, I reported to both Welles and Baker. Baker did not press me strongly for information on Jones; he said he would soon learn all Judge Advocate General Holt knew when Turner submitted his report. Though I had heard rumors that Holt and Turner, on the one hand, and Baker, on the other, didn't always see eye to eye, each managed to know what the other was doing through secret operatives in each other's employ. Baker, however, asked many questions about Clavering. He confessed he considered Clavering elusive and dangerous.

Secretary Welles was eager to know everything that had happened. His face seemed to age as I told him about Jones's confession in detail, with its implications of nationwide revolt, and he became quite excited when I mentioned the proposed landings on the Maine coast.

"Pettigrew, we must not allow that to happen. We must shut off Wilmington for good and all. I have no hesitation in saying that the importance of closing Wilmington and cutting off Rebel communication with the outside is paramount to all other questions — more important right now, practically, than the capture of Richmond."

"But from what I have heard of Fort Fisher, sir, it looks as if the navy will need the help of the army."

"It will, indeed, and the army will take persuading. But with Admiral Porter in command, we may get some cooperation from Grant. After all, Grant and Porter worked very effectively together at Vicksburg, and it is our hope that he will give Porter the troops he needs."

Mr. Welles inquired about my family, said he didn't quite share their feeling of alarm about the political situation, but admitted the situation was precarious.

"Why, Pettigrew," he exclaimed, "there were actually people here who mourned our triumph at Atlanta! I tell you, this is the demon of party politics — the days of its worst form — a terrible spirit, which in its excess leads men to rejoice in the calamities of their country and to mourn its triumphs. I simply can't believe they are so destitute of love of country. It must be that they let party prejudices and party antagonisms dominate their better nature."

The "Old Man of the Sea" was in truly rare form. I think he had missed me as someone to talk with — or actually to — which was a subtle kind of flattery, especially since he had no intention of flattering anyone.

XXXV

COURIER duty for the Navy Department that fall sent me both north and south. One trip was to Captain Carter of the U.S.S. *Michigan* on Lake Erie at just the time when a band of Confederates, operating out of Canada, had seized several lake steamers and were terrifying the Northern cities, especially Buffalo. The *Michigan*, much to Carter's anger and embarrassment, had had her engines disabled by a Rebel agent who bribed one of her crew; she was helpless now. In fact, I thought that the man-of-war's capture may have been on the Rebels' agenda, but her fourteen guns were evidently too intimidating to would-be assailants, despite her inability to move. Fortunately, Canada, responding to our government's appeals, confiscated the Rebel steamers. Had Canada not done so, or had the Rebels succeeded in taking the *Michigan*, they might well have succeeded in liberating the numerous prisoners on Johnson's Island. As it was, troops and sailors were rushed from New York to threatened cities on the Great Lakes.

Two other trips took me on the fast *Rhode Island* down to the blockading fleet off Fort Fisher. Farragut, tired and ill, had declined the North Atlantic blockading command, Rear Admiral Lee was shifted to the Mississippi command, and Porter was brought in. He took over on October 1 and started at once to gather the ships and to make the necessary plans with the army to reduce Fort Fisher and close the port of Wilmington. Porter, with his heavy beard and his intense eyes, a fan of wrinkles at the corners, radiated a kind of fierce energy. Mr. Lincoln may not have shared Secretary Welles's high opinion of him, but there was no doubt that Porter was determined to destroy Fort Fisher.

But the more I heard of Fisher — an enormous earthwork and the most powerful fortress in the Confederacy — and the more I studied it through binoculars and talked with officers who had served on blockade, the more I became impressed with the task of its reduction. For that matter, the whole area at the mouth of the Cape Fear was tricky. There were two channels to the river, one to the eastward known as the New Inlet and one to the south, the Old Inlet. Though only a half-dozen miles apart, the actual sailing distance was about forty miles, owing to the existence of Frying Pan Shoals and Smith's Island. Blockading ships, to cover both channels, had to extend in an arc of about sixty miles, and blockade runners moving out of the Cape Fear could see the squadron on station off each inlet and could choose which inlet to try an escape from. Runners coming in usually attempted the New Inlet because the water ran deep close to the shore and because of the long sea face of Fort Fisher, constructed since 1862 on a sandy spit of land, here flat and there studded with dunes, known as Federal Point. The sea face extended for thirteen hundred yards and was commanded by about a score of identifiable heavy guns, with roughly the same number covering the northern or land face extending between the ocean and the Cape Fear for nearly five hundred yards. Parapets were twenty feet high, and intelligence reports gave their thickness as twenty-five feet. Traverses, ten feet higher and sloping back for a thickness of from eight to twelve feet, were bomb-proofed for men and powder magazines. A huge pyramid eighty feet high, called "the Mound," heavily armed, commanded all approaches to the fort and the interior. The total number of guns mounted in the fort was reported to be seventy-five. The garrison, probably at this time consisting of something more than fifteen hundred men, was under the command of Colonel Richard Lamb.

Supporting Fisher were other forts. Directly across the Cape Fear was Fort Lamb and, a few miles up the river, Fort Anderson. Guarding the Old Inlet down the river were Forts Holmes, Caswell, and Pender. Common to all the defenses, but especially at Fisher, on the land approaches were land mines, palisades, and *chevaux de frise*.

Brief as my stay was on the flagship, which was the *Malvern* — the old *Ella and Annie* that had seized the *Chesapeake* — I often saw Admiral Porter also studying Fisher. He would dictate to his secretaries until tired, then come up on deck while they wrote the letters for his signature. Once he evidently thought I was impatient to be on my way with his correspondence.

"What's the matter, Pettigrew, don't you like it down here? You've been walking back and forth like a man with an itch in his feet." His voice was strong and taut and somehow compelling.

"I apologize, sir. I believe I'm just restless."

"Well, for God's sake, what is there about this ship that interests you? If I didn't know who you are, I'd be suspicious."

When I mentioned that I'd always have a sentimental interest in the *Malvern,* he asked the reason, so I told him briefly about the *Chesapeake* affair.

He nodded and grunted and pounded the railing when I finished. "Hoped to get to Wilmington, eh? I don't think Braine could have made it, but maybe he would have. God knows enough ships still go in and out of here in spite of the blockade. But if we can take that damned fort over there, there'll be no more of this nonsense."

"I see that some ships didn't make it." And I pointed to the wrecks of several runners along the shore.

"But too many have slipped through," he growled. "Still, it won't last much longer. All we're really doing now is waiting for the army, though it's taking them a damned long time."

"Yes, sir."

"Until General Grant came along, I don't think the army ever appreciated the difficulties under which the navy operates, particularly in making a blockade effective. But I don't suppose you've seen sea duty, Pettigrew."

"Some, sir." There was just enough of a suggestion of disdain in his voice, of which he was perhaps not conscious, that I couldn't let it pass. I therefore told him about my being on blockade duty off Fort Pulaski early in the war, but I didn't see any need to mention my collision with a splinter when a thirty-two pounder hit near me. I did mention, however, as an afterthought, that I also knew something of what sea duty was like from the point of view of a seaman on the *Alabama.* He turned to me with the most astonished expression on his face.

"Yes, sir, it's true. Secretary Welles can verify it. But it's a long story, and I don't think you'd be interested now."

"By God, I am interested. I want you to have supper with me this evening and tell me about it."

"But I'm supposed to take the dispatch boat back tonight, sir."

"And so you will, but that boat shan't go until I give the word."

I therefore spent part of the evening relating to Porter my experiences in London and aboard the *Alabama*. Porter also questioned me closely about the policy of procuring blockade runners in England and the role Englishmen played not only in helping finance the business arrangements, but in manning the runners as well. He expressed indignation that so many officers in the Royal Navy had obtained release from active duty to skipper blockade runners.

"One day England should be made to pay handsomely for the injury she has done us," he said.

I recalled, as I listened, that it was his father who had fought the British in the Pacific and whose frigate, the *Essex*, had finally succumbed to two British men-of-war whose captains had grossly violated South American neutral waters to get at her. Before that, the *Essex* had raided British shipping much as the *Alabama* had raided ours. David Farragut had been adopted by Porter's father and served on the *Essex* as a very young midshipman.

Not long after I returned to Washington with Admiral Porter's dispatches, I learned that one of our men-of-war had likewise violated South American neutrality. When the raider *Florida* lay at Bahia, Brazil, the *Wachusett*, under Commander Napoleon Collins, captured her at night in complete disregard of Brazilian neutrality, and took her to Hampton Roads. Though our government promised to return the *Florida* to Brazilian waters, an army transport rammed and sank her in the Roads while the *Florida* was under the protection of one of our men-of-war. My colleague Lee Judson was convinced it was no accident, and I shared his view.

But the same month that brought us word of the *Florida's*

capture and the heroism of that long-haired daredevil, Lieutenant William B. Cushing, who slipped a spar torpedo under the Confederate ironclad ram *Albemarle* and sank her in the Roanoke River, also created excitement and uneasiness, especially among those of us aware of Confederate conspiracies. Two incidents in particular were upsetting. One was a raid on the little town of St. Albans, Vermont, by Confederate soldiers from Canada under the command of Lieutenant Bennett H. Young. They killed at least one man, set fire to several houses, robbed three banks, and fled, under fierce pursuit, with seventy-five thousand dollars. Unlike Calais, St. Albans had not been warned. The other incident was the successful running of the blockade again by the *Tallahassee*, which had been renamed the *Olustee*, on October 29. She fled past Fort Fisher under heavy fire from blockaders, but though she suffered some damage, she soon left the Union men-of-war behind. Urged on by Secretary Welles, Porter, who was now back in Hampton Roads in the *Malvern*, sent every available ship after her. So did the commandants of all the navy yards. Despite the search, the raider destroyed six ships off the coasts of Delaware and New Jersey and as far north as Block Island. Heavy weather — a run of fierce gales — hampered the pursuit as well as the raider herself, and her skipper, his coal supplies vanishing, put back to Wilmington. For twenty-six hours beginning on November 5, she engaged in a running fight with the Union man-of-war *Sassacus*, before she ran under the protecting guns of Fort Fisher.

The second cruise of the *Tallahassee*, coming so close to the Presidential election on November 8, made me wonder at first if this wasn't part of the conspiracy to invade Maine. Probably it was not, but it demonstrated that such an invasion would not have been an impossibility if the Calais raid had not tipped the conspirators' hands.

The extent to which Jones's confession had alerted the government, which now sent Turner's operatives and Baker's agents into all the principal cities and brought troops into New York and Chicago, must have dismayed the conspirators. Naturally Jones's confession had not been the sole instrument in uncovering the vast network of Confederate activity. Not only were other Confederate agents active, but the state governments with their own spies, particularly in the Middle West, had been following developments closely and took such countermeasures, sometimes in cooperation with the federal government, that disloyal organizations dared not, or were unable to, rise. One result was that, though few arrests were made at this time by Turner and Baker, and new conspiracies were being expected, the Rebels and their friends were prevented by federal alertness from influencing the election through violent measures. Another and more important result was the successful reelection of President Lincoln.

For, in the end, a large part of the country rallied around the President. Even Horace Greeley beat the editorial drum for him at last. The insurrectionary movement within the Republican party broke down. The failure of the Confederate commission in Canada and subsequent ventures from Richmond to come up with a peace program palatable to the federal government, and, especially, the fall of Atlanta to Sherman, had been convincing arguments in support of the Administration's policy. Likewise, Republican victories in Maine and Vermont played their part, Frémont pulled out of the race, and the Cincinnati convention never met. Many of the radical Republicans were appeased by the retirement of one of Lincoln's strongest supporters and one of their bitterest critics — Montgomery Blair, the Postmaster General, whose family's estate at Silver Spring had been vandalized by Early's troops during the July raid on Washington.

Though the President won the election with a respectable popular majority and an overwhelming number of electoral votes, there was still a good deal of restlessness. Grant continued to pound futilely at Lee before Petersburg. Sherman disappeared from Atlanta on a march to the sea, and concern rose daily that he was heading for disaster. General Benjamin Butler had been given command of the army force which was to cooperate with Porter at Fort Fisher, and was creating so many problems that he had both Porter and Mr. Welles furious at him. Finally, discovery of evidence of a Confederate conspiracy involving plans for Rebel agents to set the cities of the North on fire, caused alarm. There had earlier been rumors that incendiaries would be active on or before Election Day, but possibly the show of force by the authorities intimidated the arsonists. Reports by government detectives indicated that the arrival of Butler with ten thousand troops just before Election Day killed the incendiary campaign and possible copperhead risings in New York. Butler fumbled many times in the field, but he could administer a city with a fair degree of effectiveness, as he had demonstrated early in the war in holding Baltimore for the Union, and as his tenure in New Orleans showed, despite his conflict with a number of that city's ladies, patriotic to the South. Yet Butler's presence in New York only served to set off sparks from both Secretary Welles and Admiral Porter; they felt that he could be doing something more solid by taking his troops down to Fort Fisher. Lee Judson, however, remarked over a whisky one night that he could certainly understand why the Massachusetts politician-turned-general wouldn't want to leave the luxury of his suite at the Fifth Avenue Hotel for the sand barrens and shells of Fort Fisher.

With November moving rapidly along, I received a letter from Henry Adams. He brought me up to date on the legation news and Confederate activities in England. Both the legation and Consul Dudley were incensed that Captain Bulloch had pulled another one out of the hat by getting the East Indiaman *Sea King* to sea, arming her off Madeira, and sending her, as the *Shenandoah*, on a cruise into the Pacific under Lieutenant James Waddell. Our New England whalers, Henry said, could be picked off like pigeons.

[391]

But it was something else Henry wrote that really caught my attention:

Our mutual friend, Tamara Ravenel, has succeeded in persuading one of England's great shipping firms to charter what must surely be one of the fastest blockade runners ever constructed. She is aptly named the *Challenger*, for she is bound to test our blockading skills to the limit. She is loading now with guns, ammunition, medicines, canned foods, and probably some luxuries in clothing, gew gaws, and choice liquers. There is a rumor that the ship may stop at Halifax and pick up one of the Canadian Commissioners of the Confederacy or at Nassau if he has already left Canada. Rumor also has it that the *Challenger* will be commanded by Charles Erskine. You may remember meeting him at the Palmerston reception at Cambridge House. He is Alexander Rushton, Lord Cromyn, one of England's few naval heroes of the Crimean War, who won his reputation in the Baltic. He belittled the effectiveness of our blockade of Southern ports, you will recall. For some time he has been on leave from the Royal Navy and had commanded several blockade runners, his first being the ship we saw him aboard with Miss Ravenel and Clavering when we returned to London from our visit to the *Tuscarora*. Remember? I am afraid he has made good on his criticism of our navy. Now he is about to dare our patrols again in this most formidable and valuable runner. Scott, if you have any influence, see that this steamer never arrives in Wilmington. What she has aboard will greatly revive Southern fighting spirit, if it is at all flagging.

Henry flattered me that I should have any influence in the Navy Department, but I could at least let Secretary Welles read what he had written. I therefore sought an interview with him and showed him Henry's letter.

He looked at me over his spectacles when he finished. "There is nothing here that we don't already know, Pettigrew, including the likelihood of a Rebel commissioner or his representative being aboard. We even know that Miss Ravenel will remain in

England and not come home on the *Challenger*. Secretary Seward has been receiving information on the *Challenger* from Mr. Charles Adams and Mr. Dudley for six weeks, and he has obligingly turned this information over to us."

"Then I am sorry to have taken your time, sir."

"Not at all. Now sit down and listen. The *Challenger* is loading at Liverpool, and she is indeed a formidable runner. She is an iron side-wheeler built on the Clyde, is close to three hundred feet long, has a beam of thirty-five feet, draws eleven feet of water, has a very sharp rake to her masts and two funnels, and can sail at her utmost, when loaded, perhaps seventeen and a half or even eighteen knots. She is registered at eight hundred tons. Young Mr. Adams is quite right, quite right indeed: she must never be permitted to reach Wilmington."

"But I doubt that we have any ship off Wilmington of that speed, sir."

"We don't. That is why we must devise other means of assuring her capture or destruction."

Surely Welles wasn't consulting me. Or was he? "Well, sir, do we know what her port of destination is from Liverpool?"

"We're not sure, but possibly, as Henry Adams says, Halifax."

"Then, if Halifax, Erskine could make a run down the coast to Wilmington."

"That's true, Pettigrew. The *Tallahassee* made it safely, but she had a long running fight. The run from St. George in Bermuda or from Nassau in the Bahamas is shorter and more dangerous, but Erskine could choose the day and the hour to make his dash. From Halifax he wouldn't have that option."

"Nassau is a real possibility, though more attractive to a runner bound for Charleston or a Gulf port than Wilmington. Bermuda is about seven hundred miles from Wilmington, and Nassau just under six hundred."

"I think we shall know before she sails where she will be heading. Dudley has operatives at work in Liverpool."

I could well imagine how Maguire and his men were mixing

with both the crew and the men loading the *Challenger*, and standing them to drinks in an effort to extract information.

"But I still don't see, sir," I said, "how you plan to prevent the *Challenger* from entering Wilmington. Our blockaders won't know when she'll appear, she'll have picked up a veteran pilot at Bermuda or Nassau, and, if she has the speed reported, she'll run away from our ships. Of course, we may score hits aboard her to slow her down or possibly blow her out of the water. But she'll make her run in at night, she'll probably be painted a dull gray, and she'll make no silhouette on water or against the land. That means we might fire a whole arsenal at her and not even start splinters flying. Unless, of course, we station a few very fast ships close in, ships with good records for marksmanship. And unless —" I stopped.

"Yes, unless what?" Welles demanded. But his voice was not urgent; in fact, it was slow and rather solemn.

"Unless someone aboard were to sabotage her engines or set her afire or show a signal of some sort that the blockaders would recognize and thereby prod them to try harder to stop her than they might otherwise do."

"Those are interesting possibilities, aren't they, Pettigrew? Now how would such a person get aboard the *Challenger*?"

I thought of my *Alabama* experience. "He might be a member of the crew, though with the *Challenger*'s crew already signed on in England and eager for money, it's not too likely there'll be need to sign on anyone else at Bermuda or Nassau."

"So if that possibility is out, what then?"

"A man might be a stowaway, but the chances of detection are high."

"So let's play that one down but not dismiss it altogether. That leaves the man as a passenger."

"This is probably the best chance of all, though he would have to have a good reason for making the trip to Wilmington. Many runners carry people back and forth between the mainland and the islands, including women and children."

[394]

Secretary Welles sighed and combed his beard with his fingers. "Pettigrew, I have talked with Admiral Porter and Colonel Baker about this situation. Both agree that you are the likely candidate for this assignment. Now I am not ordering you to take it. It is dangerous in the extreme in any event. Once aboard, you may still be discovered by someone, and if the ship should make it to the Cape Fear, you would face prison or perhaps worse. If the *Challenger* should refuse to heave to, you would be exposed to our gunfire. I don't want you to make up your mind at once."

I had no intention of making up my mind then or later to go at all. What Mr. Welles didn't know was that Captain Erskine and I had once met and that he might remember me if I boarded the *Challenger*. If I agreed to go and he recollected who I really was, he could refuse to accept me as a passenger. If I still managed to secure a place on the ship and he discovered and recognized me, he might well confine me in some secure place from which I would have no opportunity to alert the blockading vessels to the *Challenger's* presence.

When I finally broke the long silence and explained what I had been thinking, Mr. Welles nodded but did not dismiss me as I might have expected him to do, and turn to someone else.

"It is my understanding," he said, "that when you volunteered for service on the *Alabama*, even Captain Bulloch, who had met you several times, did not recognize you. That is true, isn't it?"

"Yes, sir. And I see what you mean, sir. Perhaps shaving my beard again would disguise me enough to escape detection."

"It would probably help, especially when combined with whatever civilian role would be contrived for you. You say that Erskine, as Lord Cromyn then, saw you only once?"

"Yes, it was more than two years ago, sir."

"Then I shouldn't be concerned about his identifying you now. But I don't wish to hurry you into a decision."

"I'll be glad to go, sir," I said.

He shrugged. "I'll arrange for you to see Colonel Baker. He and Secretary Seward have worked out an arrangement whereby, so I understand, Baker has several men placed on the islands. They may be of help to you. Meanwhile, you'd better get your civilian clothes in order. And, Pettigrew . . . not a word to your folks."

By mid-November, Mr. Welles notified me that the *Challenger* would go directly to Nassau, then to Wilmington, and would have someone of official importance aboard. I was to be ready to leave on a fast steam packet from New York on Monday, November 28. Meanwhile, Baker sent for me and went over the procedures in detail. He felt that what he called "Greek fire" would be the most useful means of identifying the *Challenger* to the blockaders or of setting her afire, if it came to that.

"It may not be just what the Greeks used to defend Constantinople against the Turks, but it's a compound of naptha, phosphorus, and turpentine that will burn when exposed to the air. When you reach Nassau, have the chemist by the name of Purcell prepare a few small bottles of it for you. Be sure he seals those bottles well, because you'll want to carry two or three in your pockets when you signal the fleet and you don't want the fluid spilling over yourself or you'll be a torch in no time."

"What am I to be in Nassau and on the *Challenger?*"

"You're a cotton buyer from Manchester, England. You're dissatisfied with the quality of cotton coming through the blockade and want to do your own selecting of bales. Learn everything you can about the manufacture of cotton in the next few days, Pettigrew, and practice talking a little like an Englishman — not much, but a little. I'll have papers drawn up for you that'll satisfy the most suspicious Rebel or Englishman."

"Mr. Welles mentioned that you have men available if I need assistance."

His pale gray eyes studied me before he replied. "That's right.

One is Joseph Miller, who is a ship chandler in a waterfront store. The other is a professional gambler at the casino, named Ralph Brown. Miller is a gray-haired, little man. Brown looks just what he is, and actually appearances couldn't be more deceiving. You can't miss the little white scar under his left eye. If you want the attention of either, just mention that you hate seasickness. One final point, Pettigrew. . . . While you are in New York over the weekend, don't let any hotel desk clerk give you a room on one of the upper floors."

"Sir?"

"I am not at liberty now to explain. Just remember what I have said, and don't let anything that may happen this weekend prevent you from catching that steamer to Nassau. And, Pettigrew," he added, "if by some chance our cruisers should not succeed in stopping the *Challenger* and you should find yourself in Wilmington, stick to your role and come back on a blockade runner to Nassau or Bermuda. You can always get back to the States, even if you have to go via Halifax or St. John. I'll have drafts made available for you so that you won't have to worry about the money end."

As I rose to leave, he said, "Of course, a man never knows for certain ahead of time how things will turn out, but if you have to leave Wilmington by land, I'd work my way west of the coastal region and south toward Sherman in Georgia. I think that would be safer than to try to go north. If you should really have to run for it, don't be afraid to trust the blacks. They've hidden many of our escaped prisoners."

Baker had surely given me a lot to think about, and on the train to New York, though I had the companionship of Richard Benton from Baker's office who was also going to the city, I was still thinking. In fact, his last admonition had shaken me — that I should go south to Sherman rather than north. I couldn't forget — none of us in service could forget — that in Georgia lay the most monstrous prison pen in the world, Andersonville, where thousands of Union prisoners had died of disease and

[397]

starvation. I had no desire to enter its gates and would have to weigh my options, if I had any, very seriously before following Baker's advice.

However, I hoped and trusted I would never see Wilmington. I'd prefer being exposed to Union naval guns rather than have to take any of the courses of action that Colonel Baker had suggested.

FOUR

Mission to Nassau
and Wilmington

XXXVI

My friend Richard Benton was a serious person. On occasion, he would talk in great gusts. More often, it was hard to get a word out of him. What was evident to me on our trip to New York was that he was pleased to be out of Washington. He didn't explain why he was going to New York, and I knew better than to ask. I thought it interesting that he should say, after I told him my plans, that he intended to stay at the Astor also. Though the Astor was much too expensive, I had become used to it. I suppose I like to do things with a certain style — the influence, perhaps, of my grandfather. I wasn't aware that Benton had quite such an appreciation of the comforts the Astor afforded. At any rate, we took rooms on the fourth floor.

Depositing my two valises in my room, I delivered a batch of letters from the Navy Department to Admiral Paulding and then returned to the Astor for a nap. Afterwards, I dressed and found Benton in the lobby. I recognized no one, but studied the well-dressed men and women, some of them in evening clothes. All appeared gay and unconcerned. If the country was nearing the climax of a bitter, bloody war, these people seemed in no way aware of a conflict. The front was far from New York City.

Suddenly Benton grasped my arm. "Look! — through the crowd, tipping his hat."

I looked, then stared.

"I know him only through photographs," Benton said. "But —"

"It's Clavering. No question," I said. "Can't we do something to stop him?"

"Let him go for now — we couldn't reach him through this crowd, anyway. But, for God's sake, don't let him see that he's been recognized."

We watched as Clavering worked his way toward the door. He was the soul of courtesy, stepping aside for this couple, raising his hat to that, bowing and smiling. He was a tall, striking figure in his black cloak. Several women looked back at him.

Benton went to the desk. "What's the name of that gentleman who just turned in his key?"

As the clerk, who was an overbearing type, looked up, Benton asked, "And his room number?"

The clerk shook his head. "I see no reason why I should tell you, sir."

"There is every reason," Benton insisted.

"By whose authority, sir?"

"The United States government."

"Do you have credentials?"

"Where's the manager's office?" I inquired.

The clerk flushed as people started to look our way. "Please keep your voice down, sir."

"Then answer my friend's questions."

Quickly the clerk gave us the room number, which was on the same floor as ours, and said Clavering had registered as Boyce Dunmore.

We were puffing when we reached the third floor and rounded the turn for the next flight. As we did so, two maids came running past us down the stairs.

"There's a fire! Upstairs!" one of them gasped. "Hurry, please!"

We took the stairs at a bound, and while one maid led the

way down to the burning room — Clavering's, as it turned out — Richard and I caught two buckets of water from the landing and the fire axe that had so long gathered dust there. Smoke was pouring out of the top and sides of the door, but with a few powerful blows, Benton smashed in the paneling, and we stepped inside. The bed was a mass of flame, and piled on and around it were bureau drawers, a washstand, and chairs. As I threw my bucket of water on the fire, I was reminded of the way a boarding party from the *Alabama* would stack up combustibles on a captured merchantman.

The curtains were drawn, and as the maid moved to tear them aside and open the windows, Benton shouted, "Leave those windows shut. If we get a draft through here, we're lost!"

By this time, a whole brigade of hotel employees, led by the night watchman, arrived with more buckets of water and sand. Shortly the fire was at least under control, if not out, and we went downstairs to find the lobby empty and people by the hundreds standing outside on Broadway. Then we heard the clanging of fire bells and saw the first detail of firemen approaching the building, dragging hoses. The firemen would have little work here.

The same wasn't true of the United States Hotel, near the Astor, or of the City Hotel. Both were blazing, and the crowds watching the fires were panicking. By now, Barnum's Museum, nearly opposite the Astor, was also afire, and smoke and flame burst from the windows. The museum was attracting an enormous crowd of onlookers not only because of the fire itself, but also for what was going on inside and around it. Inside, the animals were screaming with terror, and the manager appeared, beating his chest and head, and crying, "Save the animals!" Outside, two men slid down the iron pillars in front of the museum. Then a woman ran out on the balcony by a second-story window and started to climb over the railing.

"Don't jump! Don't jump!" voices called out.

She wavered, while the smoke whirled around her. Another

engine company arrived, a ladder was laid against the balcony, and a fireman ran up and brought the woman down to safety, to the cheers of the crowd.

A moment later, as if another circus act were starting, a huge woman tottered from somewhere inside to the doorway. She had a mass of black hair that flopped crazily as she let out roar after roar of fright that ended in a curiously pathetic squeak.

"By God, that's Barnum's woman giant!" Benton said.

She might have been that, but she was also a woman too terrified to move. Three men ran to the doorway to try to lead her to safety. Screaming, she knocked each one down. The museum manager and a fire-department officer then ran up to her, but unfortunately they came within the range of her wildly swinging arms and hit the pavement so hard, they practically bounced. After that, she put her head down and bulled her way straight across Broadway toward the Powers Hotel. At the entrance, a number of firemen tackled her, but she dragged them into the lobby. There, from all accounts, she fought like the madwoman she had temporarily become until borne down by numbers. After that, she was given a powder and left in a room in the Powers. When the firemen returned to their posts, two were bleeding profusely, and all looked badly roughed up.

As the firemen gradually brought the blaze at the museum under control, Benton and I caught a horsecar and headed for police headquarters.

"Now look here," I muttered to Richard, as we listened to the excited babbling of the passengers, "don't tell me you're here as just a visitor for the weekend."

"I wouldn't think of telling you anything like that. Both the Secret Service and the Judge Advocate's people have been working closely together with the New York police against this very thing happening. We expected it, we tried to guard against it, and I don't understand how all this occurred."

We found police headquarters in an uproar. Runners were coming and going, details of police were being hurriedly sent off, detectives were swarming about, and the air was thick with tobacco smoke and orders. A number of army officers were closeted with Superintendent of Police Kennedy when we arrived, but they soon emerged and dashed for their horses. Benton and I were finally admitted to Kennedy's office. Obviously he knew Benton, so I realized the liaison between Washington and New York was of no recent origin.

"We won't take up much of your time, sir," Benton said, "but is there anything further the Service can do? Do you need more war-department detectives?"

"No, at the moment everything is being done that can be done. No, no, don't hurry!" he said as Benton started to rise. "Just stay here a couple of minutes and give me a chance to catch my breath."

I studied this vigorous, capable man whose face still bore the scars of his treatment by the mob during the draft riots of the previous year. He looked angry and chagrined.

"Benton, you know right well we suspected these men would try to burn the city on Election Day. But it didn't come off, and since then, they've bided their time, with more of them coming into the city in just the last few days. We had them watched by detectives, but several behaved so well someone called off the pursuit just yesterday. Now they're raising hell all over the city, damn them!"

"They've obviously concentrated on the hotels."

"Hell, yes, maybe nineteen in all. The Metropolitan and the New England House are badly hit, so are the St. James, the Albemarle, and the Fifth Avenue, where General Butler has had his headquarters, and it looks as if the St. Nicholas, the United States, and the Bancroft are going to go up completely in smoke. Well, we'll do the best we can. General Dix has his troops and Butler's out patrolling the streets. They'll help control the crowds."

Benton stood up. "I'll check back in about midnight."

"Do that, captain. We'll catch the damned Rebels yet."

When we had left police headquarters, Richard said, "I'm just a kind of coordinating officer this weekend between the Secret Service and the police. It was to Kennedy that I went after we signed in at the Astor — and also to General Dix and General Butler."

"Were the copperheads supposed to rise at this time?"

"The Rebels must have hoped they would, but the authorities have already arrested the leaders of some of the more militant groups and are after the rest. Without a base of popular support, the Rebels setting these fires will only succeed in — well, in setting fires."

"Which is bad enough, I must say."

"Yes, but politically irrelevant. Clavering and the others should have sprung this a couple of days before the election. There was a big torchlight parade up Broadway in support of McClellan, and McClellan reviewed it on Fifth Avenue. When the parade was over, there was a monster rally in Madison Square, and you should have heard the hissing and booing of Lincoln when crazy caricatures of him were held up on the speakers' platform for the crowd to see. And the cheers for McClellan were something to hear, too, I can tell you. With all the liquor flowing and the anti-Administration feeling running so high, the city was ripe for an explosion. Evidently the Rebels weren't quite ready, and by the time they were, Butler had arrived."

"And has remained ever since, despite Porter's need for him at Fort Fisher."

"But the fact that his troops have been here has saved the city. General Dix has available only his garrison at Fort Lafayette."

"Still, according to Kennedy, the city authorities knew beforehand what the Rebels intended."

"Of course. The Rebels were betrayed by one of their own, for gold — and a lot of it. Francis Jones helped tip the Rebels' hand, but this other traitor, Godfrey Hyams, gave a full list of the leaders who were to help seize Chicago with the aid of Rebel prisoners to be released, and he also furnished full details of the plan to burn and seize New York with help from a convention of copperheads here from New York, New Jersey, and New England. They were to take over police headquarters, fortify City Hall, and blow up Fort Lafayette or, at least, the gate. With Butler's troops around, all this planning was evidently postponed until today, and now, with the election over, popular feeling has pretty well subsided."

"Was Clavering on Hyams's list?"

"He and a Colonel Robert Martin are the chief leaders, though they may take their orders from Captain Thomas Hines, who works closely with the Rebel commission in Canada. All of this year's city fires, riots, bank robberies, ship seizures on the lakes, and the threatened invasion of Maine are part of a great conspiracy. It's been our good luck the Rebels have had their share of traitors, some of our people have been effective spies, the copperhead leaders lacked guts to join the Rebels when the testing time came, and Sherman and Farragut won their victories in time. Otherwise, this country would have been in trouble that would have made the war itself look more horrible for being meaningless — between a quarter and a half-million Union lives lost in vain. Christ!"

We were crossing a street while he was still talking, and I yanked him back just in time to keep him from being run down by a massive engine, its gray horses tearing toward the North River docks.

"I talk too much," Benton said, wiping the sweat from his forehead with his sleeve, though it was a brisk night. And after that, he said very little.

At the Astor once again, we heard people talking excitedly that Niblo's Garden Theater and the Winter Garden Theater adjacent to the La Farge Hotel had also been set afire, though little damage had been done. In each theater someone had shouted, "Fire!," and people rose in panic. At Niblo's Garden, where *The Corsican* was opening, a stage manager leaped onto the stage and gave an amusing speech while boys strode through the aisles with cardboard signs on which someone had written NO FIRE! Meanwhile, stagehands and firemen extinguished a basement blaze, and the audience relaxed under the facetious ministrations of the stage manager. The Winter Garden, owned by Edwin Thomas Booth, was putting on *Julius Caesar*, featuring both Edwin and his brother, John Wilkes Booth, who was playing the role of Mark Antony. At the cry of "Fire!," an official of the fire department stood up and yelled, "That's only a drunken man! Go on with the play!" Then he went down to the basement and helped put out the fire there while the play went on.

It was nearly two o'clock in the morning before Benton reported back to police headquarters. I was going to accompany him, but he insisted that he would go alone.

By this time, the fire department had long since departed with their hoses. There was ample evidence of smoke and water damage on the fourth floor, and in my room the smell of smoke was strong with my door closed and the window open. But even the outside air was smoky. Looking out the window, I could see fires flickering at a number of points in the city. Hoses still stretched across the wet streets to the United States Hotel, and the night continued to resound with the clanging of fire engines. The bayonets of soldiers on patrol glittered from the glow of flames and the gas streetlights. Though most of the onlookers had left, many remained, and these were held back out of the way of firemen by police, assisted by more soldiers. The situation was hardly conducive to sleep, and, glancing along the face of the hotel, I saw numerous heads protruding from windows. Finally, however, I shut the window, drew the shade and lay down, removing only my shoes. In the end, sleep came, though not until after I heard a distant clock strike the hour of four.

I slept until noon, and after dinner I visited a few of the scenes of the excitement. A number of the hotels looked as if they had come through the fire attack better than appeared possible last night. I also walked down to the waterfront, where crowds of men were staring at a few burned-out craft and half-consumed piers. The comments I heard were all so sharply critical of the incendiaries, I doubted that a political rising would have been possible.

When I returned, Benton was back and in a generally cheerful mood. "How about seeing *The Corsican* tonight?"

"Why not?"

I didn't think much of the play, which was shallow and flamboyant, but it was a diversion.

The next morning, I learned that the greatest fire of all had broken out during the night at the dry goods emporium of Halsted and Haines, at Broadway and White Street.

Spreading out copies of the *Herald*, the *Times*, and the *Tribune* on my bed after breakfast, I read an amazingly full account of the conspiracy, at least as it affected New York. Included, too, was a general order from General John Dix declaring that the Rebel incendiaries would be regarded as spies and subject to the death penalty; if they were apprehended, they would immediately be tried by a military commission, and if convicted, "executed without the delay of a single day." A description of a number of the agents followed, which said a good deal for the observational skill of the hotel clerks. I had no difficulty recognizing Clavering, a tall, distinguished man "whose bombs were evidently carried in pockets on the inside of his cloak." Facial features were noted, even the color of the agents' eyes.

Benton joined me for dinner, and I asked him how the papers knew so much, even to stating that among the agents were a number of Morgan's raiders.

"Scott, the authorities have arrested many people believed sympathetic to the South. These include twenty-six who are simply copperheads or the leaders of secret organizations considered disloyal. There have been all kinds of confessions, too. And, of course, the government has released some of its information now that the attack on New York has been made."

"But is the attack over?"

"Who can say for sure? The Hotel Keepers' Association has offered a large reward to anyone giving information of the whereabouts of the Rebels, so the hotel people are still afraid. Personally, I think Clavering and Martin and their crowd have done their worst and are looking for ways out of the city."

"Where do you think they are now?"

Benton carefully placed two level spoonfuls of sugar into his coffee, poured in just enough cream to color it, and stirred until every last grain of sugar must have been dissolved. Then, raising the cup toward his lips, he said, "On the way to Canada. Our men have been watching every train out of the city since yesterday noon, and checking every passenger. But I'm convinced they managed to get aboard and conceal themselves. A conductor, if he's paid enough, can help men in a situation like theirs."

"So they're on their way back to Canada and safety."

"Probably. But with our knowing what we do about the conspiracy — and with their also knowing from the newspapers that we know — I don't see that they can contribute much more to their cause from Canada. If you ask me, I think a number of those men will start to return to the South after they reach Canada, some by land, others by blockade runner. I'm glad you're leaving tomorrow, Scott, before your friend Clavering takes it into his head to go back."

I hoped so, too. If all went well, I'd be in Nassau and off Fort Fisher and back with the fleet before Clavering could conceivably reach Wilmington, provided he came by sea. But if all did not go so well — I refused to worry over such an if.

[410]

XXXVII

Despite a run through rough weather, the *Alice Perry* made her landfall at Nassau promptly and easily, and I soon discovered that the *Challenger* had not yet arrived. Aboard the *Perry* I was James Robards, a cotton buyer from Manchester, England. If the captain suspected differently, he never alluded to it; Richard Benton, who arranged my passage, may have given him a gratuity large enough to insure his silence, both while I was aboard and after I stepped ashore.

In Nassau I saw overwhelming evidence of what a sudden war prosperity could do for what was, in times of peace, a quiet, rather poverty-stricken little port. All the great cotton companies in England had established branches in Nassau, as had many of the Southern companies trading with England before the war. Cotton was everywhere the prime commodity. Blockade runners unloaded it into lighters which plied to the wharves, where it was stacked in massive tiers of bales. It was then loaded into great merchant ships from Europe which had brought out war supplies and luxuries to be placed aboard the blockade runners.

The second day, I saw what appeared to be a rectangular box moving into the harbor. It turned out to be a small runner with six hundred bales of cotton cramming her hold and piled high on her deck. A steam process in Wilmington pressed bales to half their size, which made possible such a cargo. I learned that many runners brought in eight hundred bales and one, as many as twelve hundred — a record cargo that nearly sank her. English buyers, however, snapped up all that was available; with cotton selling at six cents a pound in the South and sixty cents on the average in England, the lure of profit was irresistible. Likewise, foodstuffs bought in Nassau sold in the South at four times their purchase price.

With only an occasional runner now coming through from Charleston, and fewer than before from Wilmington, because of the tightening of the blockade, prices and wages had risen. A bale of cotton sold for more than $400, up from $250 of two years before, while freight rates in general might reach $1,000 a ton. Wages in English or American currency were fantastic for a round trip of about ten days from Nassau to Wilmington. A captain received $5,000, his pilot $3,750, the chief engineer $2,500, the chief officer $1,250, the second and third officers $750, and the crew and firemen about $250. When I recalled that prior to the war, a sea captain rarely received pay higher than $150 a month, it was easy to see why men would take the risks involved in running the blockade. After six months in this business, provided he wasn't captured, a captain would have accumulated enough money to permit him to retire for the rest of his life if he wanted to. Moreover, despite such expenses to the owners, two successful round trips by a runner would not only pay for the runner and its maintenance, but would net the owners a tidy profit.

On the other hand, a lot of the money being earned in a hurry was being spent lavishly. Gambling halls and brothels flourished, catering to pocketbooks and tastes of all degrees. In addition to the crews of merchant ships, blockade runners, and men-of-war, ashore for the usual Jack-tar's fun, everywhere one saw men and women, some dressed in the most fashionable way, behaving as if this were their last hour of pleasure. English cotton brokers, Southern arms-and-foodstuff buyers, lawyers with their inevitable black suits and important manner, refugees from the Confederacy who had fled before the family silver and other precious possessions were lost, Northerners selling western beef and bacon as well as the prohibited anthracite coal so cherished by the blockade runners — these one saw in every daily promenade. The permanent inhabitants of the island, including even the black dock workers, appeared to be pro-Southern completely. But that is not to say the citizens approved all they saw or heard. I'll never forget the shock, even the outrage, in the eyes of one retired British army officer and his wife when they observed four flashy-looking young Englishmen, fresh off a blockade runner and well liquored, playing toss penny with gold eagles on the verandah of the Royal Victoria Hotel.

Notwithstanding the distractions of the place, one of the first things I did after arriving was to visit the chemist Colonel Baker had recommended. His little shop was on a side street, and one went down several steps below street level to enter it. A bell tinkled as I opened the door. After a few moments, I heard a shuffling from the rear, and a cadaverous man of middle age, his black spade beard flecked with white, appeared from an inner room, dragging one foot slightly behind him. He had on a long rubber apron and smelled of acid, as, for that matter, did his whole shop, with its many multi-shaped bottles and, surprisingly, heavy photographic equipment.

"Yes, sir, may I help you?" His voice was asthmatic and slow. There was just a hint of annoyance that I had interrupted him in some important process.

"Are you Mr. Purcell?"

"I am."

"Mr. Purcell, I am James Robards, and a mutual acquaintance has recommended you as the most reliable man around to make up a certain formula for me."

He bowed and asked, "And the name of our mutual friend, sir?"

"Charles Pearson." This was the name Colonel Baker had bidden me use to identify himself to any of the men who worked for him at Nassau.

He acknowledged the name with another slight bow. "What is it exactly that you wish, Mr. Robards?"

I told him that I wanted him to make up four pocket-sized sealed bottles of a chemical mixture that would burn brightly when exposed to the air and could not easily be extinguished by water.

"Ah, you are talking about a weapon, Mr. Robards." His deep-set, black eyes looked steadily at me.

I shrugged. "Possibly. But it might also have the properties of a signal."

"I see." Again he stared at me. Then he suddenly inclined his head. "How soon would you like this 'Greek fire'?"

"Ah, you recognize it."

"Am I not a chemist?"

"I should like the order filled as soon as possible, Mr. Purcell. By tomorrow morning, or not later than tomorrow afternoon."

"You may call for your order at five o'clock tomorrow afternoon, Mr. Robards."

I thanked him and left, aware that he continued to observe me as I walked up the steps to the street. I wondered as I turned down toward the waterfront how well Baker knew Purcell.

I did not feel easy the next afternoon when I called for the order and, after a photographer left the shop with several plates, Mr. Purcell brought the four bottles out of his inner room. The bottles were rather smaller than I had anticipated.

As if he divined my doubts, Purcell said, "You will find these effective, Mr. Robards. Just be sure the seals are unbroken until you are ready to use them." He then wrapped the bottles carefully in brown paper, and I paid him and thanked him.

"Thank you, sir," he said, bowing slightly. "And kindly remember me to Mr. Pearson when you see him and thank him for recommending me."

I left, holding the small package somewhat gingerly. I should dearly have liked to try one of those bottles, to test Purcell's statement of their efficacy, but this, of course, was out of the question. I disliked to trust someone I knew as slightly as the chemist.

Meanwhile, the weather was delightful, the hustle and bustle

[414]

of Nassau exciting, and the harbor a never-ending source of interest, with the big European steamships coming and going and many glasses constantly focused seaward to catch a glimpse of an incoming runner or to watch the progress of one slipping out of the harbor.

Then, one afternoon, as a crowd on the piers was observing a race by the boat crews of three English gunboats, a blockade runner hove in sight, moving with great speed toward the harbor. The peculiar feature about her was that though incoming, she looked like a runner rather than the usual box described by the stacked, brown-wrapped bales of cotton.

"What a beauty!" a man near me remarked and passed his glass to a friend.

My own binoculars confirmed the truth of his remark, and I had a feeling this was the *Challenger*, long before I was able positively to identify her. But even as people admired her, I heard a few critical comments, mostly about her color. She was a lighter gray than the usual color of the runners, almost white.

Later, as she lay at the pier, a feather of steam at her valve and her masts and stacks tilted at a rakish angle, she conveyed an impression of great speed. In fact, if one half closed one's eyes, she looked as if she were steaming right through the dock.

That very night, I joined a half-dozen others in line waiting to see her purser to buy a passage to Wilmington. Her captain had limited the passenger list to a dozen, and I was very grateful when I received the purser's receipt for my passage money. He said he didn't know when the *Challenger* would sail, but probably within three days, to take advantage of the absence of a moon. In the meantime, as the ship took on coal, we should check with him each day. We left our addresses with him so that we could be reached in the event of a sudden departure.

While waiting, I stopped by Joseph Miller's store. Colonel Baker had described Miller as a gray-haired, little man. He was that, all right, and modest and unassuming as well. Yet, after mentioning that I wished to look at a cloak for protection

[415]

against rain and flying spume, he was self-assured and confident in describing and showing me the virtues of those cloaks he had in stock.

"You must be going on a sea voyage, sir," he said as he held one for me to try on.

"Yes, a fast voyage, Mr. Miller."

I looked around the store, its shelves and racks crowded with about everything a man could wear or use at sea. There was but one other customer, and he was being waited on by a sallow, droopy-mustached clerk.

"You must have a pretty complete knowledge of what a blockade-runner passenger would need to have with him," I said.

He nodded as he shook out the folds of the cloak. "Yes, I think I do."

Then, remembering what Baker had directed me to mention, I said, "I wish there were something to stave off seasickness. I'm always subject to it at the start of a voyage, and I hate it."

"Now that you speak of it, sir," he said, "you look a little pale at the very thought. I shall be happy to have you join me in a steadying nip of brandy."

"And I shall be happy to accept, sir."

"Good." He told the clerk he wanted to check my bill with me and led me through his office, with its clutter of bills and correspondence, to a kind of little sitting room with a Turkey carpet and three chairs. Closing the door and pouring two drinks from a decanter on a cabinet, he raised his glass. "To a successful trip, sir."

"Thank you. My name is James Robards. I bring greetings to you from a mutual acquaintance, Mr. Pearson."

"Ah!" It was like a quiet suspiration, and he appraised me as carefully as had Purcell, the chemist. But unlike the somewhat malevolent manner of Purcell, Miller's was merely one of caution and intense concentration. At last, he smiled slightly. "You arrived on the *Alice Perry*, did you not, Mr. Robards?"

[416]

It was less a question than a statement, and I nodded and said, "I suppose I shouldn't be surprised that you know that, but I confess that I am."

"In a store like mine, situated as it is on the waterfront, I can't help but learn many things, Mr. Robards."

"I presume that it is good business to do so, Mr. Miller."

"Oh, I never discourage receiving information," he laughed.

"I suppose you know my destination, too."

"I know that you are going to Wilmington and that you have engaged passage on the *Challenger*. More than that, Mr. Robards, I do not know, and I have learned these facts only since you have arrived."

"Well, it is a relief to know that you are not omniscient."

"That I am not," he laughed, then added, "but please do not underestimate me on whatever occurs in this little place."

"Not for the world," I said. "In fact, I should like to test your knowledge of what lies outside Nassau. For instance, do you have available a map of Wilmington with the layout of the principal streets and industrial sites?"

"No, Mr. Robards, I do not, but, in five to ten minutes, I can sketch one for you, if you'd like."

When I told him I'd be grateful to have such a sketch, he went to his main office and brought back a sheet of white wrapping paper and a pencil. In just about ten minutes he had drawn me a map so superior in its details, including wharves and industries, to anything I had seen in Washington that I was just this side of lavish in my compliments. He looked pleased. He had a right to feel so.

But as he passed the map to me and I folded it carefully and placed it in my inside coat pocket, his face grew solemn. "Mr. Robards, I will not ask for what purpose you wish that sketch, but if I were you, I would destroy it before I entered Wilmington, perhaps, sir, even before you go aboard the *Challenger*. Strange things can occur, and people can misunderstand."

[417]

"You may be sure I will burn this before the *Challenger* sails," I said.

"I do think that will be wise."

"One more test of your omniscience, sir, if I may presume. Is one of the Confederate commissioners in Canada sailing on the *Challenger?*"

"No, sir."

This was something of a shocker, for both Secretary Welles and Colonel Baker, especially the latter, had believed the contrary. In fact, though it was desirable to prevent the *Challenger* from getting through the blockade because of the value of its cargo, it would have been even more desirable if some state dignitary of importance were aboard to be captured.

"Is there no one of political consequence aboard, a representative of that commission, perhaps?"

"No, Mr. Robards. One member of the commission, Mr. Holcombe, was originally supposed to go to England and perhaps to have returned on the *Challenger* to Wilmington. Instead, he sailed from Halifax to Wilmington on the *Condor*, which was wrecked, but he arrived safely in Wilmington in early October."

Somewhere along the line our intelligence efforts had broken down, and I felt suddenly depressed to be imperiling myself for just a cargo, however valuable. I thanked Mr. Miller for his helpfulness and told him that every time I put on the sea cloak, I'd remember him with pleasure.

I had occasion to be grateful sooner than I expected; a messenger informed me at suppertime that the *Challenger* would leave at midnight. Accordingly, in mid-evening, I packed my valise, rolled up my overcoat and stowed it away in a smaller valise I had bought, and, with my cloak over my arm, went down to the lobby where the doorman hailed a cab for me.

Aboard the *Challenger* I was shown to a tiny cabin, no larger than a very narrow closet, with an upper and a lower berth. My cabin mate, a young French captain of artillery, had evidently

[418]

been established in the lower bunk since leaving Europe. In fact, he had taken possession of the whole cabin so completely that he had to remove some of his gear from my bunk. His name was Henri Martin, and he was on a tour of coastal fortifications, starting with Forts Fisher and Caswell, and moving down to Charleston next. Hardly the dapper, handsome, sabreur type, he was a stocky man, though trim in his uniform, with his sandy mustache twirled into an imperial with waxed tips, in the style of his Emperor or Raphael Semmes. His English was generally excellent, though he had trouble with the definite article. After we talked for a while, I went on deck. I had the impression that whatever was in my valises was as safe with Martin as with one of my fellow officers, perhaps safer. But I had distributed the four small bottles in the two side pockets of my suit jacket before coming aboard, and I had burned Joseph Miller's map in an ashtray at the hotel after a compelling period of memorization.

The deck of the *Challenger* was a place for passengers to steer clear of. Though she had taken aboard most of her cargo in Europe, space had evidently been found for more items, and these were of a bulk small enough to be trucked or carried aboard by the black stevedores. The hatches were now closed and the decks hosed down. Meanwhile, the vessel had started to vibrate as she got up steam. Only a faint trail of smoke spewed from the funnels. The ship burned anthracite rather than soft coal or even the Welsh semibituminous, which reduced her chances of detection. The passengers were all aboard now, most of them scattered aft by the rail on both sides and keeping out of the way.

Captain Erskine appeared; he was unmistakably Lord Cromyn. Though I had prepared myself not to show any surprise when I saw him, I was grateful for the darkness in which I stood. A tall, erect man, his tanned face clean-shaven except for his upper lip, and his hat cocked rakishly forward and to the right, he looked the very ideal of the dashing skipper of a blockade runner. I watched with growing apprehension as he moved with authority, yet with a kind of grace, to take charge of his ship.

Momentarily his officers clustered around him, then, at a sharp word of command from him, scattered to their posts. The decks now being cleared, the gangplanks were drawn up and the lines cast off. As a gong sounded in the engine room, the *Challenger*'s paddles began to churn water. With barely an effort, the runner glided away from the dock. Once she was clear of the shipping, her deck lights were doused, and she moved, wraithlike and fleet, toward the open sea.

With Miller's sea cloak wrapped around me, I watched the lights of Nassau until distance and darkness gradually winked them out. I had not felt so alone since I had enlisted aboard the *Alabama*. However this experience might end, it was bound to be dangerous. Though I might not object to a little adventure now and then, I had no desire to be a hero. Too many heroes live long in song and story, and briefly in life. The fact that so many runners slipped through comparatively unscathed, though fewer now than earlier in the year, was not reassuring; if the *Challenger* escaped the blockaders, I was in yet deeper trouble as a Northerner in Southern territory.

The next morning, few of my fellow passengers ate breakfast. We were slashing through some rough water, and the narrow ship developed a roll. For myself, I was glad to seek the open air.

On deck, a medium sea was running, the wind fresh, and the sky cloud-studded with patches of blue showing. With her somewhat convex foredeck — to enable her to cut through and shed water with a minumum of resistance — the *Challenger* was maintaining a reasonably swift pace. Relieved to find the first officer instead of the captain in charge of the deck, I exchanged a few pleasantries with him, principally about the weather. Then, with his permission, I ran up the steps to the rail-enclosed space on the roof of the paddle box and swept the horizon with my binoculars. I saw a couple of sails to windward, and to leeward a faint trail of smoke. A glance at the lookout up in the crosstrees of the foretop told me that he, too, had spotted the smoke and was studying it with his glass.

"Is that one of your friends in the distance, Mr. Pettigrew?"

The wind blowing, created in part by our speed, whipped away the words even as it wrapped the speaker's light blue dress and dark blue cape against her form in a most alluring way. Streamers of blonde hair fluttered from under her tightly tied hat, and her cheeks glowed. But it was probably not so much the wind that drowned out speech as it was the thrashing of the paddle wheels just below us.

"You didn't answer my question," Tamara Ravenel cried, pointing toward the horizon.

"Oh, that," I said. "Who knows what it is?"

But we had to give up talking, the noise was so great. Instead, we stood there together, watching the streamer of smoke. Then, after a few minutes, we walked down to the main deck. Actually it was she who turned away first, and though I steadied her, I knew that, in effect, she was leading me down and would demand an explanation of why I was here.

What I should say eluded me, at least anything that would make sense to her. I had placed so much trust in the assurance I had received from Secretary Welles and Colonel Baker that she would not be aboard that I had never seriously considered that she might be. If she informed Captain Erskine who I was, he would be sure to confine me until he arrived. If she waited until we reached the shelter of Fort Fisher's guns, then I would be turned over to Colonel Lamb, Fisher's commandant, in any event. That she would do one or the other was certain. The time had long passed when I could impress either her or Clavering that I was anything other than a Northerner.

"Now, sir, you must admit this is a curious place for you to be."

We stood in the lee of the deckhouse aft. Her voice had a

hard ring, though she was considerate enough to keep it low so that none else could hear.

"For your information," I said, "I am James Robards."

"Indeed! I looked at the passenger list before we left Nassau, and noticed the name Robards. I believe you are from Manchester, England."

"Little escapes you."

"Not a great deal, as far as you're concerned. Did you think I would not recognize you? Come, now, I'm still waiting to know why you are on the *Challenger*. I think you must be a spy."

"That's a harsh word, Tamara."

"Yes, it is, and I'm afraid it's true. You're a Yankee from Maine."

"I may be a Yankee from Maine, as you say, but I may also be interested in cutting in on the profits to be made out of blockade running. Plenty of others are, particularly some of your English friends."

"I'm sure of that, but your role doesn't convince me. You've worked with the United States legation in London and with Consul Dudley in Liverpool. You smuggled yourself aboard the *Alabama* —"

"Hardly 'smuggled,'" I said. "I enlisted as a bona fide member of the crew."

"And deserted at Jamaica when you found there was no chance for a Yankee gunboat to catch her before she sailed for South America and Cape Town."

"Go on, you're doing very nicely."

"Then you went back to Washington and served with the Yankee Navy as a courier. And all the while you've been reporting what you have seen, and opposing whatever the South has tried to do, even to the *Caleb Cushing and Chesapeake* affairs."

"Surely you don't think I played an important role in either of those. You were witness to the *Cushing* affair, and Clavering was involved in the *Chesapeake* business, and it must have been clear even to him that I had nothing to do with the navy's recovery of that ship."

"I didn't say you had an important role. It's unlikely you would have an important role in *any* undertaking. But you acted as a Yankee navy officer both times, and that doesn't square with your present role as James Robards, unless you're acting as a spy."

"That assumes that I really was a navy officer in those two events and that I am now demonstrating more courage and dedication than I think I possess."

"I'm sure you are a navy officer, and I wouldn't underrate you as a brave man. Even Roger has come to think you dangerous."

"Both of you are too kind and trusting, Tamara. You do not realize what a timid fellow I really am and how greedy I am. You people are losing the war, you know, but there still is money to be made from trading with you, and in cotton above all things, despite the long-staple cotton now coming to English factories from the East."

She looked at me, shaking her head slightly. "Have you met Captain Erskine?" She knew I had met him as Lord Cromyn at the Palmerston reception; she had been present. The challenge in her eyes could not be ignored. If I refused to meet the captain as Erskine, she might expose me. If he failed to recognize me, she might say nothing, at least for the present.

"I would like to make Captain Erskine's acquaintance," I said.

She put her hand on my arm, and we went over to Erskine, standing by the helmsman. Tamara introduced me as James.

"Oh, yes, you're the cotton man from Manchester. Dreadful place. Don't know how you stand it."

Clipped, disdainful, very upper-class. Yet he exuded a certain warmth in his face and handshake that I had noticed in London and that kept me from disliking him. I could see why he commanded such loyalty from his men during the blockade, though he had not run it as often as Augustus Charles Hobart-

Hampden, a son of the Earl of Buckinghamshire, who was an even greater naval hero and a former commander of the Royal yacht. As "Captain Ridge," one of several aliases he used as a skipper of blockade runners, Hobart-Hampden had tried to run the *Condor* into Wilmington from Halifax only two months ago and had run aground off Fort Fisher in attempting to avoid another wrecked blockade runner. The *Condor* was the same ship on which Mr. Holcombe had been a passenger, though Washington evidently didn't know it or had misplaced the information. It was also on this voyage that Mrs. Rose Greenhow drowned by insisting on being rowed ashore; the boat was swamped, and the gold which she had raised for the South and had kept in a reticule hanging from her neck dragged her under.

As I was sifting these matters through my mind, I noticed him looking at me with an intentness that brought me to a high degree of alertness.

"Mr. Robards," he said slowly, "there is something vaguely familiar about you. I have the feeling that I have met you before."

"I doubt it, captain. It must have been someone who resembles me," I laughed. "My face is not uncommon."

"I wouldn't say that at all."

But as we stood there, his first officer called his attention to the smoke on the horizon, and he looked away, much to my relief. Though he studied the smoke a long time through his glass, he appeared in no way truly concerned. Nor need he have been. The *Challenger* was too swift for any Union cruiser on the prowl.

Meanwhile, Tamara and I moved away from him.

"Well?"

She shrugged. "You were lucky. I think he was on the point of recognizing you when the mate broke up his train of thought. You would have had a hard time explaining to him your change of identity."

She left, and the ensuing hours on the *Challenger* passed

slowly and uneasily for me. I had several conversations with Tamara. Every one of them was thrust and parry.

Once, after the French army captain, Henri Martin, saw us, he said to me, "Mr. Robards, before you came aboard at Nassau, Miss Ravenel was an enchanting passenger. I think she is something of a coquette, and she and I talked much together. But now she talks only with you, and, Mr. Robards, I do not understand why this should be."

"Why do you say that?"

He tenderly caressed his waxed mustache tips. "I do not think she likes you. There is something in her voice and in her manner. Have you offended her, my friend?"

"Captain," I laughed, "I think you have a lively imagination."

"Perhaps. But she talked differently with me."

"That's because you're a Frenchman and a gallant soldier."

He pursed his lips and shook his head, and we said no more on the subject.

Before long, we entered the approach waters to the Carolina coast. Since July, thanks to Admiral Lee, the lot of the blockade runner had been made much harder. Until then, the average ship might have made perhaps five round trips through the blockade before capture. Others might have made three times that number, while many were captured on their first or second trip. But since July, the navy had increased the number of ships off both Wilmington and Charleston, and altered their tactics. A few shallow draft ships hugged the shores and inlets to warn the main blockading cordon of runners attempting to come out, which was almost always at night. Beyond this main cordon Lee had established an outer cordon so that if a runner escaped the inner line in the darkness, ships of the outer line could seize her in daylight. By the same token, a runner headed for Wilmington had to elude the outside cordon of ships, which it could usually, but not always, do because of its speed. Sometimes, runners, owing to the necessarily wide intervals between the blockaders, could run through this line undetected. A runner

[425]

would then try to make his landfall in darkness and time his dash for one of the inlets in order to take advantage of continued darkness and high tide over the bar. While some runners attempted to scoot right through the blockaders, the more successful would hug the land to the south and steer through the Old Inlet or sail to the north of Fort Fisher and come down in the deep water close to the breakers, heading for the New Inlet. This was by far the more dangerous course, but it had the advantage of bringing the runner eventually under the protection of Fisher's guns. Owing, however, to the increasing number of ships now employed on blockade and the perfecting of coordinating techniques between the two cordons, fewer runners were enjoying success.

Tension rose perceptibly as we neared the area where the outer line of blockaders took up their stations. It was late afternoon, and we cut our speed. From our funnels rose scarcely a trace of smoke, thanks to the Pennsylvania anthracite coal in our bunkers. Presently the outer cordon came into view, large ships far apart, steaming slowly along and obviously burning a softer and smokier grade of coal than ours. The day was gray, a small sea was running, and occasional showers drifted by, blotting the ships from view. Apparently no one aboard the blockaders saw us, for we passed through them without challenge and left them behind on the horizon.

With darkness falling, Captain Erskine upped his speed and steered a course to the north between the two cordons of ships. It was clear now that his aim was to skirt the inner cordon, avoid the inshore patrols, and make his run south for the New Inlet to gain full advantage of Fisher's protection. This run would have to be timed exactly with the tide, too, because, with our draft, we needed a high tide to clear the bar. Luckily for Erskine, I thought, he had a pilot along who had a reputation for knowing the coast.

A light supper was served, but few had any appetite. Immediately afterward, Erskine told the passengers we should pack our belongings in case we needed to evacuate the ship quickly and there was time and space for them. He also advised us to remain below, or, if we insisted on being on deck, to stay out of the way of the crew. Besides, if we came under fire, it would be highly dangerous on deck.

No one paid much attention to this last point. Several of the passengers had run the blockade before, and one now said the Yankees were such bad shots in the darkness there wasn't much to fear unless they didn't try to aim — then they might hit something! Everyone laughed, though I thought it a high, nervous laughter. And when the order went out to douse all inside lights (the outside ones had never been illuminated), screen the engine-room hatchways with tarpaulins, cover the binnacle, and put out all cigars and pipes, the response was immediate and silent.

As we neared the northern bend of the inner cordon, Erskine again cut our speed and blew off steam underwater. This submarine venting of steam resulted in a furious subdued gurgling, but it was infinitely better than blowing it off through our valve next to the funnel, for the sharp hissing could have been heard at a great distance.

On the bridge stood Erskine, his chief officer, and the pilot, while in the forechains stood the leadsman. Between the bridge and the leadsman crouched several crewmen to pass along the whispered reports of the soundings.

And at this particular report, one of fourteen fathoms, the pilot muttered to Erskine, "We're still south of where we want to be. Keep north but port three points."

"Mr. Pettigrew, I think it is time Captain Erskine learned what you really are." Tamara Ravenel's voice was low-pitched but hard.

Again she had surprised me, so intent had I been on the *Challenger's* course.

"Now, look here," I said. "I've told you what I am. You must believe me."

[427]

A soft but fierce "Quiet there!" from the bridge silenced both of us.

Then she took my arm, and her grasp was by no means gentle. She had established herself as a sentry over my actions. I'd find it difficult to draw one of the fire bottles from my pocket and release the seal without her noticing it and trying to prevent me, and calling for help.

"Far enough," the pilot said.

Slowly we began our turn toward the shore.

"Psst! Ship to starboard!"

The whisper carried along our decks, and everyone seemed to freeze. Just off our beam, possibly a hundred yards to starboard, lay a dark shape, a kind of nucleus of blackness.

"I see her," Erskine whispered. "Steady as she goes."

Not a sound could be heard on the decks of the *Challenger*, though the beat of our paddle floats seemed to roar in our ears. Then we dropped the ship behind, and people began to whisper again. But only for a few minutes.

"There's another!" the pilot said.

"Right," Erskine muttered.

Off the port bow loomed another blockader, so we swung gently to starboard.

"Dead ahead, sir! Steamer dead ahead!" The whisper flew aft from the forehead lookout.

"Stop her!" Erskine said.

The *Challenger*'s engines died at once, and, as we lay like a dead thing on the heavy swells, a dark shape drifted slowly across our bow, the acrid smoke from its funnels making us want to cough.

For a second or two I considered releasing one of the bottles, but with Erskine knowing where the blockaders were and with our capacity for a quick burst of speed, we could probably elude them without much danger from their guns, except a chance shot. I therefore decided to wait until we could go in only one direction, south.

[428]

"Something's wrong here!" Erskine said harshly when the cruiser had passed. "By God, we're right in the middle of them."

"Yes, but we're through the line now," the pilot said. "Take her straight toward shore."

Our paddle wheels began to turn again, and slowly we moved forward until we saw the massive loom of the land, at which point we swung sharply to port and picked up speed to make the run down to Fisher, hugging the shore. Ahead and to starboard, close, we could see the smother of white from the breakers and hear the smash of the seas above the sound of the paddle floats and the rising wind.

"A dangerous business, my friend, don't you think?" Captain Martin said, ranging up on the other side of me.

There seemed no need to answer.

The night was now moving on, the *Challenger* nearing the breakers to starboard, and the moment approaching when I must make the signal. Would I pretend to reach for my handkerchief? Would I gently disengage my left arm from Tamara's? Certainly I would need both hands to remove the wax seal from a bottle, and if she resisted me, I would have to wrench my arm loose and throw her aside. I preferred not to do this; any violent move would be bound to bring Martin to her assistance. My right hand, however, was free, and though Martin was standing next to me, I managed to slide it into my pocket and grasped one of the bottles.

"My God, what is that?" It was Martin who spoke.

Reddish-yellow light suddenly flared up from our deck as the canvas cover over an engine-room hatchway blew off. Poorly secured, it had evidently worked loose, and the wind passing under its edges ballooned it. Several men leaped for it before it slithered overboard, and secured it in place again. The ensuing darkness was intense. So was the apprehension as everyone stared seaward.

What followed came scarcely more than a few seconds later.

High over the waters rose a trail of sparks followed by a burst of whitish light that must have illuminated us against the shore as if it were momentarily noon. This was a calcium rocket known as a Drummond Light, and it revealed not only us, but the ship that had lofted it: a low-slung steamer not two hundred yards off our port bow. Hardly had the first flare vanished when two other rockets went up. While they were bursting, the cruiser opened on us with four guns to a broadside.

"Full speed ahead," Erskine shouted.

The time for concealment and silence had passed. The *Challenger* leaped forward like the racehorse of the sea she was, her paddles thrashing the tumbling water into a furious foam.

Time and again, the cruiser fired. The shells straddled us and whistled over us, but none struck. Other rockets, however, soared skyward from a distance and indicated additional pursuers sweeping in from the sea. From them, too, shells streaked toward us, but all fell short. Yet it looked as if the cruisers were certain to cut us off before we reached shelter within range of Fisher's guns.

Meanwhile, Erskine drove the *Challenger* to a tremendous speed. At one point he shouted delightedly that we had reached eighteen knots, and at such a pace we started to pull ahead of the persistent man-of-war on our port beam. Who could but admire the skill and courage Erskine and the others showed? A blockade runner was bound by the laws of the sea to be unarmed, thus depending on the speed of the ship and the ability and courage of the captain. With a cruiser like the *Tallahassee*, the situation was different; she could return shot for shot.

Though the situation was highly hazardous, I felt so deep a relief at not having had to use a fire bottle that, though a number of the passengers and crew were crouching behind the bulwarks, I stood up as if holding inspection. To have deliberately endangered the lives aboard was a step I would have taken regardless of my feeling toward them or concern for myself, but

I was grateful to have been relieved of the necessity. The *Challenger*, for all I might have done and hadn't, was in mortal peril brought on by the alertness of the fleet and her own course.

Now our pursuers were closing in rapidly, and a lightening to the east, where a gray dawn was starting, revealed at least six ships heading in toward us. Though we had left our first pursuer behind, she continued to fire with her bow gun, and another cruiser, looking like a former runner herself which the navy had captured and armed, pressed us closely.

Suddenly a tremendous crack came from above, where a shot had slammed into the foremast and severed it just below the crosstrees. All of us ducked to avoid the shower of splinters; then men ran forward to heave the mast and tangled gear overboard. Another shot hit the after funnel, which started to sag, and a third crashed through our side and exploded in the engine room. Screams came up from below, followed by the terrifying cry of "Fire!"

"Fire crew below!" shouted Erskine, and a detail of men scrambled down into the engine room.

"Damn them! Oh, God damn them!" cried Tamara, weeping now out of sheer anger.

Still we steamed on, though at diminished speed. As long as we could move, the *Challenger* had a chance.

Suddenly a puff of smoke billowed from the land and was instantly flattened and blown inland by the wind. Then came another puff, and yet another. The great guns of Fort Fisher had opened up. Almost as quickly, our nearest pursuer drew off as one shell, barely landing short, deluged her with a shower of spray. Everyone aboard the *Challenger* cheered, but the cheer died as a lookout forward shouted wildly, "White water dead ahead!"

A savage word from Erskine to the helmsman, and the *Challenger* swung sharply to port. It was an adroit move, but even as the ship fought for sea room, I heard an ominous grating underneath. The next instant, the *Challenger* struck so hard that the sagging funnel fell to the deck; everyone still on his feet scrambled madly to get out of its way. Tamara held onto me, and I dragged her forward. At once a tremendous roller crashed against us and slammed the steamer over on her beam ends. Then a whole succession of massive seas picked us up and gradually bumped us shoreward where we stuck fast, heeled at a steep angle, starboard side down, about two hundred yards from the beach. Under the pounding the ship began to break up quickly. Worse still for those who had not already been swept overboard, the fire had broken out of all control. The stern was soon a mass of flames. And those of us who knew, could not forget, I'm sure, the explosives aboard.

The survivors who had crowded forward looked to Erskine, who was hatless, bleeding from head injuries and barely alive. All the boats were smashed or swept away. The firing from both the fleet and the fort had ceased, and soldiers were trying to launch a couple of boats from the beach. One was overturned at once, and the principal officer on the beach evidently ordered the other held back. The soldiers, however, stood ready with heaving lines if only we could make it near enough. As it was, everyone aboard hung back from being the first to enter that wild, tumbling mass of green water.

"Robards, do you swim?" Exhausted though he was, Erskine still had authority in his voice.

"Yes, sir," I said, and kicked off my shoes and tossed my coat aside.

"What about you, Captain Martin?"

"Very well."

"Then the two of you take Miss Ravenel ashore. I'm sorry, my dear," he said to her, "we did the best we could — "

I never knew what else he intended to say. A huge sea foamed over the bow and slammed several of us into the water. I fought my way back to the surface but was rolled under again and shoreward. Fighting to the surface once more, I saw a tangle of petticoats off to my right and struck out toward them.

[432]

When I reached Tamara, her head was under. I pulled her up, shouted her name, and held her close, breaking a wave's impact upon her with my back.

It seemed eons before strong arms took Tamara from me and passed her along a roped file of soldiers standing nearly to their shoulders in the water. By the time I had come ashore myself, a Confederate army surgeon was bending over her body.

"There's no hope, I regret to say."

And when I looked at him, he shook his head.

"Her neck is broken," he said. "She's dead."

XXXVIII

Loss of life aboard the *Challenger*, which finally blew up, had been heavy — an unusual experience in blockade running — and the Confederate garrison at Fort Fisher showed every possible kindness to the survivors. Colonel William Lamb, a tall, striking officer with closely trimmed mustache and beard, found odds and ends of clothes for us despite his own depleted supplies. Most of the dozen of us who survived, which included Erskine but not Captain Henri Martin, were glad to spend the rest of the day and night in the fort before going up by steam launch to Wilmington the following morning. While Captain Erskine was entertained personally by Lamb in a little cottage among the sand dunes back of the fort, where his wife and two small children lived, the rest of us shared the officers' mess.

That evening I had reason to feel grateful for the surgeon's bandage over my head and the left side of my face. Among the defenders were a number of Confederate navy personnel, and, as we were introduced to the officers by those Confederates who had been assigned as our hosts, I recognized Lieutenant George Armstrong, late of the *Alabama*.

"A gallant ship," I said to him.

"Yes, she was all of that, with a gallant captain, too."

"Where is Captain Semmes now?" a Liverpool factor asked.

"He sailed from England for Havana and then Mexico. The last we heard of him, he had made his way into Texas. There's a rumor that if he can reach Richmond safely, he will be promoted to the rank of rear admiral and given command of the James River squadron."

"Hardly as attractive a post to an ocean hero like Captain Semmes," I said.

Armstrong shrugged. "True, but except for the *Shenandoah* and the new ironclad we're trying to get from the Danes, the *Stonewall*, that's about all the navy left to us." His tone was bitter, and his face was set in sterner lines than when I had last seen him. I suspected that neither he nor his former commander would take the eventual triumph of the North with ease or grace. Not that I could blame them. In fact, I knew Secretary Welles still hoped to have Semmes tried for piracy, and hanged.

The next morning, a steam launch from the fort took us up the Cape Fear to Wilmington. Tamara's body had been placed in a coffin, and a detail of soldiers accompanied it as an honor guard.

On the way up the river we passed a number of great rice plantations, particularly on the west side, and, as we approached Wilmington, what the launch captain called "the Dram Tree." This was a great cypress which every incoming ship's crew had toasted since, early in the eighteenth century, an English ship captain had thus celebrated his safe arrival. The launch skipper, a scrawny old man, grinned as he added that many a blockade runner arrived in port with its crew staggering from the generous libations to the tree.

I had known that Wilmington had been a little town of fewer than five thousand when the war started and that it had undoubtedly grown and become a very active port during the war. What I wasn't prepared for, as we drew near it, was just how active it appeared to be, despite the blockade. Before the

[434]

war a considerable volume of naval stores — tar, pitch, resin, and turpentine — had been shipped abroad, much of them for use by the British Navy. Wilmington also exported lumber, rice, and cotton. Since the war began, the volume of all these exports increased, in spite of the blockade, or perhaps because of it, and the wharves were piled high with lumber and cotton bales. The demand for cotton was such, and the need so desperate for getting as much of it as possible aboard the blockade runners, that a large steam plant was built opposite Wilmington which pressed cotton into half its normal bulk. Two large shipyards also loomed up, though they didn't appear very active at the moment. Several blockade runners lay at the numerous wharves, which were clearly under heavy guard, judging from the number of soldiers I saw. While no bridge spanned the river, a little steam ferry puffed busily across. The town appeared to be one of many churches, of which possibly there was need if one could believe what was rumored aboard the blockaders and at Nassau — namely, that there were so many rough characters roaming the streets, many of them off the blockade runners, that honest citizens dared not go out at night. I had no intention of testing this rumor. I desired first of all to buy some clothing (thanks to my money belt with its gold sovereigns, this was possible), find accommodations, and investigate the arrangements for cotton buying that would eventually return me to Nassau or to Bermuda on a runner or, happily, to the Union fleet.

Fortunately, it was not difficult to take care of the clothing and housing problems. The first was solved owing largely to the blockade runners which had brought in a great many nonmilitary supplies. I was soon outfitted almost as well as I had been before leaving New York. Prices, however, were exorbitant, presumably far beyond the ability of most Southerners to pay, which probably accounted for so many of their clothes looking shiny and patched and darned. Finding a satisfactory place to live was a little harder. British business organizations using or operating the blockade runners had rented a number of houses, and since I was not part of such a fraternity, a place in these houses was not available. But I did manage to secure accommodations with a Confederate army officer's widow, a Mrs. Lunt, who rented several of her rooms to boarders. Thanks to the culinary skill of Hattie, her colored domestic, and to Hattie's son Ben, a fisherman, Mrs. Lunt managed to serve an acceptable table despite the shortage of supplies.

I attended Tamara Ravenel's funeral. I suppose that, for Wilmington, her death, coming after that of Mrs. Rose Greenhow, was anticlimactic. Mrs. Lunt, who attended both ceremonies, said that Mrs. Greenhow's was much more impressive, with thousands of mourners present as against possibly one or two hundred at Tamara's. But, of course, Mrs. Greenhow was a national heroine whose career as a spy in Washington and whose sacrifices were widely known. Far less was known about Tamara Ravenel and her activities; in fact, I suspect that, despite what she had written in her book in England, only a few, both Northerners and Southerners, understood the extent and value of her efforts in behalf of the South.

Services were held at St. Thomas's Church, after which her coffin was moved on a gun caisson, with a detail of soldiers as an honor guard, to interment in Oakdale Cemetery. Mourners followed on foot or in carriages. I asked Mrs. Lunt to accompany me in a carriage I had hired. A devoted Southerner, Mrs. Lunt, in her bereavement, seemed to find a kind of release in attending funerals. She wept at the graveside ceremony, one of the few women present who did. The men looked solemn, and Captain Erskine, who also attended, blew hard into his handkerchief. During the drive back, I felt much like Mrs. Lunt.

On coming to Wilmington, I had registered at the headquarters of General William H. C. Whiting, who commanded the Cape Fear River defenses, and at the customs house, as an English cotton buyer. I was a little reluctant to begin active buying, since it was likely to be a long and involved process, including the procuring of space aboard a runner. Those companies in England which owned runners had a great advantage here, and independent buyers had to rely to a large extent on their goodwill. It was usually more desirable to negotiate with the captain of one of the few blockade runners owned by the State of North Carolina, which did a thriving business but whose numbers were diminishing, owing to the stiffening blockade. The recent capture of the *Advance,* a crack runner, had evidently shaken the Wilmington waterfront.

Another reason for my reluctance to start buying was my desire to investigate other possibilities of reaching the fleet. To cross the peninsula to the sea without going far down the Cape Fear would be to find myself on a desolate coast patrolled by the military and with no means of establishing contact with the fleet. To go down the twenty-eight miles of the river to Fisher was no great feat in itself; a little steamer ran the river regularly, touching at the great plantations on the way. But how to reach one of the blockading ships was a real problem. I was convinced it could be done with a small boat, if one were careful and mildly daring. Only a short time ago, Lieutenant Cushing, who blew up the *Albemarle,* was reported to have gone up the river in a boat almost to Wilmington. And I wasn't long in the town before Mrs. Lunt, in describing to her boarders the near-professional performances of the amateur actors at Thalian Hall, told of two Yankee officers in the blockading fleet who rowed ashore, stole horses from a plantation, and rode to Wilmington to attend a production at the Thalian.

"Of course, they wore civilian clothes, so no one suspected them. I've heard they even returned the horses."

I had heard this story, too, on one of my courier trips to the fleet, but I had never been able to get anyone to identify the officers or the ship they came from. Possibly this was because of a desire to protect them from the wrath of their captain. Or, of course, the story might have been made from whole cloth. But whether true or false, it did not surprise me that Wilmington learned of it so quickly. There was no small amount of illicit trading between Confederate guards and some of our close-in ship patrols; our coffee and their tobacco often changed hands. Besides, both Nassau and Bermuda were clearing houses for intelligence and rumor. At any rate, it was the existence of such stories that gave me some measure of hope I might be able to get to the fleet if I had to.

With the prevalence of reports in Wilmington, some of them gleaned directly from the columns of Northern newspapers brought through the blockade, I learned presently that at least part of the reason for the delay in the expected attack on Fort Fisher was owing to an idea of General Butler. I realized as I listened to discussions of his idea and read the local press that the South had the greatest hatred and contempt for him. His plan was supposed to be kept secret.

Admiral Porter's ships that were not already on blockade off the Cape Fear were ready at Beaufort up the coast by mid-December, but Butler's transports had still not arrived. When they appeared, several days later, and the expedition sailed for Fisher, apparently some difficulty rose about when to carry out Butler's plan. This was to immobilize or completely destroy the fort by bringing down a captured runner, the *Louisiana* — loaded with more than two hundred tons of powder — from Hampton Roads, run her close to Fisher, and touch her off. In the midst of the delay, a tremendous winter gale struck, Butler and the transports fled back to Beaufort, and Porter and the fleet rode out the gale at anchor.

The gossip at Mrs. Lunt's boardinghouse closely resembled what I heard on the street corners and at a cotton warehouse where I had begun inspecting cotton. In short, everyone ridiculed Butler, thought his plan absurd, and had little fear the fort would fall.

Mrs. Lunt lost something of her composure when she talked about Butler. "That horrible man!" she exclaimed. "Think of how he wanted to treat our lovely womenfolk in New Orleans!

[438]

And I'm sure he has stolen all kinds of silver and grown rich off us."

"Oh, I'm sure of that," said Mr. Snavely, an elderly bookkeeper from a local emporium who ate as much as any two of us at Mrs. Lunt's table. "What a pity he can't be blown up with his *Louisiana* torpedo!"

So far as I could tell, both Mrs. Lunt and Snavely were merely expressing the sentiments of most Southerners I heard commenting on the situation. And recalling how anxious Porter had been, weeks before, to get on with the attack, I wondered if there were times when he, too, didn't wish at least something might happen to shunt Butler aside and produce an abler and more energetic replacement.

The delay in mounting an attack on Fisher began to trouble me more and more. At first, I had thought to be leisurely in exercising my role, because with the attack imminent, it seemed to me that instead of my having to reach the fleet, Union forces might capture Wilmington after the destruction of Fisher, and I should have nothing to fear. But now, with the attack delayed, the English cotton buyers were quickly trying to complete their business transactions before Porter and Butler closed in. So, to remove suspicion, I had to hasten making arrangements myself.

At the same time, I started to pay attention to Hattie's son Ben. He took me out fishing several times, and I came to know him reasonably well. I noticed that he was usually silent and subservient in the presence of white Southerners but less so among the Englishmen down on the waterfront. Slowly, cautiously, he began to respond to my questions. Mrs. Lunt had acquired Hattie and Ben from a sister who had died in a yellow-fever epidemic back in 1862, when hundreds of people in Wilmington perished. Though Mrs. Lunt was kind to him, he envied the freedom and fine clothes of English boys no older than himself, who came into port on the blockade runners. Resenting his own condition, he had tried to smuggle himself onto a blockade runner a year ago. He had been literally smoked out when the authorities down at Smithville near Fort Caswell fumigated the bales of cotton — a device to prevent slaves from escaping. He had been severely whipped and returned to Mrs. Lunt with a warning to her to watch him more carefully. He seemed so intimidated by his experience that I doubted I could persuade him to help me get away.

Along with the depressing news for the South that Sherman had entered Savannah on December 21, came word that the fleet off Wilmington was now greatly enlarged. It was reported that the North had more than fifty men-of-war off the Cape Fear, so the chances of a runner coming in or breaking out were greatly reduced. Yet this did not seem to deter the more venturesome captains.

Early in the morning of the day before Christmas, about half-past one, I awoke suddenly. It was still very dark, and I thought my window sash had rattled in the night wind. But all was quiet outside, just a faint breeze rustling the leaves in the street. I went back to bed. The explanation arrived from Fort Fisher in the forenoon. The *Louisiana* had been run ashore and blown up, but too far away from the fort to do any damage. Soldiers thought a blockade runner had blown up or that the steam boiler on a Union man-of-war had burst.

But the same wire that brought the news of the powder ship's failure also flashed the information that Porter's ships had been forming in line of battle since dawn. It looked to the Fisher command, however, that nothing much by way of a land attack could be expected, since Butler had not returned with his transports from Beaufort.

Then, around noon, as those of us at Mrs. Lunt's were about to sit down to a dinner of fish and pone, a low rumble that initially I had thought was caused by drays in the street, was soon identifiable as guns to the southward. All six of us — three

Englishmen, a Confederate major, Mr. Snavely, and I — walked to the doorway and stepped outside to listen.

"So it's come at last," Mr. Snavely said with a sigh.

Mr. Kirkbright, who was an agent for the British shipping firm of Alexander Collie and Company, turned to us and said what many people North and South must have often wondered. "Why do you suppose the Yankees waited so long to test the forts?"

I could have given him many reasons, including Secretary Welles's difficulty all through this current year in persuading the army to cooperate and to give the destruction of Fisher high priority. But, of course, I said nothing of that: I merely remarked that I, too, was puzzled as to why the Yankees had held off.

"You gentlemen seem to imply that now that the Yankees have begun to shell the forts, they'll succeed in closing the river!" snapped Major Ledyard, who was on General Whiting's staff.

"Not at all, sir. I am sure Fort Fisher is too formidable and its garrison too courageous to fall to the Yankee fleet." Kirkbright's voice and words were obviously conciliatory, and the officer looked less resentful.

"Gentlemen, your dinner is getting cold. Please come in at once." Reproach and authority were in our landlady's voice. Except for Major Ledyard, who excused himself to report for duty, the rest of us returned to the table.

All afternooon the rumbling continued, then came to an abrupt end at about five o'clock. Major Ledyard did not return for supper, and during the evening, as a number of us stood on the wharves, speculating and staring down the river, several boatloads of troops towed by a steam launch left the town, going south. I wondered if the major was among them.

It must have been a sad and meager Christmas Eve for many of the Southerners in the town. Although I was sure the children found something exciting to look forward to, for the citizens the time must have been fraught with the most dire possibilities. Still, I did hear a few groups singing Christmas carols; one group consisted almost entirely of young Englishmen, with a number of the local girls.

Christmas morning, I pressed a package of velvet cloth into Mrs. Lunt's hands. I also presented Ben with a new fishing pole and asked him to give a packet of ribbons to Hattie.

Then, shortly after I walked out into the crisp air with Kirkbright to smoke a cigar, it began again. A rumbling and thundering out of the south rose and fell, though it seemed less intense than the previous afternoon. But as the day continued, so did that distant muttering. Oddly enough, the people's mood seemed to change from concern to confidence as the battle went on; Fisher was evidently holding out, despite the combined efforts of Porter and Butler.

In the late afternoon, the guns fell silent, and the suspense mounted in Wilmington. In fact, not until mid-evening did the news arrive that although the naval bombardment had been heavy, most of the fort's guns were still intact, and Butler had become so discouraged that after his troops had made a slight penetration of the land defenses, he had withdrawn all his forces and was retreating to his transports.

Yet the real celebrating started the next day when the town learned that Butler had abandoned several hundreds of his troops, which had to be evacuated by the navy, and had sailed northward.

"How can Lincoln and Grant put up with that man?" Kirkbright asked.

"Politics," Snavely, the elderly bookkeeper, said. "Butler is a Massachusetts politician, and Lincoln had to keep him until after the election."

"But hasn't the election been over for weeks?" I asked.

"Yes, but I suppose they felt they had to give him another chance. Now they'll fire him and get a better man."

[442]

"But surely the Yankees won't be back before spring," Kirkbright said. "The winter gales will be bound to drive them off the coast."

"I wouldn't know, but I wish they'd all drown," Snavely said.

"Come, come, Mr. Snavely," said Mrs. Lunt with a grimace of distaste. "We may not wish our enemies well, but yours is hardly a Christian thought at this season of the year."

"Your pardon, ma'am, but this hasn't been a Christian war at any season of the year."

From newspaper reports in the ensuing days, a veritable war of words broke out in the North over Butler's conduct. Porter begged for another general, insisting that Butler's troops could practically have walked into the fort. Butler said the fort had scarcely been harmed by naval fire and its capture would require a siege operation. Grant entered the act by firing Butler, who declared he would take the case to Congress and prove the fort impregnable. In Butler's place Grant appointed General Alfred H. Terry, who had served under Butler but possessed a fighting reputation, according to Major Ledyard, who had returned to Mrs. Lunt's boardinghouse.

"There are reports that Terry will be bringing along more troops, too," he added.

"Then that'll be just so many more casualties for them," Snavely said, his voice hopeful.

"My, you are the bloodthirsty man!" Mrs. Lunt exclaimed. "I'm sure General Butler would have run away from you."

"The odd thing is that Butler was nearer right than Porter." And the major smiled in what looked like mock regret.

"How's that, major?" asked Snavely.

"Well, Porter may have thought he hurt us a lot, but, apart from putting three guns out of action and destroying several of our wooden structures, his fleet didn't do us much harm. If he'd selected specific targets and concentrated on them, we might have had real trouble. As it was, though we had three killed and sixty-odd wounded, we were still largely untouched and would have slaughtered Butler's men if they had mounted a real attack. But Butler, of course, didn't want to give it even a try."

That the Confederates expected a heavier attack than before was soon evident. General Braxton Bragg, who had lost most of the battles he had fought against the North and then had been salvaged by his friend Jefferson Davis and appointed the Southern President's military adviser, arrived with a strong force of troops, possibly three to four thousand, and sent several hundred of them down to Colonel Lamb. But according to Ledyard, who was certainly a garrulous citizen-soldier, Lamb was urgently requesting more men, shells, grenades, and torpedoes to plant close to the shore to hinder federal landing efforts. Unfortunately, said Ledyard, these requests were not being filled.

If Ledyard was correct, he was understandably bitter, and rumor was prevalent that General Whiting himself was so put out with Bragg, who was encamped at Sugar Loaf, a few miles north of the fort, that he proposed to take his entire staff and go down to assist Lamb in any way he could while leaving the command of Fisher to Lamb himself.

The more I thought over the defense developments and what I had heard about them, the more convinced I became that Admiral Porter should be apprised of at least two points: the probable limited strength of the garrison, and the desirability of the fleet's selecting specific targets rather than relying on a general bombardment. When news reached Wilmington on the morning of January 9 that General Terry had arrived at Beaufort the day before and that the fleet and the transports were expected to sail for Fisher on the 12th, I decided the time had come to leave Wilmington without delay. Rejecting altogether the possibility of Ben's assistance, and remembering Colonel Baker's instructions, I had previously spoken with Kirkbright about a passage out. He said the only difficulty would be whether a runner would be daring enough to try to run out of

[444]

Wilmington now that the Union fleet had been strengthened. This had been just before Butler's attack. Now, with word arriving that Porter was about to bring Terry's troops down from Beaufort, I spoke with Kirkbright again. He told me the runner *Martha* was leaving within twenty-four hours for Nassau and he would speak with the captain about me. When he later informed me that the *Martha* would take me, I went at once to the docks and paid my passage.

I boarded the *Martha* early the next morning for the trip down the river. The captain, Daniel Murdock of Savannah, hoped to make his run out of the Cape Fear that night. He was a tall, powerful young man contemptuous of the Yankees. Since this would be his eighth trip out of Wilmington, he had reason to feel confidence. A one-funnel paddle-steamer about 175 feet long, the *Martha* carried eight hundred bales of cotton and was capable of a speed of thirteen knots. At Fisher, Murdock stopped briefly to report his pending departure, then continued to Smithville. Here we picked up a Cape Fear pilot and waited for nightfall.

But just before darkness set in, Union fleet activity increased with inshore patrols easily observed off both the New and Old inlets. Though Murdock was game for making a break for the open sea, the pilot cautioned him to wait for a night when the sky was less clear. Grudgingly, Murdock assented.

I was sure he felt better about the pilot's advice when, in the early morning, we heard guns just offshore and the sky flared brightly with Drummond lights. Rushing outside, I watched a runner making her dash for safety. For a time it looked as if she would surely be taken. Then the guns from the forts opened up, and the blockaders drew off. The runner eventually dropped anchor but a few yards from us.

After daybreak on a lowery day, the crew of the *Martha* stared across at the long, narrow steamer with three funnels. She showed shell damage aft, but otherwise appeared untouched. We presently learned, however, that she had been struck at the waterline on the starboard side — which accounted for the evidence of activity on her deck and the pounding on the other side of her hull where carpenters sought to plug a leak. By mid-morning the repairs had been completed and she had steam up again.

It was then that I saw Roger Clavering. A tall, dark figure, he appeared on deck and paced back and forth, looking repeatedly at his watch. Once he glanced over at the *Martha*. Fortunately, I was in the midst of a group of men, leaning on the railing. He could not have identified me — of that I was quite sure. But I did not feel easy until the runner began to move upstream. Yet she was but a length away when Clavering conferred with her captain and both looked back at us. Even when the vessel continued on its way I was apprehensive, wondering now whether Clavering could have recognized me. All the forts in the Cape Fear were connected by telegraph and the necessary word would have halted the *Martha* before she had cleared the channel.

I can't deny that the strain of uncertainty persisted until the *Martha* began to run down to the Old Inlet about ten o'clock that evening. Captain Murdock had decided from what he had observed of the inner Union cordon to try for the western bar at the mouth of the Cape Fear. We therefore doused all lights. With no moon or stars, the night provided near-perfect cover.

Whispered warnings from the forward lookouts caused us almost at once to veer to port, though with no cutting of the engines. Not a half mile offshore and barely two hundred yards from us, a Union gunboat steamed by on patrol. Later we saw two other ships in the darkness, but neither hailed us. After passing them, we were clear of the inner cordon.

The outer cordon, twenty to forty miles at sea, usually gave outgoing runners less difficulty than those coming in. They were spaced farther apart and were generally slower. They could signal the flight of inbound runners by a towering column of black smoke in the daytime and a Drummond light at night,

[446]

thus alerting the ships of the inner cordon. The outward-bound runners, once clear of the coast, generally could outfoot the heavy blockaders.

But on this night, fog closed in when the *Martha* was less than ten miles offshore. Reluctantly, Captain Murdock reduced the ship's speed and posted more lookouts. Somewhere ahead steamed a line of blockaders at right angles to us. Though the fog might enable us to elude them, it also created a potential danger. At daybreak the thick gray shroud continued to envelop us, and Murdock pounded his hands together in angry impatience. Then, shortly after breakfast, the fog thinned and the *Martha* picked up speed.

Suddenly the cry of "Sail, ho!" turned all eyes aft. Brushing the haze aside came a big blockader under both sail and steam.

Murdock leaped for the speaking tube and shouted for full speed. The *Martha* quivered at the increased thrust of the paddles. Yet fast though she was, the pursuer gained on us. Even after Murdock hoisted his fore-and-aft sails to add to our pace, the man-of-war steadily cut down the distance between us. Presently, white smoke blossomed at her bow, and a shot splashed a hundred yards off our stern. Again and again she fired, seven times in all. Finally, a scant half mile away, she sheered and let go her broadside. Three shells roared over us; the fourth slammed through the *Martha*'s funnel.

"That does it! God damn them!" Murdock said. At once he stopped his engines and brought the *Martha* up into the wind.

The Union prize crew that presently swarmed aboard the runner was more exultant than any the *Alabama* put aboard a captive. But why shouldn't they be? Whereas the *Alabama* crew gained only promissory notes, conditional on a Confederate victory in the war, the Union sailors received hard cash from a prize taken. Twenty shares of the appraised value of a prize went to the pursuer. Of those shares, the captain received fifteen percent; the commissioned officers divided twenty per-

[447]

cent, and the petty officers thirty percent while the remaining thirty-five percent was distributed among the seamen.

It was no wonder that I found Captain Charles Boggs of the *Connecticut* agreeable to my request to be put in touch as soon as possible with Admiral Porter. I have rarely seen a man more pleased with his ship; the *Connecticut* had been built expressly for blockading duty and was one of the fastest ships on that station, with an impressive record for intercepting runners. I had a little difficulty initially convincing Boggs that I was who I said I was. He knew my name as a courier, however, and, once he was satisfied with my identification, he said that if Porter was not already off Fisher, he would put me aboard the squadron's mail and supply boat leaving for Beaufort within a few hours.

This was so much sooner than I had hoped that I felt deeply grateful, but while acknowledging the speed of the *Connecticut* and the presence of the fog, I did not neglect to feel thankful to Captain Murdock, who had dared try to penetrate the Union blockade. Naturally, however, I said nothing to him.

XXXIX

By fast steaming, the *Connecticut* was able to take her place in the great fleet which Admiral Porter deployed in three columns for the approach to Fort Fisher. Yet I was unable to speak with Porter until the fleet had anchored twelve miles off Fisher for the night. Then I was rowed over to the *Malvern*. The admiral was about to retire, and I found him anxious about the forthcoming attack and very tired, but interested to learn what information I had acquired.

After I satisfied his curiosity by a brief account of my experiences on the *Challenger* and in Wilmington, we turned to the matter of troop movements. General Bragg, I said, would probably reinforce Fisher to a garrison strength under Lamb of something above two thousand but below twenty-five hundred. General Hoke, who had the immediate field command under Bragg, was reported to be preparing to oppose the landing of federal troops.

"He is, is he?" Porter snorted. "Well, we'll give him a taste of naval gunfire and see how effective he'll be. We'd have shelled the landing area in any event. Now we'll increase the volume of fire."

I went on to give him Major Ledyard's comments on the comparative ineffectiveness of the fleet's first bombardment. "Sir, he was very explicit that a general shelling of the fort did little harm. A concentration on specific targets, he thought, would have been much more dangerous from the Confederate point of view. He said that the only really specific target, so far as the garrison could judge, was the flagpole and that, another time, Colonel Lamb would be glad to erect any number of flagpoles if that would divert the attention of our gunners from those points in the fort's defenses which our troops were supposed to assault."

I went on to tell him, though I mentally crossed my fingers when I did so, that in the judgment of the Rebels, at least according to Ledyard, General Butler's troops would have been slaughtered if they had attacked, because so few of the defenses had been damaged by the fleet's guns.

"By God, I don't believe it," Porter said, springing to his feet. "I still think the main trouble lay with Butler. He had his eye on the Presidency, and he was afraid to chance a defeat which might injure his precious reputation!"

"I wouldn't know about that, sir," I said. "I only know what Major Ledyard said, and Southerners have no reason to praise General Butler's caution, or to see any good in him."

In due course, Porter dismissed me. I left feeling that he was unconvinced by anything I had said. Since the hour was late, I gratefully accepted the invitation of Acting Master John Price to find me a place to sleep.

I awoke to the thudding of hundreds of guns. On deck, great clouds of white and black smoke towered high over the battle area. Three lines of ships covered the area south to Fort Fisher from a point four miles to the north. Off Fisher itself lay the *New Ironsides* and several ugly-looking monitors pounding away, supported by a number of heavy wooden ships. At the extreme northern point, the smaller vessels, with the big frigate *Brooklyn* in the center of the line, swept the shore with their fire. Back of this covering fire, 120 boats were loading troops from the transports. Even as I watched, the first wave of boats swept toward the beach, the sailors who were manning the oars rowing in wonderfully disciplined rhythm despite the strong swell. As one boat passed just under the stern of the *Malvern*, I could see several soldiers overcome by seasickness. They certainly would be in no condition to fight if the Rebels should counterattack when they hit the beaches. As if to make sure such a counterattack could not occur from General Hoke's division, our ships inshore increased the tempo of their firing as the boats swept in. Oddly enough, it was not the Rebels but scores of cows, flushed from their grazing by the shells, who rushed toward the shore. At first, the troops, who were wading ashore, scattered when the cows stampeded toward them. Then some well-aimed rifles soon provided fresh meat for the morrow.

By mid-afternoon, with Terry's eight thousand troops ashore, a defense line established, and troops fanning out across the peninsula, most of the fleet moved southward in two lines to attack Fisher while a third line remained behind to land field artillery, equipment, and supplies. Using the anchored ironclads as guides, the two lines of men-of-war converged on the fort, and, until darkness by five-thirty made firing imprecise, the ships pounded Fisher with every available gun. Though many of the fort's guns were silenced, others, particularly those far in, continued to fire. They were easily identifiable by the flashes, and why Porter hadn't earlier ordered a concentration on individual sites puzzled me. By this time, of course, it was too late to change his orders. The fact, however, that the fort was still very much alive seemed, in my opinion, to prove Major Ledyard's point.

In the night, during which the ironclads maintained a slow, constant firing, and in the course of the morning, captains came and went from the flagship. By noon, the first line of ships was moving in to shell the fort generally and keep the Rebels in their bombproof shelters, while the small gunboats from all three lines, which mounted eleven-inch pivot guns, steamed into a position from which they were to concentrate on those guns in the fort's north face that could menace a troop assault. When I heard this order discussed as the captains departed, I began to feel a little less futile than the night before. At one o'clock, the gunboats opened fire, silencing a number of the fort's guns, though a few continued firing and occasionally scored a hit in the fleet. Long after the light had faded, a leisurely but steady firing was maintained, with both gunboats and ironclads having their magazines replenished by ammunition boats that drew alongside in the darkness.

That night, General Terry came aboard the *Malvern* and conferred with Admiral Porter. After his visit, word went out to the ships to supply a quota of sailors and marines for an assault on the sea face of Fisher on the morrow, the 15th, while Terry's eight thousand soldiers attacked the land face. The fleet would shell the fort in the forenoon, and the general expectation was that the ground attack would start about two o'clock in the afternoon.

It was the following morning, right after breakfast, when I was watching the single-turreted monitor *Mahopac* at work — her two guns firing, then the turret revolving with the guns pointed away from the enemy while they were reloaded — that a harsh voice called down from the *Malvern*'s bridge. "What are you doing, Pettigrew? Come up here." It was Porter himself.

"I hope you noticed," he said, when I reached him and saluted, "that yesterday we concentrated on specific targets while keeping the Rebs in their bombproofs with general fire."

"Yes, sir. I hope it was effective."

"It was, though there are still too many guns over there that have not been knocked out of action. We're going to have to deal especially with those heavy guns in their mound battery and those remaining on the land face. Terry's troops could get a dreadful mauling if those guns are left by the time he attacks."

I agreed, and did not remind him this time that Butler had been afraid of that very possibility, with evidently far more reason in the first attack on Fisher than Terry might have in the second.

"The fleet as a unit will commence firing again at eleven o'clock. General Terry and I have agreed that the fleet will send a brigade of sixteen hundred sailors and four hundred marines for an attack on the palisades over there at Fisher. We've broken down most of them by gunfire. The shore party is already gathering, as you can see. Now, Pettigrew, you're unattached, you've just come through a trying experience, but I could use you."

"Sir?"

"We've made arrangements to have signalmen ashore, using the army code and working with army signalmen as liaison between the land forces and the fleet. But in case anything breaks down in communication between the shore and this ship, I want you to take the *Malvern*'s gig and stand by to assist Lieutenant Commander Breese, the fleet captain and the officer in charge of the landing party. If he can't get a message through to me because of the smoke, you are to make sure that the message reaches me by the gig. I'll see that you get a good boatcrew."

"I'll be glad to serve, sir."

"Good. The *Malvern*'s shore party has already left under

Lieutenant Ben Porter. When the gig returns, you take charge of it."

The role the admiral had cast me in was hardly the one I would have chosen, which would have been something more direct, such as command of a landing detail. But I was glad to have any role, however slight, in what seemed likely to be the most crucial event remaining in the war except for the inevitable future surrender of the armies of Lee and Johnston. Certainly it would be the last great strike by the navy.

Thus it was that when all the ships were in line by eleven o'clock and the roar of their guns and the explosion of their shells among the Confederate guns between the traverses were oppressive on the eardrums, I was ashore with the gig. I considered myself lucky to have a sprightly little veteran sailor named Sam Elliot as coxswain.

For a while, Breese was away conferring with General Terry, and Lieutenant Commander James Parker, executive officer of the *Minnesota*, was in charge. In fact, I soon discovered that, as the senior officer present, Parker thought he was in command of the sailors ashore. Hence, he formed four lines of attackers, the first of marines and the other three of sailors, according to the division of the fleet. He also sent men forward to throw up a breastwork six hundred yards from the defenses, and then advanced other men to dig rifle pits within two hundred yards, these pits being quickly occupied — some, but not all — by marines.

What appalled me was the improvised nature of the whole attack. The groups had huddled onshore as they landed, exposed to the well-aimed rifle fire and guns of the Rebels. It was only when Parker sent the individual ship quotas forward to the four divisional commanders and formed a line of battle, that order appeared and casualties fell off. Worse still, though the marines and a few of the sailors had rifles, a large proportion of the sailors were issued pistols and cutlasses, as if they were expected to board a ship in battle instead of having to move across hundreds of yards of sand, exposed to Confederate fire, before they could get near enough to the enemy to charge through the gaps in the palisades and over the ramparts of Fisher. Then along came Breese, accompanied by two sailors, one of whom bore the admiral's flag, and announced to Parker that he, Breese, was in command. I'll never forget the expression of shock on Parker's face, for he was Breese's senior in rank. But, to give the man full credit, Parker accepted the news graciously and said he would gladly serve as Breese's second.

Meanwhile, as the army advanced skirmishers against the land face and mustered attack columns at the northwest corner of the fort, the marines and bluejackets began to run through the sand into closer position. The Rebel fire was heavy, particularly from a Blakely cannon which persisted in strewing bodies in the sand. When Breese tried in vain to get a signal to the admiral, because of the smoke both from Fisher's batteries and the ship's guns, I went to the *Malvern* with his request that the admiral have our guns silence the Blakely. So far as I could see, however, the Blakely remained undisturbed by our marksmanship. But the feeling of impotence I experienced as I observed it still firing, vanished when, at three o'clock, with the army having signaled that it was ready, the ships tied down their whistles and kept only their upper batteries in action. Fifty steam whistles made quite an uproar despite the crash of cannon, and their blowing was the signal for our attack.

But if those whistles sent our two thousand bluejackets and marines forward, they also warned the Fisher defenders of our attack. Some of us, as we extended to the left flank along the beach, had from a quarter to a half mile of loose sand to charge through; others, only two hundred yards. Whether near or far, we had no sooner started than shells, grapeshot, and rifle fire burst from Fisher's parapet. Men were dropping everywhere. In the charge I became separated from Breese, and was selfishly grateful I was not with him when a shell struck into the center of the headquarters group and both the national flag and the admiral's went down. Breese, however, appeared unhurt, and the charge went on. I joined a group from the *Powhatan* under a hard-faced ensign, Robley Evans.

Then, to my amazement, many of the marines who had been sent forward to the rifle pits came flying back toward us in utter panic. Officers waved their pistols at them, shouted at them to turn around, but they ran over us. Some still had their rifles, others had thrown them away. In all fairness to them, many were new recruits and unused to the discipline and courage that were usually the hallmark of United States marines.

Luckily, the sailors refused to panic and drove forward, cheering, into the fire from the parapet. Many of the marines, rallied by their officers, soon mixed in with the sailors and charged toward the palisades. As we closed in, it seemed that most of the garrison must be facing us, as indeed turned out to be true, and I wondered what in God's name our army was doing. I could even see Colonel Lamb, the fort's commander, up there on the parapet, waving his sword and pointing at us.

Then both sailors and marines hit the sand. At least three times the officers got them up for charges. Commander Parker was a hero several times over. Yet none was more gallant than young Evans, whose group followed him devotedly to a man. We made a dash for the palisades. We clawed our way through the gaps made by the ships' shells, reached the base of the parapet, and started up the slope.

Then it was as if a furnace door burst open in our faces. A blast of blue-white fire from above cut many of us down, and those of us who survived fell back, firing our pistols futilely. Glancing over my shoulder for our supports, I saw sailors and marines everywhere retreating. In their eagerness to storm the fort, the officers had rushed far ahead, suffering heavy casualties and leaving too few behind to steady the men.

Our group had almost reached the palisade in our withdrawal

[455]

when Evans himself went down. Even as I saw him fall, I felt a blow above the heart that spun me around. An instant later, while I stared stupidly at a ribbon of blood streaming through a hole in my jacket, a bullet slammed into my left leg just below the knee, knocking me over. Fighting down a feeling of panic, I tore off the tail of my shirt and, bunching it, held it and my handkerchief against my chest. As I did so, a bullet threw sand into my face.

Then I saw my tormentors. Up on the parapet in full view, not more than forty yards away, were Roger Clavering, in a Confederate army officer's uniform, and a sharpshooter. The latter was again aiming his long rifle when, holding the navy Colt with both hands, I fired.

The bullet caught him full in the shoulder. Instantly Clavering fired. I squeezed the Colt's trigger twice, and my second shot hit him.

The crack of the second shot was still in my ears when the parapet erupted in a swirling mass of flame and smoke and sand. Clavering was thrown into the air, and simply disintegrated as the fleet opened fire on this part of Fisher. The whole parapet seemed to dissolve under the impact of exploding shells. To judge by the horrible sounds I heard, our wounded had dreadful company from the other side of the parapet.

The battle went endlessly on. I saw many of the sailors and marines rush back to join the soldiers, and the roar of the fight and the cheers from Fisher's land face seemed to indicate that our troops had penetrated the fort. But if so, it was because the Rebels had evidently thought our attack was the main assault and had weakened their defenses elsewhere.

With darkness, while the fight still raged within the fort, the tide rose, and a number of our wounded drowned, as I would have myself if little Sam Elliot, coxswain of the *Malvern*'s gig, hadn't rolled me to higher ground.

As I lay there, sometimes near fainting from loss of blood, the mismanagement of the navy's assault haunted me. Had we conducted a siege by digging saps and parallels and shoring up the sand with timbers, we could have brought mortars up and advanced our assault line to within at least one hundred yards of the fort. This, of course, would have taken more time than the admiral wished to spend on a station so exposed to winter gales. But even had all our men been equipped with rifles, it would have been an improvement over short-range pistols and cutlasses. What the admiral had envisaged was the fort as a ship, and our landing force as a boarding party. How many mistakes had been made in this war so soon to end, so many that need not have occurred, perhaps not even the war itself had men not passed the point of reasoning and started listening to the demagogue and the drum.

Sometime in the evening — ten o'clock or so, the reports said — the firing died away, and from the fleet and the transports came the din of whistles and a vast pyrotechnical display that was like a hundred Fourth of July evening celebrations at home in Maine. I needed no one to tell me that Fort Fisher had fallen. Later, of course, I learned the statistics: from the navy, nearly four hundred killed and wounded (one man out of five engaged); from the army, nearly one thousand (one man in eight). The Confederates suffered probably seven hundred casualties (one man in nearly four), including General Whiting and Colonel Lamb wounded, while practically the whole garrison was captured and the entrance to the Cape Fear closed for good to the Confederacy. But such statistics tell little of the heroism and savage fighting and anguish of that crucial little battle.

If a stretcher squad searching for our wounded hadn't found me soon after the rocket display, I might have been moved from one column of statistics to another. But it was my good fortune to be found that night; some were not discovered until morning. Before dawn, the surgeons had finished with me, and I was being taken to a hospital transport when someone, by accident or design, touched off the powder magazine of the fort,

[457]

with resulting fearful slaughter of both Northerners and South-erners. That the fleet captain, Lieutenant Commander Breese, assured me he would mention me in his report to the admiral was pleasant, but that I had seen my last of bloodshed in this war was more gratifying.

How many of those whose lives had touched mine had perished! I thought especially of three: Mel Taylor of the *Alabama*, who had died in my arms; Tamara Ravenel, who had courted violence and death — and though the specific responsibility for her loss was not mine, I could not but feel a sense of guilt; and Roger Clavering. To be sure, it had been his life or mine, but there was no satisfaction here. Even young Evans, who lay in the hammock next to mine, suffering from five wounds, was fighting for his life.

Ultimately, in the summer, when the country was recovering from the cruel loss of our great President, when the armies of both North and South had dissolved in the weeks after Lee's surrender, and when the navy had ended its long watch and was fast shrinking to its old status of lonely ships on distant stations, I went home. I journeyed by hospital transport from Norfolk to New York, thence by steamer to Portland. What shape or meaning the future might have for me I could only surmise. But for those of us who had fought in the great struggle, the issues of human freedom and the integrity of the Union were likely to have a significance far more personal and precious than they would have, had we not put our lives on the line. As the *Chesapeake* rounded Cape Elizabeth and I caught the heady aroma, off the land, of pine and new-mown hay and seaweed sun-drying on the black reefs, the tensions of the war seemed to fall away. Standing at the rail, and breathing of that air, I thanked God for my safe release.

[458]

Acknowledgments

It may be possible for me to write a book without the encouragement and criticism of my beloved wife, Elizabeth M. Wallace, but since I haven't succeeded in doing so yet, I acknowledge with profound gratitude her assistance, which included transcribing my handwritten copy into typed copy for revision. For the final copy I am indebted to Mrs. Walter Olson, and to Mrs. William Hay as a kind of liaison agent between Mrs. Olson and myself. I wish also to acknowledge my debt to Gorham Munson, with whom I have discussed this novel and who urged me to write one on the Civil War era, with some of the action based on the coast of Maine, which both of us cherish. And I cannot but express my deep appreciation for the interest, candor, skill, and unfailing good humor of my editor, Llewellyn Howland III of Little, Brown and Company. Finally, I should like to thank my brother-in-law, Dr. Walter J. Mueller of Washington, D.C.; the numerous helpful people in libraries and museums, north and south — the Olin Library at Wesleyan University in particular — and the President and Trustees of Wesleyan University for making it possible for me to devote at least a part of a sabbatical semester to finishing this novel.

Historical and Bibliographical Note

UNTIL the last generation or two, many families in the State of Maine had sons who went to sea, some to find a livelihood, others for the experience, whatever the course of their future careers. A time of national emergency naturally brought a large influx of State-of-Mainers into the navy, a number of them cast in peculiar and exciting roles. Through the memoir left by Scott Pettigrew, who is fictitious but representative of certain types of venturesome State-of-Mainers, and a descendant of a family I have followed through two previous books, I have tried to present a view of certain aspects of the Civil War that are less well known than many but of great importance, particularly part of the action at sea.

In addition to Scott Pettigrew, Roger Clavering as a historical person did not exist, but there were several prototypes on whom I drew in developing him, particularly Captain Thomas Hines, a great secret agent of the Confederacy, and George N. Sanders, former United States consul to London, who turned up in Canada and England during the war on mysterious missions for the Confederacy. He was usually persuasive, always with money, and rarely without attractive women. There was an ingratiating but faintly sinister air about him. He and Hines loathed and distrusted each other.

Tamara Ravenel, Bruce and Sally Thornton, and the various members of Scott's family in Maine are all fictitious. In Tamara, however, there are certain characteristics found in the two outstanding women spies of the Confederacy: the prominent Washington hostess Mrs. Rose Greenhow, and the dashing blonde Belle Boyd.

Research for this novel has been fascinating both in the field and in the library. Trips along the Carolina coast and to Charleston, Wilmington, and the lower Cape Fear area were exciting as I considered their historical importance. The Fort Fisher area (there is an excellent museum here) and the Cape Fear River, as one takes the ferry from Fisher to Southport (formerly Smithville), seem incredibly tranquil after reading in contemporary documents and correspondence about the blockade runners slipping by the forts, the blockaders rushing to intercept them, Porter's terrible bombardment, and the most ambitious amphibious operation until the Second World War.

Works consulted are too numerous to cite in their totality; this is not a historical monograph. Still, readers may be interested to know of a number of the sources which proved most valuable to me. First, the *Official Records of the Union and Confederate Navies in the War of the Rebellion* (1894–1922) and its longer counterpart, *Official Records of the Union and Confederate Armies* (1880–1902). Often their contents can be supplemented by the accounts in *Battles and Leaders of the Civil War* (1884–1887), edited by R. R. Johnson and C. C. Buel. Virgil C. Jones's *The Civil War at Sea* (1960–1962) proved exceedingly helpful, as did Bern Anderson's *By Sea and By River: The Naval History of the Civil War* (1962); *Mr. Lincoln's Navy* (1957) by Richard S. West, Jr.; Clarence E. Macartney's *Mr. Lincoln's Admirals* (1965); and the volumes in the Scribner's series on *The Navy in the Civil War* by J. Russell Soley, Daniel Ammen, and A. T. Mahan. Useful, too, was Admiral David D. Porter's *Naval History of the Civil War* (1885), but this warm, at times gruff man, second only in ability to Admiral Farragut, was so determined to present himself in a favorable light that one has to read his work with caution.

Gideon Welles's *Diary*, originally published in 1911 in three volumes and re-edited in 1960 by Howard K. Beale, is a unique source. No other cabinet member kept so complete or so interesting an account, or was so consistently devoted to Lincoln. But Welles, able and conscientious, was a crusty, opinionated man. There were those who loved him, many who admired him, and others who hated and feared him. Stern and incorruptible, he revealed to only a few the warmth and compassion which were so much a part of his inner nature. These human qualities, as well as those other qualities which his contemporaries saw, emerge in his magnificent diary. Along with this, one might read Burton J. Hendrick's *Lincoln's War Cabinet* (1946) and the fine biography, *Gideon Welles: Lincoln's Navy Department* (1943) by Richard S. West, Jr.

On the Confederate side, two books of a general nature stand out. One is the *History of the Confederate Navy* (1887) by John Thomas Scharf. Though published before the naval *Official Records* appeared and ill-proportioned in its emphases, it is still invaluable. I found of great help the superb pictorial history by Philip Van Doren Stern, *The Confederate Navy* (1962). Apart from an admirable selection of photographs, drawings, and sketches, it contains an abundance of technical and miscellaneous information I discovered nowhere else. In its pictorial aspects it adds a nice balance to the Union emphasis in the interesting volume *The Navies* in *The Photographic History of the Civil War* (1911), edited by Francis Trevelyan Miller.

Scott Pettigrew's experiences in connection with the *Alabama* led me to find especially helpful what I consider to be the best general study: Edward Boykin's perceptive and gracefully written *Ghost Ship of the Confederacy* (1957). Close to it is Edna and Frank Bradlow's *Here Comes the Alabama* (1958). Details of the construction and the means taken to avoid detection and detention of the ship in England are available in the account by one of the most underestimated contributors to the Confederate war effort by sea, Captain James Dunwoody Bulloch, whose *Secret Service of the Confederate States in Europe* (1883) is indispensable.

The cruise of the *Alabama*, on which Scott went part of the way, saw me turning to several firsthand sources of great interest. Foremost was Raphael Semmes's *Memoirs of Service Afloat . . . During the War Between the States* (1869). Whatever the reasons for Semmes's mediocrity before the war, he became a masterful raider during it. He also wielded a caustic, bitter pen where Northerners, especially New Englanders and above all Gideon Welles, were concerned. But he could also write vividly and tersely of the sea, and I have followed very closely his accounts of navigating the *Alabama*, particularly in bad weather. Incidentally, Semmes was paroled in April, 1865, arrested in December at Secretary Welles's insistence, and imprisoned throughout the winter. The case against him got nowhere, and he was released in April, 1866. He returned to Mobile and ultimately to a law career, and died in 1877.

Supporting, and expanding at points, Semmes's *Memoirs* are his journal in the *Official Records* and books by three of his officers: George T. Fullam, *Cruise of the Alabama* (1863); Arthur Sinclair, *Two Years on the Alabama* (1895); and John McIntosh Kell, *Recollections of a Naval Life* (1900). The most scholarly of these, as well as the most entertaining, is Sinclair's. Also helpful were W. Adolph Roberts's *Semmes of the Alabama* (1938) and the biography of the *Kearsarge*'s captain, J. M. Ellicott's *The Life of John Ancrum Winslow* (1902). Those interested in learning of the catastrophic effect of the *Alabama* and her sister raiders on the United States merchant marine should read George W. Dalzell's, *The Flight from the Flag* (1940). The *Alabama* alone sank, burned, or ransomed sixty-six ships, thoroughly intimidating Northern shipowners.

Whereas, in 1860, private shipping in the foreign commerce of the United States amounted to a total of 2,379,396 tons, of which 66.5 percent was carried by American ships, in 1865 the total amounted to 1,518,380 tons, of which American ships carried only 27.7 percent.

A good deal of dispute has occurred over whether Edouard Manet's painting of the battle between the *Alabama* and the *Kearsarge* was developed from a sketch made aboard one of the pilot boats, or from newspaper accounts. If the latter, this could explain the fact that Manet placed the *Alabama*'s funnel abaft the mainmast rather than the foremast. Certainly, if present at the battle, Manet, who had been a naval cadet for six months, would have been unlikely to make such a mistake. On the other hand, a student of his might have thought he could achieve a greater effect by misplacing the funnel, thus revealing more of the ship, which is partially obscured by smoke; and I have chosen to think a student of Manet's made the original sketch on the scene of battle. For a discussion of Manet's presence or absence, see J. C. Sloane, "Manet and History," in *Art Quarterly*, summer, 1951, pp. 93–106. The original of the painting is in the John G. Johnson Collection in the Philadelphia Museum of Art.

On the day before the sea battle, the family of John Lancaster, who owned the *Deerhound*, discussed whether to go to church the next day or watch the battle. The parents and their niece voted for church. The three Lancaster boys voted for the battle. It was the nine-year-old daughter, Catherine, who cast the deciding vote.

The *Kearsarge*'s sternpost, holding the unexploded shell from the *Alabama*, was cut away by request of President Lincoln and placed on view in Washington. It is now at Annapolis, in the museum of the Naval Academy.

Readers who like to ask, "Did this really happen?" (and I am one) may be interested to learn that, in addition to the officers mentioned aboard the *Alabama*, men such as Bartelli, George

Forrest, and Paymaster Yonge did exist, that Forrest led the mutiny on the *Alabama*, that Yonge revealed to United States officials in Jamaica and London much of what he knew of Semmes and the *Alabama*, and that Bartelli went down with the ship. Taylor and Larkin are fictitious.

Outstanding in value for my purposes among the works I consulted dealing with the Adamses in England, the diplomacy used to stop the *Alabama* and the ironclads, and the social events of the time, were the following: Worthington Chauncey Ford (ed.), *A Cycle of Adams Letters* (1920) and *Letters of Henry Adams* (1900); Martin B. Duberman, *Charles Francis Adams* (1960) — a brilliant book with some extraordinary insights; Ernest Samuels, *The Young Henry Adams* (1948); Elizabeth Stevenson, *Henry Adams* (1955); the massive *Journal of Benjamin Moran* (1948–1949) — that cantankerous secretary — edited by Sara Agnes Wallace and Frances Elma Gillespie; Ephraim Douglass Adams, *Great Britain and the American Civil War* (1925); Herbert C. F. Bell, *Lord Palmerston* (1936); Frank Owsley, *King Cotton Diplomacy* (rev. ed., 1959); William W. Wade, "The Man Who Stopped the Rams," *American Heritage*, vol. XIV, no. 3, pp. 18–22, 78–81. The last-named is an article on Thomas Haines Dudley, the United States consul at Liverpool during the Civil War.

Incidentally, Maguire, the detective employed by Consul Dudley and with whom Scott worked in Liverpool, was evidently a skillful, persistent man. Captain Bulloch, however, found out that Maguire was trailing him. So far as I know, no description of Maguire survives.

How tight the blockade really was remains a matter of statistics and interpretation. According to Union records, the United States Navy captured or destroyed more than fourteen hundred ships of all sizes, shapes, and descriptions, including 295 steamers. Yet fast steamers, specially built in England for the trade, were running the blockade as late as 1865, though there were few places left on the Atlantic coast and none of consequence to go to after the fall of the Cape Fear defenses. Gulf activities picked up, however, especially trade in and out of Galveston, with Tampico, Mexico, allegedly becoming another Nassau. Until the middle of 1864, blockade running was more successful than not. Though, by 1865, the navy had six hundred ships, many were on foreign stations or undergoing repairs; those available for blockade duty had over thirty-five hundred miles of coastline to patrol — an overwhelming task. After mid-1864, with more blockaders on station than in previous years, different blockading techniques adopted, and several great ports fallen, blockade running became tough. Lee said that if Wilmington fell, he would have to evacuate Richmond. This he finally did, though it is arguable whether the fall of Wilmington more than hastened what was already inevitable. Still, without the blockade, the South would probably have been able to achieve its political goal.

The blockade running aboard the *Challenger* that Scott Pettigrew experienced sent me to material that is thrilling to read. The best overall account by far, in my judgment, is Hamilton Cochran's *Blockade Runners of the Confederacy* (1958), which I have followed closely. Also good is Francis B. C. Bradlee's *Blockade Running during the Civil War* (1925). A most engaging book by a man who scuba-dives among the wrecks of sunken runners is Dave Horner's *The Blockade Runners* (1968). And I must also mention a splendid if somewhat controversial article by Daniel O'Flaherty, "The Blockade That Failed," *American Heritage*, vol. VI, no. 5, pp. 38–41, 104–105. Accounts of men who ran the blockade — and they are numerous — included Augustus Charles Hobart (Hobart-Hampden) Roberts's *Never Caught* (1867); Thomas E. Taylor's *Running the Blockade* (1896) — an English supercargo, Taylor made twenty-eight round trips through the blockading fleet; William Watson's *Adventures of a Blockade Runner* (1892); and John Wilkinson's *The Narrative of a Blockade Runner* (1877). Helpful for the Wilmington scene were Andrew J. Howell, *The Book of Wilmington* (1930) and James Sprunt, *Chronicles of the Cape Fear River* (1916).

For the New York City draft riots in which Scott found himself involved on returning from a trip to Maine, James McCague's *The Second Rebellion* (1968) is both sound and interesting. Contemporary newspaper accounts tended to enlarge both the area of lawlessness and the casualties. But that the riots were dangerous, destructive, and shameful admits of no doubt; and they were not suppressed until thousands of troops were used. The extent to which Southerners aided and abetted them remains a matter of speculation. John Andrews, a Virginian, and a secessionist, was an active leader. One of the most effective leaders was killed on Second Avenue, and he was found to be wearing fine clothing under workman's attire and to have soft, white hands. That he was another Southerner, is, of course, mere conjecture. The *New York Times* made too strong an accusation that Richmond was responsible for the riots, but it is unlikely that Confederate agents in New York stood by and let the riots develop without a little assistance and direction. Estimates of casualties vary widely, ranging from seventy-four to twelve hundred.

A very interesting article on the riots is by Lawrence Lader, "New York's Bloodiest Week," *American Heritage*, vol. X, no. 4, pp. 44–49, 95–98. An article that examines one of the basic causes of the riots is by Albon P. Man, Jr., "Labor Competition and the New York Draft Riots of 1863," *Journal of Negro History*, vol. XXXVI, no. 4, pp. 375–403. A more extended, confusing, but valuable account is Joel T. Headley's *The Great Riots of New York, 1712–1873* (1873), which is excerpted in *Secret Missions of the Civil War* (1959), edited by Philip Van Doren Stern, who makes admirable comments on the riots. The best account of conscription generally in the North is Jack F. Leach's *Conscription in the United States* (1952).

The capture of the daredevil Read and his *Tacony* raiders after they seized the *Caleb Cushing* in Portland harbor, is related in the naval *Official Records*, naval histories, and in Clarence Hale, "The Capture of the *Caleb Cushing*," Maine Historical Society *Collections*, third series, vol. I.

The seizure of the *Chesapeake* by John C. Braine is set forth in detail in the *Official Records*. The role assumed by Clavering in the novel was largely that, in reality, of Vernon Locke, a Canadian.

The Great Conspiracy of 1864, designed to foment internal dissension in the North during an election year, has been the subject of much writing. Frank L. Klement, in his fine study *The Copperheads in the Middle West* (1960), sees the copperheads as representing no great hazard to the North. Wood Gray, in *The Hidden Civil War: The Story of the Copperheads* (1942), and George F. Milton, in *Abraham Lincoln and the Fifth Column* (1942), take the opposite view; and I tend to agree, though I think they may push the point too far. I found especially fascinating, if a little extreme in the direction of Gray and Milton, James D. Horan's brilliant and original study, *Confederate Agent* (1954), which is focused on Captain Thomas H. Hines, C.S.A. This gives the most complete account of the Northwest Conspiracy and the only substantial published account of the Northeast Conspiracy involving the proposed invasion of Maine. Sultry hours in Washington spent with my wife in the National Archives in August, 1966, helped enlighten me further on the Northeast affair as we read in the Turner-Baker Papers, no. 4026, three important items: Francis Jones's confession, September 14, 1864; Major Turner's report to Secretary Stanton, September 16, 1864; and Adjutant General Holt's report to Stanton, November 2, 1864. Until the opening of the Turner-Baker Papers in 1953, and Horan's discovery of these items, knowledge of what he labeled the Northeast Conspiracy had practically disappeared. The raid actually occurred, and, for information about it, one should read these items and the *Calais Advertiser*. Sheriff Brown was real, but the details of the raid are so confused and obscure that I reconstructed it largely from imagination. I do not pretend that it is exact. The cruise of the *Tallahassee,* as related by John Taylor Wood (the ship's captain), "The *Tallahassee* Terrifies New York and New England," in Stern's *Secret Missions of the Civil War,* acquires added significance when set in the context of Horan's discovery. The attempted burning of New York, which Scott Pettigrew witnessed, is also related by Horan and by Lieutenant John W. Headley, one of the incendiaries, in *Confederate Operations in Canada and New York* (1906); this is excerpted in Stern's *Secret Missions.* The principal leaders of the attempt to burn New York, which was authorized by one of the Confederate commissioners to Canada, Jacob Thompson, were Lieutenant Headley and Colonel Robert M. Martin.

John Wilkes Booth, who was on the stage with his brothers, for the first and only time of his professional life, at the Winter Garden next door to the La Farge Hotel, which the Confederates had set afire, had recently been on a secret mission to Canada. After he was shot, there was found on his body a bill of exchange drawn on a Montreal bank, October 27, 1864 (Stern's *Secret Missions,* p. 266).

The Washington that Scott saw while with the Navy Department is vividly and unforgettably presented in Margaret Leach's *Reveille in Washington, 1861–1865* (1941).

The circumstances of Scott's being wounded at the second attack on Fort Fisher, as well as the nature of his two wounds, roughly approximate the experience of Ensign Robley D. ("Fighting Bob") Evans as related in *A Sailor's Log* (1901). Evans, however, received five wounds before shooting his sharpshooter assailant, nearly died, but refused amputation and lived to captain the battleship *Iowa* at the Battle of Santiago in 1898 and, as Rear Admiral Evans, to lead the White Fleet when it left Hampton Roads for its voyage around the world during the administration of President Theodore Roosevelt.

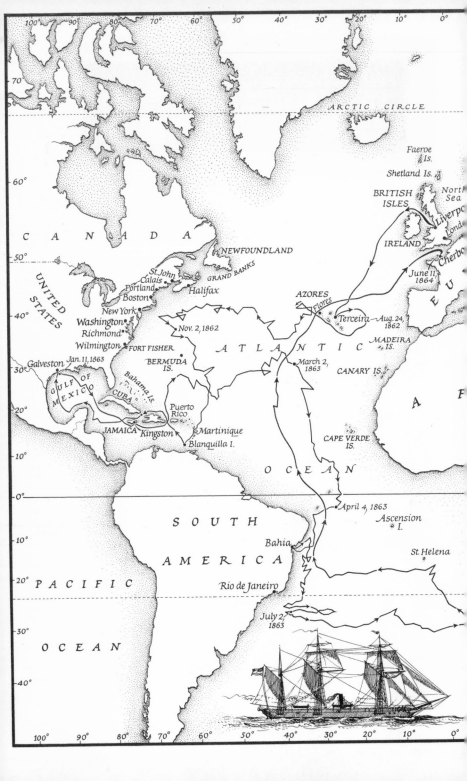